Please return / renew by date shown.
You can renew it at:
norlink.norfolk.gov.uk
or by telephone: 0344 800 8006
Please have your library card & PIN ready

D0508933

NORFOLK LIBRARY
AND INFORMATION SERVICE
NORFOLK ITEM

30129 059 621 772

David L. Robbins is the author of six previous novels.
A former attorney, he now writes full time.
Visit his website at www.davidlrobbins.com.

By David L. Robbins

Souls to Keep

War of the Rats

The End of War

Scorched Earth

Last Citadel

Liberation Road

The Assassins Gallery

THE
ASSASSINS
GALLERY

DAVID L. ROBBINS

An Orion paperback

First published in Great Britain in 2006
by Orion
This paperback edition published in 2008
by Orion Books Ltd,
Orion House, 5 Upper St Martin's Lane,
London WC2H 9EA

An Hachette Livre UK company

3 5 7 9 10 8 6 4 2

Map design by George Ward
Poem: Virginia Moore – *Psyche* from the collection *Homer's
Golden Chain*, E.P. Dutton, New York 1936
Churchill quote from *The Second World War: Triumph and
Tragedy*, Houghton Mifflin Co., Boston, 1953
Permission to reprint *The Unfinished Portrait* granted by the
Georgia State Department of Natural Resources.

A CIP catalogue record for this book is available
from the British Library.

ISBN 978-0-7528-9333-4

Printed and bound in the UK by
CPI Mackays, Chatham ME5 8TD

The Orion Publishing Group's policy is to use papers that
are natural, renewable and recyclable products and
made from wood grown in sustainable forests. The logging
and manufacturing processes are expected to conform to
the environmental regulations of the country of origin.

www.orionbooks.co.uk

For Doug, who finally lets me be his big brother.

Man's desire to be remembered is colossal.

—FRANKLIN DELANO ROOSEVELT
upon first seeing the Egyptian pyramids

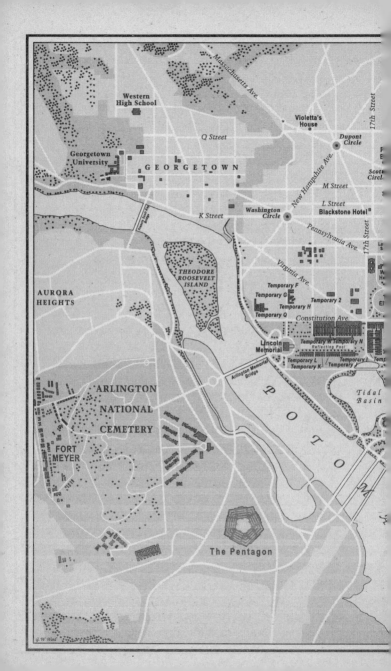

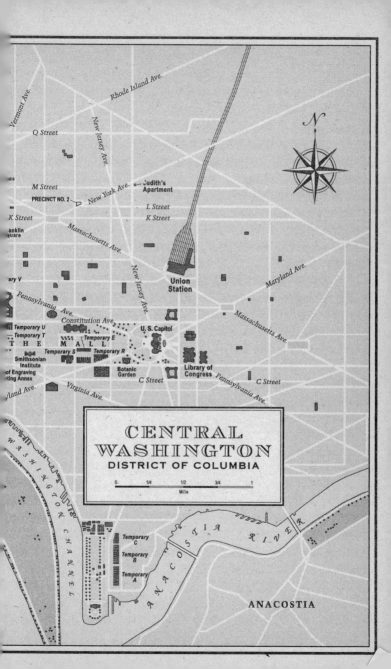

JANUARY

CHAPTER ONE

January 1, 1945
Newburyport, Massachusetts

FIVE HUNDRED YARDS FROM the beach, a gloved hand choked the outboard motor. Six black-clad men took up silent oars. They rowed toward shore, urging the raft through whitecaps with a strong wind at their backs. Two hundred yards out, where the breakers began to build, Judith in her wetsuit slid, practiced and liquid, over the side.

She said nothing to the six and they did not speak to her. She merely sucked in breath at the bite of the icy water through her rubber sheath, then pushed off from the raft. The boat eased away. She turned to kick for shore. Behind her, slaps of water against the raft faded beneath the wind.

Judith spit saltwater. The immense cold clawed her cheeks and stung through the wetsuit. She kept her arms wrapped to her chest, letting the suit and the knapsack and her fins keep her buoyant in the surging surf.

A hundred yards from shore, Judith lowered her legs to float upright. A wave boosted her. At its crest she took a quick look at the

beach under a veiled quarter moon. The coming storm flung foam
off the whitecaps, a rabid water. She lifted the dive mask from her
eyes to see better. She sank into a trough but another, taller roller
swept in fast. Judith scanned the dark coastline. She saw nothing
but vacant sand flats. No light glowed from the blacked-out town
four miles beyond.

She lowered her mask. Kicking the last hundred yards to the
shore, she went numb.

"IT'S SURE BLOWIN' STINK," she said.

With a hand on his belly, the man agreed. Spray from the surf
speckled the windshield of his pickup truck parked on the packed
sand of Plum Island.

"Nor'easter." He pointed out the direction of the wind to the
woman on the seat beside him.

"Forecast called for it," she replied. "Gonna be a bitch of a New
Year's Day."

"Yeah, happy New Year's."

"You, too."

The two leaned across the seat to the center and kissed lightly. He
had to angle down because she was short. He patted her leg when
he straightened.

"What time you got?" she asked.

He dug under his cuff for his watch. "We're getting here a little
late. We left the party a little before two. So I figure it's . . . yep,
two-ten."

"What do you think?"

"I think it's blowin' stink, like you said. You dressed warm
enough? You got a couple sweaters under them oilskins?"

"Yeah, but geez. Look at it. It's cold as a well-digger's ass out
there. Why we gotta be so gung ho all of a sudden? Who's gonna in-
vade Newburyport?"

"Honestly, Bonny, don't start. You and me got the graveyard shift this week. You knew that. Take the good with the bad, that's how it goes."

"Yeah, but..." She raised a hand at the crashing surf out in the dim light, water bashing the sand so hard that mist spewed. The pickup rocked a little with the wind, but it might have been Otto's weight as he shifted to face her.

"This is what we volunteered for," he said. "Guarding the coast-line. Think about the boys in uniform, they're doin' tougher shit than this all the time. You know that."

"Yeah, I know."

"Look, I understand we been kind of slack about this Civil Defense thing. All of us, the whole town. But I been doing a lot of thinking since that Battle of the Bulge started over in Belgium. You don't think our boys are cold over there?"

She spread her hands.

"Huh?" he prodded. "You think?"

"Yeah, but look at this."

"I am lookin' at it, Bonny. And I think it's time we started doin' our jobs here. That's all I'm saying."

"But Otto, geez Louise. Nobody's doin' nothing in this weather. You think the Germans are coming tonight? They're not gonna, okay? You and me are the only ones out in this."

"And that's a good thing. Come on, gimme another kiss. It'll warm you up."

"You. All you think about."

"Is you. Come on."

With a sigh, she considered him. "Alright. C'mere." She gave him more than a peck.

"Yeah, thatta girl," he said, pulling back to sit straight again. His gut extended far enough to rub the steering wheel. "Hey."

She wrinkled her nose at him, feigning annoyance that he wanted to get out of the pickup into this wintry, blustery night.

"What?" she asked.

"Look, I gotta ask. You don't think Arnold knows, does he? He was acting kind of weird yesterday when he came in the store. And tonight, at the party."

"Naw. Arnold's always weird. He still thinks I'm crazy for joinin' the C.D. What the hell. I told him he should join, too, you know, do somethin'. But he just goes to work and comes home and sits with his damn stamp collection. All night. Every weekend. Unless he's fishing. I swear to God."

She grimaced, exasperated with the image of her husband. Slothful, skinny, only thinks about himself and his postage stamps.

"Okay," she said, fighting her temper, "okay, I won't do that. He's not your problem. He ain't here right now. Just you and me, right?"

The big man had tilted the back of his head against the window, away from her. He watched while she took hold of herself.

"Okay," he said. "Look, you stay in the truck a little while, calm down. I'll make one trip down to the Rowley line, then come get you. How's that? Okay? You stay here, baby."

"You gonna be warm enough?"

"I'm fine," he chortled, thumping his stomach. "I got my winter fat on me. Be back in about an hour. I got some schnapps in the glove compartment there. Have a snort. What the hey, it's New Year's, right?"

"Right. You're a good man, Otto."

"I try, baby. So, I'll be back. You bundle up. I'll leave the keys, case you want to run the heater some."

He squeezed her knee before opening the car door. He moved fast into the blowing chill to shut the door quickly. With a gloved fist he thumped the hood, then lifted his hand in a wave.

Inside the cab, Bonny watched him walk up the beach. Moonlight lay across his broad back. He soon slipped it and stepped into the dark.

When he had disappeared, she pushed the starter to crank the engine and run the heater full blast. She took his bottle from the glove compartment for a single, long pull. She put the bottle away, and stared straight out to sea.

ON HANDS AND KNEES, Judith crawled over the last film of bubbles and saltwater. On dry sand, she dropped to her stomach. Her skin was so frozen she did not feel the grit of the beach against her cheek. She closed her eyes and caught her breath, angry at the frigid water but glad of the storm that blew her ashore; without the waves sweeping her forward, she might not have made it.

Inside her rubber suit she wriggled finger and toes; they felt like cadaver's digits. She hacked up a slime of mucous and salt, barely lifting her face to spit. Then she opened her eyes and rolled to her back, finding the knapsack there. She sat up and shrugged the straps from her shoulders.

The pack was waterproof and difficult to pry open with clumsy hands inside thick gloves. With her teeth, she gripped one glove to pull it off and flexed her bare hand to flush blood to her fingers. The second glove came off with trouble, too. She kicked the fins from her feet and hurried with the knapsack. The soaked wetsuit sapped her body's remaining warmth on this icy beach. Her hands trembled. She needed dry clothes, quickly.

The twin zippers of the pack slid reluctantly. Judith pinched the grips by sight, not by feel; her fingertips relayed nothing. The top item was a black wool watch cap. She peeled the hood of the wetsuit off her head, rubbed her ears hard to animate them, then tugged on the cap, tucking her wet hair under it. Her eyes probed the darkness and mist. She'd made landfall right on target. The beach road should be about ninety yards north from where she knelt.

Judith hauled down the zipper of her wetsuit. She spread apart the wetsuit from her naked chest, molting the rubber off her shoulders and arms. The thin moonlight diluted her coffee skin to a milky pallor. Her breasts and sternum prickled. From the pack she plucked a flannel long-john top and a thick wool fisherman's sweater. She brushed sand from her buttocks, skimming the hard, cold muscles there, then shoved her legs into the bottom of the long johns and a pair of oilskin pants, cinching the waist. Using socks to swipe sand from her feet, she sensed nothing of her toes. The laces of her boots were tied badly, in a rush. A dark peacoat unfolded out of the bag, and Judith was dressed like a New England lobsterman. She rolled her wetsuit around the fins and mask to cram them into the satchel. She was ready to move off the beach. The last item taken out of the pack was a long, sheathed blade. She tucked this in a boot, then covered the haft with her trouser leg.

Judith looked north and south. At her back, breakers unfurled and pounded, wind drove froth and sand; snow would fall out of this storm before morning. Intelligence stated that this part of the beach, a mile south of the Coast Guard station and summer homes of Joppa, near the head of the Plum Island road, would be clear for fifty minutes following every hour dusk to dawn. The report said the townspeople guarded their territory sloppily, like a community hobby.

Judith stood, warm now, and limber.

She took three steps and did not see or hear the idling truck before the headlights nailed her.

BONNY MUTTERED, "WHO THE hell . . . ?"

The figure caught in the headlights stopped. The guy just popped up out of the sand, maybe forty yards straight ahead down at the water's edge. How could Otto have missed him, just standing there?

And what the hell was the guy doing out in this godforsaken weather? Watching the waves on a freezing New Year's morning? Drunk?

The man started walking toward the truck. He didn't look drunk, he strode erect. A little in a hurry. He had one hand up to his armpit, tucked in the strap of a sack or something on his back. Dressed like a fisherman but he was slender; those men tended to be thick, hard, and bearded. Besides, with the war on, all the young ones were gone. Bathed in the headlights, coming on, he seemed tan-skinned, maybe one of those Portuguese up from Gloucester.

"Son of a bitch," Bonny grumbled to Otto, him and his do-the-job-for-the-boys-overseas bullshit. If he'd stayed right here in the warm truck, he'd be getting the chance, instead of leaving her alone to do it.

She opened the glove compartment. Losing sight of the stranger for seconds, she took one more pull on the schnapps. She screwed the cap back on, growing nervous, and tossed the bottle on the seat.

"Okay," she breathed. "Okay."

Without taking her eyes off the advancing stranger, she reached her arm over the seat, down into the space behind. She rattled her hand through trash, oil cans, rags, and coffee mugs until she found what she was looking for, a tire iron. She grabbed it.

Bonny clapped it once into her palm, satisfied it had enough heft. She left the motor running, the headlamps on, and got out of the truck.

"Can I help you?" she called the moment her boots were on the sand, even before she slammed the truck door. The wind blew her question back into her face. "Sir?" She shouted louder. "Can I help you?"

The figure, washed in the lights, walked closer, unconcerned. Bonny held the tire iron out where the fellow could see it. Maybe he didn't speak English.

"Sir? You understand this is a restricted area after dark? There's a curfew in effect."

Bonny took a few strides to the stranger, to put herself in front of the lamps where she could be seen and appreciated as an authority figure with a weapon in her hands. The slender man stayed silent, raising a gloved hand in greeting. He smiled.

"I need you to stop right there, sir."

He came ahead, waving, friendly but ignoring her command.

Bonny gripped the tire iron with both hands.

When the stranger was a dozen steps away from the truck and casting a long shadow on the beach, he held his position.

"I'm sorry," he said. "I did not hear you. The ocean."

He had an accent. Bonny couldn't place it. Probably one of the Portuguese.

"I said, sir, that this is a closed beach after dark. There's a curfew. I need to see some identification." Bonny enunciated clearly. The guy must be stupid and foreign since he wasn't drunk.

The stranger screwed up his face. It was a lean face on a tall frame. He raised his hand to his dark cap. He pulled off the hat and black hair tumbled to his shoulders.

Her shoulders.

Bonny eased her grip on the tire iron.

"Honey, what are you doin' out here like this? It's the middle of the damn night in a damn storm. Where you from?"

The woman shrugged, hat in hand. "I had a fight, with my husband. He tried to hit me. I took a walk, that was all."

The accent was French-like. Some kind of European, anyway. The woman had blue eyes, odd to go with that skin.

"I was here, just here." She pointed off to the water's edge. "Sitting when you drove up."

No, you weren't, Bonny thought. Otto would've seen you, missy.

"Let me see some ID." Bonny's right fist closed again around the base of the tire iron, the knobby end in her left palm. She didn't know and couldn't guess who or what this woman was, or what her business was out here in a restricted area with a damn nor'easter on its way in the dark. Or how she got here. But all that would be hashed out before this gal walked on.

"Yes, yes," the woman answered eagerly. "I have here."

She dug into her peacoat for a slip of paper, then held it out. Bonny stayed where she was, making the woman step up to hand it over.

Bonny raised the slip to the headlights. A Massachusetts driver's license, made out to Arcadia Figueroa of Newburyport. On East Boylston Street.

This woman wearing a New England waterman's clothes carried a lot of unanswered questions about her. But one thing Bonny was certain of: This gal was not living on East Boylston Street. Not with that hair and that smile and those blue eyes. Bonny would know. Every married woman in Newburyport, and maybe Ipswich and Rockport, would know if Arcadia Figueroa lived anywhere near their husbands.

Bonny returned the driver's license. The black leather of the glove the woman extended was thin, not made for warmth, not waterproof, not fit for hauling lobster pots and nets.

"How long you lived on Boylston?"

"A week."

Long enough to get yourself a driver's license, though you walked out here four miles from town in wicked cold.

"What's in the knapsack?"

The woman dropped the bag from her shoulder, settling it between her boots.

"I thought I would leave my husband. I packed clothes. Is all."

"Let me see."

The woman cocked her head. Her eyes flickered.

"Just let me go my way." Her voice had changed, withdrawing something.

"Can't do that, honey."

"Why do you want to look in my bag?"

The accent was gone.

Bonny stared at her, lit up in the headlights. The first snowflakes of the year tumbled into the beams.

"I don't know. The boys over in Belgium, I guess."

The woman shook her head. She did not understand. Bonny almost did not.

Bonny stood as firm as she could, not tall but dutiful. She held the tire iron ready, while the mystery woman kneeled to her satchel in the sand.

NO OTHER WAY PRESENTED itself.

Judith sprang. She swept the knife right-handed out of the sheath, clutching the haft so the long blade lay flat against her forearm, hidden, lunging up and forward, as though throwing a punch. Three steps away, the woman had only a second to brace herself and raise the iron bar in her hands. Judith timed her own move just slowly enough, telegraphing it to allow the smaller woman to gather her instincts and counter with a swing of the bar. This was what Judith wanted.

Ducking the rod aimed at her head, Judith jabbed her own fist up inside the sweeping circle of the woman's arms. With a snap of her wrist, the blade jutted like a jackknife, slashing across the inside of the woman's right forearm, through her coat sleeve and deep into her flesh.

Judith retracted her knife hand, flipping the hilt without thinking to a thrust grip. The woman's right arm fell away, unable to clench now, with all the tendons slit. She held the bar only with her left. The inside of her good arm lay bare to Judith's next rip. One more swift slice in the other coat sleeve dropped the iron bar to the sand.

No blood dripped yet.

The bar lay at the woman's feet. She stumbled away from it, sliding down the auto's bright beams toward the ocean. Now she was the one lit up. Snow spangled around her, a halo of fresh, dry crystals. She held her arms out, both hands dangling off the wrists like broken necks. She was open, begging. Judith closed the distance in three swift steps. The woman's lips moved but she said nothing, or Judith did not hear her.

One cut across the windpipe, and Judith could move on out of these lights.

She waggled the blade to confuse the woman about where the

final gash would be aimed. The woman stumbled backward, foolish, blood at last rolling off her dead fingers, spotty trails on the sand. Judith ignored the woman's face and focused on her neck, the flowing carotids left and right. Backhand. Forehand.

Judith leaped.

She hung stymied in the air. Her knife hand swung and missed, her own head yanked backward, eyes wide on snowflakes.

"Get off her!"

A man's bellow. A powerful hand clenched her hair.

A fist or knee buried hard in her kidney. Judith gasped at the pain, then arched. She saw false stars. The big hand in her hair combined with his other hand crushing her knife arm, forcing her to her knees.

"Otto!" the woman blubbered. "She . . . look what she did!"

"Shut up, shut up!" the voice behind Judith shouted. "I see!" The hand in her hair twisted. "Put the knife down, lady! Put it fucking *down*!"

The painful clasp in her hair hauled back more, stretching her neck as if the man had a knife, too, to slice her throat instead. Judith looked upside-down into the night, straining to get a fix on his silhouette.

The woman in front bleated, "Bitch!" Judith did not see the blow come; she fought to stay conscious when the boot smashed into her rib cage.

"Lady, one more time! Put down the knife or I swear to God I'll snap you in two!"

Judith drew what breaths she could with her throat strained backward and her ribs on fire. She could not twirl on the man and slash at him, not with her head yanked back and her right shoulder pinned, her knees ground into the sand. She bent her elbow to hold out the knife, to show her attacker she was accepting his command. She lowered the blade slowly, gaining seconds, scrambling for fragments of clarity.

The fist tightened and twisted. She felt hair rip out of her scalp.

"Put it *down*! And I fucking mean *now*!"

"Bitch!" the bleeding woman screeched again.

Judith opened her hand to release the knife.

Before it could roll from her fingers to the sand, she flipped the balanced blade—a thing she knew intimately—to her waiting left hand. The move was instant; her left arm started before the knife arrived. Judith collapsed at the waist, allowing the man's weight to buckle her. This brought him forward, locking him in place.

She stretched the blade behind him, then yanked the razor edge across the top of his boot, through the Achilles tendon. She carved as fiercely as she could. Bone scraped the blade. She pulled the knife through, then waited for the man to fall. She looked the bleeding woman in the face.

The big man bellowed and toppled to his left. His right hand scrabbled at Judith's shoulder, his left stayed in her hair. She fell with him, keeping her gaze on the woman who'd kicked her, with a look that said *I will attend to you in a moment.*

Judith let herself fall to her left shoulder, still turned away from the man. When they were both down, he tried to regain his hold on her, flailing for a grip. Before he could attach his other meaty arm, she flicked the knife back to her right hand and, blind, just by the feel of where he lay behind her, raised the knife and pounded it down in one lightning arc, pegging hard into his heart.

The man reacted like he'd touched a live wire. His big body spasmed; the gushing left calf sprayed murky blood. Judith lost her grip on the wet hilt sticking out of his chest. The woman screamed again. Judith pivoted to her. Shrieking, the woman hoisted both arms. With the loose wrists, she looked like a chimp. Judith watched her turn and run out of the headlamps.

Judith leaped from the jerking body and took off. The woman ran awkwardly. She did not get far out of the beams before Judith caught up.

From behind, Judith dragged her down by the collar. Gamely the screeching woman beat her damaged hands in Judith's face, slapping and slinging blood. Judith sat on the woman's torso and strangled her. She left the body where it lay.

This had all gone wrong. She would need help making it right.

She trod over the beach toward the man's body. He had crawled, backstroking out of the headlights. Now he lay motionless in the pale spill of the beams, only ten yards from the water's edge. The falling snow thickened, dancing on the cold sea breeze. Judith ignored the big corpse for a moment and went to the idling truck. She opened the cab door and cut the engine and headlights. Fumbling on the floorboard, she found a rag to wipe her face, neck, and hands of blood, pocketing the cloth. She picked up her knapsack and walked along the man's trail in the sand.

The knife was gone!

Judith dropped to her knees to look. He must have wrenched it out of his chest and thrown it. Some stupid, dying instinct. But where, how far?

She ran back to the pickup truck, got in, and started the engine. She shifted into gear and goosed the headlights around to stare across the body. Again on her knees, then on her feet running back and forth, she searched the ripples of sand for the knife. Nothing. She searched for as long as she dared. He must have thrown it into the water, that was the only answer. Good, she thought. In these breakers it will roll out to deeper water.

Judith shut off the headlights washing over the bigger corpse on the beach, then cut the motor. She shouldered her pack, looked once at what she'd done, and set off jogging for the road to town, to make this right.

SHE DODGED ONLY ONE car, seeing it come from a long way off on the Plum Island Road. She moved from the paved surface to wait beneath a bridge, out of the snow. She caught her breath in steaming wisps. The car rumbled overhead. Judith noted it was a police car, cruising New Year's morning, probably looking for locals stumbling away from parties, to take them home and tuck them in, in that American small-town way. She watched to make sure the police car did not go all the way out the beach road, to check on the man and woman guarding the sands with their lives. Instead, the car turned left, north toward the Coast Guard station and the few rows of ocean homes there. Judith clambered out from under the bridge and resumed her run.

On the outskirts of town, she slowed to a quick, quiet walk. The snow ghosted the streets and earth and began to build. Judith stepped through the blacked-out central village, keeping to the narrow residential lanes of old clapboard seamen's homes from another century, pastels and battered shutters, some finer homes in brick. She located Woodland Street, and found the house on a rise with a view of the river.

She crept behind the house to the garage. The combination in her head worked the lock. She parted the slat doors and peered inside. The building smelled musty and unused, but there in almost complete darkness sat the car. Judith slipped inside the garage, feeling down the driver's side for the door handle. She opened it. The keys were in the ignition.

Closing the garage, she crunched across the mounting snow to the back door of the house. An old step creaked under her boot. Before she could reach the knob of the screen door, the inner door flung open. The hammer of a pistol cocked.

"What are you doing here, dearie?"

Judith stopped at the bottom of the steps.

"Something went wrong at the beach. I need to come inside."

"No. You need to get in that car and drive away, like you're supposed to. Now be a good girl."

The voice issued through the screen door, from the blackness of the house. Judith could make out only the snub barrel of a revolver and a white, steady hand.

"I need your help."

"I've been plenty of help already. You've found the car. A map's in the glove compartment with a gas ration book. The registration's over the visor and it's an excellent fake. Everything else you asked for is in a bag in the trunk. That's all I was told to do, and I've done it."

Judith moved her hand to the screen door handle.

The voice hissed, "If you open that door, my dear, I will shoot you where you stand and tell the police you were a burglar. You're certainly dressed like one."

Judith pulled open the screen door and spoke up the peeling painted steps, into the inky house and the black eye of the pistol.

"If you do that, I think someone might come and ask for their money back. And perhaps a bit more than money."

Judith laid her boot on the step.

"Ten minutes. No more. Then I'm gone. Now put that away before I take it from you."

Judith strode into the house. The revolver floated backward, still trained on her, then disappeared. A match scratched and flared, drifting to a lantern on a table. Judith stood in a kitchen, facing an old woman in a cotton nightdress.

The old woman said, "Wait here. Don't touch anything." She set her gun on a countertop beside a toaster and left the kitchen. Judith eyed the revolver, an out-of-place thing, like her.

The woman returned garbed in pants and a blue flannel shirt.

"What happened?" she asked.

The old woman pulled out one kitchen chair for herself and sat at the table. She slid the lantern out of the center of the table, and in this way told Judith to sit opposite her. Judith did not know her name and would not know it.

Judith pulled off her wool cap, letting her hair fall. The gesture was intended to tell the woman she was the younger and more powerful, and for the woman to be careful. Judith shrugged off her knapsack, dropped it, and sat.

"Your information was wrong."

"No," the woman denied. Judith gazed at the liver spots on the woman's hands spread on the table, tiny shadows between the creases of her knuckles. The hands flexed.

"No, I'm sure everything was right. Two o'clock to six, every night. Mile-and-a-half walk each way, one hour back to the truck. I been taking cookies and coffee out to that goddam beach in the middle of the night a dozen times. Every time the same. No."

The woman stirred in her chair. She wiped a hand over her lips. Judith watched.

"Tonight was Bonny and Otto. I know those two. Otto's a stickler; he would've been on time, no matter what."

The woman put her hands in her lap, below the table. An unsteady breath escaped her. She took the measure of Judith with a searching glance, then said:

"Oh, my God, girl. What'd you do?"

Judith would remember them now as Bonny and Otto. She had their blood in her pocket, on a rag.

"Bonny stayed in the truck tonight. She saw me leaving the beach."

The old woman dropped her eyes.

"Otto?" she asked.

"Both of them."

The lantern guttered, the room jittered to the flame. The old woman looked up. "Don't tell me. I don't want to know. I'll find out when everyone else does."

"I wasn't going to."

The old woman cut her eyes across the kitchen to the pistol on the counter.

"This wasn't my fault," Judith said.

"It doesn't matter."

The old woman looked confused. She could not tell if this was forgiveness. Judith passed a hand between them, a gesture to wipe away blame. The woman nodded.

"What next?"

"I need more information."

"Then?"

"Then you do what I tell you. After that, you go back to sleep." The old woman snickered at the notion.

Judith said, "Bring me some water."

"Get it yourself. Cabinet to the right of the sink."

Judith rose. She found a glass and drank from the tap. She kept her back to the woman, looking out at the flurries. She imagined the beach, snow flattening and covering everything by now. It would be useless to go back and search. No, that was done.

"Were Bonny and Otto lovers?"

Judith waited, assuming some silent reaction behind her back, marvel perhaps. The old woman could not know what emerges in the last seconds of a stolen life. Secrets, truths, purity. This old woman knew only coffee and cookies, lies and greed, and this little town.

"There might've been something going on. Everyone figured."

"They were both married?"

"Yes."

Keeping her back turned, Judith asked, "Can this pistol be tracked to you?"

"No."

"Where do you keep your knives?"

"Left of the sink."

Judith slid open the drawer. She chose an eight-inch blade and pressed her thumb to the sharp point. Lifting her boot to the countertop, she slid the knife into the empty sheath.

CHAPTER TWO

January 2
Tomdoun
Highland, Scotland

LAMMECK POINTED INTO THE dusk.

"There, *there*!"

The driver slammed on brakes. Bodies and curses jumbled in the truck bed.

"You missed the turn," Lammeck chided.

The driver, a soldier half Lammeck's age and a fraction his size, said "Sorry" and shifted to reverse.

Lammeck shouted behind him to the men riding under the tarp. "You alright back there? It's dark; he missed the turn."

"You think so?" answered a droll French voice. "Christ, mate," returned a Cockney.

The truck backed to the sign, almost lost in the thick shadows of wild forest growth. The last of the highland afternoon retained only frosty strands of light, snared by the hills and branches of the Lochaber foothills. The air bore a wet chill that only a snug pub and lukewarm ale could disperse.

Down a pebbled track a hundred yards off the narrow road

stood The Cow & Candle. An inviting yellow glow stemmed from ancient windows; wood smoke screwed from a chimney.

Lammeck lowered the tailgate. Eight of his trainees jumped out.

"Hey!" he shouted. "Don't forget Hunk."

The last soldier, a kilted Scot, smacked a palm to his head and jumped back into the bed to retrieve the sandbag dummy.

All of them filed into the tavern, ducking to enter except the tiny driver, an Irish kid. They swarmed to a poorly lit corner, borrowing tables and chairs to make themselves a camp. Hunk, carried in on the Scot's shoulder, was plopped upright in his own seat. The dummy had been dressed in the fatigues of a Royal Marine, swiped from the trunk of a teetotaler who wouldn't come out tonight. Lammeck ordered Hunk a stout.

With cigarettes lit and beers delivered, Lammeck held court. Around him sat three Englishmen, one Irishman, two Canadians, one Frenchman, one Scotsman, and one dummy.

Lammeck raised his mug. These boys were Jedburghs, the name for the multinational clandestine teams recruited and trained by the British Special Operations Executive, the SOE, to operate behind enemy lines.

"To you, my lads, and to all the Jedburghs who've come before you." The young men lifted their glasses and clinked all around. The Scot hoisted Hunk's arm and stout for him.

"Alright, alright," Lammeck said, wiping foam from his beard, "what do we have here? I know most of you specialize in Weapons. What else do we have?"

"Wireless and ciphers," said one of the Brits.

"Ooo, ciphers. Riddles." The crew laughed.

"Tell us a cipher," Lammeck ordered.

"Zero three one zero five four."

"You are now The Sphinx," anointed Lammeck. "Next."

"Languages," answered the Frenchman.

Lammeck asked, "Which?"

"Japanese."

"Really?"

"And, of course, Burmese."

"Of course."

"After all, we are going to Burma, *n'est-ce pas?*"

"And he speaks French!" shouted the Scot. "Bloody talented."

"Say something in Burmese," Lammeck egged the Frenchman.

"Ein tha beh ma le?"

"What was that?"

"I said, 'Where is the toilet?' "

"Loo!" Lammeck christened him, and the Frenchman's nickname was permanent. The Frenchman attempted to contest it but the rest of the boys cheered and slapped him on the shoulders, crooning, "Looooo."

Lammeck took a sip. He set the beer down hard like a gavel, then tilted his chair back from the table to take more room for his belly and chest.

"You." With a jab of his hand, he indicated the Scotsman. "Specialty?"

"Sabotage."

"Careful, Hunk," the Irish lad said, leaning across the table to the sandbag dummy. "He'll piss in your beer."

"Hesperus," said Lammeck.

"Crikey, man, what the hell kind of a name is that? Hesperus? Let me be something else, Professor."

" 'The Wreck of the Hesperus.' Longfellow. Our greatest American poet."

Lammeck waited for the connection to sink in, and got nothing.

"The Wreck?" one of the Canadians pitched in. "Get it? Wreck? You're a saboteur?"

"Ohhh." The Scotsman understood. "Yeah, okay. I like that. Hesperus. A bleeding poet, too."

"In a skirt," the Frenchman muttered.

Lammeck spread his arms across the backs of the chairs on each side. He was easily the largest man at the table. These SOE Jedburgh boys were going to be parachuted behind Japanese lines in three-man paramilitary teams, as guerillas, W/T operators, underground liaisons for resistance, and wreckers. They needed to be fox-quick, steel-nerved, and clever, not brutes.

"Then the rest of you are Weapons, yes? Good. Let's see what you wee lads know before we start you out tomorrow. Sphinx, Loo, Hesperus, you pay attention. When we're finished training, you'll need to know as much as everyone else. Alright, favorite weapons. Who's first?"

He indicated the Canadian who knew about Longfellow.

"Yukon?"

The young man grinned, accepting the label.

"A silenced M3 submachine gun, .45 caliber. The weight of the silencer adds balance to help keep the muzzle down. Inaudible at two hundred yards. Wonderful stopping power. Lightweight. Sturdy. Excellent for indoor use."

Nods accompanied this choice. Lammeck sipped his beer and said nothing, gazing at the Canadian.

"Oh, oh," muttered The Sphinx.

Lammeck shook his head, mocking sadness.

"Two things I don't like about the M3 SMG. One, the silencer needs to be cleaned of carbon every three hundred rounds or it'll actually sound louder than if you didn't even have the damn thing on. In the jungle you may go through ten magazines in ten minutes or ten weeks, but either way you better keep track. And two, that's an American OSS gun, not available to Section 136. Next. You."

Lammeck stabbed a finger at the small Irishman.

"Easy," the soldier said, an eager and devilish twist in his eyes. "But it's another Yank gun, Professor, so don't tear me an arsehole over it. The Thompson SMG with a 230-grain .45-caliber round. Hundred-shot drum magazine, 879 rounds a minute. It can be stripped and reassembled in sixty seconds with no tools. Loud, powerful, reliable, balanced, spits flame. And the best-looking goddam gun ever made."

"True, true, and true," Lammeck agreed mildly. "It also weighs twenty pounds with that magazine. You want to lug that son of a bitch through the jungle with Jappo on your tail, go ahead. I think it'd be better just to shoot yourself with it and be done."

The Irish lad was not defeated by the laughter and clinking glasses. Lammeck smiled.

"Your name will be Capone. Next. Anyone actually want to use a British-made gun? Since you're being equipped by Britain, I recommend it."

A handsome English boy raised his beer.

"Sten gun. Lightweight, inexpensive 9mm. Can be used with a silencer—" The Brit glanced across the table at Yukon, who also favored a silenced submachine gun. "—but the Sten silencer works with baffles, not screens, so it requires less cleaning and upkeep. Makes more of a hiss than the regular clap of a firearm. Durable, withstands mud, sand, and water better than any other SMG."

The Brit paused. Lammeck waited him out, to see if the boy knew. He did.

"And, yes, Professor, the silencer does reduce the penetrating power of the 9mm round."

"And?"

The Brit sighed.

"And it has an alarming tendency to loose off an entire magazine if dropped."

"The solution, fellows?" Lammeck challenged.

Everyone chimed in, "Don't *drop* it!"

"And you, my lad," Lammeck raised his ale to the Englishman, "I dub Thumbs. Now who's left? You."

The other Canadian, the largest of the soldiers, a muscled young man with carrot hair and thick hands, pointed at the dummy. Hunk's sand-filled hand rested around a stout that mysteriously had been half drunk.

"I want to hear what Hunk has to say," the Canadian replied. "I mean, he's been shot by every weapon SOE has. What's he think, Professor?"

Lammeck waved away this diversion. "Hunk prefers hand-to-hand. He's a knife man. Alright, then...hmm...let's see...You, my boy, shall be Grizzly. Alright, no dodging. Favorite weapon."

The newly minted Grizzly shrugged. "I like the Welrod 9mm Parabellum."

"Ahhh, yes. A real killer's weapon. Continue."

"Silenced pistol. Six-round magazine, three and a half pounds. The stock and barrel can easily be detached and concealed. The most effective close-quarters weapon in SOE's arsenal. Accurate to fifty yards, virtually silent. Cheap to manufacture."

"Yes." Lammeck nodded. "Excellent choice. You all hear this, you blazing machine gunners? Grizzly here wants a weapon that's almost incapable of hurting anyone unless the muzzle is pressed against their fucking forehead. This Canuck is the only real man among you. And the one least likely ever to see home again. My condolences to your family for your courage, Grizzly. Now, who's bringing up the rear? You, my lad. You're awful quiet. You're going last, so I expect a reasonable choice from you."

The young Brit grinned shyly into the table. He had wavy hair, light eyes, and looked to Lammeck to be a good boy, someone's treasured son.

"Silenced sniper rifle, .22-caliber LR round, fourteen-shot magazine. Lethal to one hundred yards. Less stopping power than a 9mm or a .45, but reduced recoil, plus less bang and flash. Lightweight, sturdy, easy to maintain. Ideal for special forces work in jungle conditions."

The boy braced his shoulders, waiting for the rebuttal the whole table knew was headed his way. Lammeck grinned.

"Well, at last. Somebody finally picked one of my favorite weapons."

Everyone groaned. The shy Brit raised his head. Lammeck pointed across the table.

"So, you are...The Wizard."

"Shite," groused the Irish Capone, "he got the best one."

"I dunno. Hesperus isn't so bad." The Scot preened. "I rather like mine."

Grizzly raised his big hands, baring his teeth in a playful swipe at his countryman Yukon. The Frenchman Loo pretended to take the temperature and pulse of The Sphinx. The table swelled with calls for another round. Somehow Hunk's beer got finished.

Lammeck set his glass on the table. Under cover of the young soldiers' horseplay, he dipped his hands below the tabletop. He laid his left hand over his right forearm, then bent his right elbow.

Beneath his shirt, an elastic band stretched. He cupped his right-hand fingers to snag the inch-and-a-quarter pipe sliding into his palm. The weapon was called a Welwand, or sleeve gun. Just twenty-six ounces, 9mm, essentially a silenced, single-shot Welrod without the pistol grip. Ejected no telltale cartridge. Great care had to be exercised to avoid shooting oneself in the foot.

"Proprietor!" Lammeck called. He thrust his left hand high to join the others barking for another round. His right forearm hovered an inch off the table. He set his thumb on the Welwand's trigger near the muzzle. The silencer coughed. He shot Hunk in the chest. No one noticed.

Lammeck let go of the Welrod. The elastic lanyard tugged it back up his sleeve.

He stood. "I've got to hit the WC, boys. Wizard, make sure I get an India Pale. And another Guinness for poor Hunk. He looks like he's sprung a leak."

Lammeck shuffled off to the toilet. When he returned, the entire table was in an uproar.

"Professor! Hunk's been shot. Poor bugger."

Thumbs wriggled his index finger in the hole of the Royal Marine's tunic. "How in blighty . . . ?"

Hesperus laid an elbow on Hunk's shoulders. "Drink up, my lad, that looks bad. Here, let me help you with that." The Scot guzzled Hunk's stout.

Lammeck set his hand on Hunk's other shoulder. He patted in

sympathy, squeezing a small flexible tube he held secreted in his palm. Instantly, the chemical in the tube squirted onto the dummy's neck.

"Oh, for the love of Christ!" Hesperus leaped from his chair. "Hunk, old sod, you've soiled yourself!"

Chairs scraped back from the table, soldiers shot to their feet, waving open hands to ward off the reek. Lammeck's knees bent with glee. He stumbled to his chair and sat, well accustomed to the strong fecal smell of the chemical.

A few in the ring of repulsed and grousing Jedburghs pinched fingers over their noses. Lammeck wiped away tears and fought to find his voice through his laughter.

Again he slipped the Welwand into his right hand. He held it up for the boys to see, then with his open left hand palmed the tube of the substance christened by SOE as "Who, Me?" It was well known that the Japanese found the accidental odor of feces particularly offensive and humiliating. Locals could use this chemical agent to cause disturbances, as well as embarrass and assault the morale of Jap guards.

"What the hell are those?" Yukon inched closer to get a look. The others braved the stench to return to their chairs. Hesperus smacked Hunk on the back of his sandbag head for the offense.

Lammeck laid the weapons on the table.

"These," he said, still chuckling, "are my other favorite weapons. Now which of you is buying this round?"

January 3
Lochaber Forest
Highland, Scotland

THE ANCIENT PICTISH FOREST clutched the gloom of the highland dawn to itself with bare limbs and thick evergreen. At sunup, Lammeck and a dozen Jedburghs tramped out of stove-warmed barracks into the woods. They climbed a shallow, frosted hill to SOE's shooting range.

The dozen soldiers spent three hours with 9mm pistols inside a heated Quonset. Some of the boys lamented that one of the sandbag dummies at the far end of the hut might be their pal Hunk, now anonymous and naked before them. Lammeck assured them that Hunk gave gladly of himself for the war effort and they should do the same. Before heading to the open-air rifle range for scope training with .22s at one-hundred-plus yards, Lammeck gave them a coffee and piss break. When they'd regrouped, he handed out nicknames to the few who were not in attendance last night at The Cow & Candle. Outside, wind swirled on the hilltop, the temperature stalled just below freezing. Lammeck suspected none of the boys would score better than seven out of ten with the sniper rifles until he had them versed in windage and friction. He knew he could expect a nine from himself, hoping as always to be lucky as well as good.

Lammeck let his boys have a half hour to themselves while he sat alone, watching. In addition to teaching weapons, his job was to help assess who worked well with whom, and to advise on how to split them into three-man teams. In two months all of them would drop into occupied Burma. They were not to be spies, but resistance saboteurs and killers.

A year ago, Lammeck's fellow Americans made up a third of the Jedburghs. Those teams had been dropped into France and the Low Countries, from June through November. Once the European theater moved to the German border, the American Jeds stayed in the States to train with their own OSS for drops into China and Indo-China; at the same time, the British SOE formed Section 136 for operations in Burma, Malaya, and the Dutch West Indies. Lately, most of the French Jeds were dropping into Vietnam to protect their interests there. With the war progressing into the new year, each of the Allied nations seemed to be going her own way. This multinational-effort training in Scotland, once a mainstay of the Allied guerilla agenda, was becoming a rarity.

Lammeck leaned against a woodpile in the Quonset, cleaning his nails with a switchblade. He watched and admired these young Jeds while they tested each other and weighed who was fit to parachute in with whom. Lammeck envied the certainty of their impending months, the uncertainty of their outcomes. He wondered what was in store for him, and wished that it be different from what he expected. Then he grabbed a rifle and moved to their center. He smacked the stock on the ground. The gun made a cheap jangle.

"It's a good bet," Lammeck said, "that if you get killed in Burma, this is the weapon that'll do it."

He tossed the gun in the air and snatched it with one hand.

"The Japanese Arisaka Type 99. It fires only a 7.7mm round, which isn't exactly a show-stopper. However, as you will find out, the Asian soldier believes his willingness to die fighting is sufficient to make up for any deficiencies in his weaponry. Your job, of course, will be to prove him wrong."

Lammeck hefted the 99 into firing position at his shoulder.

"The 99 weighs about the same as any other rifle, just over nine pounds. The lighter-caliber rounds reduce recoil and muzzle flash, and are judged to be more suitable for the smaller physiques of your typical Japanese. Although the rounds are of lesser power, be advised they tumble in flight and break on impact. That means when one hits you, it makes a mess. So, what is the solution, my boys?"

"Don't get *hit*!"

Lammeck grinned. "Where do they come up with such clever lads? Correct. Now, do not suppose you will find these rifles just lying around the jungle. Your Jap grunt does not drop his gun and run. He breathes his last holding it. You see this chrysanthemum emblem here on the receiver? This is the symbol of the Japanese emperor Hirohito. If a Jap soldier surrenders his weapon, he will first scratch out this mark, because it's a humiliation to surrender a gun belonging to the emperor. On this 99, you see the mum is untouched. That tells you it was taken off a dead Jap. You will seldom discover a scratched-out chrysanthemum.

"The Arisaka 99 is for the most part a lousy weapon. It's a bitch to disassemble. It may fly apart on firing due to compromises in Japanese metallurgy this late in the war. So I suggest you just shoot the little man holding it with your lovely British weaponry and keep moving. Questions? Good. Now let's head out into this brilliant Scottish afternoon and fire the damn thing."

"Professor?"

"Yes, Thumbs?"

"One question, sir. The chaps and I were all wondering. Well, we know you're an American, of course. If it's not impertinent, the lads and I would like to ask why you're in the Scottish outback doing training for the SOE, instead of in the States working with your own blokes. Sir."

Lammeck looked about the seated ring of Jeds.

"The U.S. wasn't in the war when I wanted to be," he replied. "England was. So I came over in '40 to do my part. I took a position at the University of St. Andrews. And I volunteered with SOE. Now everyone on their feet. It's time to go play with this rotten Japanese rifle."

Yukon asked, "What made you do it, Professor? I mean, you left your home in the States, your family..."

Lammeck sighed. He tapped the stock of the 99 on the floor.

"What made *you* do it, son?"

The Canadian glanced around, not eager to reply. He swallowed and plunged ahead.

"Well, no offense, sir, but we all signed up to fight. You're a bit too..."

"Old? So I am. You might as well mention fat while you're at it."

"Sorry, sir. But what made you come all the way to Scotland?"

"I was born in Prague."

The Jeds all nodded. Each man knew the portion of shame his own country would suffer in history over little Czechoslovakia. How, six years ago, each of their nations turned their backs when Hitler first cast his hunger at his eastern border. England and France violated their own treaties by refusing to defend their hapless ally. America had not yet stiffened its will to stand up to the Nazis, to engage again in another bloody European conflict. In a span of six months, Czechoslovakia had been gobbled up, carved into slices, parceled out to Germany, Hungary, and Poland.

"I was not happy that Czechoslovakia was sacrificed to the Hun for a few paper promises, a few more months of peace. Peace for who? Not for the Czechs. And I am still unhappy about it. So here I am. With you lads. Doing what I can."

Hesperus, in kilt, asked, "So, you've been with SOE since the beginning?"

"Yes."

"Then you must have trained ANTHROPOID."

Lammeck kept his surprise from his face. "Yes, I did."

Hesperus aimed a solemn glance around the ring. "They were the best, laddies," he whispered. "The *best*."

A few of the Jeds agreed. Amazing, Lammeck thought. A myth had sprung up.

The boys all seemed curious. Certainly they'd heard the story, everyone in SOE had. But clearly they were not aware of how badly it ended.

"Tell," the Scot said.

Lammeck hesitated, considering that it might be better to herd everyone outside with the Jap rifle. ANTHROPOID's tale was not going to help their morale. It had done little for his.

"Professor?"

"It's not pretty."

"Neither are we, man. Tell."

Lammeck shrugged, admitting he was in no hurry to stand outside and watch the boys shoot a poor weapon on such a dismal day. He folded his legs and took a spot on the floor. The Jeds shifted on their rumps to settle in. Most lit cigarettes.

Lammeck told them first of the hundreds of displaced Czech volunteers, who came from their betrayed land in 1940 to defend France, looking for places and ways to fight the Nazis. When France capitulated—Loo winced at this—the Czechs made their way next to England.

The Czech government-in-exile and SOE selected from the Czech Brigade three dozen commandos to return to their occupied nation. These thirty-six men would show the Soviets and British that the Czechs were still in the fight, and that an active underground existed that could be brought into play against the Germans there.

"Josef Gabčik and Jan Kubiš," Lammeck said, remembering the faces of the two boys, both young and smooth. Blue eyes. Best friends.

"Gabčik and Kubiš made up the team code-named ANTHROPOID. I had them here in Scotland for Weapons. They were not my best students, but they were the most enthusiastic. They dropped into Czechoslovakia, I remember, on December 29, '41. Their assignment was the same as yours, my lads. At the right time and at the right place, to perform sabotage or terroristic acts. But their job description went a little further. They were instructed to do something so big it would be known outside Czechoslovakia."

"And that's what they did," piped up Hesperus. "Wait'll you hear."

Yes, Lammeck thought. Wait.

"Gabčik and Kubiš spent months in the Prague underground, moving from safe house to safe house. Finally, they sent word to London. ANTHROPOID had chosen their target. They intended to kill Reinhard Heydrich, Reichsprotektor of Czechoslovakia."

The Jeds stirred and murmured. They'd heard of the killing of Heydrich. Lammeck guessed that was all these boys knew.

"ANTHROPOID gathered intel from Heydrich's house staff and gardener in Prague. The decision was made to attack the

Reichsprotektor's car as he was driven into the city to his office in Hradčany Castle. Gabčik and Kubiš picked a hairpin turn Heydrich had to pass on his way to work. The car would have to slow to make the turn. Right beside it was a tram stop where civilians gathered."

Lammeck paused. He recalled both boys on the weapons range. Gabčik was a below-average marksman with every weapon he picked up. He practiced extra hours but never improved. Kubiš was the better marksman, smarter with the machinery of guns. Both boys enjoyed a pub. Gabčik was a fine dancer, Kubiš a comic.

"Gabčik was like you, Thumbs. He preferred a Sten Mark II. On May 27, 1942, he carried it to the tram stop under a raincoat, with an extra clip, a grenade, and a .32 pistol in his pockets. Kubiš had two modified Type 73 antitank grenades in a briefcase. The grenades were packed with a pound of nitro each."

They did it backward, Lammeck thought. Kubiš should have had the Sten.

The Jeds leaned in, elbows on knees.

"Two Czech paratroopers from other teams were already on site. One kept a lookout to the south, the other had a mirror ready to signal Heydrich's approach. They expected the Reichsprotektor at 9:30 A.M. He was an hour late. The mirror flashed. A dark green Mercedes convertible slowed to go into the tight curve. Gabčik dropped his raincoat, stepped into the street, and pointed the Sten at Heydrich in the rear seat." Lammeck shook his head. "Nothing."

Some Jeds sat upright, some clucked tongues. Capone elbowed Thumbs. "I told you the Thompson was better. But no. Now look. Oh, sorry. Go ahead, Professor."

"In this case, Capone, I agree with you. The Sten malfunctioned."

Hesperus spit into the center of the circle. "I didn't know this part. Damn."

"The car sped up into the turn. Kubiš ran forward and threw one of his grenades. The thing exploded near the Mercedes' running board, tearing up the right-hand side of the car. Heydrich and his driver jumped from the car. The driver took off after Gabčik, who ran to a butcher shop. He got into a gunfight and wounded the driver. The butcher chased him out of the shop, and Gabčik disappeared into Prague. Kubiš lit out on his bicycle. The other two paratroopers did the same on foot."

Loo asked, "But Heydrich, he is dead, *oui*?"

Hesperus piped up, peeved, "Of course he's dead, you silly git."

"No." Lammeck raised a hand to soften Hesperus. "He's not. And Hitler was furious at the attempt on his governor's life. As punishment, he ordered a million-Reichsmark reward, and the execution of ten thousand Czech hostages."

"What?"

"By the next day, the Gestapo had collected enough evidence, like the dropped Sten and the British grenades, to figure out that the attackers were British-trained parachutists and not from any Czech underground or resistance group. So the Nazis held off on Hitler's orders. Instead, they started a massive manhunt for Kubiš and Gabčik."

"And Heydrich?" The Sphinx asked.

"He died in the hospital a week later from his wounds. An autopsy blamed blood poisoning from the grenade fragments. Probably he died from bacteria and lousy medical care."

"Good," the boys said. "Bastard."

"What about ANTHROPOID? Did they get away?"

This was the crux for these Jedburghs, for every boy going to war. These keen lads around Lammeck would surely do their jobs in Burma, Malaya, Japan, wherever they wound up. They'd been chosen by SOE on that basis. They would die if they had to. They wanted to know if Gabčik and Kubiš had.

"No. They did not get away."

The Jeds reacted with disgust. A few gazed away from Lammeck, who pressed on to make the ending quick, though it had not been for Kubiš and Gabčik, and a thousand others like them.

"Twenty thousand police and Gestapo started a manhunt across Prague for the four parachutists. A reward of twenty million crowns was posted. Every resident of the Czech Protektorate over the age of fifteen had to register with the police by May 30. In the first three days of June, a hundred and fifty violators of this rule were shot."

"Black-hearted Nazi rotters."

"What about Gabčik and Kubiš? How'd the Nazis get them?"

"The four parachutists who attacked Heydrich tried to get as far underground as they could. The Gestapo's house-to-house sweep almost nabbed them. They changed their appearances and looked for a place to hole up until the search died down. On June 1, they found an Orthodox priest who agreed to hide them in the basement of his church. Three more parachutists from other teams managed to get to the church, too. There, they were all betrayed."

"By who?" Every one of the Jeds was mesmerized. A stab in the back was the worst of fates. Each of these boys would soon be working in secret far behind enemy lines. Keeping that secret was the ultimate priority, for their missions and their lives.

"Hitler worked himself into a fit that his Reichsprotektor's killers hadn't been discovered. He upped his ante. Now he threatened to execute thirty thousand Czechs. Amnesty was promised to anyone who came forward with information on the assassination. Tips poured in to stave off Hitler's temper. One letter came right out and named Jan Kubiš and Josef Gabčik as Heydrich's killers. It was sent by an SOE-trained parachutist."

Curses burst forth. "Son of a bitch." "Bastard." "Bloody coward." Lammeck let them rage, before going on.

"On June 16, KarelČurda walked into Gestapo headquarters in Prague. The Germans established he'd been trained by us and parachuted in. Čurda told them he wanted no more reprisals against innocent Czechs, and that he wanted to save himself and his family. He gave them the names of every SOE operative and Czech underground member he knew. At dawn the next day, the raids started."

The Jedburghs were silent. None could meet Lammeck's eyes.

He continued: "I had Čurda here, too, with the rest. No one knew he'd turn out to be a weasel. He seemed like a good enough chap."

Lammeck resurrected Čurda's angular face for an instant. It was one that would have been forgotten, along with Kubiš's, Gabčik's, and the rest, had it not been for their brief roles in history.

"Several in the Prague underground, folks who'd hid or helped the parachutists, bit their cyanide capsules with the Gestapo at the door. More were rounded up and thrown into cells and interrogated. One young man was shown his mother's severed head floating in a tub of water. He broke, telling the Gestapo that his poor mom had warned him that if things went south and he needed shelter, he should head for the Orthodox Cathedral of Saints Cyril and Methodius."

Yukon muttered, "I don't fucking believe this."

"At dawn on the eighteenth, Gestapo and local police cordoned off the church and entered. A firefight broke out in the choir loft. Two of the parachutists were killed. Kubiš used his last bullet on himself. The priest was forced to show the Germans the small door leading down to the crypt. Čurda was brought in to talk the four remaining parachutists into surrendering. Then he had to duck from a machine gun blast."

Grizzly rattled a big fist. "Good."

"The fire department flooded the church basement. The water seeped out through drains and cracks in the floor. The police tossed tear gas canisters down to the crypt and the parachutists threw them back out to the street. Finally, after six hours of this, the Gestapo lost patience. They blew a big hole in the main entrance to the crypt. When they rushed in, four shots rang out. The parachutists killed themselves. The Germans found eleven weapons in the basement and not one round of ammunition left."

Lammeck had never told this story, gathered over the past two years from fragments of intelligence smuggled out of Prague. Now, seeing the way his Jedburghs were affected, he made up his mind that relating it would be a permanent fixture of his training regimen. Opening these boys' eyes and tearing a piece of their hearts was as important as instructing their hands.

"Then Hitler took his revenge."

The boys moaned.

"In June, the Führer ordered the destruction of the villages of Ležáky and Lidice. All the adult inhabitants of both villages were executed, about five hundred men and women. Lidice was obliterated. A road and a creek were diverted so no trace of the town would ever be seen again. Later, two hundred and fifty friends and relatives of the seven parachutists were executed. All the officials of the church where the parachutists hid were executed. Čurda the turncoat collected a five-million-crown bounty."

"Someone needs to cut that lad's throat."

"Or stretch it."

Lammeck surveyed the twelve young men around him. This would be all for now. He'd lead them back to the warm barracks and let them have the afternoon off. He didn't feel up to taking more weapons in hand, either. He wanted to put his feet up on the woodstove in his quarters and consider the human math of sending these boys, not much older than children, to murder one symbolic figure like Heydrich, resulting in so many subsequent deaths. Was it fair, even necessary? Yes. History, he thought, is built on bones. The lucky bones at least get to keep their names attached.

Lammeck gave his Jeds the ending to the tale.

"The skulls of those seven parachutists are kept on a shelf in the Gestapo headquarters in Prague."

"That's good enough for me." The Wizard rose from the circle, impatient. "Lads, what say we tell SOE to sod off on Burma. Let's drop into Prague. A bit of work left to do."

Capone shouted, "Here, here!"

Lammeck got to his feet, creaky from the cold floor. "The Japanese, boys," he told the Jeds. "Focus on the Japs. They're next for you."

"Professor, someone's got to take care of that bastard Čurda."

"He'll be dealt with, I suspect. Let's head back to the barracks."

The boys picked up their gear and filed for the door. Hesperus, his Scots face scarlet, wasn't done.

"Alright, laddies, it's the Jappos for us. What say we swear right now, every one of us, that if we get one shot at fucking Hirohito, the professor here can drink an ale out of our bloody skulls, and that's bloody alright with us. Hey? I swear."

All the Jedburghs formed a ring and piled their hands into the center. Hesperus led them to repeat, "I swear."

Lammeck stood aside, knowing he'd done his job today. He'd taken a step toward making these boys into assassins. He walked into the cold day, following their swagger, listening to their oaths. And, silently, as he had with Gabčik and Kubiš, he envied them.

January 8
University of St. Andrews
St. Andrews, Scotland

LAMMECK STEPPED TO THE podium.

His classroom windows looked north across St. Andrews Bay. The world outside shone blue and tranquil, glinting off riffles on the water, a calm and rare Scottish winter morn. Inside, his walls and chalkboard bore a pink cast, the reflection of the sun off the many ruby gowns of his students.

He smoothed the folds of his own black masters gown and pressed his belly against the lectern.

"Good morning, scholars."

Lammeck marveled, as he did at the beginning of every semester during these war years, that Britain could somehow field enough young men and women to fill his classroom. The University had weathered the six-year storm well, with only the Botany and Geology labs destroyed by bombs. Though blackouts remained in effect, and the staff worked overtime to cover for war-absent colleagues. St. Andrews reflected Churchill's admonition to his countrymen: "KBO"—Keep Buggering On. Spirits stayed high, especially on opening days as glorious as this, with the promise in the air that the war might end sometime this year. But no one at the University forgot The Count: So far, 153 students who'd left campus for National Service would never return from their graves in Europe, Africa, and the Pacific. Lammeck often regretted his extraordinary ability to recall their names and faces.

This semester's class held more new faces. At the desks were a fresh round of Air Force cadets, always clean-shaven and eager young bucks; a handful of Polish officers billeted in the area who were granted access to the University; two wounded veterans mustered out honorably—one lad wore an eye patch; a few young ladies from the London Medical School for Women, relocated to St. Andrews after bombs damaged their buildings down in London; and the usual smattering of bejants and bejantines, the ancient name here for first-years.

"Just so we are all on the same page, and to be certain no one has wandered in by error, this class is Beginning World History. I am Dr. Mikhal Lammeck. So rise now and retreat, or hold your place and away we go."

None of the cardinal gowns stirred. Lammeck left the podium.

"Right. Let us dive into the bloody mess that is human history. We'll start with a question. It is the single most important query for any historian, because the answer determines your point of view, the lens through which everything you study and decide about history will be colored. Tell me: Do you believe that history is made by men or by events? By this, I mean to ask, can a single man change or direct the course of history, or must history inevitably be the result of massive inevitabilities?"

Lammeck paused. The students cocked their heads and rubbed their chins. Lammeck searched for which smart child he might call on first if no volunteers presented themselves.

"Hmmm? I'll give you an example to help you along. As you may know, my area of expertise in world history is the assassin. The political killer. There have always been two types of assassination. First, it has been the work of an individual or individuals who kill for only two reasons: They might be deranged, or they might be revolutionaries. Either way, the murders they commit are motivated by a great, uncontrolled obsession for God, country, power, social change, or sometimes just to quiet the voices in their heads."

The class snickered at this last classification. Lammeck would have laughed, too, had he not known of so many examples.

"The second type of assassination is a bit colder: state-sponsored assassination. Every nation on earth has at one time or another utilized political murder as a way to further the state's ends."

One red-clad arm attached to a pimply bejant lifted.

"Yes?"

"*Every* nation, sir?"

Lammeck laughed. "Oh, yes, every nation. My own dear and brave America, for instance, has done this sort of thing many times, and not always with finesse. The first recorded instance of state assassination in America happened in 1620. Myles Standish, one of our stalwart Pilgrim leaders in Plymouth, invited the local Indian chief, the chief's younger brother, and two braves to a feast. Once the four were inside and seated, Standish locked the door and personally hacked one of the braves to death with his longknife. The chief and the other brave were murdered by several other Puritans in attendance. The chief's young brother was allowed to live long enough to be taken to the colony's edge and hung as a warning to the other Indians in the area. Now, was this the work of patriots? Or madmen?"

A few students uttered "Madmen." The older ones, the Poles and the veterans, said nothing.

"Madmen? Perhaps. But let's not forget that the Plymouth colony survived to become one of the few permanent colonies in the New World. And the New World became America. So, the question stands: Can even a bloodthirsty madman determine the course of history? Would the Plymouth colony have survived anyway without this atrocity? Or would the Indians have swept it away, and taken the one in Jamestown, Virginia, with it? Would America then have become not a British colony, but perhaps Spanish? How would that have affected the world's path? Incredibly, you must admit."

One of the medical students raised her hand.

"Yes?"

"Professor, doesn't it seem logical that if a country can go to war, and send millions to kill other millions, that it can also send one person to kill one particular person? Isn't assassination just a smaller act of war?"

The class nodded, appreciating this question. Lammeck approached the young woman.

"Could you do it? Assassinate someone, if you were convinced your own survival and the survival of your culture or country required it? And I mean kill a king, a queen, a president, the prime minister. A great leader, admired and followed by many, even millions. But you and your side, you disagree with his leadership. So: Could you kill a king?"

"I don't know. I...I don't think..."

"Yes, I understand, you're an aspiring physician. Life is precious and all that. And your hesitation is also history's hesitation. This quandary has tormented some of the greatest minds and commenters of history. On the battlefield, circumstances determine who must die. There's something random and, therefore, fair about it. But selecting one person? Marking one leader for death? It doesn't seem cricket. Who determines if a ruler must die? Who is the proper moral judge?"

Lammeck ambled his wide waistline through the desks.

"Saint Thomas Aquinas had no problem with killing a usurper to the throne, but he balked at murdering a legitimate monarch who'd become a tyrant. Here in Scotland, in fact, right here in St. Andrews, the great Calvinist John Knox preached that anyone, royal or otherwise, who did not share his faith was prime for assassination. Knox was quite incensed that Queen Elizabeth did not knock off her Catholic rival, Mary Queen of Scots. And of course, Niccolò Machiavelli made perhaps the best, and certainly most frequently cited, arguments on behalf of assassination, in his sixteenth-century book. Anyone know the piece?"

"*The Prince.*" The answer came from the lad with one eye.

"Correct. Machiavelli's main assertion was that religious and ethical notions have no place in politics." Lammeck quoted from memory: " *'It must be understood, that a prince cannot observe all of those virtues for which men are reputed good, because it is often necessary to act against mercy, against faith, against humanity, against frankness, against religion, in order to preserve the state.'* "

He let this notion settle with his crimson students, so bright in the early light.

"On the other side of the argument, no less a writer than Leo Tolstoy was quite clear in his disdain for Napoleon. The old Russian wrote in his epic *War and Peace* that Napoleon had led nothing, had changed nothing. The emperor was merely a figurehead on a great ship of state, only a name and face put out front before the great momentum of events, all of which would have happened with or without him."

One of the Polish officers timidly raised his hand.

"Professor."

"Yes."

The boy simply said, "Hitler."

"Of course, Hitler. There's a perfect example. Do you think if we could pull the little bastard up by the roots, if he'd been hit by a truck or gotten the clap early on, before he became *der Führer,* could this war have been avoided? You." Lammeck indicated the Brit veteran with both eyes, wondering where this boy's wound hid. "Go back in time and kill Hitler for me."

"Alright, sir."

"Now, what have we got? War or no?"

The boy hesitated. Lammeck watched him blink. Memories or pain—something—redirected him from this sunny, safe classroom away to the battle where he got whatever bullet or shard had been destined for him. Lammeck was about to relieve the soldier of the question when the lad replied:

"War, sir."

"Tolstoy agrees with you."

"And you, Professor?" The question came from the eye-patch soldier.

"As an historian, I straddle the fence. Machiavelli could argue that it might've been a good job to send a few of Hitler's pals to Hades with him, like Goebbels and Himmler. I think we might actually have spared ourselves a lot of trouble by erasing that crowd from history sooner rather than later. I agree with our lovely med student here that state-sponsored assassination can be viewed as an act of war. But I cannot be convinced that poking knives into Julius Caesar altered anything along the lines which Brutus and Cassius anticipated. In fact, ending Caesar's dictatorship did not result in the republic but only in Augustus and the long line of autocratic Caesars who followed. Later, the murder of feeble Tiberius served to open the door for that SOB Caligula. Or take little Gavrilo Princip and his Serbian band of Black Hand assassins who plotted against, then plugged, Archduke Franz Ferdinand. This act toppled all the dominos to start The Great War. Even so, historians agree that that war was just waiting for a spark, and it would have found one even without Princip's pistol. No one seriously pretends that Ramon Mercader, Trotsky's ax-murderer in Mexico City, was not an agent for Stalin. Trotsky's dead, Stalin is Stalin, and the world keeps spinning Russia's way. The message here is that it's hard to imagine anyone worse than Hitler. What if the plot last July to assassinate him had succeeded? Some argue that that would have accomplished nothing but to end the war last year instead of this year. Then Germany would have been able to cry that it was betrayed and that's why it lost, the way it did after the last war, instead of having its fanny kicked on the battleground fair and square and for good. What if we could have eliminated Hitler in his cradle? Might that have changed history for the better, or worse? Or would it perhaps have just put a different and equally loathsome figurehead on Tolstoy's ship of state? A good many historians and philosophers believe that, sooner or later, here we'd be, right where we should be."

For a moment, Lammeck thought of hauling before this new crop of students the bodies of Gabčik and Kubiš. The sacrifice of the two young Czechs had been sponsored by the British state, and by Lammeck personally. They'd certainly been successful assassins. Heydrich was dead. And what was the result? The martyred Reichsprotektor was celebrated on stamps in Nazi Germany. Czechoslovakia remained brutally occupied. The towns of Lidice and Ležáky had been erased. Nothing had changed, not for the better.

Even realizing this might happen, Gabčik and Kubiš hadn't straddled any fences. Nor do any of those boys up in the Highlands, training on this fine morning to kill.

What was the lesson?

Lammeck shrugged, to show he did not know, and to end this part of the discussion.

A hand went high from one of the Air cadets.

"Yes?"

"What about the others, Professor? The lone actors."

"Ah, the zealots and avengers. The crazed gunmen, poisoners, and stabbers. Yes, what about them? They're my favorites. They are history's wild cards. The ghosts in the machine. Impulsive, always oddly timed. Sometimes they act at a pivotal moment, when teetering history just needs a slight nudge to fall hard. Sometimes their targets are marked for death anyway; history was simply done with them. Other times the assassination is a tragedy, marked by woe the world over, because it served nothing but hatred. John Wilkes Booth's handiwork falls into this category."

"Lincoln," added one of the med students.

"That was an easy one, so don't look so smug. Some say Lincoln was our greatest American president. Booth's plan was to kill both Lincoln and Ulysses Grant, who was supposed to be in Ford's Theater that night with the President. Other conspirators were to murder a few more officials in the government on the same evening, Good Friday, April 14, 1865. None of them pulled it off, though Secretary of State Seward was stabbed in the throat. Booth was the only one to score big that night. Grant was not in attendance at the theater with the President because Mrs. General Grant had grown tired of Mary Lincoln's hysterical outbursts—Mrs. Lincoln was not a well woman—and begged off. After the play began, Lincoln's only bodyguard, a member of the Washington police force, left the presidential box for a nearby tavern. By now, the Civil War was over. The only thing Booth, a Southerner, could achieve was revenge. He walked unhindered into Lincoln's box, cried out *'Sic semper tyrannis'*—Ever thus to tyrants—and with a derringer shot Lincoln behind the left ear."

Another of the Air Force cadets piped up. "Are you saying nothing changed in America with Lincoln's death?"

Lammeck strolled the sunny classroom.

"Always difficult to tell, of course. This sort of inquiry is a brew of fact and speculation. But no, Andrew Johnson stepped in as president and the sun came up the next morning. Secretary of State Seward recovered. However, after studying assassinations for twenty years, I have my own little theory. I believe that history anticipates certain acts. She readies herself for them to keep everything on track. But I don't think history saw Booth coming. You can always spot when history is annoyed, when one of her favored sons or daughters is killed before their time. She steps in and does something exceptional, to make certain the assassins get caught. Here's what happened. After shooting Lincoln, Booth leaped over the railing to grab a curtain and slide down to the stage floor. But his spur got caught on the fabric and he fell to the stage, breaking his left leg.

Without this injury, John Wilkes Booth might have ridden fast out of Washington and gotten himself lost among the rebel soldiers flowing home after Lee's surrender. As it was, he needed medical attention. He got that attention from a Maryland physician named Dr. Mudd. This unfortunate country doctor appears to have been in the wrong place at the wrong time. Implicated in the conspiracy, he was sentenced to life in prison. The doctor also gave rise to an American saying. When someone's luck abandons them, we like to say 'Your name is Mudd.' History has a sense of balance, you see, even fair play, and is not without humor. She accepts but does not like caprice. History does not pout; she picks up her skirt and moves on. That's why she fascinates us."

Lammeck returned to his podium.

"This is the question, my scholars. Do great men and women create their times, or do great events identify the people needed and simply allow them to take the credit? The list of the great who have been cut down before their time is ludicrously long. Pancho Villa and Zapata, Thomas Becket, Nicholas II, Shaka Zulu, American Presidents Garfield and McKinley, Rasputin, Wild Bill Hickok, eight popes, and more Chinese and Roman emperors, English and French kings and queens, shahs, tsars, and Latin American dictators than you can imagine. And let's not forget the lucky ones who dodged assassination attempts. Hitler, Lenin, both Teddy and Franklin Roosevelt—a list as lengthy as the roll call of poor buggers who bought the farm. But not once did history pirouette and dance off in another direction just because one of her actors had left the stage."

Lammeck stopped to look over his charges.

"Or did she?"

The students all seemed breathless at the scope of carnage among the famous and important. They sat eager and baffled by the answerless question. Lammeck could have continued at this pace for hours, casting famed and obscure names and episodes, near misses and fatal luck. On this first day of the semester, however, he decided they were going to be a good class and rewarded them. He'd dismiss them early. He'd go back to his flat, work through the rest of the day, then leave at dawn for the Highlands, for tomorrow's weapons session with the Jeds.

"I'm going to let you go a bit early today. You have the reading assigned for Wednesday? But first, one more tale. Then off with you."

Lammeck pointed to a small poster tacked to a corkboard hung on his classroom wall. The poster depicted the painting by the artist David of Jean-Paul Marat, knifed in his bathtub.

"At fifty years old, Jean-Paul Marat was a doctor turned journalist and revolutionary. His writings are widely held to be responsible for helping unleash the Reign of Terror which cropped up to defend the French Revolution. Marat approved of the slaughter of thousands, stating that the guillotine must stay busy in order to keep the revolution alive. He composed death lists. He demanded that the French king be executed. On July 13, 1793, a twenty-four-year-old Girondist, Charlotte Corday, arrived at Marat's door in the turmoil of revolutionary Paris. She was stopped by guards, but Marat heard her insist and called out to admit the girl to his bathroom. He sat soaking, working on his lists, in a disgusting medicinal mixture designed to relieve a festering skin disease, now believed to have been a wanking case of herpes. Miss Corday told him of antirevolutionary activities in her hometown of Caen. Marat shouted, 'I shall send them all to the guillotine in a few days!' Taking this as her cue, young Charlotte produced a six-inch knife from her bodice and plunged it into Marat's lung and aorta. At her trial, held two days afterward, she steadfastly refused her lawyer's plea of insanity, crying out that she had committed an act of assassination. 'That,' she declared, 'is the only defense worthy of me.' Only four days after killing Marat, the brave girl faced the guillotine. The historical result of Charlotte's act was that, in the frenzy that followed, many thousands more were sentenced to death than Marat at his best might have been able to order murdered. A sad outcome. But dear

Charlotte Corday had one of the nicest moments in all my studies of assassinations and assassins. Shall I tell you?"

The rapt students shouted, almost indignantly, "Yes!"

"Alright, settle down. Listen to this. After the guillotine had lopped her off at the neck, Charlotte's executioner held up her head to the crowd. And slapped her."

The class sat agape. Someone coughed. Lammeck chortled by himself.

"No?" he pleaded. They stared. "You don't think that's just perfect?"

Lammeck sighed, resigned that, even with a promising class, he alone might appreciate history's beauty, that a century and a half later he would even know Charlotte Corday's name. This was splendidly unpredictable, human, and seductive.

"Alright, go home."

LAMMECK POURED A DRAMBUIE. He swirled the tastes of Scotch whisky, heather honey, and herbs over his tongue. The window beside his desk looked down over Muttoes Lane, a brick alley where scarlet academic robes mingled with drab townsfolk. He set the glass on the sill to inspect the afternoon light through the amber liqueur.

He flicked a finger against the sheet of paper, upright and blank in his typewriter, to punish it for being blank. Below his window, some students laughed.

Lammeck sat back in his chair, knitting fingers across his stomach. On his desk, lunch waited uneaten. The plate was partially covered by the pages of a book. He gazed at the ceiling of his apartment, also broad, white, and empty.

What was the answer? Lammeck wanted to know, or at least take a position. If he could muster a convincing argument one way or another, he could capture it on the pages of his book, intended to be the scholarly last word on the impact of assassinations throughout history. Thereafter he'd be hailed or reviled in academia; he didn't care which.

An old historian's instinct and common sense told him the times *must* change if the leaders are taken away. How could they not? The voices of insurrection silenced, the conqueror's sword dropped to the sand, a throne toppled? These were more than the personalities of history: They were her engines. But the weight of evidence didn't support this conclusion. Not when history was viewed in the long term, across the decades and centuries. Other leaders inevitably stepped in. Other forces rose to counteract. Even Nature intervened, with storms, volcanoes, earthquakes.

Lammeck had spent his adult life chasing the answer. He'd pored over annals and archives, studied not just assassinations and their ripples but the killers themselves, their mind-sets, private lives, customs, tactics, conspiracies. He'd trained himself in the assassin's weapons and ancient craft. He collected images, pinning them up on the large corkboard covering one wall of his office, slayer beneath the slain, matching them for his book the way history had.

As much as he knew, he was convinced of very little. This was why the treatise he'd been writing since he came to Scotland five years ago was unfinished.

He stared at the corkboard. The hundreds of withholding faces gazed back. With his finger, Lammeck again snapped the naked page in his typewriter.

A knock sounded at his door.

Lammeck scowled. Who would bother him at home during lunch and his work? He left his cluttered desk to head down the hall, ready to blister someone.

Opening the door, he found the man in the foyer was no student, no soldier, but a civilian in a rumpled mackintosh and a beat fedora.

"Well, well. Look at this bad penny showing up on my doorstep."

"Professor."

"Mr. Nabbit. Do come in."

Lammeck stood aside. The man strode into the small flat, looking around.

"Nice," he observed.

"Small. But well located. I have a pub twenty steps away."

The man did not remove his hat. "I owe you," he said, narrowing his eyes.

"Me?" Lammeck feigned innocence. "Whatever for?"

"It stuck. That damn nickname you gave me. I can't get away from it."

Lammeck laid a hand to his former Jedburgh's shoulder.

"Honestly, I had no choice. If someone came to you with the last name of Nabbit, what else could you call him?" Lammeck shrugged, helpless. "Really. Now have a seat and I'll get you a drink."

Lammeck smiled, then turned away to fetch the bottle of Drambuie.

When he returned, Dag Nabbit had taken off his hat and raincoat. He'd tossed them over the sofa arm. His shirt and tie needed either a good pressing or an incinerator. Lammeck shook his head and went to the kitchen to fetch another glass. He called into the den, "Before I ask what you're doing here, how'd the mission go?"

"Lousy," Dag said. He accepted the glass, then held it out while Lammeck poured. The two clinked glasses and swallowed.

Lammeck eased into a rocker. The chair creaked to his girth. Dag took the sofa.

"You're still a bear," Dag remarked, pointing his Drambuie at Lammeck.

"And you've lost a stone, at least. What happened in France? That was last April, yes?"

"April Fool's Day. Perfect. I lost my radio man on the drop. Lost our equipment in a bog. Got captured after three days of wandering around ten miles from where we were supposed to meet the resistance. I didn't stay long. Didn't like the Nazis' accommodations."

"How'd you get out?"

"Actually, pretty much like you taught us. Amazing the things you can make a garrote out of."

Lammeck raised an inquiring eyebrow.

"Shoelace."

Lammeck nodded. "Excellent."

"And a belt."

"Of course."

"And a vine."

"Dag, that's . . . that's quite a specialty. Would you like to come to the Highlands with me tomorrow and teach technique?"

"Nah."

"Of course. I assume you're in St. Andrews on business. Too cold to play golf. Although these Scots will tee off in a blizzard."

Dag drained his Drambuie. Lammeck noted the man still had his nervous energy.

"So, Dag, who has the pleasure of employing you at the moment?"

"I'm with the Secret Service."

Lammeck raised his glass. "Special Agent Dag Nabbit. That is a far cry from crawling in the mud with a shoelace between your teeth. How did this plum fall your way?"

"When I got back to the States, I took their test. After two months with you in the damn hills shooting every morning at dawn, I was pretty crackerjack with a firearm. I asked for my discharge to join up and the Army let me go. I'm on the President's security detail."

"Ah, FDR. How is the old son of a bitch?"

Dag met his eyes squarely. "Okay. Knowing how you feel about Czechoslovakia, you get that one for free. But no more. Alright?"

Lammeck let it go; he'd taken his shot and hit center. "Certainly.

Anyway, congratulations, Dag. I assume everyone calls you Dag. I take pride in that."

"Let's just say you're never far from my thoughts."

The two grinned at each other.

"Professor, I came back to get you."

"Get me?"

"Take you back to the States. We might have a situation."

"Who is we?"

"I can't say."

"Why not?"

"There's four people in the whole United States who know what I know. Before I make you number five, you're going to be standing on American soil. I'll send a car for you in an hour."

"I'm going back to the States? You're joking. What about my university classes?"

"I've already talked to your department head. He's not happy but he understands who I work for."

"And the Jedburghs?"

"Same."

Lammeck rose from the rocker. On his feet, he looked back down the hall to his office.

"But my work."

Dag looked up at him, chuckling. "You still on that book?"

Lammeck glowered. Dag was a philistine, an unrefined American killer now working for the other side. Lammeck couldn't expect him to appreciate a scholarly work like his, of import and historical breadth.

"Yes. *The Assassins Gallery.* I'm still working on it and I plan to continue."

"Well," Dag grunted, rising from the sofa, "you're just gonna have to get back to it later."

"You seem pretty sure I'm coming."

"I figure you know who I work for, too. Anyway, trust me. It's right up your alley. And you're the best man on the planet for what I need."

"Tell me what you've got, Dag. Or no deal."

Dag screwed the felt fedora on his head. Lammeck wanted to swipe it off and reshape it, then plant it back on the man's messy crown.

"I'll tell you what's public," the Secret Service man said. "The rest you get when you step off the plane. We got two dead Civil Defense wardens on a remote beach, a man and a woman in Newburyport, Massachusetts. Both were knifed to death around two-thirty on New Year's morning. And we got the husband of the dead woman, committed suicide in his house. Gunshot to the temple. About three-fifteen that same morning. A big kitchen knife with blood on it was found in his sink."

Lammeck watched Dag don the rumpled raincoat. "Sounds open-and-shut."

"It isn't."

Dag headed for the door, lips tight. Lammeck didn't move.

"So what got the attention of the Secret Service? Why do you need me?"

Dag turned the doorknob to let himself out.

"Pack a bag, Professor. Quick. I'll tell you in Boston."

CHAPTER THREE

January 9
Washington, D.C.

JUDITH STEPPED OUT THE front door of the Commodore Hotel. Across the street, beyond the corner of North Capitol and F, sprawled the immense station house and acres of rail of Union Station. She'd come to enjoy the sounds and dark diesel exhaust of the trains coming and going at all hours. Taxis and crowds arrived and departed; many times Judith waded into the tides of people to listen, walk like them, observe their clothing, and speak on occasion.

She'd spent the last six days in shops, in restaurants, on sidewalks, listening to the radio, reacclimating to America. She'd practiced her Midwestern flat tones and her Negro accent. She'd made herself facile at the humility of the colored girl, the springy step of the pretty American white girl, and could instantly switch between the two. She'd assembled a small wardrobe for her poses in both races.

This morning, a blue and crisp day, Judith was ready.

She wore a dark blue woolen dress with a ribbon at the throat, bought at a thrift store in the Trinidad section of the city, along with a cobalt pillbox hat and blue flats without nylons. Before leaving her room, she'd made sure to put on a mismatched brown coat, slightly but unmistakably secondhand.

The walk to the Public Welfare Building lasted only eight blocks and took her closer to the White House. The last time she'd been in Washington, this nation was not yet at war, and this city was not the capital of the Free World. Now, the classic dome rose high against the sky with a deeper meaning, a sort of proud puffing of America's white chest at a world saved by its hand. Judith nodded at the dome. She relished the increased power of Washington and America now, better adversaries than the last time they met.

At the P.W. Building, she found the listing on the wall for the District Housing Assistance Office. Moving deeper into the building, she rounded a corner and halted at two signs. Arrows pointed different directions: right for WHITE, left for COLORED. Judith turned left.

Quickly she stepped into the rear of a long line. Most of the Negroes waiting in it were dressed like her, in proper but worn clothes, while a few of the men stood out in pressed suits and fedoras, carrying leather briefcases. More brown men and women filtered around the corner to fill in behind Judith. Several in the line recognized one another, but voices stayed low. The corridor smelled of hair products, soap, and wool.

Judith listened to the talk in the line. The Negroes made smiling reference to yesterday's *Amos 'n Andy* radio show, at how Kingfish had snookered Andy Brown again and landed in hot water with wife Sapphire. A few held open the *Washington Post;* many nearby leaned in to read the spread pages. They remarked on the banner headline: **U.S. Forces Land on Luzon, Philippines.** They tapped the pages approvingly over articles describing the imminent victory, mostly Patton's credit, of beating back the Nazi winter offensive in Belgium. One proud lady's boy was "over there." The sports section gave rise to laments about the Redskins' heartbreaking season. Quarterback Sammy Baugh got hurt and only played eight games, and had his worst statistical year. The Redskins got knocked out of the championship by losing twice to the New York Giants at the end of the season; the last game, without Sammy, was a 31-0 humiliation. A few women knit from bright balls of yarn secreted in oversized handbags. Most of the folks just stared ahead and shuffled forward when the line crept ahead.

Forty minutes passed before Judith reached the head of the line. She stepped through an open door into a small room divided into two cubicles. The desk on the left was busy with the woman who'd been in front of her in the line. From behind the righthand desk, a squat, sharp-faced white lady beckoned her.

"Over here, honey."

Judith took the seat before the desk. The woman greeted her with eagerness, an odd energy since she'd likely seen several dozen people in Judith's seat already this morning.

She put forth her hand, tweeting, "How're you? I'm Miz Sanderson."

Judith took the lady's hand for a firm shake.

"What's your name, honey?"

Judith hesitated, needing to adjust to the thickness of the woman's accent, a southern twang Judith had not heard before. To Judith it sounded as if she'd been asked for her *"nime."*

"Desiree Charbonnet."

"My, that's a bee-utiful name. Where your people from?"

"New Orleans."

Miz Sanderson touched her breast with an open palm. "Oh, my stars, I was there once before the war and I am *still* tryin' to recall how much fun I had. Well, welcome to Washington. You just get in?"

"Yes, ma'am."

"Where you stayin' now?"

"A hotel."

"Well, that cain't be cheap. Let's us see if we cain't find you someplace to live..." she scrunched her features and turned her face sideways, "...a little more reasonable. Okay?"

Judith watched the woman work through the typewritten sheaves on her desk. While she dug, Miz Sanderson asked questions: "How much education you got, sweetie?" "What kind of work you expectin' to do?" "How much experience you got?" "Your folks sendin' you any money to help out?"

Finally, she lit on two specific pages that she felt best matched pay and expectations to Judith's abilities.

"Okay, we ought to have somethin' here. You're a nice-looking girl, I'm gonna bet you'll find some good job lickety-split. Now, Desiree, as you know, the federal government works with a couple hundred real estate firms here in the District to help find places for folks just like you."

"You mean blacks."

Miz Sanderson reached across the desk with a touch to Judith's arm. "Honey, I'm sorry, but yes. Even so, you've done yourself a big favor by coming to this office. It's gonna save you a lot of heartache. Comin' from New Orleans, I'm sure you understand."

"Yes, ma'am. But isn't this America's capital?"

"You sound surprised, darlin'. Don't be." Miz Sanderson considered Judith for a long moment. She looked up at the long line waiting to follow into Judith's chair, then made some decision to spend a few extra moments with this pretty and naïve colored girl.

"Desiree, let me tell you how things work here in America's capital. You know Washington is a federal district, don't you? We don't have our own city government; Congress administers us. And to be honest, Congress, in the middle of a war, couldn't care less about us." Miz Sanderson lowered her voice. "The District Committees in the House and Senate are the two worst assignments in Congress. All they got is junior members or ol' bastards they're tryin' to punish. And let me tell you, sweetie, sometime you should meet the ancient sumbitch who heads the District Committee in the Senate, the honorable Theodore Bilbo from the enlightened state of Mississippi. He hates everybody—Communists, unions, Jews, foreigners, and, of course, coloreds. Last month he recommended on the Senate floor that all America's Negroes be deported to Africa, and that Mrs. Eleanor Roosevelt be sent with them as their queen."

Miz Sanderson put her fingers to her lips, fearing she'd said something too volatile for Judith's ears. But Judith laughed, squelching her own grin behind her fingers. It was too ludicrous to believe, this secret America.

"Go on," Judith prodded.

"Well, honey, honestly, it's not going to get better for a while yet."

"What about President Roosevelt? Hasn't he done anything for the colored people here?"

Again, Miz Sanderson paused in scrutiny of Judith, a hint of surprise on her face. Judith reproached herself: She'd exposed her lack of knowledge about being an American Negro in the South. And no mistake, Washington, D.C., was southern.

The woman answered, "For all the good works of the New Deal, racial issues were left out. There's no way Roosevelt is ever going to antagonize his power base, and that's the southern Democrats. So no, Desiree, don't look to the President for much help. Not this president, anyway."

Judith repeated the phrase in her head. *Not this president.*

Miz Sanderson lifted the two pages. Looking over them, she smiled sympathetically.

"Desiree, I trust you are not looking for the Ritz-Carlton. This city is crowded, tight enough to bust. Once the war started, D.C. grew by leaps and bounds, it seemed overnight. There's work here, there's opportunity, yes. But I want you to know, it's not all good. Our murder rate is twice that of New York's. Last year alone there were more than fifty thousand cases of venereal disease. The telephones and water systems are ready to explode from overwork.

Traffic is terrible. And, like you noticed, this city is still very segregated. Washington is packed solid, confused and doggone stubborn. Half the places I can offer you have no indoor plumbing. The other half are only a little bit better, but twice as expensive. Everything on this list is run-down and in a dangerous neighborhood."

The woman paused, blinking at Judith with concern.

"One last thing. If you've come to Washington to find a romance, honey, forget it. With almost every man good enough to hear thunder gone off in uniform somewhere else, the ratio of women to men here is about eight to one. So before I help you find a room, I got to ask if you're sure you want to be here?"

Judith stood from the chair. She'd taken more than her share of this kindly woman's time. The others in the line, the coloreds who would make the real difference in this city and country, stirred expectantly.

She stretched out her hand.

"Thank you, ma'am. I'll take the list, please."

January 10

JUDITH RESTED HER LUGGAGE. This was her second frustrating day of hauling her two bags around Washington's inner city, working her way down the rental list in her purse. She stood on the porch of the only apartment she'd found that was available for a single colored woman. Everything else on Miz Sanderson's list had already been rented when she got there, or was shared space like a dormitory.

On the porch next door, an old, dark woman wrapped in a patch quilt tilted in a creaking cane rocker. The woman pulled a corncob pipe from her mouth and raised it in greeting.

In front of the locked door, the landlord fiddled with a ridiculous ring of keys, jangling and cursing under his breath. He had a lazy eye and a bristled gray chin. Behind him, his teenage son had the same wandering eye. The eye probably kept him out of the military. He wore a black-and-white jacket too thin for the weather.

"Jus' a minute," the landlord muttered, not looking up. He tried several keys. The old Negro woman chuckled in the cold afternoon, shaking her head behind her pipe. At the man's rear, his son edged into impatient fidgeting, waiting for the door to be unlocked. The boy ran hands along his temples to smooth down his slicked hair. He chewed a toothpick and lightly tapped a foot to a song in his head, as if he were standing at a microphone. Judith smiled at the boy, who jerked his shoulders in response, cool, eager to be older and not standing behind his clumsy father who was keeping them all waiting.

Another three keys were rejected by the lock. Before another could be slid into the slit, the boy stepped up. He snatched the key ring from his father—Judith thought it impatient and disrespectful—to locate the proper key. The man raised his hands to surrender to the boy and sighed, but did not scold his son.

Waiting, Judith looked up and down the alley of rotting steps and tar-paper shingles, careful to keep her face impassive. Litter rolled across the old cobbles; two Negro boys chased a paper cup caught in a wind devil. The only other time Judith had been in Washington, D.C., had been winter, too, four years ago, ten months before Pearl Harbor. The weather then was just as freezing and damp. But she had seen none of this squalor, only the central train station, a trolley, the lobby of the Bellevue Hotel, room 310, and, again, the train station.

With a triumphant grin, the boy found the right key. He jiggled the rickety door open. The glass pane in the door was spiderwebbed and held together by tape.

The father did not touch her bags, but the son made a show of lifting the heavier of the two. The boy held the door for her to enter first, crooning "Missy." The father, oblivious, stepped inside ahead of her; the son grimaced at his back. Judith hefted her smaller bag and followed into a dim hall lit by one bare dangling bulb. The smells of greasy cooking clung to the green walls. The man led her to the third door. The son stayed one stride behind. Judith smelled the fustiness of cigarettes on them both.

"Here you go." This time the man had the room key ready. When Judith flattened her palm to receive it, he drew the key back.

"First month's rent."

"May I see the room first?"

"Sure, but I got three gals just like you waitin' for it, if you don't want it."

Judith cut her eyes to the boy, who made a scrunched face and nodded sharply, telling her to take it. She set down her bag and took from her purse a small wallet, to give the man a ten and four ones.

He pocketed the money, handing over the key. The boy winked; his toothpick jumped on his lips.

The father said, "I'll be around the first of every month. Cash only."

Judith asked, "What if something breaks?"

"Fix it or wait to the first of the month to tell me about it."

She smiled prettily into the wandering eye.

"Or, you know," the son piped up, pulling out the toothpick and sliding in front of his father, "you can leave a note at the front office and I can maybe drop by, if you need somethin' bad enough."

"Thank you."

"I can fix most anything."

The father elbowed the son aside. "Alright, Josh."

The man turned away. Josh the son lingered long enough to wink again and mouth "Anytime" to her. Then he followed his father down the hall.

Judith slid the key into the lock. Opening the door, she caught her breath at the condition of the room; nothing seemed without a stain. The doorknob came off in her hand. She stood beside her bags in the threshold, then awoke, striding for the front door, hoping to catch them to at least repair the knob. Reaching the porch and the cold slap of air, she saw father and son already far down the alley, turning a corner, and gone. Judith looked above the tin roofs of the alley. One mile to the south, the white dome of the U.S. Capitol jabbed into a sulky sky.

The old colored woman in her rocking chair nodded, still sucking her corncob. Judith acknowledged her, raising the doorknob in her hand. The woman laughed.

"Oh, I can see already. You gon' love it here, darlin'."

JUDITH MOVED DOWN THE hall, matching sounds to closed doors. At the wail of an infant, she knocked and found a hefty black woman with a fat baby on her hip and two others on the floor. Judith borrowed a broom and dustpan. Next, she followed the sound of a radio and scored a box of suds, given to her by a large yellow-eyed man in a torn undershirt. From a third door, oddly hiding a practicing violin, she secured a scouring brush and a sponge. The little pigtailed girl who gave her these was alone.

Judith cleaned her room. Hot water flowed amply in the sink, where she soaked the bed linens in the soap powder. She chipped baked clots off the hot plate and used the wet sponge to lift dust from shelves. She unpacked her bags into an old chifforobe and bureau, both of them peeling veneer. Driving south from Boston, she'd passed through New York City. In Harlem she'd purchased the luggage, two dresses, a winter coat, slacks, shoes, undergarments, a sweater, and the pillbox hat. She shoved her passports, identifications, cash, and kits under the blue tick mattress. The Nash she'd driven from Massachusetts waited in a rented garage three blocks away.

Once the room lost its musty odor, Judith scrubbed the floor. She stood after an hour on hands and knees, ignoring the curtains on the dingy window. She'd wash them some other afternoon. She walked outside to let her floorboards dry.

The old woman had not left her rocker but had finished her pipe.

Judith walked to the railing separating the porches, determined that it would hold her weight, and sat. She swept a curl of hair from her face.

"Girl," the woman said, "you bes' go back inside and put some clothes on. You catch a death out here."

"I'm alright. Thank you."

"Come over here and set with me, then."

Judith left her porch and took a stool beside the woman.

"What's your name, child?"

"Desiree Charbonnet."

"That's pretty, that's nice. Kinda rhymes. Everybody calls me Mrs. P. My husband was Mr. Pettigrew."

"Pleased to meet you, Mrs. P."

"Where your people from?"

"New Orleans."

"Laws." Mrs. P. rocked and cackled. "I love *that* town! Bourbon Street. Yes." The woman composed a memory and did not share it. Judith put her arms around herself. Her sweat began to chill in her clothes. Mrs. P. undid the comforter and wrapped it around Judith.

"Thank you."

"You jus' skin and bone. But we gon' fatten you up. I used to look just like you, 'cept them pretty blue eyes. What are you, girl, one of them Creole Negroes?"

Judith had no reason to object, it seemed a fine explanation.

"Yes, ma'am."

"Well, welcome to the capital of America. When you get here?"

"Last week. I've been staying in a motel, looking for a room to rent."

"A mo-tel? That must've been 'spensive."

Judith thought of the six thousand dollars she'd just stashed under her mattress. In addition to her fee, she was allowed to keep whatever she did not spend.

"Yes, ma'am."

"You gon' stay long?"

"I'm not sure."

"Yeah, I wasn't sure neither, forty years ago when I come to town. Things sure done changed."

Judith accepted the respite beside this affable old woman. Nestled inside the quilt, which smelled crisp and clean, she let Mrs. P. ramble.

"This war is what done it. Yes, ma'am, jus' six years ago this was nothin' but a sleepy little town. Then people start comin' after that Pearl Harbor. White people comin' on trains and buses, like pigeons goin' after corn, flockin' here."

She waved her cool pipe to encompass all around her, the capitol spire in the sky.

"Gubmint workers. Throwin' up temporary buildings all over D.C. You seen 'em, big ugly things on the Mall and both sides of the Reflecting Pool. Oh, my, this war is big business. And black folks, too, comin' here lookin' for work, like I reckon you doin'. City got twice as many people since the war. Now, tell me somethin'. Where everybody gon' live? Where they gon' put all them new office buildings to run they war? You think the whites gon' knock down *they* homes? No, ma'am."

Mrs. P. pointed her pipe west. " 'Cross the river, they knocked down homes of two hundred Negro families to put up that Pentagon. And more Negroes was kicked out when they took more space for Arlington Cemetery. Black homes been busted up all over this city, for offices and highways and homes for white folk. Like in Foggy Bottom where I lived for nineteen years. Kicked out so the gubmint could build theyself some buildings and such. Same thing over in Georgetown, blacks just been shooed out. And we ain't got nary a thing back from them. Didn't build us nothin'. Jus' about every new home goin' up is restricted."

Judith did not know this term or idea. "Restricted?"

"Girl, whites only. Can't sell to no black folks; it's the law. What you talkin' 'bout, you don't know restricted?"

Mrs. P.'s surly moment passed. She patted Judith's knee.

"So here we are, right where we supposed to be, I reckon, right where we started out. These alleys been here since the War Between the States. White folks been ownin' these shacks for a hundred years, makin' a dollar off of black folk. Coloreds been on these stones since Abe Lincoln, and it ain't gon' change no time soon. You can hang on to that quilt. I'll get it back sometime after you settle in."

Judith nodded her appreciation.

The old woman stood on swollen ankles and bowed legs. She asked, "Desiree, you don' talk much, do you?"

"No, ma'am. I don't have much to say."

"Child, everybody got somethin' to say."

The woman stepped close. She lifted a hand to Judith's chin, moving her face side to side, examining. "Mmm, somethin'," she said. "Somethin' here, I dunno."

Mrs. P. stepped back. "Jus' not everybody uses words to say it. That's all."

Judith smiled. "Yes, ma'am."

The woman pivoted on her legs, so arched she seemed to straddle a barrel. She opened her own door, and before stepping off the porch said, "You need anything, you come see Mrs. P."

"I will."

"That's right. Whatever you come to this capital to do, girl, now you got a friend."

POVERTY WAS SHOT THROUGH the veins of this capital city, not unlike Cairo or Algiers. But when Judith walked onto the broad boulevard of New York Avenue, the poorness of the alleys vanished; the city's Negroes and their shantytowns were neatly tucked away. The ten-block walk to the White House took her along a streetcar route, past many large buildings, many of them still glittering with Christmas decorations, among them the Hippodrome

Theater, a department store called Goldenberg's, a Greyhound bus station, and, closer to the White House, more theaters and play-houses. The one-mile walk was trivial; Judith could have run it full bore. But the flashing green and red bulbs and golden bows from the holiday colored the sundown and slowed her gait. Streetcar bells tolled their stops. The stroll was pleasant.

Traffic on New York Avenue thickened as the end of the business day neared. The sidewalk buzzed with pedestrians, mostly women in rich fabrics and furs. Judith ducked into a store just before it closed. She did not speak with a Negro accent and did not avert her eyes, so the salesclerk was pleasant. She bought a scarf and thicker woolen gloves than what she'd been wearing.

At a quarter to five o'clock, Judith stood on the lawn of the Ellipse, the vast oval expanse two hundred yards south of the President's residence. Guards manned two gates left and right, checking the credentials of cars pulling onto the grounds. In the dis-tance, other guards patrolled the vast green expanse at the foot of the big columned building. Judith pulled up her scarf against the wind, narrowing her focus.

Tonight she watched only the southern face of the White House. For the past week, she'd walked the perimeter, studying the routes in and out, the State Department and its barracks, the Treasury building, the guards, gateways, the visitors and how they dressed, when they arrived and left, where they came from, the types of cars and limousines allowed to enter, the security checks. Tourist groups entered, too, gaggles of schoolchildren herded by teachers and parents.

How to get inside? How to get to the President of the United States? Then, when the time came, how to kill him?

The building across from her and the man inside were the most heavily guarded in the world. Judith felt no impatience. Every lock had a key, no matter how hard to find. That was her profession, and her heritage, finding the key, the way in. Franklin Roosevelt might be the most powerful man on earth, but no power in history had yet been great enough to avoid an assassin. That required luck. And Judith knew her luck was as good as Roosevelt's.

This thought of luck was rewarded. At precisely five o'clock, the southern gate to the White House swung inward.

A large black Ford rolled past the checkpoint. The Marine guards saluted, ramrod-straight. Judith counted four men inside the car in overcoats and felt hats. Another Ford followed, but larger, heavier, perhaps armored. At the rear, a third car matching the first, with four serious-looking men, closed ranks. The little motorcade turned left, past the statue of some old American general, and headed into the windy warren of the city.

"So," Judith murmured inside her scarf, "every once in a while, the great man comes out."

CHAPTER FOUR

January 11
Boston, Massachusetts

LAMMECK STEPPED FROM THE cargo plane as soon as the props quit spinning. He'd been the only passenger. His welcome back to America was a broad tarmac as wind-scoured as any place in Scotland, and an idling black Packard.

Dag unfolded out of the car. Lammeck plucked cotton balls from his ears. He lifted his collar against the New England chill.

Dag grabbed his duffel to stow it in the trunk. "How was your trip?"

Lammeck answered with a sour tone. "You mean trips. By car to Glasgow. Night train to Leeds. Plane to Dublin. Plane to Newfoundland. Plane to Boston."

Dag slammed the trunk lid. He patted the Packard. "And now car to Newburyport. Get in."

Lammeck slid into the passenger side. Unbuttoning his overcoat, he noticed the government vehicle was not a mess yet, with only two manila folders on the rear seat. Shabby Dag must have just picked the car up from the motor pool.

"You look beat," Dag said.

Lammeck snorted. "Why the hell weren't we on the same plane? I haven't talked with anybody in three days. This is the first time in two days I've taken the damn cotton out of my ears."

Dag smiled and dipped his head, acknowledging Lammeck's discomfort. "We had to travel separately."

"Why, for Christ's sake?"

"You remember I told you that only four people in the world know what I have to tell you? Well, that was to make sure at least one of us got here alive. Sorry."

Lammeck accepted the answer as the secret and labyrinthine logic of the government.

Dag circled a finger in the air. "You're from around these parts, if I recall."

"Providence."

"Nice town?"

"A hole. Maybe someday someone will do something with it, but for now if you want a fight or a whore, call the mayor's office."

Dag laughed. "Got his number?"

Lammeck closed his eyes.

Dag asked, "You want to talk now?"

Lammeck waved this off. "Let me sleep to Newburyport. I don't want to be half dead when you show me whatever it is you dragged me across the planet to see."

"Trust me, Professor. Half dead's a lot better than what I'm going to show you."

Lammeck opened his eyes for a moment, a little startled, but too tired to remark. He closed his eyes again and slept.

He didn't wake until Dag tapped his shoulder. Lammeck looked out the windshield at an intersection bounded by sooty slush, dull storefronts, and cars steaming exhaust into the frosty noon. Newburyport was a waterman's town, no question. Stacks of lobster traps rose in the parking lot of the filling station, knotty nets lay tangled outside a hardware store, sun-bleached driftwood decorated

front porches and windows. Every face on the sidewalks bore the
etches of salt, wind, and sun. These were tough people. Lammeck
knew them. He felt the returning embrace of America in this northern town.

"You spent a few years in these parts, didn't you?" Dag asked.

"Yes."

"Your old man, didn't he teach up here somewhere?"

"At Brown. European history."

"That's right. I remember you telling us about him one night in a
pub. That first night when you shot the dummy. That was slick."

"Thank you."

"How is your father?"

"He died. Just before the war broke out."

Dag nodded and quieted.

Sitting up straight in the car, taking it all in for the first time in
five years, Lammeck told America not to get too cozy with his return. He was still mad. If his father were alive, he'd be mad, too.
Lammeck missed the old man, but was glad his father had not lived
to see his native Czechoslovakia occupied, the massacres, and
America's failure of will to stop Hitler early, before the entire world
caught fire. Lammeck had abandoned America. He was not ready
to get chummy with it again.

Dag drove through town, to the outskirts. He headed east, toward
the ocean, taking the government car along a three-mile stretch of
sea oats and dune. The road was empty. Out here, the snow lay pris-
tine. All the ripples of sand were smoothed in a blank jacket and the
shoulders of the Merrimack River were round and soft.

At the end of the paved surface, Dag took a right turn onto the
beach road. Here, a police barricade stopped them. One bundled-up
local cop stood guard. The man greeted Dag by name.

Dag shut the engine and leaned to the backseat to snag one of the
yellow folders.

"Time to work your magic, Professor."

Lammeck climbed out of the car to the hiss of a tame surf and little wind. The day was socked in and gray. He walked beside Dag onto the sand. The snow here was only a thin gauze; the ocean wind blew most of it away. They came to a site, fifty yards square, marked by sawhorses and a sagging string hung with damp red ribbons. Inside the cordon, small yellow stakes had been driven into the sand.

"This where it happened?"

"Yep. Take a look. We've got pictures of everything."

From the folder Dag handed him, Lammeck pulled a sheaf of eight-by-ten black-and-whites. The first photo showed this same empty bit of beach, not empty on the morning of the pictures, but filled by murder.

A pickup truck had stood just to the right of where Lammeck gazed at the photographs. A rectangle of stakes outlined the location now. The truck's grille had been aimed directly at another phantom of stakes, a large body in the photo, flat on its back, arms palm down. The body lay exactly thirty-seven feet from the front bumper of the truck, according to a line drawn on the photo and a notation. A second corpse, a woman's, lay also faceup, almost in the water, seventeen feet past the man's remains. Her arms were bent up to her shoulders, like she was showing off her biceps. There were no stakes visible for the woman. Her death place lay below the afternoon tide.

Another set of photos displayed close-ups of the area around the truck. A crowbar lay in the sand four feet in front of the hood.

Lammeck tapped the picture. "Anything found on the crowbar? Blood?"

"Negative."

"Footprints?"

Dag shook his head. "Dead end. By the time the next shift of Civil Defense wardens showed up at six A.M. and found the bodies, then ran all over the scene, then add to that the local cops tramping it up, there were fifty different prints in the sand. No go."

Lammeck flipped to another series of photos. These showed the wheel tracks of the pickup truck in the sand. The photos marked the truck's approach and stop. Lammeck paused at a photo that illustrated how the truck had been moved in a small arc, coming to rest directly facing the man's corpse. Another picture showed the keys in the column ignition.

Lammeck surveyed the remaining photographs, mostly differing angles and zooms of information he'd already ingested, shots of bodies and wounds. Dag waited without speaking until Lammeck returned the black-and-whites to the folder.

"What do you think?"

Lammeck handed over the pictures before replying. "You're saying the husband did this? The guy who shot himself in the head?"

"I'm not saying anything, Professor. I'm just showing you what I've got. I have a few theories. But the local cops, yeah, they're pinning it on the husband. I take it you don't agree."

"If you thought I would agree, you wouldn't have brought me all this way. Where is he?"

"Morgue. Town Hall. With the other two."

"Let's go see."

They returned to the Packard. The local cop at the barricade stood smoking a hand-rolled cigarette, casual in the bitter cold. Dag drove away from the beach, back through Newburyport. Lammeck watched the odometer, 3.9 miles to the center of town.

Dag parked in front of a brick three-story building below a tall spire, in a space marked POLICE VEHICLES ONLY. He grabbed the second folder from the rear seat and pushed open his door. Lammeck sensed pedestrians ogling them as he climbed out of the Packard. A multiple killing like this in a small town would definitely put everyone on edge. Big Lammeck with his beard, alongside lean, crumpled Dag—they'd stand out in Newburyport as strangers. To a local, that could not bode well. Lammeck had only been back in America for two hours, in this town for less than one, and already he found his situation unsettling.

* * *

THE MORGUE LAY IN the basement of the Town Hall. Lammeck and Dag descended steps in cool fluorescent light. They entered through a swinging door into a gleaming room of silver implements, linen-draped tables, and vials. Lammeck wanted to pause, his academic interest engaged by the room's tools, but Dag headed across the gleaming linoleum, past a secretary, and straight for another door marked STORAGE. Lammeck reluctantly followed. They stopped at a bank of white portals, lacquered and pearly like refrigerator doors, even with the chrome handles of refrigerators. Strange, Lammeck thought. Of the thousands of dead bodies he'd studied in photos, illustrations, and his imagination, he'd never seen a real cadaver except for his father in his casket. Dag stepped forward, reaching for one of the shiny white doors. Lammeck's stomach turned over. There'd been no moment to prepare himself for the proximity of a murdered body; Dag just marched up to the silver handle and tugged. Lammeck's gut skittered. He was tired from the long trip, still annoyed at being dragged so far from his work, and now he was reluctant and squeamish. He drew a shaky breath, smelling the room's soapy air.

Dag slid out the long silver tray.

Lammeck stepped back.

Dag glanced at him. "Something the matter?"

Lammeck didn't answer. Instead, he asked, "This the husband?"

"No. The Civil Defense guy. Otto Howser. You okay?"

Again, Lammeck made no reply. He stepped up to the drawer and the cadaver.

The naked corpse rested on its back, a, sizeable man with a belly rising off the tray. The skin was blanched except for the bottom few inches, a blue bruise running from heels to neck, pooled blood. A mild odor of meat rose from the flesh; the body had been washed, then preserved in this cooler. Lammeck fought to hold his ground, convincing himself that the smell was not awful and the look of death on the frozen face was not too gruesome. The man's eyes were closed. His mouth hung slightly open, a last gasp. A clean slit marred the big chest. Dag casually probed a finger near the cut, left-hand side, a heart stab. Lammeck tried not to flinch.

"The coroner figures an eight-inch blade, one and a quarter wide. Straight-in angle. Plenty of force. Otto here didn't die right off. You remember the photos?"

Lammeck nodded.

"He crawled backwards, nine feet. His heart was still pumping for a minute maybe. Then he was done. Look here."

Dag pointed at the corpse's left leg, above the ankle. The Achilles tendon had been sliced deep, a slash that likely went down to the fibula.

Lammeck stared for another minute. The beginnings of a theory had already arranged themselves in his head, but he said nothing, to let Dag believe he was thinking through the crime rather than simply enduring.

Once he'd taken a better hold on himself, he asked, "Where's the woman?"

Dag put Otto away. The platform slid into the wall with a whisk and click. He pulled out another drawer.

The woman's short body was equally antiseptic and drained. It bore the same azure pooling of blood along her entire backside. Lammeck fought off a twinge of embarrassment at her nakedness. He gazed away to the floor, as if to give the body a moment, then raised his eyes, figuring he could best serve her by looking. Like Otto, she was full-figured. But her wounds, and her face, were very different.

Both forearms had been cut in identical diagonal lines. Dag stepped back from the body, tilting his head at Lammeck for him to step up for a closer examination of the wounds. Lammeck licked his lips. He moved closer, to slowly dig a finger into one of the furrows in the flesh. He spread the cut and peered down into severed cords of muscle and tissue. His heart raced.

"Bonny Chapman," Dag told him.

Lammeck took his fingers from the fissure; the flesh eased shut.

He bent to examine her face. Bonny's features were distorted, stained cherry red by her murder, the remnant of broken capillaries in her cheeks and nose. Her eyes bulged in an inhuman fashion, as if she might pop. Her mouth was fixed wide, the tongue stiffened over the lower teeth, which were slightly yellow.

Lammeck wiped the back of his hand across his lips.

"You ever seen this before, Professor? Know what does this to someone's face?"

Lammeck nodded.

Dag answered anyway. "Strangulation."

Bonny's face had frozen in her last struggling seconds, begging, straining for air. This was confirmed by a series of empurpled bruises around her throat.

Lammeck did not speak. Dag seemed callous. The woman's brutal choking, Otto's stabbed heart, scarcely seemed to touch him. Lammeck moved back to let Dag slide her away. Watching his former Jedburgh, Lammeck wondered if coldness was an unavoidable side effect of being a killer.

The third body proved the most difficult to look at. A chunk of the left side of the man's head had been blown out. The gaping wound was jagged and raw, a grayed shade of pink. Lammeck pinched his lips together, and this time made no disguise of his queasiness. Not even Dag could chastise him for being averse to this wreckage of a human skull. Lammeck ducked for a quick look inside the brainpan and involuntarily sucked a sharp breath. Beside him, Dag murmured, "Hang in there, Professor."

Lammeck leaned across the body to view the right temple. The sideburn had been punctured and scored by a blast at close range. The rest of the corpse bore no marks. Lammeck straightened and retreated two steps, mopping his brow.

Dag said, "Arnold Chapman. Skinny little cracker, isn't he?" He pointed out the man's pocked nose. "Drinker, I bet."

Lammeck nodded, ignoring Dag's cavalier tone. "Probably. Was alcohol found? Suicide note?"

Dag held up the second folder. "I got shots of the guy's house. Yes to the booze. No to the note. And I got close-ups of all three stiffs before they were cleaned up. This guy in particular."

"Cordite on the right hand?"

Dag nodded. "He was holding the gun, no question. You need to see the gat?"

"Yes. And I want to see the knife." Lammeck indicated the jagged exit wound in Arnold's head. "Where did you find the spent round?"

Dag dug into the folder for several photographs. He held the black-and-whites out to Lammeck, pointing while he spoke.

"This is where they found him, in the living room."

In the photo Arnold lay spread-eagled in the center of an oval hook rug. Blood splattered the fabric. Around the body were the normal domestic articles: lamps on doilies, framed pictures on an upright piano, prints on the walls, a Victrola radio, a sofa and chair. On the fireplace mantel were trophies, a bunch of photo albums, and some signed baseballs. The dead man lying in the middle of his possessions seemed an even sadder sight than seeing him here on a morgue slab.

"Flip to the next one," Dag instructed.

Lammeck brought up the next glossy, a close-up of a baseboard. A slug was buried into it. Dag reached across and tapped the picture.

"He was lying down when he did it."

Lammeck agreed. He turned quickly through the rest of the photos of Arnold and Bonny's home. It felt wrong and tragic touring their house like this in black-and-white, after their lives had been snuffed out, peeking in their cabinets and drawers, the state of their housekeeping. Lammeck handed back the pictures.

"Any need to go over there?" he asked.

Dag shook his head. "Nah. The cops have gone over it pretty good. You think we're done here?"

Lammeck flicked both hands at Arnold Chapman to have Dag slide him away. Once Dag had pushed the corpse back into its dark cubby, Lammeck followed him out of the room and up the steps, buttoning his coat against the chill. Dag led him from the Town Hall to the sidewalk. Lammeck welcomed the frigid air and distant sun. Dag eyed him and gave him a quiet moment to restore his nerve.

A block away, the Newburyport police station seemed almost vacant. A double murder and suicide must have shaken this town to its roots. Lammeck guessed all the cops were out, collecting clues, interviews, and more pictures, running in circles that would bear fruit for them because they wanted to prove Arnold was the killer. It made sense: Close the books quick and go back to being a quiet fishing village.

Dag showed his federal ID to a desk sergeant, saying Lammeck was with him. The cop raised an eyebrow at the Secret Service badge but made no comment. He let them pass into the station's inner offices.

"Wait here," Dag told Lammeck at a worn sofa in a dingy outer room. A coffee pot steamed on a hot plate. Lammeck poured himself a cup. He was unable to find cream or sugar, and regretted it with the first sip. The cop coffee was strong and old. He sank into the cushions of the battered sofa.

Waiting for Dag, Lammeck sifted through his conclusions. Unlike the police, he was unchained from procedure and probable cause, free to roam through possibilities and likelihoods. Neither he nor Dag would ever be faced with proving a case in court. He suspected what had happened, and was certain of what had not. The weapons would confirm him.

Dag returned. He set a cardboard box on the sofa, then turned to pour himself some coffee. Lammeck warned him off it. Dag ignored the advice.

The box was marked EVIDENCE: DO NOT REMOVE in a thick black scrawl. Lammeck marveled how Dag managed to dodge the rules, the same way his clothes managed to avoid an iron. He recalled how this skill had made up a large portion of the Jedburghs' training in Scotland: Use the land and what's at hand to your advantage; exploit opportunities; seize the initiative. Lammeck had taught them how almost any common item can be used as a weapon. Apparently Dag had learned well.

Dag sipped the coffee and made a sour face. Lammeck shrugged, having done his duty. Dag pointed at the box.

"No surprises in there, Professor. The pistol—"

"—a .32 revolver, judging from the wound."

Dag paused, impressed.

"And?"

"The serial number has been filed off."

"Go on."

"The knife is probably just a big kitchen carver. No blood on the handle, only on the blade."

"Give the Professor a kewpie doll."

Dag set his mug on the counter. He reached in his coat for a pair of cotton gloves. He tossed them to the sofa. Lammeck put them on, then dug into the box.

First, he lifted the pistol, a nickel-plated four-inch-barrel Smith & Wesson .32 revolver. The serial number had been obliterated. He broke out the emptied six-shot cylinder. Five unspent round-nose lead cartridges rolled in the bottom of the box.

He set the pistol aside and took up the knife. It was nothing more than a kitchen blade, brand name Wüsthof, an old German cutler. Lammeck handled it carefully, to check the sharpness and study the rusty bloodstains on the steel. As he'd guessed, the handle was unblemished.

He returned the knife to the cardboard box, then peeled off the gloves. "What else have you got to show me?"

"I'm keeping the best for the end."

Lammeck grimaced. His peevishness returned. Dag must have spotted this, because he spoke quickly.

"You did real good in there with the bodies, Professor. But don't get cranky on me. I just want to see what you make of all the odds and ends first, before I show you the last piece. You've got the best mind I've ever seen for this sort of thing. You know, I've read every paper you ever published."

This disarmed Lammeck. "Really?"

"I had to. And in three days. I had to convince my boss to let me go to Scotland to get you. I wrote a nice report on you, real flattering."

"Because you don't think we have a run-of-the-mill domestic murder here in little nowhere Newburyport, do you? Husband-catches-wife-with-lover sort of thing. Kills self in despair and guilt."

"Nope."

"You believe we have an assassination attempt brewing. Starting on that beach."

"I do indeed."

"Who do you think is going to be assassinated?"

Dag picked up the box. "Who do *you* think?" he challenged.

Lammeck stood from the sofa. "I'll meet you at the car. Let's head back to the beach and I'll show you."

LAMMECK STOPPED BESIDE THE rectangle of yellow stakes pinned in the sand that signified the pickup truck. The afternoon had worn on and the wind had picked up. Tonight would be frosty, maybe a front moving in. He looked to the slate sky. Dag, bundled up, stared at him in the freezing breeze. Knowing his ex-student was growing impatient, Lammeck watched low clouds scud on the northerly gusts.

"Alright," he said.

"About time," Dag grumbled.

"Let's take this in the order of events."

"Go."

Lammeck pointed to the sand, at the front seat of the make-believe pickup.

"First, Bonny was in the truck alone."

He paused, expecting Dag to say something like "Check," or

"How do you know?" But Dag kept silent, rubbing his hands in the cold.

Lammeck continued: "The slashes in her forearms tell us she was the one holding the crowbar, not Otto. If they'd been in the car together, if Arnold Chapman had come up to them threatening with a knife, Otto would have grabbed it, not Bonny. Those cuts were to make her drop the crowbar. Otto was up the beach somewhere, doing his job walking the shore. Bonny stayed behind. It doesn't matter why."

Lammeck moved to the front of the yellow stakes.

"She was surprised by an intruder. Someone she didn't trust, so she grabbed the crowbar out of the truck and walked up here."

Dag added, "Someone she didn't trust, or maybe didn't recognize."

"Exactly. Bonny got out of the truck with the crowbar and moved in front of it. Here. Let's assume that was because the headlamps were on. If it had been her husband coming up to the truck in the dark, I don't think she would have grabbed a weapon before she got out to talk to him. Besides, if Arnold was planning on murdering her, I think he would have attacked her as soon as she got out of the truck, right here on the driver's side. Or she might have run away. But Bonny had time and a reason to grab the crowbar and move in front of the headlights, to see who she was talking to. And it wasn't Arnold."

Dag nodded.

"Okay. So we can figure that whoever did kill Bonny, she saw him coming." Again, Lammeck aimed his finger at the sand. "I'm going to guess this is where she got knifed, because this is where she dropped the crowbar. As far as we can tell, no one got hit with it, right?"

Lammeck didn't wait for an answer, but stalked to the next set of stakes, the ones depicting Bonny's corpse, exposed by the receding tide. Dag followed.

"Bonny takes off, cut bad, scared out of her wits. She's bleeding, can barely defend herself. The killer catches her by the water, knocks her down, and strangles her."

"Where's Otto?"

"He shows up sometime during the fight with Bonny. Or the killer waited for him afterward, then ambushed him when he came back this way. My guess is Otto got back here during the fight, because of the cut on his Achilles tendon."

Lammeck left Bonny's markers and trod over to Otto's large yellow silhouette.

"Otto pulled the killer off Bonny and knocked him over. Otto was a big guy. My guess is the killer lashed out while on the sand and brought Otto down with that slice on the leg. Then he finished him off with a stab to the chest."

Dag said, "Otto didn't die right off."

"No. That's another thing that tells us Otto got back before Bonny was killed. He tried to get up off his back to defend her."

"Tough guy," Dag mused. "Fucking shame."

Lammeck shook his head. "He didn't stand a chance. That's why we know it wasn't the husband."

"I'm with you all the way, Professor. Keep going."

"Did you see those wounds? Let's do Bonny first. Come here."

Dag stepped up to Lammeck.

"Make like you have a crowbar."

Dag lifted his hands in the manner of a baseball player gripping a bat.

"Try to hit me."

Nimbly, Lammeck ducked Dag's two-handed swing. With his right hand, he thrust the outer edge of his palm up against Dag's forearm, then hacked downward. In a flash, he did the same to Dag's other forearm passing overhead.

Dag opened both hands, as though they'd been rendered useless.

"That blade you showed me at the police station. That thing didn't make those cuts on Bonny. That was a single-edged kitchen knife. What cut the insides of her arms was a two-sided dagger. Forehand, backhand. Instantly, before Bonny even knew what hit her. That's why the crowbar was dropped in front of the truck." Lammeck mimed the motion again for Dag, sweeping down once in the air, then, reversing direction, up and down again. "Just like that. Can't do it with a kitchen blade."

Dag took this in. Lammeck didn't slow.

"Also, I find it hard to believe that little Arnold Chapman could make the move I just did. That was special, years of training. Kali, Escrima, Arnis de Mano, maybe Balisong. I learned it from an old Brit named Fairbairn before the OSS grabbed him as a Weapons teacher."

"What are you telling me? This is some kind of ninja shit?"

"I wouldn't have put it in those terms, but yes, Dag. Ninja shit. Not the sort of thing you expect from little Arnold."

The look on Dag's face told Lammeck that now he had left the trail Dag had sniffed out.

"Now let's take Otto's wounds. The cut across the Achilles tendon was the perfect disabling blow. A jealous, crazy husband who's just been knocked on his butt maybe hacks away in the air, cutting up the guy's leg. Maybe he scrambles to his feet and keeps fighting. But he does not come up with one clean, specialized move to bring a larger opponent down. And he does not dispatch that opponent with a single drive deep into the heart. That kind of finish requires a brutal sort of calm, and that only comes from training. I assume Arnold was not a commando."

"No."

"Your killer was."

Dag chewed on this. Lammeck could see he agreed. Dag tossed out one more obstacle.

"The husband. He shot himself, Professor. No doubt about it. And a big-ass knife was in his sink, with blood on it."

"I haven't figured out how Arnold managed to pull the trigger. It'll come to me. But the knife? Like I said, it was a single-edged

Wüsthof, with blood only on the tang. My guess is the killer wiped it in Bonny's and Otto's wounds after the fact, then took it to Arnold's house. If that knife was the actual murder weapon, there'd be blood on the haft as well. The murderer made four cuts in two people, all deep. In a hand-to-hand struggle, there would've been blood spraying everywhere, especially from Bonny getting strangled with deep gashes in both arms. The killer would certainly have gotten blood on his hands. If he took the time to clean the handle, he would have cleaned off the blade, too. Doesn't make sense to do it any other way. And why choke Bonny instead of knife her and just finish her off? He'd already cut her twice."

"You tell me, Professor."

"Because the blade was still in Otto. But the cops didn't find that kitchen knife stuck in Otto's chest, did they?"

"No."

"Then the kitchen knife is a plant."

"So you're saying..."

"Three things. One, our killer is extremely good. Trained. Smart. Fast. Two, he makes mistakes."

"And three?"

"There's a knife missing."

Dag grinned. Turning to walk from the beach, he jerked his chin for Lammeck to follow.

"No there isn't."

A FRESH POT OF coffee simmered on the hot plate. Lammeck tried another cup while he waited for Dag. This sample was no more palatable than the last.

"I need sleep," he mumbled, emptying the mug into the sink.

He put his feet up on the police station sofa and lay back. Just as he dozed off, Dag entered, startling Lammeck awake by setting a box on his chest.

"You can go to sleep that fast?" Dag asked.

Lammeck sat up, grabbing the box so that it didn't fall. Again the cardboard was labeled EVIDENCE: DO NOT REMOVE!

"It's a skill you learn as a teacher. I can do that and lecture."

"Stay awake long enough to figure this one out for me, will ya, Professor? Here."

Again Dag tossed Lammeck a pair of cotton gloves. Lammeck tugged them on.

"Is this my surprise?"

Dag poured himself more coffee. This time, Lammeck did not warn him off.

"There are three reasons I brought you back from Scotland, Professor. To help me figure out the crime scenes on the beach and to confirm some ideas I had. Consider that halfway done. Arnold is still a mystery."

"It'll come to me."

"I'm sure it will. What's in this box is the second reason. You're the only person I know who can untangle this one."

"The knife?"

Dag waved his coffee at the box. "Take a look."

Lammeck peeled back the flaps. He caught his breath and realized he'd gasped loud enough for Dag to hear.

He reached a gloved hand in to take up the knife. Lifting it into the light, he thrilled to the feel of it. Weight and balance, perfect. Even the blood dried on the blade and in the crevices of the handle made it ideal. He put both hands beneath the knife and held it across his white palms for Dag to see.

"You don't know what this is, do you?" he asked. Dag slurped the bad coffee, reflecting none of Lammeck's awe.

"Nope."

"This is an Assassin's dagger."

Dag shrugged. "Well, I knew that. I mean, it's got blood all over it."

"No, I mean with a capital A. Assassins. As in the twelfth-century Middle Eastern cult that fought the Templars in the Crusades. This is one of their knives."

The Secret Service man put his coffee on the counter and sat on the sofa next to Lammeck.

"You're kidding. How old is that thing?"

Lammeck handled the dagger, shifting it to look closer.

"I can't be sure. But it's an exact specimen. It could be a replica, though I doubt it. The tang looks like Damascus steel. Diamond-shaped in cross-section down to the point. Ornate brass cap and hilt. Engraved onyx grip. Absolutely perfect weight distribution. Someone who knows what they're doing could throw this knife and bury it in your neck from thirty paces. I could."

Dag snorted, apparently thinking Lammeck was kidding.

Whether it was eight hundred years old or just a remarkable re-production, the knife contained a marvelous lethality. Lammeck was convinced an analysis of the brass and steel would prove it a bona fide antiquity. But authentication would have to come later. For now, this knife was evidence. It was going nowhere beyond a cardboard box and a police station storeroom. Holding the razor-sharp dagger, Lammeck in his imagination invested it with a millennium of intrigue and murder. The thing tingled in his hands.

"Where'd the cops find this?"

"You remember Otto, the big guy?"

"Sure."

"He must've yanked this out of his chest just before he croaked. Probably he threw it away. Then . . ."

"He crawled over it. He was lying on top of it."

"Yep. Ain't that something?"

Lammeck thought back to the pictures of the crime scene: Dying Otto had slithered backward across the sand. The killer went after Bonny next. He finished choking the woman by the water, then re-turned to Otto to retrieve the knife. But it had vanished.

The tire tracks of the pickup showed the truck had been shim-mied to the left, to shine headlights across the corpse. So the killer had gone to the truck to light up Otto's body, looking.

He hadn't looked under Otto.

History. Lammeck grinned. History does this when she's displeased, little things to give an edge against the killers. Lammeck felt a thrill at this close brush with the forces he'd spent a lifetime studying.

"What do the local cops make of it?"

"Nothing. Arnold was a collector of stuff—stamps, comics, baseball cards and whatnot. They figure he had this antique knife because it was interesting and maybe valuable. Everyone knew Bonny hated his collections. They reckon Arnold used it on her out of spite, dropped it, then did Otto with the kitchen knife. Poor Arnold."

Lammeck did not pause for poor, unfairly blamed Arnold. They'd square his name later if they figured this mystery out.

"Look here. Carved into the handle. This is onyx."

Lammeck put fingers gingerly beneath the blade, careful not to rub away any of Otto's and Bonny's blood.

He pointed into the onyx grip, delicately carved with a bas-relief of little murders. Many of the tiny scenarios were scabbed by clots of dried blood, but the theme of the carvings was clear: One man drove a blade into another. In the center of the haft, with the cameos of stabbings surrounding it, was an emblem:

Lammeck touched a gloved finger to the symbol.

"This," he said, eyeing Dag for a reaction, "is the key."

"What is it?"

"The symbol of the Assassins. It's an offshoot on the Freemasons' emblem, sort of a compass and square piercing a heart."

Dag leaned to examine the knife more closely. Lammeck held it motionless, then told him, "Put it away, before it gets missed."

Dag disappeared with the box. Lammeck celebrated by pouring another cup of the awful coffee and making himself drink. The coffee helped buoy his flagging energy to match his excitement.

When Dag returned, he said, "Come on, we're getting out of here."

"Where?"

"Doesn't matter. Let's just go. I don't want to talk about this in a police station. I don't want anybody overhearing this. It sounds crazy enough when it's just you and me."

Lammeck followed the Secret Service agent out to the cold and the car. Newburyport's sidewalks and streets held little traffic. A few kids rode bikes. Most of the men were gone to the military or their boats. The women were at home or in a factory.

Dag started the Packard's engine. He pulled away from the police station and drove west through town.

"Put it in a nutshell for me, Professor. Who were the Assassins, and why is one of their goddam knives in that box?"

"There's a lot of history here. It doesn't fit easily into a nutshell."

Dag took an idle turn, down a residential street of close-knit and humble homes. "Cram hard, Professor. I'm driving; you don't want me to go to sleep."

"In the twelfth century, returning Crusaders brought back home to Europe stories of an odd sect of Saracens they'd met in Syria. These were Ismai'lis, an offshoot of Islam. You know about the Sunnis and the Shi'a?"

Dag gave Lammeck a withering look that said, *Of course not.*

"Fine. Muhammad died in 632. Because Muhammad was a prophet, he couldn't be succeeded by another prophet; they don't come along that often. But someone had to take the reins of Islam.

Muhammad had appointed no successor, so the first leader, called a *caliph,* was named from his inner circle. The fourth caliph was Ali, Muhammad's cousin and son-in-law. But Ali was opposed by a rival clan, the Banu Umayyid. In 661, Ali was murdered and the caliphate was taken over by the Umayyids. The majority accepted this; the followers of Ali did not."

"Civil war," Dag said.

Lammeck nodded. "Centuries of civil war. The Umayyid followers took the name of the community, or *Sunni.* The Ali opposition called themselves the *Shi'at Ali,* or just *Shi'a.* The Sunnis were the majority and became the Islam establishment. The Shi'a were persecuted."

"Heard that story before," Dag growled.

"The Sunnis continued to be led by their caliphs. The Shi'a pinned their hopes instead on the descendants of Ali, calling them *Imams.* The sixth Imam after Ali had a son, Ismail. This one apparently got a little radical and was booted out of the family business. But not without his own set of followers."

"The Ismai'lis," Dag offered.

"Dead on. The Ismai'lis were another opposition group, but this time within the Shi'a. They were extremely well organized, pious to a fault, secretive, traditionalist—in other words, perfect for anyone disenchanted with Islam in general and the Shi'a in particular."

"These Assassins were Ismai'lis?"

"Yes. But by the time the Crusaders met them in the Holy Land, the Ismai'lis were already a hundred years old and very powerful in Islam. The sect was strongest in Persia, led by a brilliant young revolutionary named Hasan-i-Sabah. He was the founder of the Assassins. You've heard of him, yes?"

Dag glanced away from the road. "Who?"

"Have you ever read Arnold of Lübeck? Or Marco Polo?"

Dag sent Lammeck another of his *"You're kidding"* looks, then put his eyes back on the narrow neighborhood lanes.

"Remember," Dag reminded him, "nutshell."

"I'm trying. But it's a big story."

Dag raised his palms from the wheel in surrender.

"In the middle of the eleventh century, Islam was weakened by the invasion of the Seljuk Turks. In 1090, to protect his Ismai'lis from the Seljuks, Hasan-i-Sabah took to the Elburz Mountains south of the Caspian Sea. He and his disciples conquered Alamut Castle, built on a massive rock six thousand feet above sea level. From Alamut, Hasan could dominate the entire valley, three miles wide and thirty miles long. There, his followers took ten castles in all, plus dozens of outposts and watchtowers. This became known as the Valley of the Assassins. Marco Polo brought back from Persia the story of Hasan-i-Sabah and the Assassins, and put them in his book, *Travels*."

"Okay, that I've heard of."

"Good. The educational system hasn't completely failed you. From a prison cell in Genoa after his return, Marco Polo wrote about his twenty-seven-year journey on the Silk Road. One of the wonders he claimed to have encountered was a society of killers who seemed to murder their enemies with ease and extraordinary tactics. The story went that, high in the mountains, the lord of the Assassins raised a thousand sons of peasants from childhood. He had these boys taught Latin, Greek, Turkic, Arabic, and every language of the realm. They trained for years until they became masters of the many secret ways to kill—by blade, arrow, poison, and hand. These young men were instructed that they had to obey the word of their lord, The Old Man of the Mountain, and that if they did, he would assure them paradise in the afterlife."

Dag snickered. "Nice retirement plan." He wheeled the car into another random turn.

"Visitors to Assassin castles came back reporting that they had seen Hasan direct his disciples to jump to their deaths from the parapets, just to show off their loyalty before dinner."

"I take it back," Dag said.

Lammeck continued. "The legend goes that when acolytes were

finally brought before Hasan-i-Sabah, they were asked if they would do anything Hasan required of them. The answer was always yes. Hasan maintained a huge pleasure garden at Alamut. The lads were taken to the garden, given every earthly pleasure, and messed out of their brains on hashish. After a few days of rapture, the boys were drugged and awakened in front of Hasan, who told them they'd been transported to Paradise. If they wanted to go back, he'd say, take this knife and go kill what's-his-name."

"Did this nonsense work?"

"Apparently like a charm. The first Assassin murder was the Turkish vizier himself, Nizam al-Mulk, in 1092. In the disguise of a Sufi mystic, one of Hasan's boys waited months for his chance, until he got close enough to knife al-Mulk while he was being carried to the tent of his women. When Hasan got the report, he said, 'The killing of this devil is the beginning of bliss.' To the Turks, the Assassins were criminals. In Islam, they were hailed as patriots fighting the occupation and enemies of the faith. The killers were called *fida'i*s, which means devotees."

"Where'd the name Assassins come from? The hash?"

Lammeck shrugged, though Dag was not watching.

"That's the story. They were called the *hashishin*. Their cult was considered to have the greatest fighting abilities in the ancient world. It was said they could predict the moment of a man's death by reading the stars. Assassins could shape-shift into animals, and mastered flying carpets."

"Uh-huh."

Lammeck was near the finish of both the tale and Dag's attention.

"Want to hear how the story ends?"

"Alright. Finish up."

"By 1250, Islam was in trouble. The Mongols had invaded Asia, and Genghis Khan's grandson Hülegü was mopping up. He sacked all the Muslim lands as far as Egypt. In 1258, he took Baghdad. The final Ismai'li Imam was Rukn-al-Din. Hülegü wiped out the Assassin castles in the valley. He had the Imam murdered."

Dag said, "Sauce for the goose."

"The last that was heard from the Assassins was the words of the Islamic chronicler Juvayni, who wrote they had become 'a tale on men's lips and a tradition in the world.' Great stuff, you have to admit."

"Especially the flying carpets."

"It's a mixture of myth and fact, Dag."

"I don't give a shit about myths, Professor. You can keep Marco Polo and the Mongols and whatever else for your history books. I just want you to explain one fact to me: How did one of their knives wind up in Massachusetts?"

"It's an Assassin knife, Dag."

Dag's patience was at an end. He jerked the car to a quick stop at the curb.

"Meaning?" he demanded.

"Meaning someone thinks he's an Assassin. And that someone is highly skilled with an Assassin knife, and extraordinarily cold-blooded. So that someone just might be."

"A hired killer from the twelfth-century." Dag looked incredulous.

"From this century, but using twelfth-century tactics and disciplines. In addition to what we've seen of his ability with this knife, he's probably also a master at open-hand combat and poisons. He's not likely a shooter; it's not the Assassin way. But I would duck if he pointed a gun at me, in case I'm wrong."

"This is so fucking unlikely."

"But not impossible. In fact, the Alamut valley is still called the Valley of the Assassins. Your killer could be Persian. Or he could be a copycat."

"Like I said. Unbelievable."

"It's the only explanation I can come up with. You asked. I told you. Our guy's an Assassin."

"Our girl," Dag said.

"What?"

Dag jammed a hand into his coat pocket and produced a wadded brown paper bag. He unrolled the opening and reached inside. Between pinched fingertips, he withdrew several strands of long dark hair.

"I found these."

"Where?"

"On Otto's coat and pants leg. The yokel cops didn't even bother to check him for forensics. So I went over his clothes with a magnifying glass and found these. I even found bits of hair stuck under the fingernails on his left hand. Christ, Professor. Our killer's a woman."

Lammeck took one of the strands from Dag. He stretched it to its length and held it up to the window to get the color. Shoulder length. Slight curl. Black as pitch. Definitely not Bonny's.

"Is this the natural color?"

"Not sure. I'll have it checked for dye back in D.C. But my guess, since you're talking about some Arab assassin, is yes."

Lammeck shook his head. "No, Persians aren't Arabs. They're Aryans. That's why in 1935, Shah Pahlevi changed the name of their country to Iran. It means Aryan."

Dag blew out a breath, gazing at the strands between his fingers. "It could still be a man with long hair, but I doubt it. This whole thing just smacks of a woman to me. The cuts on Bonny's arms, that was skill instead of strength. The knife in big Otto's chest—she didn't drive the blade deep enough to finish him in one stroke. Even Arnold. He might not have opened his door to some strange guy in the middle of the night, but a woman? Who knows?"

"And if this is a hired assassin, a major part of doing the job would be to blend in. A man with hair this long would stand out."

Dag carefully tucked the strands back into the paper sack.

"So, Professor. What's your crystal ball say? Who's her target?"

Lammeck gazed out the window at clapboard houses and bare trees. He considered a dark woman, stealthy, dangerous, clever, trained, making her way through the American countryside, anywhere, to kill someone, anyone. One lone woman in all this land, a nation distracted, at war, slipping unnoticed into place, waiting, striking.

At whom?

Lammeck opened his vast vault of knowledge on assassinations. What figure in history had ever been safe? Who had been too high and untouchable a target? No one. How could he predict who this Persian woman was locked in on when history dictated that every single person in America was prey? Even the first half of the bloody twentieth century was dripping with examples. In June of '43, Churchill dodged an attempt on his life when he didn't board a plane that had been marked by Nazi agents, then shot down over French waters. Instead, actor Leslie Howard—Ashley Wilkes from the film *Gone With the Wind*—died on that plane. In 1918, after a factory speech, Vladimir Lenin was shot twice by an anti-Lenin revolutionary. Lenin survived, but died five years later from lead poisoning seeping out of the two rounds still in his torso. Louisiana senator and presidential hopeful Huey "Kingfish" Long was shot down in 1935 by an angry doctor in a corridor at the state capitol in Baton Rouge, while surrounded by bodyguards. In 1912, Theodore Roosevelt, entering a car in Milwaukee, took a bullet to the chest, fired by a deranged saloon-keeper. The would-be assassin claimed that President McKinley's ghost, the day after his own assassination in 1901, came to him in a dream and accused Teddy, McKinley's vice president, of his murder. A fifty-page speech in Roosevelt's pocket, along with the metal case that held his spectacles, slowed the bullet. Teddy, bleeding, ignored those who pleaded with him to get medical attention, and delivered his speech. He died seven years later in his sleep, with the bullet still in his body. And of course, there was the botched assassination of Hitler last summer, the bomb in the bunker. But what about the earlier, lesser-known attempt on the Führer's life? In 1939, a Swiss master carpenter built a bomb into the wooden pillar of a Munich beer cellar that exploded twelve minutes after Hitler left. Hitler had not felt well, and had shortened his speech, and had also not followed his custom of lingering afterward with beer-drinking comrades. After his arrest, no one believed the carpenter had the skills to do this alone, until he demanded access to a woodworking shop, where he re-created for the Gestapo the entire mechanism.

Lammeck caught Dag glaring at him. The agent was waiting for a response. What could Lammeck say? That this Persian woman was implausible? That she was also classic and perhaps historic, and that whatever she had in mind to do, she could very well pull it off, against any target she chose? Because the more unlikely the assassins, the more history seemed to favor them.

The problem for Dag was that he'd be looking for a specter assembled out of interdependent guesses. One wrong assumption and everything toppled, a house of cards. Every bit of evidence the two of them had amounted to nothing but bare speculation, starting with their assumptions about the crime scenes, all the way to the long black hairs. And what about the dead ends? Like, how did Arnold die if it wasn't a suicide? Or who sent the assassin? And what if he and Dag pursued this woman based on a wrong guess of her target, then it turned out to be someone else? That would be the same as a free pass for her, and a death sentence for whoever she was really after. Finally, Lammeck couldn't completely rule out the chance that the local cops were right, that this was a domestic murder-suicide. Or that the assassin might be a man, or not exist at all, just some local nut-job with an eye for antique knives.

Still, despite misgivings and traps of logic, Lammeck sensed that he and Dag were on a trail. This was a plot; he felt it in his gut. A conspiracy that aimed high.

Lammeck did not answer Dag's question, but asked another of his own: "Why'd she kill Bonny and Otto?"

"Because they caught her."

"Doing what?"

Dag hesitated. Lammeck filled in the response.

"Arriving. In the middle of the night. On a remote coastal beach in the dead of winter. It was just bad luck. Bonny, in the wrong place at the wrong time, saw our gal pop up out of nowhere, so she grabbed a crowbar and got out of the truck to do her job and challenge her. The woman tried to talk her way past. For whatever reason, Bonny didn't believe her. They fought. Otto showed up too late."

"She came out of the ocean," Dag said.

Lammeck nodded. "Dropped off by a sub. Then swam or got rowed ashore."

Dag asked, "And who has subs?"

Both men spoke:

"Governments."

"It's a shot in the dark, but what the hell, everything else about this case is." Lammeck raised a finger to make his point. "The target has to be really high up. Why go to all that trouble for anyone less; who else rates that kind of risk? At this point in the war, getting a sub close to an American shore has to be next to impossible. The Germans, the Japanese, some nation wants someone big out of the way."

Dag rubbed a hand into the furrows of his forehead. "This is such a stretch, Professor." He lowered his hand. "And son of a bitch, if it isn't exactly what's happening. Now, tell me, honest. Who do you think she's after? Somebody in Boston? It's only about forty miles from here."

Lammeck shook his head. Dag fell back against the car seat. Lammeck did the same. Both men seemed to give way to the exhaustion of travel, the dire weight of Dag's question, and the precarious balance of any answer based on such impossibly fragile deductions.

"Let me put it this way. Let's not assume it's the President of the United States. But my advice to you is, do everything you can right now to protect him."

Dag thinned his lips. "Shit," he said, snapping his head with the curse. "I was fucking afraid you'd say that."

Lammeck patted his former student on the shoulder. "Dag, my

boy, protecting Roosevelt's your job now, and I expect you're good at it. You're poking around in this because you think Roosevelt's her target. But how in the world did this come to your attention in the first place? I mean, a double murder and suicide in a dinky Massachusetts sea town? A love triangle gone sour? What made you look in to it?"

Dag appeared weary past a simple physical letdown. He looked suddenly depressed. Lammeck couldn't figure why. Dag's efforts and intuition could well have thwarted an attempt on the President's life. Doesn't that get a man a ticker-tape parade?

"A week ago, I read in the D.C. paper about the New Year's killing of two Civil Defense wardens north of Boston. I wondered, why murder a man and a woman guarding a remote beach? Seemed fishy to me, maybe because it's just the sort of thing I was trained to do myself, by you and the SOE, right? I called the Newburyport cops and heard about the two knives and the husband's suicide. The dropped crowbar, with no sign that anybody got hit with it. Those weird cuts on Bonny's arms and the one on Otto's ankle. Something smelled bad about this. Didn't add up to be just a husband-wife domestic murder to me. I hustled up here for a look. I made a few guesses from the photos, the bodies, and that creepy knife. I didn't like the fact that Arnold laid down to shoot himself either, and left no note. It all gave me a bad feeling. I reckon I smelled a rat most when I pulled those long black hairs off of Otto's clothes. Didn't belong to Bonny, sure didn't belong to Otto or the husband. I went back to my boss, laid it all out, and he gave me permission to get you."

It was time to wrap up. Dag would be driving him back to the airport, a job well done for them both. Lammeck patted him on the shoulder.

"Well, you'll be a hero now. You'll get a medal or something. A promotion. Maybe they'll let you guard someone better than Roosevelt."

Dag looked away, dour. He put the car in gear and pulled from the curb.

"This is another one of your jokes, right?"

Lammeck stared at the side of Dag's head. "I'm not following."

"Professor, come on. You're a smart guy. Use your head. Do you really think I can go back to the director of the Secret Service and tell him that some twelfth-century assassin from Persia was dropped off by some sub and is *maybe* headed to kill the Boss? Based on the wild-ass guesses you and I just came up with?"

"But, we both agree . . ."

"Yeah, we agree." Dag shifted the Packard higher, going too fast down the narrow street. "But that doesn't mean my boss is going to go for it hook, line, and sinker."

"But you were put on this assignment, right?"

"After a fashion."

"What does that mean?"

"It means they let me start this investigation without a lot of what you call enthusiasm."

"Then take it to the FBI. They'll follow it up."

"No way. If Hoover got wind of this he'd yank the whole thing from us. No, this is a Secret Service case, such as it is. Look, maybe now's the time to tell you."

Lammeck gazed blearily at Dag, suddenly tired again.

"You remember I said there were only four people in the States who knew what I had to tell you? One was me. The other two are the Director of the Secret Service and the chief of the President's security detail. The fourth is whoever killed those three people. I've been instructed to keep it that way. That was the deal I made."

"What deal?"

"In return for letting me bring you into the case, I'm on my own with this. I'm sort of regarded as a crackpot on this one. So I reckon it's just you and me."

Alarms went off inside Lammeck.

"You and me? Dag, no. I have work to do. I'm a weapons trainer, an historian, and a teacher. You know this. I'm no secret agent."

Dag took his eyes off the road just long enough to grin.

"Yeah, but admit it, you always wanted to be."

This remark struck home. Lammeck's objection was derailed for a second. Before he could recount his many good reasons to be left out of this, Dag spurred the car away from the neighborhoods and onto the main Newburyport road.

"Look, Professor, I really need your help. I can put you up in a D.C. hotel for as long as it takes, until we get something concrete. We will, and you know we will. Then I'll take that to my boss and he'll give me a task force to track this woman down. But until we dig up something better than us scratching our heads and ginning up facts, we're on our own. I went a long way to get you. And I'm positive that was the right thing to do. Tell me I was wrong and I'll take you straight to the airport. Tell me I was right and we're heading to D.C."

Dag halted at a stoplight. He did not move when the light turned green. Behind them, a car horn blared. Dag watched Lammeck, still waiting for an answer. He didn't get one, so he continued, insistent now. "Your country's at war, Professor. Someone's here and planning to kill somebody important. I figure the target's gotta be Roosevelt. Who else is worth the risk? Who else gets a trained killer dropped off on a beach in the middle of nowhere by a goddam sub? What single person in America today can you remove that'll make any difference in the war? All the big generals are in Europe or the Pacific. You'd have to kill a hundred scientists spread over a dozen top-secret places to make even a dent in whatever they're coming up with. No, it's Roosevelt, if only because I can't figure out who else it could be. And protecting Roosevelt's my job. So I don't give a goddam if you live in Scotland, Prague, or Timbuktu, or if you happen to think Roosevelt is the devil in a red dress. I don't care what your reason is, but will you please come up with one for staying and helping me stop this?"

The car to the rear honked again.

"Go," said Lammeck.

"Where?"

"South. Washington."

"Good. Thank you."

Lammeck crossed his arms and waited until Dag had the car running out of Newburyport, toward Boston.

"Just so you know, crackpot—"

"What?"

"I'm not doing this for God or country, or apple pie and the flag, or that arrogant SOB in the White House. I'm doing it because you're a friend and you asked."

Dag laughed, a full-throated guffaw.

"And I'm a belly dancer. Don't kid yourself, Professor. You're doing this so you can put yourself in your own damn history book. This is a career move for you. But nice try."

Lammeck said nothing, grappling with whether Dag was on the money.

"Trust me," Dag said, still chuckling, "that's the only part of this whole fucked-up case I am *sure* about."

CHAPTER FIVE

January 12
Washington, D.C.

JUDITH DID NOT ROCK in Mrs. P.'s creaky porch chair, wanting to wake no one.

She laid the clay pipe across her lap, covered by the quilt Mrs. P. had given her. Unscrewing the top to a tin, she used a penknife to cut a small chunk of resin. Smearing this bit into the bowl of the pipe, she shook from another tin a portion of shredded Egyptian tobacco. With the small blade, Judith blended the tobacco leaves with the hashish. She flicked an American Zippo lighter and sucked the flame into the bowl.

She held the first white breath, waiting for the sense of unfurling behind her eyes, then in her groin. At this time of the morning the dark alley was vacant, with no human strays, dogs, or trash. The Capitol dome glowed mightily above the roofs.

Judith exhaled. She preferred the blond Moroccan kif. Its intoxication was milder and more active. The black Indian hashish made her euphoric and laconic. That was for another time, to celebrate the inevitable completion of her task.

The drug breezed in her blood. She sucked on the pipe again, rising, a carpet ride from the old tales. She thought of how far she was from her home, not only in distance. Here in America a woman could sit on a porch and smoke a bowl, even in a Negro neighborhood, and be left alone. She wore what she liked, boots and an undershirt, a wool coat and seaman's cap, stretchy underpants, and the gift of a warm quilt. No one cursed her or tried to chase her inside.

J'aime cette liberté, she thought. *I like this freedom.*

Judith cleared her mind except for the flight of the hashish. Even with the debacle on that freezing beach, she was still an unknown quantity, and that was the best weapon at her disposal. Satisfied, she closed her eyes to the world and the mission.

Once the clay pipe lost its warmth, Judith stood. The quilt hung in a cape around her shoulders; the cold nipped her bare thighs. The drug's heat in her midsection melted the cold on her skin. She ran a hand beneath her shirt across her belly, then down into her underpants. She stood like this, robed in the quilt, facing America and its bright dome, pleasing herself.

She returned to her apartment, careful not to drag the hem of Mrs. P.'s quilt across the porch and hallway. Inside her room, she lapped the carpet over the bed, then moved to open the rickety door of the chifforobe. In the floor of the old cabinet, she pried loose one of the heart-pine boards, where she'd hidden her documents, cash, and poisons. Laying the clay pipe in its leather case along with the tins of kif and the Zippo, she replaced the board.

Inside the chifforobe hung her coat and three suits of Western clothes, purchased on New York Avenue. Judith looked at the fine American skirts and jackets of wool, one blue, one black, and her favorite the color of desert sand, slightly browner than her own skin. Beside the suits hung two white linen blouses. These were cut too tight for her shoulders—she could not move well in them—but the designs showed off her breasts and narrow waist, which seemed to be the purpose of *Ferangi* garments. Below them sat two pairs of shoes, both leather with buckles, straps, and heels. Western shoes were not made for walking so much as showing off a woman's legs to men. She thought of the cloth-soled *giva*s she wore as a servant girl. She admired both, the shoes of her memory and these. Both were the same, a woman's disguise.

She'd been able to purchase no hose this time in America; due to shortages of nylon because of the war, most women had forsaken them. Judith had worn stockings the other time in America, before the war, and liked them. But her favorite American things were the undergarments. Western underpants and bras were the most excellent items for women the world over. With regard, Judith slid the underpants off her hips and unclipped the brassiere, laying their smoothness aside.

She walked to the foot of the metal cot. With both hands beneath the frame, she lifted and tipped it up, leaning the mattress against the wall. A rope, tied to a thick nail driven into the wall then bent into an eye, hung beside the frame. She tightened the line across the bottom of the frame, knotting it to another crooked nail on the other side. She let go. The bedstead stood balanced, firmly held.

From the corner she grabbed a broom, bought for its sturdy handle. This she set across the legs of the frame protruding at head height.

Naked, she approached the tipped-up bed frame, looking down into the exposed cot springs. With both hands she gripped the suspended broom handle, collapsed her knees and hung. She pulled, chinning on the handle, five, ten, twenty pull-ups, until the muscles in her back and arms burned. She stopped and sat, her buttocks warm on the cool, scoured floorboards. She spread her legs and bent her forehead until her breasts touched the floor. She reached, stretching the muscles she'd worked on the broom handle, then rose and repeated the set of twenty pull-ups, and the stretch, three more times.

For the first time since arriving in the U.S., twelve days earlier, Judith improvised ways to work her muscles. The hashish in her system powered her and, in the heat of exercise, slipped away unnoticed. She filled a pail with water and lifted to strain her biceps, then her shoulders. She squatted in the center of the room, hands on hips, building a fire in her legs and bottom, until she closed her eyes and breathed through the pain. The pain is where I begin, she thought, and willed herself through it, doubling the time she spent in this position.

After an hour working like this, she lay flat, breathing through gritted teeth, sweat slicking the boards. She listened to her heart race in her temples and tread through her extremities. Even so early in the day, the smells of cheap cooked food and spoiling lives crept in from the hall under her door to reach her lying, panting, on her floor. Judith did not mind the odors or judge the people who made them. She was glad of all of them, because this poor place hid her. When they came looking, who would think to look here?

When her pulse calmed, she took from her closet a carved bit of wood she'd made to replace the knife lost on the Massachusetts beach, with the same shape and weight. Taking it in hand, she went through her exercises, an arduous series of Kali katas. For another hour she swept in and out of the stylized stances and movements of the katas, aping combat with knife, fist, and foot, against one, two, and several opponents. She did not allow herself the martial grunts and bellows called for to accompany the fiercest strikes—the hour was too early and the sounds were designed to harden the spirit and unnerve an opponent. She would have been heard out in the alley.

The katas left Judith dripping. Toward the end of her routine, as her naked legs spread wide and solid, the wooden knife plunged into a shadow heart, her free hand poised to fend off an attacker from behind, the door to her apartment opened.

Judith held her position. At the slight sound, she turned only her head to Josh in her doorway.

"Wow," the boy said.

Judith completed the move, retracting the knife in the air. She lowered her hands, crossed them at the wrists, and took a deep, composing breath with eyes closed, a last martial moment before speaking.

She did not look at the lanky boy until she had put the knife down and wrapped her bare body in Mrs. P.'s quilt. She walked to the door, where Josh stood keen and grinning.

"Close it," she said.

Josh started, unaware that he'd left the door open. His façade failed him for a moment while he turned eagerly to do as he was told. When he faced Judith again, he remounted his attempt at a sneer.

The boy was again dressed in clothes unfit for the freezing temperature outside. He wore baggy charcoal pants and two-tone shoes, below a cream square-shouldered suit coat and matching white bobby socks and pocket kerchief. The look was that of a band leader, but the face was that of a pimply boy unfit for the army.

"What are you doing here, Josh?"

He held up Judith's busted doorknob. "I saw your note at the office that you was having a problem with this. I was up early so I thought I'd pop by and fix it for you. Then I saw your lights on and figured, what the hey, you must be up."

"So you used your father's key to simply walk into my apartment?"

"I knocked."

"No. You didn't."

The lazy eye the boy shared with his father took in the room. He was only an inch taller than Judith, and no more than a few pounds heavier.

"Josh, those aren't the clothes someone wears to come out and fix a doorknob."

"What, these?" The boy widened his stance to show himself off. "I don't wear nothin' else, honey. Hey, do you like Frankie?"

Many days waiting in her car outside the White House, Judith had listened to Frank Sinatra on her radio.

"He's fine."

The boy corrected her. "He's tops."

"Josh, do you need something?"

He ignored her question. "So, you do that stuff buck-naked, huh? Pretty swell."

Both stood staring. Under the quilt, Judith continued to sweat. Josh saw this.

"It looked hard. Maybe I'll get you to show me sometime."

Judith nodded. "Sometime."

Another pause fell between them. Clutching the quilt, Judith kept her face and movements empty, to draw the boy out. Slowly, he grew uncomfortable with her stillness.

"You got anything to drink?"

"No."

"Why don't you take a shower or something?"

"I intend to."

"Go ahead. I'll wait."

"Wait for what, Josh?"

The boy pointed. "You."

Judith did not move. Josh shifted his weight to one hip, tucking his thumbs in his pockets.

"Way I figure it, you need this apartment pretty bad, seeing as how you took it without even looking at it. D.C.'s real crowded these days, and coloreds ain't got too many places to rent this good. So, I guess if you want to stay here, you just got to be nice to me once in a while. I got my own set of keys, y' see. I can pretty much come and go as I see fit around here, if you get my drift. My dad don't care. And don't worry, I'll take good care of you."

Judith loosed a long, resigned breath.

"I don't have anything to drink," she said. "I have something else."

She turned her back on the boy. Inside the chifforobe, she pried up the loose plank and selected the tin of black kif.

Judith prepared the pipe, using the penknife to split a sliver of resin from the little dark brick. She mixed in tobacco so the boy could take the drug better. She turned, and grabbed the Zippo lighter.

"Here." Judith held out the pipe and flicked the lighter.

The boy straightened, unsure.

"What's that?"

"Hashish."

Josh blinked at the Zippo's flame. He made an effort to wipe the reluctance from his face, then clamped his lips around the pipe stem. Judith lowered the lighter to the bowl.

"Breathe deep," she whispered.

Josh coughed once; he brought up his free hand to smother the cough, polite and for that moment so young. Judith pressed the pipe back to him, urging him to inhale more.

When she saw Josh's eyelids bat and his knees soften, she took the pipe away. Again she turned her back to set it and the lighter on the dresser.

Behind her, Josh asked, "Aren't you going to have some?"

"No, that was for you."

Still facing away, she dropped the quilt.

Josh cleared his throat and stifled a cough. Judith waited, listening. "Wow," he said again.

Seconds passed. Then the floorboards squeaked under his shoes. Judith relaxed.

His right hand slipped into the bare curve of her waist, below her ribs. His left hand crept to her shoulder, almost as if, from behind, taking her in hand to dance.

Josh's breath brushed her neck; the sweetness of the pipe blended with cigarettes on his tongue and the spicy oil in his hair.

Judith laid her open right hand over his fingers at her hip. Josh gave a little gasp in her ear.

"Josh?"

"Yeah, doll?"

"Is this going to happen more than once?"

The boy snickered. "You bet it is."

Judith nodded against his pressing cheek. She encircled his thumb in her grip, opened her eyes, and whirled.

Still clasping Josh's thumb, she clamped both hands around his, swiftly raising the wrist in an arch across her face, past the boy's shocked features. She twisted his arm to bend the hand down and turn the elbow up. Josh, shocked and wrenched out of his embrace, made no move to counter. In an instant, Judith had him bent at the waist, facing the floor, the tendons of his shoulder and wrist near snapping.

"Ow, goddammit!" he cried at her bare feet. "What the—"

He did not finish his curse; Judith's naked knee crashed into his face. She felt teeth give way and the cartilage of his nose dissolve. She tightened her grip on his hand, bent it more and held it high to increase the pain shooting up his arm, then slammed her knee harder into his head. Josh's legs buckled, he sagged. Blood spilled from his open lips.

With the boy crumpling, she freed her right arm, reached it high, and with all her strength hammered her elbow down into the top of his neck, the spot where the spine joins the skull. Josh collapsed to the floor, five seconds after putting his hands on her.

With her foot she rolled him over. Above a smashed nose and mouth, his lazy eye dodged her, seeming to seek a way out, even while his good eye fixed on her in wild panic. His bloodied lips tried to form a word, a W sound, a Why or a What. Perhaps a Who. It made no difference.

Judith lifted her foot, sighted down the long length of her brown calf, and stomped on the boy's Adam's apple. The windpipe collapsed beneath her heel. The boy convulsed at the blow. She ground her heel into his throat, snuffing his breath. His body jerked again, then settled. She bent to lift one eyelid, to watch the boy's one good pupil dilate.

Judith got dressed in the New England fisherman's pants and shirt, then tugged on boots and the watch cap. She cut a soft slice from the black Indian kif. This piece she stuck in the boy's pants pocket; and the rest she returned to the tin. His other pocket she turned inside out. In his shoe she tucked a hundred dollars in cash.

Judith padded into the dim hall, then trod quietly to the porch. Dawn lay five hours away; the alley remained dark, empty, and cold. She checked Mrs. P.'s window to see that the old woman was not awake, then returned inside.

It was easy to heft the body across her shoulders in a fireman's carry. Silently, to barely a creak of the floorboards, she hustled Josh outside. Twenty yards into the alley, at a pile of overturned trash cans, she laid him down.

Back in her room, Judith scrubbed her floor again.

ONE HOUR AFTER SUNRISE, Judith pushed aside the garage door. She let the Nash warm, then drove off to follow the morning's first streetcars down New Jersey Avenue, to New York Avenue, on to Twelfth Street. After fifteen minutes, she drove past a huge temporary building set on Constitution across from the Commerce Department. This was one of the hundreds of massive sore thumbs hastily flung up, flimsy and unadorned wartime necessities to house the sprawling administration of war. The buildings seemed even uglier among the great and arrogant Grecian temples of America's white capital.

Judith wove through early traffic to compete for one of the parking spots beside the Commerce Building. Already, with two hours to go before the workers reported for their day, the streets thrummed with life, buses jammed, people jousting in their automobiles. Judith dove into one of the last available spots just ahead of another car, a uniformed sailor who banged his steering wheel.

She pulled on her long overcoat, tied a kerchief around her hair, and got out to walk. A cold gust blew from the south across the Potomac and Anacostia rivers. Judith had made herself learn these and other names and locations; she'd driven behind the trolleys to

grow familiar with the city. She patronized the clothing departments at Woodward & Lothrop and Hecht's, where they saw her
money and believed she was a white woman, so they let her try on
items in the dressing rooms. She visited no monuments or museums.
She felt no curiosity for what was here except the President. This
morning, to move among the people on the sidewalks and do what
they did, she wore the favored brown suit with square padded
shoulders and tan leather shoes. From a corner stand she bought a
Washington Post, black coffee, and an egg sandwich for fifty cents
total. She did not return to her car but strolled, chewing and carrying the paper folded beneath her arm, listening to the women talk.

It didn't take long to see that what the lady at the Public Welfare
Building had said was true: Females far outnumbered males in this
city. They were clerks and secretaries, assistants, couriers, and typ-
ists, civil servants in suits like Judith's or in uniform. They called
them GGs—the government girls who made the war small enough
to be fought on paper by men. They'd come in tens of thousands
looking for work and even, despite the slim chances, romantic
matches. They found a city crammed with themselves.

Judith slowed to catch snatches of conversation. Most were
laments. The women were paid far less than the men. Costs were
high. Acceptable living quarters were rare and too pricey. The girls
were homesick, lonely, and strapped for cash. Their jobs were bor-
ing and six days a week. Their bosses were lechers. Their typewrit-
ers were old. They had a date but their roommates wouldn't leave
them alone long enough. There were dull parties at the USO, the
Stage Door Canteen, the YWCA, at churches and synagogues.

Judith circled north to Lafayette Square, then south past the
Ellipse. Here men ate and smoked in their cars, waiting for their offices to open. She drew smiles from the many who looked up. She
returned their smiles and strode on, driving her pumps into the hard
sidewalk, making the *click click* noise of an American girl.

She walked until the sun rose enough to empty the cars of their

men and the women finished their cold puffs of chatter, to herd to
their desks and filing cabinets. Judith stood near her car. As she did
every morning, she threw away the newspaper without reading a
word. She cast one long glance at the White House four blocks off
and made a decision.

No. Enough.

She left the Nash parked. She'd return late in the afternoon. Now,
she strode away, to the corner of Fourteenth and Pennsylvania.
There, she caught the trolley—a rickety wooden retrofit from the
nineteenth century, taken from retirement and pressed into service
to help move the masses of Washington—to go shopping.

BY NOON SHE RETURNED to her alley. She strolled past the
place where she'd dumped the boy's body. Judith shouldered
through a crowd of ogling blacks pressing against police sawhorses
set as a cordon around the spot. District cops milled everywhere, fat
white men with nightsticks in their belts, keeping the gawkers at
bay. The boy was gone; the people were gaping at trash cans.

Judith went to her room and slept for two hours. Waking, she
dressed in a plain skirt, cable-knit sweater and mittens, lace-up
leather flats with a rubber cobbled heel, and a dowdy wool coat, all
bought in secondhand shops. She put her hair in a ponytail to keep
it out of the wind and walked back to the Nash, parked on
Fifteenth. Along the way, she sensed a difference in how the people
passing looked at her. Men in cars did not smile; women going in
and out of shops did not allow room for her on the sidewalk. Judith
walked on in her noiseless shoes.

She reached the Nash and climbed in from the cold. The city
coursed past, busy and tending to itself and its war. The South
Portico of the White House gleamed, patrolled and impregnable. An
hour passed, watching passersby pause to raise their Brownies to
snap photos of the building or barrel ahead into the wind. Judith retreated into her own singularity. She was like none of these people.

She was the object of nothing from this city, not the war or the work of it, the careers crushed or made by it, not the wealth, poverty, or society of it. Another hour passed quickly in her chilly car. She turned on her radio to the station WTOP and listened to American music: "This Is the Army, Mr. Jones," "I Left My Heart at the Stage Door Canteen," "Der Führer's Face," and "Don't Sit Under the Apple Tree."

Then Roosevelt appeared.

His armored limousine emerged out of the east gate, preceded as before by one black car, tailed by another. Judith started the Nash and swung out of the parking spot; the vacant space was filled in seconds. Roosevelt's little convoy sped past. Judith had to interrupt traffic to do a U-turn. She moved behind, three cars back, wondering where Roosevelt was headed. The President had never before emerged before three o'clock for his motoring forays. Yesterday she trailed for an hour and ten minutes while he and his guardians rode aimlessly through the city, out Rock Creek Parkway, then back to the White House. The evening before, Roosevelt had left the east gate at 7:33 P.M. Judith tailed him to the Statler Hotel where, according to a marquee, a Broadcasters Dinner was to be held. She did not wait for him to leave the dinner, and went home.

Today the ride was brief. The President's convoy turned left on Constitution, right onto Fourteenth, headed past the spire of the Washington Monument. Straight ahead, the cars entered a garage leading beneath the Bureau of Engraving. Behind the complex lay a small railroad switching yard. This meant Roosevelt was headed north by train to his family home in New York State. He would not come back until after the weekend.

Judith drove on, returning the Nash to its garage before the rush-hour traffic stymied every block. Her walk from the garage was through a dusk dimmer than days before; all the holiday lights of the neighborhood had finally been taken down.

Mrs. P. sat in her rocker, smoking. "Desiree."

Judith slowed.

"Hello, Mrs. P."

"Come over here, girl."

"Yes, ma'am."

Judith sat on the steps below Mrs. P.'s knees.

The old woman pointed the bitten stem of her pipe at Judith's face.

"You hear 'bout the landlord's boy?"

"Yes, ma'am."

"What you hear?"

"That he got himself beat to death in the alley last night."

"You hear what he got beat for?"

"No, ma'am."

"Police say drugs. Found some on him. And money, too."

"That's a shame."

Mrs. P. sucked her pipe on this notion. "That boy won't no harm to nobody. Couldn't even get drafted with that bad eye. He was just too big for his britches is all. Poor soul. Who'd do that kind of mess to him? What kind of people?"

"Bad people, I suppose."

Mrs. P. shook her head in disbelief.

"Mm-mm-mm. Don't make sense. I never heard nothin' 'bout that boy doin' no drugs. Mercy, you think you know some folks. And look what happens."

"Yes, ma'am."

The old woman fixed her dark eyes on Judith. "Do I know you, Desiree?"

"Yes, ma'am, I think so."

Mrs. P. whipped a hand before Judith's face. "Go on. What you take me for? Stupid? Well, I ain't."

Judith blinked, taken aback. She composed herself but took care to retain the genuine surprise on her face.

Mrs. P.'s voice had grown firm. "You know anythin' about this kind of goings on?"

"No, ma'am. Why would I?"

"You breakin' my heart, girl."

"How am I doing that?"

"You lyin' to me. I know what you doin'."

Quietly, Judith tensed.

"You think I don' see you comin' and goin' all hours? You think I don' know what you smokin' sittin' out here in my rocking chair? Girl, that shit be smellin' up the whole alley. I know what it is. I been to Harlem, New York, and all over, so I know. You lucky somebody don' tell the po-lice, what with that boy bein' beat so bad for the same damn thing."

Judith kept silent.

"No, you ain't got nothin' to say to me, girl, you just keep sittin' there bein' lucky."

Judith measured Mrs. P. The old woman rocked, agitated and glaring.

"Look here, Desiree, I ain't your mama. But your mama not here, so I got to step up for her. You listen, I'm far from stupid."

"I never said—"

"Hush up. My reckon is you know somethin' you ain't sayin', and that's fine. You go on 'bout your business. But it looks to me like you might be hangin' out with them bad folks you talkin' 'bout. We know Josh was. You hear what I'm sayin'?"

Judith nodded, letting Mrs. P. again build for her a better cover story than she would have constructed for herself.

"I know you been out lookin' for work every day. I see you goin' every morning trying to look all dolled up like you ain't colored. But them gubmint folks, Desiree, they ain't gonna hire no colored girl outta New Orleans for no office job. Pretty blue eyes and all. They ain't gonna look no further than your skin, and then you still gonna git some low-class work. No, child. You never gonna dress up good enough for some folk, and that's the truth."

Judith hung her head, portraying what Mrs. P. suggested.

"Mind, you can't go and let them get you down so much you wind up sitting out here in the middle of the night smokin' that nasty weed. Dealin' with criminals and such. Them people gon' hurt you one day, you see what they done to that white boy. If your mama knew, she'd take a switch to you. Damn, girl, you keepin' *me* up worryin'."

"I'm sorry. I'll stop."

"I know you gon' stop, 'cause I'm gon' help you out. If you want my help."

"Yes, ma'am."

"I'm gon' give you two choices. Number one is I'm gon' call the po-lice and you can tell them what you ain't tellin' me. Young Josh didn't deserve no killin' like that. I reckon maybe you know somethin' about it. But that's white folks and that's they problem, 'less you gon' make it yours and mine. Then I got to do what I got to do. You understand me?"

"Yes, ma'am."

Mrs. P. studied Judith's contrite expression skeptically. "Mmm-hmm. I think you gon' prefer number two."

"I reckon I will."

"Alright. I know a white lady. She can't keep help. But she's alright if you stay out her way. She got a husband with some big job in the gubmint, do somethin' for the President, is all I know. They got them a place in town nearby and another in Virginia. I do some cleanin' and cookin' for her couple times a week. I can't stand her much more'n that. But you need a steady job, something to keep you busy and off that stuff you smoking. She'll take you on if I say so. But you got to promise me you gon' straighten up. Now, you want me to get you work?"

Judith had figured she might have to wait weeks, she was prepared for months. Only this morning, with the White House mere blocks away yet denied to her, she'd changed direction. Now, though she sat on a splintering porch in a ghetto, with the authorities sniffing the alley for the boy's murderer and Mrs. P. dangling the police over her head, events turned the same way they had the last time she'd been in Washington. That job had moved fast, too.

Everything seemed to fall in place in America. People knew what they wanted here; people got what they wanted.

She rose from the porch steps and knit her fingers in front of her. Judith, an assassin with a dozen successful operations in her portfolio, a walled compound in Cairo paid for by clients around the world, with hours-old blood on her hands, knew to get to her feet at this moment. This was what no assassin could be taught, not through any training of weapons or tactics, but only by instinct and experience: the sense when something perfect and improbable was about to be delivered, when the path inward opened. One stood for that, humble and thankful.

Mrs. P. asked again, "You want me to get you a job or not?"

Judith smiled, not at Mrs. P.

"Yes, ma'am."

CHAPTER SIX

January 12
Route 1, 50 miles north of Baltimore

AT MIDNIGHT, DAG PULLED in to an all-night convenience store for a Coca-Cola and a bag of salted peanuts. He bought Lammeck, who had no dollars yet, a Grape Nehi and a roll of Life Savers. Walking to the car, Lammeck watched Dag take a swig of cola, then pour the peanuts into the bottle. Dag chewed Coke and floating nuts with each tip of the bottle.

"What?" Dag asked, testy when Lammeck grimaced. "We're headed south. This is how to eat peanuts in the South. You drive now."

Lammeck got behind the wheel. On the passenger's side, Dag covered himself with his wrinkled overcoat. Lammeck pulled out of the store's parking lot into the road. Dag sprayed foam and nuts on the dash.

"Right lane! Right lane!"

Lammeck spun the steering wheel. No traffic had come close but Dag continued to grumble. "I got it," Lammeck assured him. "Get some rest."

"Yeah, sure, I'll try that with one eye open."

Dag could not sleep. Before Baltimore, he took the driving back. Lammeck made no comment when he gave up the wheel. Driving on the right was nerve-wracking after five years of rolling on the left side of the road. He figured he'd get reacquainted with this part of America later.

Lammeck pulled Dag's overcoat up to his chin. He could not snooze either; his internal clock still ticked on Scottish time, hours ahead. Instead, he flipped through the files in his brain, furiously separating the known in this case from the guessed at.

He found very little in the known column. Two dead Civil Defense wardens, both killed expertly; one suicide, done suspiciously. A knife that might date back to the age of Hasan-i-Sabah, but was at the very least directly inspired by the Ismai'li Assassins of Alamut. That blade was probably the murder weapon on the beach. An untraceable .32 revolver definitely used in the husband's staged suicide. A kitchen knife that was definitely planted in the husband's sink.

What else?

Lammeck's next set of facts drifted away from certainty like a rowboat cut loose from a dock. The crowbar dropped in front of the truck's headlamps. A strand of black hair found in Otto's hand. Tire tracks in the sand. The matching gashes on Bonny's forearms. The fatal bullet lodged low in Arnold's wall, and the stab that didn't stop Otto's heart right away. Every one of these was just a hint. Not one sure bet in the bunch, but now he and Dag were playing all of these to win.

Next came the harebrained hunches. A sub. A woman. A Persian. FDR as the target, Washington the place.

Finally, he chewed on the revelation that he and Dag were the entire force committed to this case. Skepticism was probably too mild a word for how the Secret Service was approaching this snipe hunt.

Even so, with the dark southeastern seaboard skimming past the Packard's cold window, Lammeck could not shake the same sensation that Dag had expressed. As thin a case as all this added up to, son of a bitch if it wasn't exactly what was happening.

History had never shied from improbability. What were the odds that on the one wrong night in Ford's Theater, Lincoln's bodyguard would saunter off for a beer? That in 1835, both pistols of Richard Lawrence, the first man to attempt an assassination of an American president, would misfire on the Capitol rotunda, at point-blank range of Andrew Jackson? Who could have predicted last year that an explosive briefcase in Hitler's bunker would be placed behind a table leg so thick it spared the Führer? Or that in '33, FDR himself would finish a speech in Miami from the backseat of his touring car, then lean forward to view a telegram at the exact second the little Italian anarchist Giuseppe Zangara—who believed killing Roosevelt would cure his stomach ailments—opened fire, hitting instead and eventually killing the mayor of Chicago?

Lammeck wondered about the patchwork assassin they were chasing. This—what? Persian woman? phantom?—was clearly not mad. History provided only two classic reasons for political murder. Madness and power.

The lion's share of assassinations served this second purpose, power. Romulus killed his brother Remus, co-founder of Rome. That great city-state stood as the high-water mark in history for political slaughter. In A.D. 37, Emperor Tiberius had his rival Sejanus and his entire family murdered, including Sejanus's fourteen-year-old daughter who, as a virgin, was exempt from execution. So, the girl was publicly raped by her executioner before being strangled. In A.D. 69, Rome celebrated four emperors in a single year: Galba succeeded Nero, then had his arms, legs, and lips cut off by his successor Otho, who committed suicide to avoid being slain by Vitellius, who was later pelted by dung from the crowds, dragged by a meat hook, and tossed in the Tiber by Vespasian, who died in bed a decade after.

Nor had history reserved the role of assassin solely for men. Agrippina poisoned husband Claudius to protect the Roman crown for son Britannicus against her other son Nero. After Caesar elevated both Cleopatra and her brother Ptolemy XIV to co-rulership of Egypt, Cleopatra had Ptolemy murdered to assure that the son she shared with Caesar, named Caesarion, would succeed her. And so on.

Lammeck's thoughts wobbled with the gentle swaying of the Packard. He shifted under Dag's coat, letting his mind idle toward sleep. He considered what lay ahead, the search for a needle in an enormous haystack, an assassin embedded in the nation's capital. If, in fact, this woman did exist and had been sent by another nation, she'd have ample funds and intelligence. She may or may not be working alone. She would not act carelessly; she'd plot, bide her time, and exploit. But exploit what? What would she spot in Roosevelt's schedule or routine that would expose him to killing? Lammeck surmised from her skill and cunning—the disabling slits in Bonny's forearms, faking Arnold's suicide to cover her tracks— that she was not in the classic mold of a martyr, like Charlotte Corday or Trotsky's ax-murderer Mercader. Was she a patriot killer, the kind to lie low for months, waiting for the opportunity to stand on a corner and blast away at the President's car like Gabčik and Kubiš? Or would she insinuate her way in gently and slip away un- noticed, a professional with no desire to die in the act like the an- cient disciples on Alamut with their tickets punched for Paradise?

Lammeck sat up with a snort, so suddenly that Dag cursed and the car jerked.

"What?" Dag barked. "You almost gave me a heart attack."

"She had help, Dag. She had someone waiting in Newburyport. That's why she landed there in the first place."

"Professor, come on. I don't think I can swallow one more the- ory. Let's go get some hard facts, okay? Get some shut-eye."

Lammeck whipped Dag's rumpled coat off and into the backseat.

"Hey, easy with that," Dag said.

"Bonny and Otto. Were they lovers?"

Behind the wheel, Dag shrugged. "That's what the cops said. Everybody in town seemed to know about it except poor Arnold."

Lammeck took a deep breath to awaken himself fully. "That's

right. Poor Arnold. Tell me something. How did someone who got dropped off by a submarine in the middle of the night, from Germany or Japan or wherever, know about Bonny and Otto? How did she know where Bonny's husband lived? How did she get inside Arnold's door at three in the morning unless he saw someone on his front porch ringing his doorbell that he knew?"

"Aw, shit," Dag said. The Secret Service agent hit the brakes and swung the car to the shoulder.

Lammeck asked, "What're you doing?"

"We've got to go back, Professor. Why the hell didn't I see that two weeks ago? Damn it, she had an accomplice. Fuck!" Dag smacked the wheel with the flat of his palm. "I never even asked myself why she would be in Newburyport. I just figured the place was remote, or there was some connection to Boston that'd come out later. Or . . . whatever. Shit, I don't know. I got carried away with the crime scenes and that weird fucking knife, and then going to get you . . ."

Lammeck waved at the windshield. "Calm down, I missed it too 'til now. Don't turn around, let's keep heading for D.C. I've got another idea."

"Dumbass," Dag continued to abuse himself.

"Don't worry about it. This whole thing's like a crossword puzzle. Every time we figure something out, two or three more clues open up. We've got no choice but to do it one guess at a time. Just stay flexible."

Dag nodded, hardly pacified. Lammeck knew from training him that Dag wasn't the flexible type, but a straight-ahead charger; he'd garroted three Germans and would have killed more or died to get out of captivity. His single-mindedness was probably how he'd overlooked the fact that the assassin had a confederate. As to why he didn't figure it out earlier himself, Lammeck blamed fatigue and the distraction of being back in America, and let it go.

Dag accelerated again into the southbound lane of Route 1. The outskirts of Baltimore thickened in the darkness. Blacked-out garages and warehouses fled by in clouded moonlight. Lammeck rubbed through his beard, then launched into a flight of logic he accepted at the outset would be sketchy.

"What time were the murders on the beach? Two, two-thirty?"

"About that time, yeah."

"Okay, stop me if this gets too thin to hold water. We're assuming the assassin arrived on the shore, killed Bonny and Otto, then made her way into town. She found Arnold and did him. But she didn't plan for any of that to happen; it was an emergency response to something that went wrong. If she arrived on the beach around two-thirty, how long would it take if things had gone according to plan?"

Dag calculated. "Let's assume it was all done on foot. Five minutes to hit the sand and change clothes. Fifty minutes to walk to town. Call it an hour."

"And from town, we're figuring she headed straight for Washington."

"Check," Dag said glumly.

"What time was the first train out of Newburyport?"

"New Year's morning? I'll find out, but you can bet the farm it wasn't before seven A.M."

"Good. Now, Dag, follow me. If you were designing this mission for the SOE, if that was you swimming ashore, what time would you arrive on that beach if you were planning on making a seven o'clock train out of a small town? No attention, no suspicion, just get ashore, make the train, and head south?"

"Definitely not 'til just before sunup. Four-thirty, maybe five. I'd try to hit the middle of town just at dawn, no sooner. Find the station, keep my head down, and wait for the train. New Year's Day, figure there's no one else out, so you wouldn't want to be hanging around town with everything closed and nobody going to work. You'd stick out like a sore thumb. Someone would see you and remember you. Maybe a local cop would check you out. No, you wouldn't risk showing up at two-thirty. Too early. Too much exposure."

"Unless . . . ?" Lammeck waited for Dag to take the bit and run.

"Unless you had somewhere to cool your heels 'til the train left."

"Or . . . ?"

"Or . . ." Dag mulled a moment, then lifted a hand off the wheel. "Or you weren't taking the fucking train!"

Lammeck sat back with a sigh. "A kewpie doll for Agent Nabbit."

January 14
Washington, D.C.

THE PHONE RANG.

"Yes?"

"Dr. Lammeck? This is the front desk. There's a Mr. Nabbit who says to tell you he's out front waiting."

"Tell him I'll be down in a minute."

"If I may, Doctor, Mr. Nabbit is sitting in his car. He's been honking the horn."

"I'll hurry."

"Thank you."

Lammeck grabbed his coat and headed for the elevator. In the driveway of the Blackstone Hotel, Dag sat hunched in the idling Packard.

Lammeck climbed in. Dag pulled onto Seventeenth Street before he spoke.

"I asked you to be ready at ten to noon."

"I was ready."

"I meant in the lobby."

"What's the matter? You nervous?"

Dag snagged a manila envelope off the seat between them. He rattled it as if threatening Lammeck with it.

"This," he said. "This is going to get me fired. I can't believe the frigging report I had to write. It reads like a Raymond Chandler story. No. No. It doesn't even make *that* much sense."

Lammeck did not reach for the envelope.

"The worst that can happen to you, Professor, is a plane back to Scotland. Me? The worst they can do is put me on it with you."

"Don't worry. We'll be convincing."

Dag dropped the folder and set his jaw. Lammeck was pleased to see the agent did not look like a hanky out of someone's pocket this morning. He wore a pressed suit and tie. Aesthetics clearly mattered at the White House. Dag almost passed for handsome.

He drove to the West Gate and showed his ID to a guard, who checked Lammeck's name against a list. They parked and entered the West Wing.

Marines in dress uniform held doors for them. Walking a long corridor lined with portraits, Dag explained the security blanket around the President.

"Washington, D.C., is Secret Service District 5, out of fifteen districts nationwide. The White House is its own district, number 16. There are seventy agents permanently assigned to District 16, and another hundred and thirty-five White House police. For the first years of the war, up until late '43, there were blackouts across the entire city, machine guns on the White House roof, and antiaircraft batteries on the grounds. Those are gone now. There are air raid shelters and vaults under the residence. To make a long story short, the President is not going to get hurt while he's on the premises."

Lammeck took long strides to keep up with Dag, whose pace betrayed his nerves.

"What about that guy back in 1930 who walked right up to President Hoover while he was having dinner here in the White House?"

"You know about that?"

Lammeck grinned. "It's what I do, Dag."

"Okay, that was fifteen years ago. Since then, Congress has put everybody protecting the Mansion, all the cops and agents, under the Secret Service. Coordination's better now. Security's airtight."

"I should hope. Assuming you're right, where do you think the President is most vulnerable?"

"Definitely when he travels. We don't worry so much about when the Boss goes home to Hyde Park or down to the Little White House in Georgia. We've got those routes covered. But when he heads overseas or makes one of his political stops, you'd be amazed how much advance work gets done. Weeks before he gets to a destination, we check everything and everyone. Thousands of man-hours. But no question the toughest place to protect him is in a slow motorcade through a city for some big public event. We keep one car in front, another behind, and armed agents on the running boards of his limo. We've got agents in the crowd, agents on roofs, you name it."

"Is the limo armored?"

Dag chuckled mirthlessly without slowing his gait.

"Yeah. Back in '40 the Service kinda borrowed Al Capone's armored limo after it was confiscated. That was a little embarrassing, so the next year Henry Ford gave the Boss his own car. It's like a tank. And when he travels by train, five minutes after leaving the White House we can have him in his own specially built railcar at the underground siding in the Bureau of Engraving."

"I assume the railcar is armored, too."

"It can survive a four-story fall without a dent."

"What about the rubber knife?"

"Geez, you know about that, too?"

"Just a rumor."

"Yeah, fine. In Erie once during his second campaign, when the Boss was standing on the rear platform of the train, some guy threw a rubber knife at him. It missed and hit the guy next to him."

"That's funny."

"No. It's not."

"I assume measures have been taken to prevent these sorts of things from happening again."

"*Yes*. Professor. For the record, now's not a good time to aggravate me."

Lammeck walked on, considering that Dag was always aggravated, but thinking mostly about the company-sized troop that guarded the President in his own home, plus the armor and firepower that accompanied him when he traveled. Even with these protections and hired guns in place around Roosevelt—surrounded by a cadre of short-tempered, wary men like Dag, eyeing every possibility—there were cracks in the wall, uncovered in dangerous and comic ways by isolated individuals who just wanted to scare the President, watch him eat, or kill him.

Without more prodding, Dag continued the defense of his agency.

"Every month, Roosevelt gets forty thousand letters. Five thousand of those are threatening, ranging from guys who just want to punch him in the nose to people who say they'll shoot him dead on sight. Each of these letters is investigated by Secret Service field agents. If FDR makes a trip to a city, every one of the local nut jobs on file gets his picture handed out to the agents on the detail. A few days before the President arrives, agents pay a call to the hate mailers' families, asking them to keep their relative off the streets until the President is gone. If Aunt Sally can't control Cousin Tom, we put a tail on him. And if the guy is a real pinwheel, we swear out a warrant with the local cops."

Lammeck marveled at the amount of hate mail FDR generated. Not even Lincoln got that many threats. Lammeck recalled how Andrew Jackson, also a well-despised president, used to sign his best bits of hate mail and have them published in the Washington newspapers.

"I get the picture. You're thorough."

They arrived at a door in the West Wing blazoned with the Secret Service five-star emblem. Dag waggled the envelope again.

"We'll see," he said glumly.

They entered a windowless anteroom manned by an austere woman behind a desk. A few framed certificates broke the white of the walls. The mood was reminiscent of the principal's office. A placard on the secretary's desk read: *Assistant to the Supervisor, White House Detail.*

She peered over her pince-nez. "Agent Nabbit."

Dag approached, clasping the report behind his back. "Mrs. Beach."

"Go right in. Dr. Mikhal Lammeck?"

Lammeck stepped beside Dag. "At your service."

The woman indicated one of the hard-backed chairs.

"Charming. Have a seat."

Lammeck gave Dag an encouraging thump on the shoulder and did as he was told. Dag passed through the interior door, looking sheepish.

Lammeck spent ten minutes watching wiry Mrs. Beach scribble and answer her phone with a clipped manner. He decided the woman might be two or three times the age of their Persian assassin, and would still be a handful in a fight.

The inner door opened. Dag waved Lammeck inside. Mrs. Beach did not look up.

Lammeck entered a warmer office, small but leavened with leather chairs and photographs of the man behind the desk with many world leaders. A quick scan of the pictures revealed Churchill, Haile Selassie, Stalin, and King Ibn Saud, before Lammeck put his attention on the thickset Irishman who rose and offered a hand in greeting.

"Professor Lammeck, thanks for coming such a long way. Mike Reilly."

Lammeck shook hands. "Chief."

The report lay open on Reilly's desk. They all sat. Lammeck looked between Dag and Reilly, waiting for one to begin. Both seemed to be waiting for him.

"Okay." Lammeck lifted his palms in an opening gesture of surrender. "I know there's some leaps of logic in there."

Reilly laughed outright. "Leaps? Yeah. Like Superman."

Lammeck liked the man and played along. "Tall buildings in a single bound."

The detail chief chuckled. Beside Lammeck, Dag sat looking flayed.

"Professor, Dag speaks highly of you." Reilly patted the report. "And your résumé is impressive. You're an interesting man. You specialize in assassins, the exact sort of people Dag and I, and a thousand other men and women with us, are dedicated to stopping. I look forward to reading your *Gallery* book when it's done. Now, if you don't mind, I want to ask you some questions."

"That's why I'm here."

Reilly grilled Lammeck about the gashes on Bonny's arms, and his conclusion that the wounds evidenced a special martial training by her killer. He inquired into the dropped crowbar and the tire tracks in the sand. The timing of the murders. The mystery of Arnold's suicide, for which Lammeck and Dag had no explanation, not even an implausible one. The possibility that the assassin had a local accomplice. The long black hairs. The two bloody knives, one from the twelfth century, the other from a kitchen.

"And in your estimation, all this," Reilly concluded, "adds up to some foreign female killer coming here to Washington to murder the President. Right?"

The man's tone was patient. It was also indulgent.

"No, Chief. It doesn't."

Dag moaned. Lammeck continued.

"What it does add up to is unknown. But when Dag and I connect all these dots, we can't rule out the possibility that the President is the target of an internationally driven plot to assassinate him. Since we can't rule it out—and with all due respect, Chief, I trained Dag and I know when he's on to something—then you have a duty to listen to him, and to make sure the possibility gets run to ground."

Reilly narrowed his eyes. "Thank you for reminding me of my duty, Professor. Now give me the truth. What are the odds?"

"Slim."

Dag dug his fingers in his eye sockets.

Lammeck pressed on. "Keep in mind, Chief, that every president who's been assassinated died from odds just as slim. Maybe even slimmer. That goes for kings and queens, too. If you like, I can give you chapter and verse."

Reilly measured Lammeck, then nodded.

The chief said, "You're saying she's a level six."

Lammeck returned Reilly's nod.

Dag righted himself abruptly. "What the hell is that?"

Lammeck answered. "She's so good, there's no evidence that she actually exists. She's a theoretical assassin."

Dag mulled this, shaking his head. "Great. Frigging great. So we have to defend the President against a theory."

Reilly and Lammeck said nothing, but looked at each other. Lammeck watched the chief consider what he'd heard, while Dag rubbed his forehead in mounting misery. Then Reilly spoke.

"Dag, I can tell you're serious about this case. You went to the dry cleaners before you came to see me. So here's what I'm going to give you."

Reilly scooted the papers and photos of the report together into a sheaf. He tapped them into shape and dropped them back into the envelope.

"I haven't got a Chinaman's clue if this is a plot, a frame, a hoax, or just botched police work in Massachusetts. You tell me you've got some Persian doll who was dropped off by a sub to come and kill FDR. I say prove it better than this."

"Yes, sir."

"But Dr. Lammeck's right. There's nothing here that lets me rule out your premise. Nothing but common sense and a dose of reality.

Be that as it may, I'm going to let you keep the good professor here at the Blackstone Hotel as long as you need him, or until I get tired of this case. I'm going to let you work on it for the same duration."

Dag sat upright. "How about manpower?"

"Denied. It's still just the two of you. And for the time being, I'm not going to alter any of the President's protection. However, I'll put some subpoenas to work for you. Tell me what you need, and I'll see if I can get it. But quietly, Dag. I don't want this investigation on anyone's radar, you understand? The FBI stays out of it, the newspapers don't get even a whiff, and most of all, the Boss doesn't hear about it. Okay?"

"Yeah, Chief. Thanks."

Lammeck jumped in before Dag could say more.

"One thing. We need your Boston agents to run down every car purchased in the Newburyport area in the eight weeks before the murders. Check the buyers especially for German or Japanese surnames or ancestry. Also tell your boys to look for someone who bought a car and titled it, or their own car, over to someone else in short order."

"You think your Persian gal was given a car to drive south?"

"I think our Persian gal is already here in D.C. somewhere. But I think her associate in Newburyport is still in Newburyport. The car angle is the only thing I can figure for right now. So that's where I want you to look, while we try to find the assassin here. Under the radar, just as you say. Once we get some hard evidence, we'll be back for more help."

Reilly plopped Dag's report into the in-box on his desk. He tossed Lammeck a twinkling Irish smile.

"You say the most ridiculous things like you're sure, Professor. Do you know that?"

"I'm a teacher. It's part of the job."

"Anything else?"

"I'll need my own vehicle and gas rations. And a stipend for food and expenses."

"I'll take care of it. Dag, anything?"

"Nothing. Thanks, sir."

Reilly stood, the interview concluded. He shook hands again with Lammeck.

"Professor, I know this is a long way from your classroom in Scotland. Thank you for coming home. I can't tell you how much I hope you're full of shit."

Lammeck grinned and headed for the door.

"Professor?" Reilly called.

"Yeah, Chief?"

"I'll get those car sales records for you. Then I'm headed out of town for a few weeks. I'll be in touch with Mrs. Beach. She'll handle anything you need while I'm gone. I know that thrills you, Dag."

"Couldn't be happier, sir."

"I'll expect glowing reports. Tell me something, Professor. How do you figure on finding your assassin?"

"I'm not going to look for her."

Dag's jaw dropped. The agent was not having a pleasant afternoon, even though they were not walking out of Reilly's office empty-handed or rebuked, as Dag had feared. Lammeck decided to buy him a beer afterward to cheer him up.

"Chief, I'd never find her by looking for her. The woman's good. She's ruthless. And she's in no hurry. The only shot I have is to cross paths with her."

Reilly laid palms on his desk, intrigued. "And how do you intend to do that?"

"The only way I can."

Lammeck glanced to the picture of FDR hung behind Reilly's head. He imagined the President with eyes closed, lying in state.

"I'm going to hunt Roosevelt myself."

ALL THE WAY DOWN the corridor, Dag ranted in Lammeck's ear.

"You're going to *hunt* Roosevelt? Are you out of your..." He controlled himself enough to drop his voice, but his hiss bounced off the walls in the West Wing, ". . . out of your fucking *gourd*?"

"I'm not going to kill the man, Dag."

"You're goddam right you're not! But Jesus, did you have to say *hunt* in front of Reilly?"

"He took it okay."

"Then you didn't see the look he gave me. It was his 'He's-your-problem-Dag' look. I almost choked you on the spot."

"Thank you for sparing me."

"Don't get cute, Professor. Look, don't go off half-cocked like that again. I don't sleep well as it is."

Dag kept up his streaming plaint to the parking lot. At the Packard, Lammeck stopped.

"I'll walk."

Dag grunted, exasperated. "Don't start pouting on me. I'm sorry I jumped on you. Get in."

"It's okay. I need to do a little thinking. I'll meet you for dinner at the hotel. And Dag, when you arrive, don't honk, don't bitch, just come in and sit down in the lobby."

Lammeck strolled away, enjoying the scowl he left on Dag's face. He exited the lot and walked south along Executive Avenue. The afternoon bore a crisp blue clarity. He passed perhaps five hundred people, every one bundled against the cold, on their way, on the clock, all anonymous to him. He strolled to the center of the Ellipse, then stopped. Four baseball diamonds were laid out on the big circular meadow. Lammeck stood in the patch of grass that was the center field shared by all four diamonds.

Lammeck had spent the last five years in Scotland; the White House viewed from a baseball field on a postcard afternoon was a peculiarly patriotic image. Lammeck scanned all four directions, spotting an uncountable number of vehicles and people moving within sight of where the President sat. He breathed in the winter nip of the day, and began with the thought that she had drawn the same cold breath.

CHAPTER SEVEN

January 16
Washington, D.C.

JUDITH LIFTED HER NEW dress out of the chifforobe, tore the thin paper sheath off, and spread the fabric across the bed.

The outfit was bought yesterday on New York Avenue, intended for this morning. The cut was a belted waist, mid-calf, of shimmering cornflower-blue silk. Beaded embroidery adorned the short-sleeve cuffs and a bow set off the neckline. The saleswoman had assured her this was the latest fashion, just like the dress Claudette Colbert wore in her latest film, *Practically Yours,* a comedy costarring Fred MacMurray. Judith took from a drawer a matching scarf and arranged it on the bed atop the dress. On the floor, she set new high-heeled patent leather shoes dyed cobalt, and for her head she placed a navy, brimmed felt hat boasting a pheasant's feather. Judith stood back from the bed and hoped that, when she left Washington this time, she might be able to take some of her outfits with her. Putting the clothes on, she doubted this could happen. She donned a new fur-collared winter coat.

Mrs. P. waited on the cold porch. When she saw Judith emerge, the old woman tightened the knitted green muffler at her throat.

"You lookin' awful sharp to be goin' to ask a white woman if you can polish her silver."

Judith said only, "Good morning, Mrs. P." She followed the old woman to K Street.

Workers crowded the bus stop. Most were black domestics. Mrs. P. seemed to know every one of them. She introduced Judith to a few, but Judith took no part in the conversations and swapping of stories rippling around her. She learned nothing by talking. Mrs. P. leaned in close to her listeners to tell them what she knew and surmised about the beating death of her landlord's son in the alley four days before. Her listeners cooed at the scandal; Judith heard nothing mentioned about herself. The ladies' talk switched to gossip. Mrs. P. jiggled her great bosom with laughter and swatted her hand through the air with her responses: "No you did *not*! Go on with yourse'f."

When the bus came, Mrs. P. trundled up the steps with the other maids. Judith lagged and saw no seat with the old woman in the packed rear. She took a seat near the front next to a light-skinned girl in cornrows. The girl was too young to be scrubbing for others. She exchanged a smile with Judith.

"I like yo' dress," the girl said, pointing at the hem exposed under Judith's overcoat.

Judith said, "I like yo' hair," trying out the dialect.

The two traded no more words until the girl rose for her stop at M Street in Georgetown.

"Bye, pretty lady."

Judith shifted her knees to let her slide past. She watched the girl walk away. The next few stops were in a neighborhood of brick-and-ivied homes, where the bus emptied itself by half. Most of those stepping off were Negro women in powder-blue skirts, white aprons, and mobcaps. The bus took on more passengers, but these were whites. They all sat in the front around Judith. One man eyed her and winked. Judith lowered the brim of her hat.

The bus continued west, following the road onto a bridge across the Potomac. Judith glanced to the rear seats where Mrs. P. prattled with her friends. Along the north bank, the Gothic towers of a grand university rose. Judith was looking at these buildings when the bus pulled to the shoulder and stopped.

The driver turned in his seat, studying her. Judith was unsure why this was happening. The driver looked puzzled. Judith lowered her chin so the brim of her feathered hat hid her eyes.

She heard the shuffle of the driver's feet, then watched the man's boots square up in front of her.

"Missy?"

Judith raised her face.

"Yes?"

"We're not in D.C. no more. We're in Virginia now."

Judith blinked and stared.

"You need to move to the back."

From the rear of the bus, Judith heard Mrs. P. "Oh, my lands."

"Why?" Judith asked the man calmly.

The driver crossed his arms over his chest. Judith looked about her. The white people who had ridden near her across the Potomac glowered; a few whispered to each other. The man who'd winked at her shook his head as if he'd been tricked.

The driver said, "You're colored, aren't you? You came on with the coloreds."

Judith got to her feet. The driver did not back off but remained close, within arm's reach. Judith retreated one step for distance. She kept her arms loose at her sides. The driver kept his eyes fixed on hers, fearing nothing. Judith looked away, down his torso, then to his feet. He tapped one foot, his balance on his heels.

"What if I'm not?"

"Then I apologize and you sit back down."

She lifted her gaze to his.

"And if I am?"

"Then you need to go to the back with the rest."

"That makes it very easy for you. It must be wonderful."

Judith waited, locked on the man's eyes. The bus idled. Whispers in the seats became voices. Again, she lowered her face to watch his boots.

The driver said, "Missy, I got no idea what you're talking about. But I don't make the rules. And you don't break 'em."

With that, the man's weight transferred to his toes, stepping forward. Now he was committed, he could not retreat.

Judith raised her eyes and measured him in a fraction of a second. She straightened her right hand, firming the fingers into a rigid knife-edge. Her left hand she balled to a fist. She watched his boots; when the rear foot came off the ground, when he stood for a moment on one leg, rooted, the fingertips of the right hand driven into his throat would throttle him, her left knuckles into his sternum would stun him to his knees. After he buckled, a fist hard to the temple would incapacitate him. The three-inch blade in her brassiere would finish this soft, stupid, unafraid man.

A hand gripped Judith. She flinched at the unexpected touch. The hand jerked her backward, off balance, out of her unseen coil.

"Girl, get yo' parts to the back of the bus with the rest of us. What you doin' up here?"

The driver nodded. "You'd best talk some sense into this girl. I'll kick her off the bus and she can just walk her ass to work."

Mrs. P. tugged again on Judith's elbow.

"Desiree, get movin'. Mister, I'm sorry. She from out o' town. I don't know what-all she got in her head sometimes."

The driver pivoted to return to his seat. Judith held her ground in the aisle with Mrs. P. attached to her arm and tugging. Judith met the driver's eyes reflected in his big rearview mirror, the one above his head looking back into the seats. The look in his eyes asked: Did she want him to come back? The look in her eyes answered: Yes.

Mrs. P. yanked Judith away. No one else on the bus, black or white, moved while the driver made a show that he would not drive one inch farther into the state of Virginia until this colored girl sat in the back where the law put her. Mrs. P. spat in her ear, "Come on, Desiree, or I'm gon' whup you myse'f. You remember, we done talked 'bout you gettin' a new attitude." By this, Mrs. P. meant, again, the threat of the police.

Judith allowed the old woman to pinch her arm all the way to an empty seat in the rear. The heavyset maids clucked their tongues when she sat, and talked about her as if she were not there. "Where that girl from, Mrs. P.? She gon' buy herse'f a *peck* o' trouble."

Mrs. P. did not answer. She softened her grip on Judith. Then she leaned close and spoke only for her ear.

"What's goin' on wit' you, girl? You gon' tell Mrs. P.?"

Judith worked her jaw and hands, grinding off the tension.

"I know one thing," the old woman murmured. "You ain't from no New Orleans."

Slowly, Judith turned to Mrs. P. The woman patted Judith's hands.

"That's alright," the old woman said. "You tell me when you ready. I'll be waitin'."

The bus heaved forward. The others, black and white, quit looking at Judith and rode on together, south from the river, in their proper places.

Aurora Heights
Arlington, Virginia

MRS. P. CAME TO a stop on the sidewalk in front of a wide brick home. Old trees arched bare branches above them. Judith imagined in summer how lush and private this neighborhood must be. So many robust houses on this street, just one of a hundred streets in this enclave a mile from the river. This was America living well, very well.

Bringing her eyes down to Mrs. P., Judith was reminded that only one part of America blossomed on this street. Standing in front of the big house, the old woman altered. Her shoulders sagged under these trees and assumed the yoke of her station here.

"Girl, you done?"

"Done what, Mrs. P.?"

"You know what I'm talkin' about. Done bein' Miz Uppity. That lady in there got no truck wit' them kind o' airs. You want this job, you come off that high horse you think you ridin'. I don' know how you come by it, but you leave it outside."

"Yes, ma'am."

"You keep in mind what happened to the landlord's boy. Alright? You better'n that."

"Yes, ma'am."

"Good. You jus' keep sayin' 'Yes'm,' and you be fine."

Judith followed to the front door. Mrs. P. rang and they waited on the stoop.

A tall, thin woman opened the door. Judith was struck immediately by her fluttering manner when she greeted Mrs. P. She seemed overly friendly and breathless.

"Mahalia, good morning! And you must be Desiree! Yes, come in, come in. You certainly are as pretty as Mahalia said you were."

Judith stepped into a high foyer. Crystal chandeliers, velvet curtains, and heavy furniture anchored the rooms on both sides, brown and bland spaces as though parched. Judith in her own home sat on cushions and plush carpets, with day and moonlight and luminous fabrics, open windows, market smells and noises invited in. This house was glum, a quiet cage around this birdy woman. Mrs. P. took Judith's coat.

"Desiree, come sit. Mahalia, there's coffee on the stove."

"Yes'm."

The woman took an overstuffed chair in the dour parlor, indicating Judith sit on the nearby ottoman.

"I'm sure you know, my name is Mrs. Jacob R. Tench. My husband, of course, is the assistant secretary of the Navy, under Secretary Forrestal. It might interest you to know that my husband holds the identical position President Roosevelt himself held under President Wilson during the first war. Did you know that?"

"Yes, ma'am."

"You did? How excellent. Well, we'll get along just fine. I suppose Mahalia told you the pay. Three dollars a day, and I'll need you five days a week plus some evenings and weekends when my husband and I are entertaining. I will pay an extra dollar and a half when you work at night. Those are extremely fair wages, Desiree. I assume you are a firm hand with a broom and a dust cloth?"

"Yes, ma'am."

"Good. You look like a fine worker. Mahalia will handle the kitchen. Do you know how to serve?"

Judith did not know what she meant.

"Food, Desiree. Have you served at formal dinners before?"

"No, ma'am."

Mrs. Tench steepled her fingers. "Oh, dear. Hmm, well. We'll have you taught quickly enough. You seem like a bright girl. Aren't you dressed nicely, though? I'm afraid you'll need to wear something a bit less frilly, however. Those are not appropriate clothes for housework, dear."

"No, ma'am."

"Good. Finally, my husband travels quite frequently. On those occasions, I often visit my family out of town, or I simply stay in our Georgetown home. You may be asked to come with Mahalia out here to Arlington to prepare the house for my husband's and my return, or sometimes to our Georgetown residence. That means I will be trusting you in my home in my absence. Can you be trusted, Desiree?"

"Yes, ma'am."

"Are you sure? I've had some unfortunate experiences with help."

Judith and this woman were the same height and build, though Judith was held together by muscle and this one by nerves.

"You can trust me."

"Good. Now, do you have any questions for me before we start the day?"

"Yes, ma'am. I'll need an apron for today."

Mrs. Tench sat erect, with a disapproving pinch of her lips.

"Dear, it is your job to provide your own work clothes. Just be careful in that pretty dress today and tomorrow wear something more sensible."

Judith paused, to stay placid. On board the bus, she'd been tempted. That would not happen again.

"There'll be some weeks I can't work past two o'clock. I can come early. Or I can come back in the evenings, but never before six."

Mrs. P. entered the parlor with a china coffee service on a silver tray. She leaned the tray forward for Mrs. Tench.

"Desiree, what do you do between two and six?"

Judith told as few lies as she needed. Lies only complicated matters.

"It's a private matter, ma'am."

The thin white woman shook her head, disheartened with Mrs. P.

"Mahalia, you didn't mention this girl had other obligations."

Mrs. P. glowered at Judith while the assistant secretary's wife reached to pour herself a cup. With a scolding face, the old black woman mouthed the word "Uppity!"

"First I heard of it," she answered. "But all the housework be done, I promise, or I won't let that girl walk out the door myse'f."

Focusing on her coffee, Mrs. Tench spoke. "I suppose so long as everything is finished, Desiree, you may leave. But not unless. If you're as industrious as Mahalia says, I foresee no problem."

The thin woman sipped. Attempting a private smile, she said, "I declare, keeping this house in order is going to be the death of me yet."

Judith ignored the irony, keeping herself—in the best tactic of a maid and an assassin—blank.

CHAPTER EIGHT

January 20
Washington, D.C.

THE CLOSEST LAMMECK COULD get was Constitution Avenue. The Capitol police had cordoned off the south lawn, reserving the baseball fields on the Ellipse for five thousand family, friends, and the influential.

Around him on the street, hundreds jostled for a view. Youngsters puffy in warm layers rode high on the shoulders of their dads. Cameras dangled from necks. Street vendor carts hawked coffee, chestnuts, and hot dogs. People pressed in, Dag pushed them back, and Lammeck followed the agent through the crowd, watching.

Lammeck decided this was a small crowd for the inauguration of a president. But there was to be no inaugural ball, no military parade, no entertainments. This was Roosevelt's fourth swearing-in. Maybe the shine had worn off.

Lammeck searched faces, not knowing what he looked for, trusting an alarm to go off inside him, some instinct.

She was here; he was certain.

A thousand yards away, on the South Portico, a red-clad Marine band struck up "Hail to the Chief." On either side of the White House's curved staircase, stately magnolias hefted fat baubles of snow. Below the bunting-draped portico, fifty soldiers in wheelchairs applauded. Out of the well-dressed crowd on the dais, Roosevelt hobbled into place on the arm of a young man.

"That's his kid. Colonel Jimmy," Dag called above the cheers.

Lammeck grabbed Dag's coattail to stop him forging forward. He halted to look across the long lawn at FDR, the first time he'd seen the man in person.

"He looks like hell. Even from this far off."

"He's holding up okay," Dag said. "His legs are failing him, that's all."

Lammeck was aware that FDR had been stricken with polio almost thirty years ago. The ailment and the politican's efforts to rehabilitate were well documented. But Lammeck had no idea the President had become so crippled; Roosevelt took the few steps to the lectern like the rusty Tin Man from *The Wizard of Oz*. Clearly he would collapse if his son took away his supporting arm. More amazingly, nothing ever appeared about the President's health in any newspaper or on radio, not here in the States or in Britain. FDR was waning, you could see it plain as day. But if Lammeck were not standing here himself, he could not realize the degree of FDR's deterioration. This fascinated Lammeck, that America at war deceived itself in order to believe their President was strong enough to lead them. Even seeing the same feeble, staggering man that Lammeck saw, the crowd murmured to itself, "He looks great. The old man's fine."

Reaching the lectern, Roosevelt raised a hand to the throng on the Ellipse and the street beyond. The people answered with a roar, drowning out the Marine band. Son James never left his father's side while the crowd quieted and the oath of office was given by Harlan Stone, Chief Justice of the Supreme Court.

"You know," whispered Dag, "this is the first time he's had his leg braces on in over a year. The Old Man's got gumption, I'll give him that. Those things have got to be killing his legs."

Lammeck did not look away from the oath-taking. "How bad is he, Dag? I need to know."

"I told you, he's good. He's just tired. You try being President."

"This isn't idle curiosity," Lammeck insisted. "I need to know what she knows."

Dag waved away the suggestion, but kept his voice low. "She doesn't know any more than you do, Professor. Only what she can see for herself, and that's not going to be much. The press has had a total blackout on photos of him in a wheelchair for twelve years, so hardly anyone even knows he uses one. Reports of his health are a total taboo and top secret to boot. As far as anyone can tell, he's a guy who had polio when he was young but gets around fine now. He's got an unattractive wife and four kids in the service, like the rest of these Joe Blows out here. He's stiff, that's all. Ask anyone in the crowd, that's what they'll tell you. You're just making it worse than it is because you don't like him."

"Dag."

"What? Leave me alone for a minute. I want to hear the speech."

Lammeck poked him. "Does it dawn on you that we've determined she's working for a government? Remember, the folks with subs? If that's the case, then that same country also has spies, and that means she has access to intelligence. We have to assume she knows everything you do. Maybe more."

Dag blew out a defeated breath. "Okay, in a minute. Let me listen."

"Fine. Stay here."

Lammeck moved out of the crowd to one of the hot dog carts. He bought a coffee and watched FDR from farther off, where the man appeared smaller, but erect and stronger. America had voluntarily moved this distance from Roosevelt to keep faith in him. In return, Lammeck wondered, how did the distance affect the President? Was the Old Man as blinded to his nation as they were to him? FDR repeated the oath today to begin his unprecedented fourth term as President. Was the country growing tired of him, even as he was tired of being President, but with a war on neither of them could quit on the other? Lammeck considered the thousands of threatening letters FDR received every month. Millions of Americans were so displeased with their leader they refused to even say his name, calling him "that man." Roosevelt's economic policies had long smacked of socialism, angering the powerful Wall Street interests of America. His entry into a second European war hurt families still reeling from their losses a generation earlier. His waiting so long to join that war had offended those—including Lammeck—who believed America should have acted sooner to relieve the plight of England, France, the Jews, Poland, Czechoslovakia, even Russia. Roosevelt's multiple terms validated the claims of his critics that he was an imperial president. Even in England, Roosevelt was far less than beloved. There, the veneer that he was Churchill's boon friend and companion was threadbare: The common man on any London, Glasgow, or Dublin street was grateful that America had risen to Britain's aid, but was keenly aware of how this assistance had arrived late and at a high price. America under FDR was no supporter of England's old colonial ways; the future for Britain would little resemble its imperial past, thanks in great part to Roosevelt's vision of a new world order when the war was done, where America and Russia would be the only ones on top of the smoking heap. Americans had the luxury of buying into the ruse of Anglo-American mutual affection, like they swallowed the deception over Roosevelt's wheelchair. But the English were a savvy, jealous bunch. And they were prickly. The first chance they got, they would probably blame Churchill for their long fall from prominence, and the rise of Russia and America in their place.

Lammeck looked across the small gathering. Somewhere in those winter coats and wool hats was an assassin slinking out of the twelfth century. Someone in the world was very weary of Franklin Roosevelt, enough to order him killed. The Germans and the

Japanese, the known enemies, were the first choices, of course. But who else?

"Damn it," Lammeck said aloud. "I know you're here."

The cart vendor shushed him to hear FDR's acceptance speech, broadcast over loudspeakers.

Lammeck warmed his hands on the paper coffee cup and continued to survey the crowd, the security police, every lawn, building, and bush for a half mile in all directions. One thing he was sure of: The Persian woman was not sitting behind a rifle scope right now, waiting for a trough in the wind. No marksman could hit Roosevelt from beyond the White House grounds. And she was certainly not hiding inside the cordon. Dag's Secret Service brothers patrolled every inch.

Besides, Lammeck's gut had told him from the start that this assassin wasn't a shooter. She was a different type, an older mold of assassin, perhaps the oldest. She hadn't gunned down Otto and Bonny on the beach. Instead, she had knifed them, then pulled off some magic trick to put a bullet through Arnold's brain and make his death look like suicide. Guns were for the beginner, the untrained malcontent. She was no Zangara, Booth, or Lawrence; no Leon Czolgosz, the anarchist in Buffalo who'd hid a pistol inside his bandaged hand, then shot McKinley point-blank while the President was shaking hands. Or Charles Guiteau, the deranged office-seeker who fatally plugged Garfield in the D.C. train station.

She'd have nothing in common with those petty killers.

Except one thing.

She would do her work in close.

She was an Assassin of the Alamut, trained in silent killing. She would come privately, in disguise or shadow, emerging and receding like the weapon she preferred: the blade. Slide in, out; wipe the blood; disappear.

The President finished his speech. It was a short performance, five minutes' worth, underscoring how poorly the man must be feeling. FDR limped away on the arm of his son while the crowd cheered him off the stage.

Dag found Lammeck and came beside him. Lammeck bought him a coffee.

The two watched the crowd disperse. Would she walk away or linger?

"Dag, what kind of people get in to see Roosevelt?"

The agent lifted his coffee cup and extended a finger, pointing at the milling crowd on the Ellipse and the White House grounds.

"Them. His wife and family, their guests. World leaders and ambassadors. Senators. Congressmen. Cabinet members. White House staff."

"Secret Service agents."

Dag nodded. "Yep. Marine guards. White House police. The press corps. Some soldiers and heroes."

"How about when he's out of the White House?"

"He really only goes a few places anymore. His office next door to the White House in the executive building. He motors to that. Some weekends he goes by train up to Hyde Park. Once in a while, he heads south, down to the Little White House in Warm Springs, Georgia, where his polio clinic is. Whenever he's in New York or Georgia, the only folks who see him are staff, guests, and local people he's known forever. And you can bet we've got agents around him thick as thieves the whole time."

"What about business travel?"

"Not as often as he used to. Like I said, his legs are letting him down. Once in a blue moon, he'll leave the White House for an event here in the District. The last time was two weeks ago, to a Correspondents' dinner at the Statler Hotel. We had a full security detail, private elevator, the works. Untouchable. And then there's the big trips, cross-country or international. Again, the advance work is incredible. Reports of his itinerary are blacked out in the press. No one knows where he's going or where he's been until he gets back. You'd have to be deep on the inside to get a handle on Roosevelt's schedule. And if you were on the inside, you'd have passed a pretty hefty background check first. I don't think our little Persian gal with a knife between her teeth is going to make the cut, pardon the pun."

Lammeck gazed at the vendor's cart. Charcoal embers cooked a grill loaded with hot dogs, chestnuts, and pretzels.

"You said the Statler event was a dinner?"

"Yeah. You should see reporters eat when it's free. Locusts."

"Where was the food prepared? On-site?"

Dag sipped more coffee.

"Yep. We got that covered, too. Every waiter and cook who serves the President goes through a security check before he's allowed to work the event. Last year, just after I joined the Service, we did a check on one hotel before a banquet and found thirteen Italians, eleven Germans, and one fugitive American murderer on the dining room staff. We deep-sixed the whole event. We even look into the guests at every hotel the Boss visits. One time this guy at the Drake in Chicago was registered with his wife. The couple was from Decatur. We checked back in Decatur and found his wife at home. Uh-oh."

Lammeck asked, "How about the food?"

"At the White House and on the road, every bite the President eats gets analyzed by lab technicians first. He likes game and fish, and the stuff gets sent to him from pals and leaders all over the goddam world. We toss most of it and just don't tell him."

"Ever catch any poison?"

"Just once. Someone slipped strychnine into a batch of marlin shipped up from Cuba. The guy who sent the fish was above suspicion, so it was obvious someone in the mail chain did it. Never caught 'em."

Lammeck watched the last of the inauguration assembly disperse. Every woman walking alone, he imagined, was her.

With a steamy breath, Dag shook his head. "So no dice, Professor. I know what you're thinking and she ain't getting to him inside the White House. Not unless she runs for office, gets a presidential appointment or a job at a newspaper, joins the military or the Secret Service, or dates one of FDR's married sons. Or she's really the Queen of fucking Sheba."

For the past six days, Lammeck had walked the perimeter around the White House, looking across the open lawns. Every footstep, he probed for the way in, knowing she was doing the same. What kind of cover story was available to her, to get close? A job? What work could she do that didn't require a serious background investigation by the Secret Service or FBI? Clerical work, certainly; the war administration was brimming with girls who typed and filed, but she had no shot in any of the sensitive agencies and no hope of a high position. Cooking, cleaning? Again, even those jobs around Roosevelt required an intense background scrutiny, both inside the White House and at any location the President visited. Not even the most convincing fake identification papers could get her a real mom and a dad and a high school diploma and a tenth-grade teacher to testify what a good kid she'd been.

Dag's right. She won't get inside with a government job. She'll have figured that one out by now.

Sex?

What if Dag's joking reference was right? Could she be busy seducing someone high up, someone who might unwittingly introduce her to the President? That might be motive enough to take a menial task in some government sweatshop.

Lammeck told Dag this.

Dag said, "If that's what you want to check out, I'll talk to Mrs. Beach about getting us all the government hiring records in D.C. for the past two and a half weeks."

"I know you'll enjoy that."

Dag spit in the sooty snow piled beside the sidewalk.

"And she'll tell me that the two of us will be the ones to check out every one of those girls. So clear your schedule, Professor."

"I get your point."

Lammeck took Dag's coffee cup back to the cart for a refill. The vendor stopped shuttering his kiosk to pour the last of his coffee before wheeling away. There'd be little business on a Saturday afternoon now that the ceremony was over.

Dag accepted the refill. The two of them stood bouncing on their toes in the emptying street. The D.C. police began to dismantle traffic barriers and yellow sawhorses.

"That was a shitty inauguration," Dag observed. "Depressing."

Lammeck asked, "If you had to pick someone to sleep with to get to Roosevelt, who would it be?"

"Some guy in good shape. A good listener. And no smokers, I hate that."

Lammeck nodded understandingly. Dag punched his shoulder, spilling coffee. "Hey, I was kidding."

"No, I agree. Smoking is a filthy habit."

"Screw you. Listen, Professor, you got any idea what you're asking? If I go to Mrs. Beach and ask her to clear it with Reilly for that kind of info, who's banging who, what high-up has got himself a new girlfriend, it'll be the first time in sixty years that old bat has laughed. This is D.C., the center of the free world. Power's like money in this town, and these guys spend it on a lot of things. Women is one of them. They'd rather see Roosevelt dead in the street than have us check if Senator Bullshit is getting laid outside his home, you know what I'm saying? And even if we do get some leads, again..."

"I know. It'll be just you and me running them down. Dag, do you like baseball?"

"Yeah. What's that got to do with anything?"

"Because it's becoming clear to me we're not going to hold her to a single. We might not catch up to her until she's already rounded third."

"A play at the plate?"

"If we're lucky. We'll need a break if we're going to change the odds."

"We'll get one."

"Why so sure?"

"We got time. In two days the President's on his way out of the country to a big meeting. That's where Reilly's off to. They're not back for a month. So the Persian broad can't do a thing to the Boss because he won't be here."

Lammeck wondered if the assassin knew this.

"Where're they going?"

Dag shook his head. "Can't tell you."

Lammeck began to object.

"Hold it right there," Dag cut in. "I know that bit about how you need to know everything she does. But some of this stuff is classified and I flat-out can't tell you. If she knows and you don't, then good for her. But she didn't hear it from me. Okay?"

Lammeck tossed his coffee in the trash bin. This was rotten news, that Dag kept information from him. He was sure the assassin's sources didn't hold anything back from her. So he was at another disadvantage, as if there weren't enough shackles on him already.

Roosevelt was leaving town. That meant she had a whole month to do nothing but embed herself even more deeply into the city. To get into position while the two of them flailed at nothing but her shadow.

He surveyed the White House, the bare winter streets, the warren of buildings on all sides. He turned away.

"Where are you?" Lammeck asked into the cold air.

· · ·

"THERE YOU ARE," JUDITH murmured under her watch cap.

The two were just like they'd been described. The old woman in Newburyport was doing a much better job now with her intelligence. Judith had given her good reason to improve.

The two men stood beside a vending cart, sipping coffee with the crowd falling away. They seemed to be having a squabble. Both were speaking with their hands, waving their coffee cups to make points. The smaller of the two kept his eyes on the White House in the distance. The bigger one kept scanning the dispersing crowd. He looked only once at Judith. His eyes skipped off her quickly, and why wouldn't they? He was looking for a woman. She had wrapped down her breasts, pulled the wool cap low over her hair and ears, and walked to the inauguration garbed in laborer's boots and overalls beneath a bulky overcoat. She wore glasses, drank coffee, smoked cigarettes, and stood in the street with the colored workers who'd come because they idolized Roosevelt.

Again Judith glanced at the pair standing next to the hot-dog cart. The smaller one was the tip-off. He fit the description exactly that the woman from Newburyport had forwarded. A disheveled-looking man, battered fedora on his head, raincoat wrinkled like a dried fig. Six foot, lean and pale. He had a mistrustful face. This was the Secret Service agent who'd made a week's worth of inquiries in the little fishing town. Went to the beach every day to stare. Ate in the same restaurants, took notes, talked to no one but the police. Tried to be discreet and was noticed because of it.

But it was the larger man who caught her eye. He was good-looking behind his trim brown beard. He carried a large frame, a worthy chest and belly. He looked a bit of a fop, but she guessed at an agile mind from his owl-quick glances, and a harder body than his girth suggested. According to the old woman's report, he'd appeared nine days ago in Newburyport and stayed only one day before leaving with the other one. So the larger man was the expert.

With the President's speech finished, Judith drifted with the crowd, to watch the pair from a distance. The two stayed side by side even after the vendor packed up and departed. They continued talking and gesturing, oblivious, as if no one were looking for them.

Finally they split up. Judith could follow only one. She chose the big man.

This period was the most distressing in the whole of my experience as White House physician. The President did not seem able to rid himself of a sense of terrible urgency.

—LT. COMMANDER HOWARD BRUENN
FDR's doctor

FEBRUARY

CHAPTER NINE

February 10
Aurora Heights
Arlington, Virginia

MRS. TENCH LEANED OVER Judith's shoulder.

"You have such lovely handwriting, dear."

"Thank you."

"Where did you learn that? In school?"

"In New Orleans, yes, ma'am."

"Shall I tell you who all these names are?"

Judith set down her pen while the woman pointed out the place cards Judith had been inscribing.

"This is my Mr. Tench's boss, the Secretary of the Navy. He'll be without his wife. This is a general who's quite high up at the Pentagon. I don't know what he does but it's extremely hush-hush. And his wife. This man is an absolute drunken bore but he does something with the budget so everyone in Washington has to be tolerant of him. That's his wife, poor thing. And," she added prettily, "me. And Mr. Tench."

Judith sat at the table where the evening's dinner would be served in two hours. From the kitchen, behind the swinging door, Mrs. P.'s preparations sent aromas through the brick house. Judith tried to stay out of the kitchen; every time she entered, Mrs. P. came up with a chore or a barb. The old woman had been in a bothered state all afternoon.

"Don't you look nice," Mrs. Tench said. She tugged a lace frill at Judith's shoulder to make it lie more evenly on the powder blue uniform.

"Now, remember, always serve food from the left and drinks from the right. Keep an eye on the water and the coffee, let the men at the table pour the wine and liquor. Never take a dish away until someone nods for you to do it. Say 'May I,' not 'Can I.' And please don't try to carry so many dishes at once, dear. You have very strong hands, but it's just not ladylike. This is a private home, not a hash house."

"Yes, ma'am."

"Now, set out each of the place cards where I showed you. Then go help Mrs. P. in the kitchen. I'm going to lie down for a while before my husband gets home. Alright?"

The woman swept out of the dining room. Judith completed the task at the table, then pushed on the kitchen door.

Mrs. P. stirred a great pot of soup, steam swirling around her. She looked up only briefly when Judith entered.

"Peel me some garlic," the old cook told her.

Judith found the cloves and a paring knife. She checked the knife's sharpness. Unsatisfied, she took a whetstone from a drawer. Sitting, she drew the blade's edge over the surface with slow satisfaction.

"Where my garlic?"

Judith ignored her.

"Girl? I asked you for somethin.' "

Judith stood, taking the knife with her, absentminded that it was in her hand.

"Why are you so upset with me?" she asked the old woman.

Mrs. P. kept her angry eyes on the bubbling pot.

"I didn't bring you into this house so's you could keep gettin' in trouble. No, ma'am, I did not."

Now Judith became aware of the knife in her grip.

"What trouble am I in?" she replied evenly.

The cook pulled the wooden spoon out of the soup. She tapped it on the rim, then shook it in Judith's eyes.

"Look at you. I know what you doin'. Got that top button on your blouse all undone. I know you done took a inch off the hem o' that skirt. You walkin' around this house like you got the hots for someone, Missy, and I know who it is."

Judith stayed still, the best way to draw the other out.

"Don't you gimme no sassy look neither. You ain't no Miss Innocent, we *know* that. You stay away from the mister. This household got its share o' trouble without you addin' to it. An' you know what I'm talkin' about. I swear, girl, you got more nerve than a bad tooth. Now you abide me and shave me some garlic. And you button up that blouse."

The soup spoon stayed between them until Judith turned away.

She walked back to the table to set down the knife. She did not want it in her hand.

She pivoted to Mrs. P., who had her back turned and the spoon working the broth.

I fucked him already, she almost said.

Instead, she clamped her mouth and buttoned her blouse.

An hour before the dinner party, the mister still had not come home. The house throbbed to ticking clocks; unlit candles on the table and the mantel, plus the smells from Mrs. P.'s cooking, lent the downstairs an air of anticipation. Judith had shined every silver service piece and set them now on the table according to Mrs. Tench's diagram. She made amends with Mrs. P. by sampling her soup and breads, flattering them, asking to be taught their various secrets. Judith walked around the large dining room, straightening flatware and crystal, stopping when she heard a cry.

She waited, to see if Mrs. P. might come out of the kitchen. The swinging door stayed closed. Again, a wail wafted from deep in the big house. Judith moved from the dining room into the den, padding quietly on the Oriental carpet. Something heavy thumped on the floor; Judith heard it and felt it in her soles. She moved along a hallway, lit by sconces, walls tiled by framed photos of the Tench couple in happy times.

At the library door, she paused and listened to Mrs. Tench bawl again. Judith stood through a caterwaul of anguish behind the closed door, focusing not on the despondent woman but down the hallway, in case Mrs. P. should come and see Judith here, eaves-dropping.

After a minute, Mrs. Tench reduced herself to sniffling and a miserable mutter. Judith gave her another moment, then turned the doorknob and strode in. She made a point of not seeing the woman curled on the leather couch. From its perch on a short pillar, in an alcove between high, crowded bookshelves, a marble bust had fallen to the floor.

"Mrs. Tench, are you in—? Oh, pardon me." Judith paused, in a show of concern. "Ma'am, are you alright?"

Hastily, the older woman sat up on the sofa, smearing a palm across both cheeks.

"Yes. Please go back to your chores. I'll be out shortly."

The woman sniffled again, making a poor attempt at composure. Judith did not leave the room. Instead, she walked to where the bust had tumbled from its column.

"That's heavy," Mrs. Tench said. "I knocked it over by accident. I'll have Mr. Tench put it back."

Judith returned the figure to its place. It was heavy, but she lifted it with ease. "No need for the mister to see this."

"Thank you, Desiree."

Judith turned the bust's face carefully to the exact position it had been in. She smoothed her servant's apron.

"Your daddy was a handsome man."

A plaque on the stone identified the figure as Senator Rutherfurd B. Potts, Indiana. It also gave the dates of his tenure in government. Mrs. Tench shared her father's jawline, and little else.

The senator was marble and imperial; she was a red-faced wreck, pampered and delicate.

"Yes. My papa was. He was quite a great man."

Judith stepped into the library's bathroom and returned with a glass of water for Mrs. Tench. She closed the library door to keep Mrs. P. from stumbling on the two of them, then stood beside the sofa.

"What's wrong?"

At her question, Mrs. Tench looked into space, perhaps seeing her troubles there. She must have counted them and found them few because she suddenly brightened. She finished the offered water in a few gulps as if it were an antidote, then she wiped her mouth with a lace-trimmed kerchief, and rose from the sofa. She drew a full breath and tugged down her skirt. Judith looked at the woman's narrow hips and veined neck, whittled too thin.

"Honestly," she said, oddly refreshed, "I don't know what comes over me sometimes. I'm fine." The woman patted Judith's arm. "Thank you, Desiree. You have a wonderful calming way about you. Your people back in New Orleans must be very kind."

Judith merely nodded, pretending some grief of her own to keep Mrs. Tench from asking further, requiring more lies. For a moment she reflected how much better the fictitious family in New Orleans was than her real one in Persia.

"Well," Mrs. Tench rubbed her palms, "that's that. Needless to say, this little episode stays just between us girls. As you said, there's no need for Mr. Tench or our Mrs. P. to hear of it. I just had myself a little cry, as we girls do once in a while. I'll make sure there's a little something extra in your pay envelope this week, alright?"

Mrs. Tench extended her hand toward the door, inviting Judith to leave the library first. The thin woman followed and went upstairs, Judith back to the kitchen.

Mrs. P. had the oven door down. She poked at twin roasting geese and spooned juices over them.

"See what I mean? This house got trouble enough already. Now you know."

Judith breathed in the aromas and almost didn't ask, the smells were so transporting. Nothing had just happened that did not play into her hands.

"Know what, Mrs. P.?"

"Why that woman can't keep no he'p."

"Why is that?"

The old cook closed the door on the browning fowl. She shook her head and wiped her hands on her apron.

"Woman's crazy, that's why."

BY TEN O'CLOCK, MRS. P. had cleaned the last of the plates and pots. The dinner guests had retired to the sitting room for coffee and brandies. The men lit tobacco while the women set up a card table for a game of three-handed bridge. Judith stayed within earshot to mind their coffee cups and absorb gossip.

Mrs. P. needed to leave, to catch the last bus across the Potomac. Mrs. Tench had asked Judith to stay behind. They would call her a taxi when the evening was done, she said. At the back door, Judith helped Mrs. P. into her winter coat. The old woman narrowed her eyes disapprovingly, then bussed Judith on the cheek.

"Girl, we all got to do what we got to do. Jus' be careful. That's a snake pit in there. They ain't yo' people." The old maid took firm hold of Judith's shoulders and held her at arm's length. "But I knows you up to somethin'."

Judith leaned close. She lowered her voice, conspiratorial. "You're amazing, Mrs. P."

The old cook shrugged, pleased, and buttoned up her coat.

"Laws, don't you go and tell me neither. I don' want to know nothin'." Mrs. P. wrapped her red scarf around her neck, mumbling mournfully to herself, "I swear, I saved you from doin's with drug dealers jus' to get you all mixed up with white folk. Lawd have mercy. Your mama gon' skin me she find out."

Before opening the door, Mrs. P. touched Judith's cheek.

"You a good girl, Desiree. But you a sneak."

Judith smiled at the reproof. "And you're a wonderful old woman. But you're nosy."

The cook nodded, agreeing.

Judith closed the door behind the old woman. The service bell rang. Arriving in the sitting room, Judith was informed that the general desired another slice of Mrs. P.'s rhubarb pie.

For another two hours, Judith hovered in and out of the sitting room. The budget official proved himself the inebriate and boor Mrs. Tench had labeled him. The general was an up-and-comer, with little battle experience but a great administrative background. He expected to move up fast in the peacetime military. Naval secretary Forrestal spoke often and admiringly of Roosevelt, thinking him a great leader and gracious in person. Forrestal had witnessed the American landings in Normandy, had visited the Pacific theater twice. He was very suspicious of Stalin and communism. The Soviets would be the next great threat to world freedom, he declared to everyone's agreement. Mr. Tench played host, pouring and cajoling, conscious of making himself popular. None of the women talked of anything beyond their homes, children, husbands, and clothing. Mrs. Tench's voice was the giddiest of the ladies.

At midnight, the guests left together. Judith wore white cotton gloves as she fetched the women's coats and handed them to their husbands. Once the wives were cloaked, she helped each man into his overcoat. In the moments while she loaded Forrestal into his, Judith evaluated him, judging weight and height, the thickness of the skin on his wrists and on the back of his neck, where she touched him without his notice.

Mr. and Mrs. Tench said their good-byes. Judith faded to the kitchen for her own coat. When she returned, Mrs. Tench had already gone upstairs to bed. Mr. Tench wore his winter jacket.

"It's late," he told her. "I'll drive you home."

.   .   .

Washington, D.C.

JUDITH CLICKED ON A small electric light beside her bed. At her back, he said, "It's very clean here."

"Thank you."

"Small, though. I can put you in a nicer place."

She held her hands out for his coat. He turned to let her slide it from his shoulders. "I don't want a nicer place," she said, standing behind him. "I don't want any of your money that I don't earn."

He turned with a smile at the statement, at the double meaning it took in his head.

She frowned. "I don't mean it like that."

The time was after midnight. Jacob Tench and Judith put on no pretense about why he was here in her room. She took him out of his clothes, arranging them neatly on a chair to show she shared in the subterfuge; he could not return home in wrinkled clothes. He succumbed to her hands but remained her master. She played the servant again, in a different fashion from her maid's blue uniform and white apron, but another discipline she'd been taught long ago. Jacob Tench lay naked on his back across her narrow bed. Judith sealed his lips with a finger to save talk for afterward.

She massaged him, kneading the folds of his privileged life. His torso was soft; in it she felt desks and automobiles, social dinners like tonight's. His forearms and shoulders had for too many years labored only in politics. Judith did not undress to sit across his hips; she kicked off only her shoes. He reached up for her uniform a few times to tug it, but she stayed clothed awhile longer. She preferred to keep her power hidden until the time she chose, for her purposes.

When she did undress, she stood beside the bed in the slim glow of the one lamp. At first she did not allow his touch, once more pretending shyness. Their first sex had been a rushed encounter four days ago in his Georgetown house, in his office there. She'd stood beside his desk, still in her uniform and apron, and he took her from behind while his wife napped upstairs. He'd dropped her underpants and rubbed the brown orbs of her bottom like great gems, that was all she'd allowed him to see of her. Now he lay in her room catching his breath at the stages of her nakedness.

In the same way she'd treated his clothes, she folded hers in an attempt to appear self-conscious. She lapped one arm across her breasts and laid the other over her belly. She stepped to the side of the mattress where Tench rose to an elbow. She let his fingers play over her stomach. She dropped her arms and stood for his review.

"My God," he whispered.

Judith did not lie on the bed, but spread her legs for him. Her own aroma reached her nostrils off his hand. She stared down and waited, letting him feel the promises of her.

"I can't stand this," he moaned.

"Good."

"What do you want, Desiree? Everybody wants something."

She left the question unanswered. Instead, she straddled him, matched him, and nestled down. She fixed his eyes and held them, keeping her heels on the floor, her breasts at his face as she rocked. His hands gripped her buttocks and thighs and shoved her to the rhythm he wanted. He did not last long. Judith muffled his mouth with her hand, not because she cared if a neighbor might hear but because she did not want to. Never once did she kiss him.

She lay beside him while he stared at her ceiling and slowed his breathing. He uttered how incredible that had been and said nothing of affection. She didn't expect him to. Her role as Desiree was to please him; his was to accept it and pay her in pittances.

She rolled to lay her head on his chest. She listened to his heart, so close to the surface, easy to reach.

"I think your wife might know about us."

Tench drew a sharp breath.

"Why do you say that?"

"She cried today in the library, something awful."

He snorted, joggling her head on his chest.

"My wife is what they call a manic-depressive. She cries every afternoon. She's like the rains in the fucking Amazon forest. You could grow ferns around my wife's feet with how much she cries. Don't worry. She doesn't know about us. If she did, there'd be hell on earth, I guarantee you."

"Is she that unhappy?"

"Unhappy's got nothing to do with it. She just swings back and forth so far I can't keep up half the time."

Judith endured his sigh, a man with a troubling wife, in the bed of his maid.

"Let's talk about something else," he said.

"Tell me about your boss. Mr. Forrestal."

"What's to tell? Man works like a dog. Amazed I got him out for dinner tonight. He made a fortune on Wall Street in the twenties, managed to hang on to most of it during the crash. He had my job until Secretary Knox died and he got promoted, then I took his spot. All in all, I'd say he's a cold fish, but he's on the way up. He and I get along because we both have nutso wives. His was a Ziegfeld chorus girl."

Judith smoothed a palm across Tench's abdomen. "So, if he died, you'd get his job?"

Tench laughed. "Forrestal's not dying anytime soon. He's got too much work on his desk."

Judith sat up and crossed her legs.

"But let's play a game. If he died tomorrow, who would be the new Secretary of the Navy? You?"

"We're in the middle of a war. Who else would they get? Yeah, me, I guess."

"Then you'd meet with the President?"

"I already do."

"But every day, you'd meet Roosevelt?"

"Sure."

"Would the President come to Forrestal's funeral?"

Tench scooted back against the wall, fluffing a pillow for his back.

"What an odd question. Is that some kind of New Orleans voodoo thing, who comes to whose funeral?"

"It's just a game, Jacob. I'm just imagining."

He stroked her thigh. "Alright, don't get upset on me. Yes, if his health was good that day, Roosevelt would most likely go to Forrestal's funeral."

Judith smiled at Tench. She could make him naval secretary, could have done it tonight in his own home. Six drops of cyanide blended with dimethyl sulfoxide to open the skin pores, mixed with lanolin as an emulsifier. She would have worn condoms under the fingers of the cotton gloves. The lemon oil on them from her polishing and the lanolin would have hidden the poison's telltale almond scent. She could have rubbed the cream on Forrestal's neck while she pulled his coat up over his shoulders; she practiced tonight and he'd felt nothing. Ten minutes later, after he'd driven away, the secretary would have become short of breath, then dizzy and nauseated until he fainted. His thin body would convulse. He might have wrecked the car and killed himself that way, but that was wishful thinking. In any event, he'd be dead a half hour after leaving the Tench house. It would look like a heart attack. And if somehow the poison were discovered in an investigation, it would not be in his stomach. The source would be indeterminate, but the motive would lie with the ambitious assistant secretary, or his unstable social-climber wife, in whose house he'd spent the evening. By the time any eyes were turned on Judith, she would be long gone, hopefully with her task accomplished.

Judith smiled at a private irony. During dinner, Forrestal had made it clear how much he loathed Stalin. But it was Stalin now keeping him alive. At that very moment, Roosevelt was with the Soviet leader, along with Churchill, in the Crimea. The President could not attend an important state funeral if he was out of the country.

Tench eyed her. "Why're you grinning like the Cheshire cat?"

Judith cleared her thoughts. She returned her attention to her bed, her body, and the soft man lying with her.

"Just thinking of you as Secretary of the Navy. You'd be wonderful."

"I would, thank you."

He rolled his feet off the bed.

"I've got to go. I can convince her I stopped off for a beer, but not if I stay away much longer."

"I understand."

Tench stood, droopy and white, so unlike her own russet body. He dressed while she lay languorous on the bed, exposed, to keep him interested and to keep her control of him.

"You know," he said with a chuckle, stepping into his trousers, "you talk about whose funeral would get Roosevelt out of the White House? I'll tell you the truth—if my wife died, the whole goddam city would attend. Her father ran the Senate for thirty years. Roosevelt would be there."

Judith tilted her head. She waited for him to button his starched shirt, then stood. She wrapped him in her arms, to lay her skin and scent against his expensive suit. He would have to hide these clothes from his wife.

"You know how you asked me what I want?"

Tench squirmed inside her grasp. He seemed to consider taking his clothes off again. He cleared his throat.

"You come up with something?"

"I know you're married. I'm not asking for anything like that."

He nodded, relieved. "That's good." He kissed her. She licked around his lips, as if to clean away icing.

"What?" he whispered.

"I want to meet President Roosevelt."

Tench stood slack-jawed and greedy while Judith worked her tongue and hips on him. He took a deep breath, sinking into her again. She loosened her arms around him so he could leave. She stepped away. He looked as if he might fall forward to her.

"I want to shake the President's hand," she told him. "Just once."

CHAPTER TEN

February 16
Washington, D.C.

THE WAR WAS GOING well for America.

In Lammeck's hands, the front page of the *Washington Post* trumpeted the first bombing raids over Tokyo. A naval task force was tightening the noose around the Japanese stronghold on Iwo Jima island. In Europe, every bit of ground the Germans took in their Christmas bum's rush, now called the Battle of the Bulge, had been rolled back and bloodily reclaimed by Allied infantry. Patton had launched an all-out assault on the Rhine. Yank bombers had burned the German city of Dresden to cinders.

And the first words were leaking out of a secret meeting between the Big Three—Stalin, Churchill, and Roosevelt—from the Crimea, at Yalta.

The *Post* said, "The President is to be congratulated on his part in this all-encompassing achievement." On pages one through six, FDR's supporters crowed over his diplomacy, the supreme achievement of drawing all three Allied leaders to the table, where they could discuss and concede. The paper listed major victories for the

U.S. at the conference: The Soviet Union promised to begin attacks against the Japanese as soon as Germany fell; Stalin backed off his demand for sixteen votes in the newly created United Nations, accepting instead only three; Russia accepted a French zone of occupation in defeated Germany, plus France's permanent status on the UN's Security Council; Stalin would allow "free" elections in Poland, while postponing the settlement of that war-torn nation's western border until the war was over. Excerpts from other news organs around the world chimed in, overwhelmingly praising the triumph and accords of Yalta.

Not until page seven did FDR's critics vent their spleen. They bayed that the President had been hoodwinked at Yalta. He never seemed to grasp that he was the rich uncle caught between two squabbling, poorer relations. Roosevelt did not so much bargain with Stalin as try to persuade the stubby dictator to accept less than the Russian hungered for. Yalta did not change Stalin's insistence on the old Curzon line from 1919 as the official boundary between him and Poland, despite America's and the Polish government-in-exile's demands. Russia managed to hold on to multiple votes in the fledgling UN. And Britain, our bravest ally, who'd fought Germany alone for three years, received at Yalta little for her part in the war but more dismantling of her teetering Empire, and a ringside seat to watch the American President sweet-talk the Russian dictator to preserve the USSR's participation in Roosevelt's legacy, the United Nations. Yalta, the critics derided, was nothing more than the cobbling together of an agreement between three ideologically opposed nations, who'd banded together out of exhaustion and a short-lived euphoria, and only for so long as the war lasted. Once Germany and Japan were beaten, politics and power plays would surely undo these vows of freedom and mutuality. In short, FDR had traded hard concessions to Stalin for the gossamer of promises, and Churchill, the lion of England, was forced to sit quietly chewing his cigars while his old American ally did so.

But for now, these dissenting notes were shoved to the back by admiring headlines. Roosevelt was the golden child. No mention of his health at the meeting surfaced in the newspaper pages. The old man was pictured smiling in his navy cape, his long cigarette holder tilted jauntily. He was reported somewhere at sea, resting well, steaming for home.

Lammeck set down the paper. He walked to the window of his hotel room, gazing through the slanting afternoon sunlight to the north façade of the White House, a half mile off. That pale palace had been Roosevelt's home for almost thirteen years now. It would soon welcome him as a returning hero from faraway lands. The President was on top right now, perhaps more than he'd ever been.

That, Lammeck thought, is when they come for you. When you're at your strongest, a threat. Your enemies have always hated you. But now your friends fear you, too.

He thought of Caesar, at the peak of his power, stabbed by his senators in his own white palace, the Roman Senate. In 1935, Dutch Schultz, one of the most powerful gangland figures in America, had been murdered in Newark, New Jersey, by his associates in the New York crime syndicate to keep him from pursuing his plot to assassinate prosecutor Thomas Dewey. In 797, the popular Byzantine emperor Constantine had his eyes gouged out and was cast into a cell by his mother in a lethal struggle for the throne. Every one of them was at the top of his game, when he was cut down by betrayal, by trusted allies, by loved ones.

Lammeck turned to a knock on his door. He opened it, then backed away as Dag surged into the room. The Secret Service agent staggered under the weight of three boxes stuffed with files and manila envelopes. The top carton obscured his head.

"Put them on the bed."

Dag dumped his burden on the mattress. Lammeck dove forward to keep them from spilling. Empty-armed and red-faced, Dag glared at Lammeck as if assigning blame.

"What?" Lammeck spread his arms.

"Down at the front desk." Dag jerked a thumb over his shoulder. "Two more boxes. You go get 'em."

Lammeck headed down two flights to the lobby. The boxes were waiting, jammed and heavy. He returned to his room huffing, understanding Dag's irritation.

Dag was slumped in the overstuffed chair. His scuffed shoes rested on Lammeck's bed.

"It's all there. From January 3 to yesterday."

Lammeck set his load beside the desk. "I see we have to watch what we wish for. Good old Mrs. Beach might get it for us."

"That's every new federal hire of a woman in the whole stinking city. We got job histories, school transcripts, security clearances, background checks, typing tests—you fucking name it, your United States government has a record of it. If she's working for Uncle Sam, she's in one of those boxes."

Lammeck grabbed a random folder. He opened it to a swamp of typefaces, illegible handwriting, rubber stamping, and black-and-white photos. Somewhere on these pages, he thought, was that good, clean fact that would let him start his "NO" stack; or there might be some small and fishy item that didn't add up and he would set it on what he hoped would be a very short "MAYBE" pile. The determination might bob to the surface in seconds, or it might dodge him.

"How many are there?"

"About a thousand."

Lammeck's heart sank. His eyes felt glazed already. They stuck on the photo of a gap-toothed gal from Kentucky. She was skinny and timid, dipping her face as if terrified of the flashbulb that had gone off to freeze her image. She had light brown hair but it could have been dyed, no way to know. Lammeck dragged his finger down the first page. Fresh out of a two-year secretarial college. Single, one brother overseas in the Marines. How could this shy American girl be a foreign assassin who'd carved up two people on a beach and stage-managed the murder of a third? Lammeck wanted to toss this file out. His gut knew immediately this girl wasn't the one. But the very notion of the murderer they were trying to track down was so implausible, how could he rule out any of these women? He had to read this file, and these thousand files, and he'd better get started.

Lammeck pivoted his chair to face the desk. Spreading the folder in front of him, he flicked on the lamp. Lifting the girl's picture, he imagined her out there right now bundled in the chilly Washington dusk, fresh from Kentucky or Persia—which was it?

Dag rose from his chair.

"Whoa," Lammeck put out a hand, "where're you going?"

"Out to the car. I got Chinese take-out. And a bottle."

BY MIDNIGHT, LAMMECK HAD a "NO" pile of over two hundred files. Before he fell asleep, Dag had thumbed through half that many. They'd both tossed only one folder each onto a "YES" stack.

Dag lay snoring across Lammeck's bed, tuckered out by reading and the bourbon. He'd rolled over, cocooning in the blankets and sheets. Dag disheveled things even in his sleep.

Over the past several hours, Lammeck had developed a system in his paper chase through the folders. As soon as he noted that the job application required a background check, he discarded that file. There was no choice but to trust the FBI and each government department to handle this low level of security. Certainly, they could spot a girl whose entire background was a fabrication. Also, instinct told him his assassin would never put herself in a spot where she would show up on the government's radar. She would seek an unobtrusive hiding place. Her first job in America was to blend in.

But security checks only deleted 20 percent of the applications. The rest were for garden-variety typist and clerical positions. These had no hiring procedures other than an application, an interview, and a skills test. Lammeck's training as an historian stepped in.

After years of research, he'd learned to look for similarities in the eras and personalities he studied, and to use these trends to uncover the anomalies. In these personnel files, he swiftly figured out the prevailing theme of the thousands of women flooding into wartime Washington.

Essentially, with few exceptions, there was only one woman in these folders. She had high school and some college, rarely a degree. She had one or more siblings, and her brothers were most often in the military. It seemed the Only Child did not leave home to come to the nation's capital to seek her future. She was not Rosie the Riveter; instead of manual labor skills, she could type. She was more likely to be from a farming state in the South or Midwest than from New England or the far West. Apparently, she took typing classes as her way out of the small town or the farm. She was trim, even pretty. She probably viewed Washington as the last Mecca for romance in a nation where all the other men were gone to Europe or Asia. She came alone. She came to serve her country but not in uniform, so she was not the most intrepid of women. Still, she was an achiever, bright, and convinced she was bound for good things.

Lammeck read school transcripts and teachers' recommendations, work histories, descriptions of school sports teams and extracurricular activities, family backgrounds, health status and allergies, driver's license numbers and other identification papers. In his view, none of these mundanities served to disqualify an application enough to toss the file aside. Each of these items was easy to falsify, and besides, none of them would be back-checked. He scanned for the extra ingredient, that one scrap that told him this girl was authentic and no threat to anything but some boy's heart. He read the brief essays, typed and timed, about the girl's dreams and hopes, her hometown and kin. He looked for clumsiness and misspellings in the answers to simple questions, a hominess that spoke of an American girl on her own in a new, big town. He looked for nerves, discomfort, quirks, the little discrepancies about every person that do not add up, and so make up a complex and real whole. An assassin would not write these things. She would not make errors. She would be letter-perfect in her fraud.

The pair of files flagged by Dag and Lammeck had two items in common. First, they were both girls without families. One hailed from an Ohio orphanage; the other claimed her whole family had perished in an Oklahoma tornado. Second, both young women looked on paper too good to be true. Dag and Lammeck decided these needed another sniff. Dag wanted to find them both and, if they were not killers, ask them out on dates.

Dag griped for five hours, until he asked Lammeck for fifteen minutes of shut-eye. That was two hours ago.

Lammeck forged on. He peeled through the files with an increasing efficiency and sharpening instinct. Now it was midnight. With almost half the files rejected, he sensed that she was not in these boxes. She'd slipped him again.

Even so, he was only a step behind her. Lammeck felt it, stronger every day. He needed to get a handle on what that step would be, the stride that would finally bring him even with her. She would follow the path of least resistance to the President. Lammeck racked his brain to find that path.

He set the files aside and picked up a book he'd bought that afternoon at Garfinkel's department store across from the Treasury Department, *The Travels of Marco Polo*.

To the sawing of Dag's snores, Lammeck read again the passages about Hasan-i-Sabah and the Assassins of Alamut. Polo reported how the Old Man of the Mountain controlled his region and defended his faith by murder:

> ... *when any of the neighboring princes, or others, gave offense to this chief, they were put to death by these his disciplined assassins: none of whom felt terror at the risk of losing their own lives, which they held in little estimation, provided they could execute their master's will. On this account his*

> *tyranny became the subject of dread in all the sur-*
> *rounding countries.*

Polo described the Mohammedans of Persia as *"a handsome race,*
especially the women who, in my opinion, are the most beautiful in
the world." Hasan had put these comely native women to his uses,
drugging his cadre of killers, then seducing them with *"elegant and*
beautiful damsels, accomplished in the arts of singing, playing upon
all sorts of musical instruments, dancing, and especially those of
dalliance and amorous allurement."

Lammeck left the book open in his lap, but his mind traveled beyond the words. On the page, walking through Polo's prose, he
imagined her. She was both sides of Hasan-i-Sabah's deadly coin: a
seductress and a martially trained assassin.

He lingered on the great temptress killers of history. Catherine
the Great. Cleopatra. Salome, who danced in payment for the head
of John the Baptist. Delilah, betrayer of Samson. The Jewish princess
Judith, who on the eve of a great battle gave herself to the Assyrian
general Holofernes, then emerged in the morning with his head in a
sack, saving her Israel.

Lammeck set Marco Polo down. He sighed and dug into the
cardboard box for another file. He was going to find her. Lammeck
stayed awake, searching toward dawn.

February 17
Washington, D.C.

LAMMECK OPENED HIS EYES to where he'd left them, in the
white width of an open file across his lap.

Dag's voice greeted him to the morning. So did cotton mouth and
a stiff spine. A dejected mood had settled on Lammeck's spirit just
before sunup; it was there still.

He set the file on the desk, then turned to see Dag on the phone. The man had slept in his clothes and looked no different than he would at midafternoon.

"Uh-huh," Dag said into the receiver. "Uh-huh. Yeah, well, it's a Saturday, so may as well do it this weekend. I'm hitting nothin' but dead ends here anyway. Yep, stayed up all night. Hey, do me a favor. Have those dropped off at the front desk of the Blackstone Hotel. Yeah, that's where I spent the night. I holed up over here with the professor. No, very funny. I took the bed, he slept in a chair. I must have bad breath or somethin'. Okay."

Dag hung up. He answered Lammeck's stare. "What?"

"Was that Mrs. Beach?"

"Yeah. Apparently I misjudged her. She has a sicko sense of hu- mor. Anyway, sorry I conked out on you last night. You stay up late?"

"Yep. All night. Don't you remember? You were right there with me, apparently." Sarcasm fit Lammeck's frame of mind.

Dag ignored the jibe. "How late?"

"Long enough to get through all but one box. And to be pretty sure she's not working for Uncle Sam."

Dag yawned. He pointed at the only two files separated from the rest.

"What about them?"

"My money says no. Waste of time."

"I'll have Mrs. Beach run those two down anyway. We can take that last box with us."

"We going somewhere?"

"We're heading back to Boston."

"Why?"

Dag began to unbutton his shirt and peel the tails out of his belted waist.

"What are you doing?"

"I'm gonna take a shower. You mind?"

"That depends. What did she tell you?"

"We got word back from the Newburyport cops. Mrs. Beach's real impressed with you all of a sudden. The cops up north have pulled seventeen auto records on locals who bought themselves a second car between November 1 and January 1. In eleven of those, the old car was traded in or titled to someone else. Those titles were checked out and turned up legit; we found the new owners and everything was hunky-dory. In the six other cases, the folks hung on to their original car. In three out of those six, both cars have been accounted for. In the other three, the ones we're interested in, the folks only have one car now. But there's no record or explanation where the other car went. Honest to hell, Professor, it's just like you said."

Dag seemed enthused. This sort of investigation was more his style, getting out on the street, combing through people's lives, raking stories and events, not poring over files and records like Lammeck the historian.

"Are we really going now? I just got an hour's sleep. In a chair, as you've noted."

"Mrs. Beach's getting us a flight out of the Naval Air Station. Come on, we'll grab some java on the way. Besides, our girl isn't going to bump off Roosevelt today. He's on a navy ship out in the Atlantic."

"Dag, look—Maybe this is just another snipe hunt."

"You don't want to go?"

"I'm not saying that."

"Then what are you saying? Remember, Professor, you're the one who came up with this notion about the cars. It seemed cockamamie to me at the time, but now we got ourselves three of 'em to talk to up there. Three little mystery Indians. So let's go. What the hell else have we got to do?"

Lammeck shook his head, still edgy from lack of sleep and the fallow files. He needed a glass of water, a piss, and a day of thinking about something else. "That's just it. It's cockamamie. Like the idea

I had that she's working for the government. She's not. We wasted a lot of time and resources getting these boxes. I guess I should just tell you. If you haven't noticed, I'm making a lot of this stuff up as I go. The government-job idea. The suggestion that she drove instead of taking the train. This notion that she has a connection in Newburyport. Just about every bright thing I've come up with in the past five weeks has come out of my ass. I'm grasping at straws, trying to unravel this whole thing."

Dag yanked his shirt over his head and tossed it on the bed. Then he sat on it. He tugged off his right sock.

"Professor, don't go goofy on me, alright? She's an assassin. You're an expert on assassinations. You're trying to figure it out on the fly. So is she. The fact that you're both making it up as you go along is our best shot at finding her, you said so yourself. If we're lucky, you're hitting the same dead ends she is. And maybe, just maybe, you'll come up with the same path in to Roosevelt that she does at the same time. Then boom, there she'll be. Plus, keep in mind, if it's tough for you, it's tough for her. That's a good thing, alright? The President's not supposed to be easy to kill."

Lammeck nodded.

Dag sniffed his socks and made a face.

"No one's been interviewed in Newburyport yet about those cars, just some snooping on the Q.T. by the police there. So let's head up and have a chat with folks ourselves. We'll have a local cop along with us, for jurisdictional concerns; the guy will know his way around. No big deal. We'll be back tomorrow."

"Did they find any Japanese or German connections?"

Dag stood from the bed, rising off his flattened shirt. He laughed.

"Okay, now that part of your idea really was screwy. Turns out half of Newburyport's got Irish or Scotch grandparents, and the other half had an ancestor on the *Mayflower* and is real happy to tell you about it. Oh, and maybe there's fifty Portuguese in the town. They spend so much time on the water they don't even know there's a war on. So, no dice."

Lammeck needed a shower himself. "Alright. When do we leave?"

"Sooner the better."

Lammeck glanced around the hotel room, scattered with boxes, government folders, cartons of stale food, paper cups, all of it just a useless mess. In the middle of the disarray stood Dag, dropping his pants. Lammeck felt very far away from his classroom.

Boston

LAMMECK DIDN'T TALK AND didn't take the cotton out of his ears until the naval plane had stopped taxiing. A police car from Newburyport, a battered Ford with a cherry on the roof and the town's name on the door, waited on the tarmac.

The cop was named Hewitt. Tall and uncommonly thin in his khakis, winter coat, and badge, he was young and in his second year on the force. Lammeck watched him fold uncomfortably behind the steering column, his bony knees jackknifed up to the wheel.

As soon as Dag took the front seat and Lammeck the back, Officer Hewitt said without being asked, "I'll tell you right off, I wanted to go in the army. But I got flat feet. That's why."

"I'm sure that's the case, Hewitt." Dag hooked his thumb over his shoulder toward the backseat. "The professor over here didn't go 'cause he's got a flat ass."

"Better than the flat nose I'm going to give you."

Dag turned to scowl at Lammeck with a look that asked, *"Are you going to cheer up or am I going to have to screw with you all day until you do?"*

Hewitt laughed at the exchange, unaware that both men were squarely on each other's nerves. He drove them away from the cold landing strip into a gray Boston day.

"I brought sandwiches," the young cop said, pointing to the

glove compartment. Dag ate two while Lammeck closed his eyes for the drive north.

Lammeck drifted in and out. He listened to Hewitt ask about why a Secret Service agent and a teacher were so interested in Newburyport and the killings on the beach. Dag told him it was confidential, and whatever Hewitt saw on this trip was also completely under wraps. Hewitt liked that. Without being asked, Dag spoke of his affection for Roosevelt, the man whose protection was his profession. FDR was Dag's hero, the way he'd handled everything from the Depression to the war, the greatest leader America had ever known. Lammeck kept his mouth shut and thought of the many dead heroes he knew who would not agree. Hewitt inquired about Roosevelt's personal life. Dag told him the President liked his cocktail time, which FDR called the "children's hour." Roosevelt made all the drinks himself, often experimenting with concoctions that produced the worst martinis in Washington, though no one told him so. The President's health came and went, but a strong will carried him most days. Dag confided that FDR and wife Eleanor were a great team for the country without being a super couple. "Some water under the bridge there," was all he would say.

"Oh, hey! I almost forgot," Hewitt said. "You remember that knife, that one we found on the beach you told us to check out? We just heard back from Harvard. They did a . . . what was it?"

From the backseat, eyes closed, Lammeck interjected, "Spectrograph."

"Yeah, that," the young cop enthused. "Turns out their best guess is the damn thing is like a thousand years old. And the eggheads are sure it wasn't made in Europe."

Lammeck sat awake in the back now.

"Watch this, kid." Dag poked the cop in the shoulder, then turned to face Lammeck. "Hey, Professor, why isn't the knife from Europe?"

"High-carbon cast iron is almost unheard of in Europe prior to the fifteenth century. Before that, it was just low-carbon alloys. On the other hand, the Chinese have been making high-carbon iron since the sixth century B.C."

"So our knife's Chinese?"

"Maybe just the blade. More likely it was made by a Chinese craftsman or with Chinese techniques somewhere else, because of the motifs on the handle. And the Chinese probably would have used jade or something other than onyx for the haft. Onyx is more of a classic Middle Eastern material."

"So we're still sticking with . . . ?"

"Persia."

With a smile, Dag turned back to Hewitt.

"That's something, isn't it, kid? He's like a party trick. Fuck those eggheads at Harvard. That man back there has forgotten more than they'll ever know. Right, Professor?"

"You say so."

"I do."

Lammeck raised both palms, to surrender his bad mood to this wrinkled agent, his former student who'd killed three German guards with improvised garrotes. Who now relied on Lammeck to save his hero, Roosevelt.

The remainder of the ride to Newburyport rolled gently by. Lammeck rested easier, and when he opened his eyes in the town, he was slightly revived.

"How do you want to do this?" Dag asked Lammeck when Hewitt had pulled to the curb. The police car idled in a tight street of grimy woodframe houses. Icicles dove from gutters. Yards lay blanked out under a crust of snow. Lammeck had grown up on a New England street like this, where for four months a year trash cans and hydrants became shapeless humps and the snow turned sooty the day after it fell.

"Hewitt, you do the knocking. I'll take over soon as we're inside. Dag, did you bring a gun?"

"A piece? Aw, hell. No."

Lammeck rubbed his forehead, fighting off the resurgence of his black mood. "Officer, have you ever fired your weapon at a real person?"

Hewitt's gaunt cheeks flushed. For a moment the skinny kid reminded Lammeck of the actor Jimmy Stewart, gawky and easily embarrassed.

"No. Am I gonna have to?"

"Always good to be prepared, son. Check your load. Just stay calm but in range."

"I guess we're not just checking on car-title violations, are we?"

"No, Officer, we're not. We're investigating a plot to assassinate the President."

Dag almost exploded in the front seat. "Hey! Goddammit, that's classified. Hewitt, you didn't hear that!"

"Yes, he did, Dag. We're trying to find an accomplice to a multiple murder. I'd like my bodyguard to know what we're up against. Hewitt, you can be trusted, right?"

The young cop's jaw hung slack. Lammeck asked him again. Hewitt shook off his shock. He gave Dag a wary glance, then said to Lammeck, "Yes, sir."

"Good. Right now you know all you need to know. Don't get curious beyond that or you'll answer to Dag here. Let's go."

The house was one of the humbler structures on the working-class street, but with a wide front yard. Parked at the curb on this frosty Saturday afternoon sat a cream-colored two-door coupe with fat whitewalls and a rounded cowling that came to a pointed snout.

"What is that?" Lammeck asked. "Studebaker?"

"1940 Studebaker Champion," Hewitt answered. "It's their economy model. Started making them in '39, stopped in '42. Won't be making any more 'til the war's over."

The boy had a quick acumen. Dag seemed to soften toward Hewitt's inclusion, saying, "Exactly."

"I don't fish, and I ain't in the army. In this town, cars is all that's left."

Lammeck let Hewitt precede them up the snowy sidewalk. The cop climbed the stoop alone and knocked.

A small man opened the door with a weekend beer in his hand. He wore a brown cable-knit turtleneck, stained work pants, and boots.

"Mr. Lazenby? I wonder if we could have a moment, sir? These gentlemen are from Washington, D.C."

Lammeck did not hear what Lazenby asked, but Hewitt replied, "No, sir, you're not in any trouble. We're investigating a car theft ring here in Newburyport. These two gentlemen are from a federal agency, just observing our local police work. May we come in for a minute?"

Lazenby stared at them for a long moment, then stepped aside.

They filed in behind Hewitt. The short man stashed his beer behind a lamp, then rubbed his mitts on his slacks before shaking hands all around. Lammeck stepped up and asked:

"Mr. Lazenby, is that your Studebaker out front?"

"Yes, sir."

"It's a beaut. I understand you had another car before that one, but we can't quite determine what happened to it. There's no record of a sale and no one has seen it in months."

Lazenby shrugged. "I didn't steal nothing."

"Of course not, sir. But can you tell us what happened to your other car? It was a . . ."

Lammeck expected Lazenby to answer but it was lanky Hewitt who jumped in with, "—a black '34 Hudson Terraplane Series K Special."

Lammeck paused for Lazenby's reply. The little man turned his attention away from Lammeck, stabbing a finger at him and speaking instead to the local kid cop: "I thought you said he was just observing."

Hewitt held his ground. "Just answer the man's question, sir, and we'll get out of your hair."

Lammeck said, "The Terraplane, Mr. Lazenby. Where is it?"

Lazenby looked confounded. He glanced behind him, as if he might make a break for it. Lammeck saw Hewitt's finger brush the holster clasp over his revolver. Dag saw this, too. He moved in Lazenby's path to the back door.

"Car's in the garage."

"May we see it?"

Lazenby shrugged again. "I don't give a fuck."

Lammeck invited Lazenby to lead the way.

He took them through the tiny kitchen to the corrugated tin garage in the backyard. Lazenby unlocked a metal door to the hut, revealing a thirty-foot boat on jack stands, in the latter stages of re-habilitation.

"There she is."

"Sir," Dag said, "that's a boat."

The man made no reply but climbed a ladder to the deck. Lammeck moved to follow, but Hewitt stepped in first, patting his sidearm.

When Lammeck reached the deck, Lazenby lifted a panel in the floor to reveal the boat's engine.

Hewitt whistled. "A Deluxe Eight."

Lammeck gazed into the compartment crammed with pipes, hoses, and an engine block. He knew nothing about cars. Hewitt made it simple for him.

"That's a Hudson '35 high-compression eight-cylinder. No question."

"I even got the hood ornament on the bow." Lazenby beamed at Hewitt, who clearly appreciated the skill it took to retrofit that engine to a marine use. "I cut the body up and sold it for scrap. Gave the tires to the government. Kept the transmission. I can show it to you."

Lammeck turned away, Dag followed.

"Named her *Aquaplane*," Lazenby said. "You know, like Terraplane, but like that fella said, it's a boat."

Hewitt explained how they appreciated his cooperation, and bade Lazenby a good afternoon.

Back in the police car, Dag chuckled. "Aquaplane. That's good. That was clever. Hey, Hewitt. Did that guy look like an accomplice to an international assassin to you?"

"No, sir, he didn't."

"Damn sure did to me. I was fooled. I figured we had him. How 'bout you, Professor?"

"Next," was all Lammeck said, simmering.

Hewitt drove them to the western part of town, down a more affluent street than the first. He stopped in front of a Victorian with elaborate columns and a wide wraparound porch. Again, Hewitt knocked while they waited below. A pleasant-looking woman, maybe in her fifties, answered the door. Hewitt spoke, using the same cover story about a local car theft ring. The woman nodded, turned, and motioned them inside.

They sat in the parlor. Hewitt introduced Lammeck and Dag as officials from Washington, D.C. Before he could say another word, the woman fell apart. She burst into tears, dabbing at her face with her bare hands, searching as she bawled for something more proper to wipe her eyes with. She pointed a shaking hand at a table on the far side of the room, to a box of Kleenex. Dag fetched them.

Her story, told between sniffles, unveiled a crime, but nothing like the one Lammeck sought. In October, her only son had returned from the army, on leave from France. All last summer the boy had fought through the terrible hedgerows of Normandy. He told her he couldn't take any more; he was going AWOL. She'd begged him not to, then gave him the keys to her car. Her husband was furious with them both, but did not report his son. He bought another '41 Pontiac, same make and color, which he had with him right now at the hardware store. Her son had telephoned once, at

Christmas, from somewhere in Nevada. She begged Lammeck and Dag to promise that her son would not be hurt.

Dag stood, saying, "We'll see what we can do, ma'am. Good afternoon." He headed out the front door with Lammeck in his wake. Hewitt stayed behind to mop up.

Dag climbed in the police car and honked the horn.

"Check that out, Hewitt," Dag said when the cop had folded behind the wheel.

"She's telling the truth," Hewitt replied. "I know her son. He was always a shitheel."

Lammeck caught Dag's eye; the two agreed to stay silent. Dag knew, and Lammeck understood, that a man had limits. He can hit those limits—many did in the hedges of France, many more would on the German plains and the beaches of the Pacific—without being a shitheel. Hewitt, with his bad feet, would never know.

The last house stood near the river, on Woodland Street, close to the town's center. Hewitt drove past the police station, then the Town Hall and the morgue where Bonny, Otto, and Arnold had been kept in cold storage. Lammeck wondered how their deaths had affected little Newburyport. He hoped the three had been given good funerals, even under such dour skies and into rock-hard earth. He pondered if Bonny had been laid near husband Arnold, the wretched man accused of murdering her and her big boyfriend.

Again, Hewitt parked and led the way. Snow had been shoveled from the drive and sidewalk. The little house was neat; the open garage held a late-model Buick. Lammeck walked over to set a hand on the hood. Warm. Someone had just come home.

The woman who answered Hewitt's knock had gray hair but appeared youthful and cherry-cheeked. She wore fur-lined boots and a bright sweater that looked hand-knit. To Lammeck she seemed the ultimate New Englander, hardy and capable.

"Come in, come in," she commanded, cheerfully waving, "don't stand out there."

Inside, Lammeck already sensed their efforts were going to come up empty and the flight back to Washington would be sullen and tired. This Newburyport woman would have yet another plausible explanation and again he'd be out of ideas. This time tomorrow he'd be back to thumbing through files, to staring across the chilly grounds of the White House. Wondering on more nights, with folders in his lap, or a map, or a book, or nothing, if their assassin even existed, if she were only theoretical and nothing more, and if he'd been stupid, too eager to believe. Or worse, if she did exist, and he wound up being fatally stupid.

For the third time this morning, Hewitt told his fairy tale about car thefts. The woman sat them on her sofa and chairs. She remained standing, asking about tea or coffee. All three requested coffee. She disappeared into her kitchen. Dag jutted his chin at Hewitt to stand and not lose sight of her. The cop unfolded from his chair and moved to where he could keep an eye on her.

"So, you're from Washington?" she called, over the clink of mugs and water running at the sink.

"Yes, ma'am," Dag answered.

"Why on earth are two fine-looking men like you all the way up here in our little town worrying about car thefts? Isn't that what we have our little police department for?"

Hewitt hitched his belt at this slight. "Yes, ma'am. They're just observers."

"I see." She emerged with a tray of cups and a piping coffee pot. She poured, none for herself, set the pot on a trivet, and stayed standing.

"Now, talk to me, boys."

Dag looked at Lammeck, but he lacked the heart this time. Dag took over.

"Is that your Nash out in the garage?"

"Yes, it is."

"Was it recently purchased?"

"Just last November."

"Ma'am, what happened to your previous automobile? There's no record of a sale or other disposition of it. Can you tell us, or maybe show us, where that car went?"

The woman stared at Dag for a long moment, unblinking. Then she clasped her hands under her chin as if some message she'd waited a long time for, and feared to receive, had just been delivered.

"Would you like biscuits for your coffee? I just got some from the store."

Lammeck sat straight. "No, ma'am. We'd like to know what happened to your car."

Hewitt reminded her, "A burgundy '39 Nash."

"I'm going to get a biscuit for you boys." She turned decisively for the kitchen.

Lammeck and Dag shot off the sofa. Hewitt fingered his holster.

With the three men crowding the doorway to the kitchen, the woman opened a cabinet, searching among boxes on a high shelf.

Lammeck stepped into the room. He asked, "Where do you keep your knives?"

She froze, arms raised toward the cabinet overhead. Without turning, she answered, "Left of the sink."

Lammeck slid open the drawer. He pulled out a four-inch knife, one of a set. He held it up for Dag to see. "Wüsthof."

The woman found what she looked for. She turned to them.

Lammeck and the woman stared at each other. She held no tin of biscuits in her closed right hand. Her face took on a sorrowful look.

"Well, good job, boys. You're very clever."

Lammeck said, "Talk to us."

Her eyes flicked back to Dag. "Mr. Secret Service agent. How much trouble am I in?"

"Accomplice to two murders. Probably three. Maybe more, depending on what happens from this point on. Lady, I'd say you got a world of trouble and you don't want to add to it."

"I agree," she said, evenly.

Lammeck set down the knife and closed the drawer. He stepped aside so Hewitt could come into the kitchen to take the woman in hand. She did not open her right fist.

"You know," she said, "I think not."

"Pardon?" Hewitt asked, stopping.

The woman's head shuddered.

She addressed Lammeck. "I didn't like her very much."

Lammeck felt a thrill tag his chest.

"Her?"

"I liked Arnold. He was an inoffensive little man."

"Yes, ma'am." Lammeck kept his voice level. The Assassin was real!

"So, I've decided," she said. She smiled, showing fine teeth. "Her name is Judith."

"Judith," Dag and Lammeck repeated, both stunned. The young cop stayed motionless.

"Now, gentlemen. Good-bye."

"Ma'am," Hewitt said, patiently, "I'm pretty sure you're coming with us."

"It'll be alright," Dag added, trying to disarm the tension coiling suddenly in the small, crowded kitchen.

The woman shook her head, gazing straight at Lammeck.

"Well, well," she laughed richly, "maybe you boys aren't as clever as all that."

Lammeck sprang forward, knocking the cop aside. He grabbed for her arm but reached her too late. By the time he clamped on the woman's right wrist she had tossed the capsule into her mouth and bitten down.

As Lammeck lowered her limp body to the kitchen floor, the bitter odor of almonds swirled from her nostrils.

CHAPTER ELEVEN

February 19
Washington, D.C.

MRS. BEACH SET HER scrawny elbows on her desk, fingers steepled over her lips.

"Judith," she repeated.

Dag nodded. "Just Judith."

Lammeck watched the two Secret Service employees hold themselves in check while they bounced between them the name and the new reality of a confirmed and identified assassin.

Mrs. Beach muttered, "Joseph, Mary, and Jesus," just the way her Irishman boss would have. Then she asked Dag, "And a cop heard her say this?"

"I can get the kid on the horn if you like. I got his written statement."

"Later." Mrs. Beach pulled her hands from her lips but kept them joined, fingertips pointing at Dag. "Tell me again. This happened ...?"

"Saturday afternoon. Around three."

"And right now it's noon Monday. You've got some crazy

woman coming to kill the President and it's a day and a half later. Where in hell have you been?"

Lammeck opened his mouth, to remind Reilly's right-hand woman that their assassin was not insane but highly intelligent and superbly skilled, probably more than Dag, Reilly, and him combined. That he and Dag had been nowhere except on this case and doing nothing else since he'd stepped off a plane five and a half weeks ago. He'd gotten no sleep except what he could cobble together out of hours spent in cars and airplanes and on police station sofas.

Both Dag and Mrs. Beach shot him a glance and he bit back his response. Lammeck was not Secret Service, and he was not responsible for the President, not like they were. Dag answered the question.

"Look, first this woman keels over dead right in front of us. So then we had to go through her house, I mean with a fine-tooth comb. Plus we had to sanitize the whole situation. I laid down the law with Hewitt, told him not one peep gets out about this or he doesn't want to know what we'd do to him. All he's gonna tell his bosses is the lady was under government surveillance, he doesn't know for what, and she dropped dead during our visit, he has no idea why. Then I had to come up with a cover story about the old woman for the neighbors. She had a heart attack when she found out her car had been stolen, blah blah blah."

"What about the body?"

"Way ahead of you. I had it flown back here; she's at Bethesda. That way we control the autopsy report. She'll be buried tomorrow in a government cemetery out in Maryland. Hewitt'll spread the story she had kin there."

"Cyanide capsule?"

"No question. She went down like a sack of dirt. And the smell. Like French coffee."

Mrs. Beach aimed her pince-nez glasses at Dag, not ready for Lammeck yet. She was not in need of more speculation or a history lesson. She dredged the agent first for facts. Lammeck saw why Reilly could leave town with the confidence that she could handle things.

"Who was the woman?"

Dag opened his briefcase for papers. He shuffled up a few sheets and skidded them onto Mrs. Beach's desk.

"Birth certificate, driver's license, Social Security, passport. Her name was Maude Lily King. Born in Scituate, Mass. Went to Wellesley. Lived in Newburyport the past twenty-two years. Retired schoolteacher, owned a local bookstore. Age sixty-three. Never married. One sister, deceased. Traveled some between the wars but nowhere controversial. Paris, London, Rome—retired-old-lady kind of trips."

Mrs. Beach glared over the top of her glasses. "I beg your pardon. Sixty-three is not old, and those are lovely cities of the world for any person of any age."

Dag backed off with a shrug.

"Continue," she ordered.

"Parents, sister, her, all squeaky-clean. No commie meetings; in fact, she was known to be extremely anticommunist. No suspect associations."

Mrs. Beach raised an eyebrow at this last statement.

Dag admitted the mistake. "Okay, well, obviously that last one is incorrect. Not so's we can tell yet, is all."

Mrs. Beach accepted the retraction in silence. She mulled the open file, tapping a finger on the paper remains of a seemingly average New England woman's life. Where was the crossroads in that life? Lammeck wondered. What had radicalized Maude Lily King enough to make her part of an assassination plot? Madwoman, patriot, hireling: Where did Maude fit in?

"Judith." Mrs. Beach slowly rolled the assassin's name on her tongue like a cognac, as if it might release some secret. "What's the story with that name, Dr. Lammeck? Is it made up?"

Lammeck explained the story of Judith the Jewish princess,

slayer of the Assyrian Holofernes, one of the many saviors in the warrior tales of the Israelites.

"I thought you said she was Persian. Aren't they Muslim? Why would she take a Jewish name?"

Lammeck wanted to answer: *Welcome to my world, where nothing adds up; the assassin's a ghost, I'm confused every day, and I'm still the one with the best chance of finding her before she kills the President of the United States.* Instead, he replied, "Maybe she sees herself as some kind of heroine. Maybe she's a Jewish girl from Brooklyn. I'll ask her when I meet her."

Lammeck watched the woman work up a sour grin; he expected a scold for being a smart-ass. Instead, old Mrs. Beach eased her thin smirk into a smile.

"Do that for me, Doctor."

She stood. The two men followed suit.

"Alright," Mrs. Beach said. "I'll report everything you've said to the chief. I'm sure he'll tell me that you can expect all the help you need, money and manpower, but that everything goes through this office first. Dr. Lammeck, I know you're a private citizen but we'd appreciate it if you'd see this through with us. Dag seems to think you're a whiz. From what I've seen, despite your cavalier mouth, you might well be. At any rate, you seem to make the ideal partner for Agent Nabbit here. You have similar... attitudes."

Lammeck nodded. Even if Mrs. Beach had told him to go back to Scotland he would have kept searching on his own for Judith.

"Now listen, the both of you. The President knows nothing about this, and when he gets home next week he will not be told. The job is to make our precautions invisible to him, but impenetrable to our little assassin. Chief Reilly is going to want this kept out of the paper and out of the White House. No snafus. Also, your killer might have confederates around Washington just like she did up north. There may even be more of her associates left in New England. It's impossible to tell how wide her network might be.

Keep your ears to the ground, and we'll get on it from our end. Chief Reilly will be back soon. Doctor?"

"Ma'am."

"You've come up with a humdinger of a lead. Keep it up. Is your hotel suitable?"

"For as much as I'm in it."

"Fine. Let me know if that changes. Dag."

"Yes, ma'am."

"I know I speak for Chief Reilly and the entire free world when I say I don't give a good goddam if you catch this woman or kill her. But we want her stopped. Do what you have to do, and we'll sort it out later. Understood?"

"Yes, ma'am."

A moment later, Mrs. Beach looked up and said, "You're still here."

February 20
Washington, D.C.

JUDITH STEPPED OFF THE Ninth Street trolley at Pennsylvania. She folded the *Post* under her arm. The front-page photo showed U.S. Marines raising a flag over Mt. Suribachi on Iwo Jima. On the trolley she'd read about Russian advances through Poland, Americans charging to the Rhine against crumbling German resistance, and an earthquake in Iowa. Roosevelt had not returned to Washington, though the paper said he was expected next week. An address to Congress reporting on his mission to Yalta had been announced for next week.

Rubbing shoulders with dozens of overcoated clerks and businessmen, Judith entered the Apex Station Post Office. She found her mailbox, kneeled, and looked through the little glass pane into her slot. No letter waited inside, though it was due yesterday. She spun the combination lock anyway and reached in her hand to feel the cool confines of the empty little cubby. The postal service, she felt, was the best part of America. If there had been a letter from Newburyport, it would have been delivered.

She slammed the small metal door and jostled the lock to reset it. Her agitation caught the attention of a man kneeling near her. He smiled when he caught her eye. He probably thought her boyfriend had failed to write.

She strode out of the building, headed west. After six blocks, she stood on the eastern rim of the White House grounds. She cursed herself.

She'd been fucking Tench. She'd been cleaning house, shining silver, reading the *Post,* doing push-ups in her room at night, waiting for Roosevelt to return, plotting her next step.

And she had not noticed the security on the White House grounds had doubled.

February 21

A BURGUNDY '39 NASH. Massachusetts plate SCR-310.

For all the excitement of finding out they'd been right about an assassin, and the grim spectacle of Maude Lily King dropping dead at Lammeck's feet, they'd come away from Newburyport with only two clues: The killer was in fact a woman, and she drove a '39 Nash.

That pair of hints might be enough. But Lammeck had little faith they would be. Judith was an apparition. She showed herself only for moments before vanishing again. Though she was now real, she remained incredible. He still had no inkling how she'd murdered Arnold, who she worked for, what she looked like, where she was hiding, or how she would make her move. He and Dag were barely closer to finding her than they were before Maude King named her and swallowed poison.

Despite Lammeck's misgivings, Dag seemed excited, keyed up for Lammeck's next insight. Lammeck was glumly certain the man's eagerness would prove short-lived. He'd gotten lucky, and by definition that didn't happen often.

Lammeck fired up the engine of his borrowed government Chevy, to run the heater for a few minutes. Washington was in the grip of a late winter cold snap. He was on a stakeout, listening to the two-way radio, watching East Executive Avenue. Dag in his own car sat on the western side of the White House directing the surveillance. All the agents' and Lammeck's radios were tuned to Dag on a secret frequency; he was the hub. Other agents motored around town in unmarked cars, keeping Dag apprised of their whereabouts while they searched for Judith's vehicle. Lammeck listened to their chatter while looking across the street to the White House grounds, where the security detail had quietly been increased. Mrs. Beach had kept her word. She'd given Dag his manpower. The manhunt was in full swing, but all they could do was patrol D.C. in the faint hope that Judith would foul up, and close ranks around Roosevelt without him noticing it when he returned from Yalta. In the meantime, Professor Lammeck dug deep to come up with another lead.

In his lap sat an all-too-familiar folder of photographs, the black-and-white close-ups of the bodies in Newburyport. The last few showed the Assassin's knife in detail. Lammeck peered at the bloodied onyx handle, at the friezes of ancient Assassin murders carved into it. The artist had taken great care to display each killer wearing the costume of his victim's household. One emir was stabbed by a man holding the reins to his horse. Another by his cook. A third by a pair of his bodyguards while he rode on a palanquin. In every instance, the murdered man and bystanders shared the same looks, not of pain, but incredulity, that someone they had deemed invisible had so mortally betrayed them.

This strategy was the trademark of Hasan-i-Sabah. His followers were taken into his castle and Pleasure Garden at an early age.

There they were indoctrinated and trained, but not schooled or pedigreed. They could get close to their targets only through the barn, kitchen, or field. They could not pose as great men themselves to sidle alongside the powerful enemies marked for death by Hasan. Was this the same path Judith was on? She came to America armed with immense killing skill, but what else? How did she plan on getting close enough to Roosevelt to strike?

Somewhere, here in D.C., this woman was invisible. Lammeck was certain of it.

And what of Marco Polo's observations about Persian women? Was Judith also beautiful? Wasn't beauty a weapon? Of course it was. And Judith would use it, the way she would use anything or anyone, brutally.

The pivotal question was: At this moment, who was she using it on?

Lammeck wanted to discuss this with Dag. But he guessed Dag would scoff at one more of his far-flung theories based on tortured logic and arcane knowledge. Over the past few days, on the heels of the first strong leads they'd gotten out of Newburyport, the investigation had taken a more conventional turn. Dag finally had something tangible to sink his teeth into, something to show Reilly and the severe Mrs. Beach that he was not only keen but correct. Dag, sitting blocks away, kept himself eagle-eyed for a glimpse of that one burgundy Nash. He had two dozen other agents assigned to his case. Lammeck had become just one of Dag's resources.

Lammeck knew he'd been lucky up north finding Maude Lily King, a shot in the dark that had somehow hit home. Now, in his warming car, he knew what steps he had to take, and he figured he would take them alone. More important, he had a sense—for the first time since Dag had rapped on his door in St. Andrews six weeks ago—that he'd set his foot down on a trail that had been hidden to him, and seen beside his own big shoe, at last, a footprint.

.   .   .

February 22
Georgetown

SHE BUTTONED HER BLUE maid's dress, then slipped the cord of her apron around her waist to tie it at her back. Smoothing the apron's lace edges against her thighs, she stepped into her black crepe-soled shoes.

Tench lay naked across his bed. One arm was lapped over his face like a man hiding his eyes from grief, but she knew whatever it was he felt, it wasn't sorrow. He glistened with sweat, though the bedroom bore a chill. Judith looked down at him, motionless with his eyes covered and legs spread, still deep in his body where she had driven him, savoring the last dregs of pleasure she'd loosed in him.

She looked on Tench without disgust. He was an adequate lover and attentive enough, even to a maid, to a Negro. He was in a marriage of power, not love, and Judith understood this bargain. He sought ways to be kind to her within their respective boundaries. Tench was an intelligent and liberal-minded man. But his wife, like the old Muslim saying, was both horse and burden. Judith didn't blame Tench for his weakness, and so used him well in her sympathy.

His breathing slowed. She covered him with the quilt, but did not want him asleep. She sat on the mattress. He shifted and murmured. She set a hand to his bare chest. He did not move again, pretending sleep; she slid fingers slowly downward, under the edge of the quilt, playfully threatening to attempt a resurrection. This he could not do, so he awoke suddenly, playfully, and grabbed her arm.

"Nope," he said, eyes wide, "we're all out of stock. You'll have to come back later, lady."

She pretended to pout. "Shoot."

He looked up at her with what she determined was genuine affection. He laid a moist palm to her neck.

"I wish," he said.

"Wish what?" she asked, but she knew.

"Nothing."

She squeezed his hand at her throat, then stood.

"Well, Mr. Tench, a man who wishes for nothing is either happy or hopeless. Which one are you?"

He grinned broadly. "Neither. Where do you come up with these things, Desiree? You don't talk like a maid."

She bent to slap at him. "And how does a maid talk? How many you talked with?"

They laughed. He sat up, keeping the quilt over his lap. He glanced around for his pants.

"Oh, hey," he said, "I just heard something today. About the President."

Judith's attention perked. "Uh-huh."

"Pa Watson died two days ago, on the boat back from the big meeting with Stalin and Churchill. It's not in the papers yet. FDR asked to keep it quiet 'til he gets back."

"Who was Pa Watson?"

"General Edwin Watson. Roosevelt's military aide and secretary for years. And a real close friend. He had a heart attack out in the Atlantic. Christ, can you imagine being at sea with one of your pals dead like that on board with you? Poor old Roosevelt. It's gotta be rough on him. And just when things were looking so good." Tench bit his lip. "I guess life balances out."

Judith sat on the bed. This was delicate.

"When's the funeral?"

"Maybe next Wednesday, is what I hear. At Arlington."

She paused and lowered her eyes to be demure. "Can I go with you?"

"Desiree." He shook his head. "Be reasonable. The President's burying one of his best friends. That's not a good time to be shaking hands with the guy."

"In other words, you'll have your wife with you."

"And yes, to be honest, if I go I'll have her with me. It's a funeral but it's also politics. How am I supposed to explain you coming along?"

"Explain me to who?"

"My wife, for starters."

Judith shook her head, dismissing this. She could handle the wife. "Who else?"

"Jesus wept, everybody else."

Judith nodded. "Politics."

"Look, you know if it was up to me. But people in this town ... Why don't I just take Mrs. P. along too?"

Judith sat beside Tench on the bed, to drag the back of her nail gently up his spine. He writhed.

"Just an invitation, Jacob. Your wife won't even see me. I'll hide. I just want to see the President up close. Once. That's all."

"I can't."

"You can." She dropped her finger from his skin. "But you just won't."

Judith rose from the mattress to stand in front of Tench. She swayed her hips below his chin.

"You said for me to come back later, Jacob. How much later?"

Tench's gaze tumbled from her face, locking on the motion of her hips. With the fingers she'd run up his back, she reached behind her to tug on the shoelace knot that held the apron cord about her waist. The cord loosened, then dangled free.

"A lot later, Jacob?"

February 28
Arlington, Virginia

JUDITH DROVE HER CAR into Virginia. She parked a quarter mile from the Tench household, then took a bus to the big gates of Arlington National Cemetery. She wore a mourning dress at calf

length and a new black overcoat and felt hat. She sat on a front
bench of the bus.

Stepping off, she followed a phalanx of limousines and olive drab
army sedans through the stone gates, all the vehicles puffing exhaust
into the cold noon, matching her breath. The funeral procession
came across Memorial Bridge nonstop; Pa Watson must have been
beloved. Judith watched for Roosevelt's heavy car and security detail to rumble by, but did not see them. She quickened her pace into
the wintry paths of the vast graveyard.

She had not been here before. She was taken with the seeming
endless fields of white crosses, the occasional Jewish star, granite
spires marking great men, and the fatness of the trees, the placid,
eternal view of the river. Death, her trade, was treated grandly here.
She liked the place.

She easily found the funeral for General Watson. A crowd flowed
among the headstones to gather under tent tops set against the chill
and the possibility of rain. At a hundred yards away from the grave
site, a half dozen men in dark suits and overcoats eyed men and
women filing past, checking credentials of those they did not recognize. Judith approached and showed the pass Tench had written her.
The guard glanced at her face, then passed her onward.

Judith moved with the mourners, slowly, nodding somberly at
quizzical others who caught her eye. She located Jacob and his
wife and avoided them, circling wide to their rear. Roosevelt was
nowhere to be seen.

She stayed back from the hole in the ground and the shining dark
coffin resting on its black bier. The crowd, perhaps two hundred,
shuffled into a ring around the burial spot. Seven Marines in brilliant blue, red, and black uniforms formed a stiff line beside the
coffin, rifles at ceremonial parade rest. Pa Watson's family sat on
folding chairs, the women in veils, the men all in ebony broken only
by white pocket kerchiefs. Judith, in the outer reaches of the crowd,
kept her face down. The gathering waited; a chaplain stood near the
hole with a Bible closed in his hands. Then Roosevelt appeared.

A Secret Service agent rolled the President's wheelchair through the furrow opening in the crowd. Much closer to him this time, Judith felt the President looked no better than he had at his inauguration. The man's eyes appeared sunken and rimmed, his cheeks caved in. He slumped in his chair, accepting without lifting his head the pats on his shoulder from people he glided past. The ungainly woman walking behind was Eleanor, recognizable from her pictures. Hale and upright, touching offered hands on all sides of her and smiling appreciatively, his wife made Roosevelt appear by contrast even more collapsed.

The ceremony began as soon as Roosevelt and his wheelchair were settled beside the grave. Only family members sat for the chaplain's words, and the President. The burial service droned on for ten minutes; Pa Watson's career had been stellar and he'd affected many lives. Judith watched Jacob and Mrs. Tench from behind. They did not touch.

When the chaplain was done, the Marine honor guard fired their salute, three deafening volleys in the silence. The reports shook a few birds off bare branches, and nothing else moved until the echoes were finished. The casket was lowered on ropes into the grave. The chaplain folded shut his Bible. The crowd began to unravel, drifting past older graves, back to the warmth of their cars. Limousine and military drivers cranked engines to prepare for the returning riders.

Judith held her ground. Men and women eased past her. She waited until Jacob Tench and his wife finished shaking hands with several well-wishers, then watched the couple make their way to their own idling limousine. She eyed a small clot of dark-clad people beside the grave. At the heart of them, accepting hands and words, sat Roosevelt.

No line formed before him. People simply walked up, shared a quiet second with the seated President under the intense gaze of several agents, then moved off. Judith did not step forward yet, but opened her black purse.

Onto her right hand, she slid a white cotton glove. Quickly, over the index and middle fingers of her left, she stretched condoms, then stabbed the hand into a thin silk sheath. Over this she slipped on the matching left-hand cotton glove. From her coat pocket, she palmed a small bottle of cyanide mixed with dimethyl sulfoxide and lanolin. She walked forward.

The President was lingering beside the grave, working a separate klatch of dignitaries from his wife, who stood five yards behind him. When Judith was twenty steps away, still moving in, she unstoppered the little bottle to drip the contents onto her coated fingertips. The white glove instantly emitted the almond waft of the poison. Judith breathed it in and knew the odor was too slight and unexpected to be noticed. She tucked the emptied glass back into her coat and advanced with her head up, her expression sad and sympathetic.

Roosevelt did not look to see her coming; his attention was held by an old courtier gripping his hand and wagging his gray head. Judith stepped close, scrutinized by an agent who made no move to interrupt her progress. Judith halted five feet from the President's wheelchair. She brought her left hand up, to lay it on Roosevelt's the instant he swung his attention to her. The almond aroma fluttered past her nose.

Roosevelt nodded to the older man, who finally released his grip, still talking. Judith studied the President's open hand, the distended veins on the back where she would wipe the cyanide while she squeezed with her other hand, smearing the toxin on the thin and spotty skin into his blood. Inside of a hundred minutes after her touch, he would be dead.

Roosevelt glanced back at his wife, who nodded, agreeing it was time to go. A Secret Service agent stepped behind the wheelchair to roll the President away. Judith took a step forward. She opened her lips to say, "Mr. President."

A strong grip encircled her left arm. Before she could react, she was tugged off balance, away from the President's wheelchair. She almost stumbled under the dragging grasp, then turned, a spike of anger in her chest, to face a large, bald man. He did not look at her but pulled her several steps from Roosevelt. She cut her eyes back over her shoulder to see the President had now been taken in hand by the Secret Service and was rolling away from the grave.

Judith yanked her arm to be let go. The big man held firm; he was at least six and a half feet tall and powerfully built. She could have made a dozen moves to escape him, and another dozen to take him down and end his life. She saddled every one of these impulses; this was absolutely the wrong time and place. Judith held her tongue in check as well. She did not know who this man thought she was, a white guest at a power funeral or a Negro maid interloper? She could have swiped his hand with the poison-damp glove and paid him back hours from now for thwarting her. Again, Judith curtailed all her instincts to act and waited instead for information. She surrendered to the man's pull and silently trod beside him far from the remains of the crowd, past many grave markers.

When he let her loose, Roosevelt was long gone. Judith stepped away and glared up at the man.

"What the hell you think you're doin', missy?"

His voice trickled with arrogance.

So, Judith thought. She was colored to him. She lowered her eyes.

"I wanted to just say hello to the President and say I'm real sorry for his loss. The man's friend died. Folks got a right to tell him they're grievin', too."

"Folks do. You don't."

"I got a right to be here. I got this." Judith produced the pass handwritten by Jacob Tench with her right-hand, unpoisoned glove.

The man crossed his arms over a great chest, refusing to examine the note. He shook his head.

"No. You got no right whatsoever, little girl. And that paper ain't worth shit to me."

Judith tucked the page away into her pocket, beside the empty cyanide bottle. "Who are you, mister?"

He unfolded his arms. Beneath his coat, Judith glimpsed the leather edge of a handgun harness.

"You a cop?"

"Not at the moment. But yeah, most days I'm a D.C. cop. Right now I'm talking to you because of the other people I work for. They don't want you here. That means I don't want you here."

"Who are they?"

The man reached into a pocket for a pack of Lucky Strikes. He lit up, not offering a cigarette to Judith. He made her wait until he'd struck his match.

"Let's just say," he breathed with smoke that hid the hint of almonds around them in the cemetery, "that no one gives a damn if you screw Jacob Tench in your cruddy little apartment in that nigger alley. But when you start coming out in public, when you start appearing at the same places he appears with his wife . . . well, then, missy, some folks got a big problem with that."

She had her answer: Mrs. Tench's family. The dead senator's clan. Apparently Jacob had been a bad boy on other occasions, as well.

"You understand what I'm telling you, little girl?"

"Yes, sir."

The tip of the cigarette glowed hot from a long suck, while the man considered Judith. He nodded.

"I can see why he bothers with you, though."

Judith shuffled. "You been following me?"

"I been following Tench. And I seen enough to know it's time for you to quit your job in his house. You just tell the missus you're movin' on. No explanation necessary. Go sweep some other white folks' floor. It's all the same to you."

"I don't want to quit. But I'll quit screwing the mister. I don't want no trouble. Alright?"

"Too late for that. You got to go. And I mean today."

Judith lifted her chin, to measure him. She could make him agree to have his employers pay her some fee, a month's salary, and in return she'd leave the Tench household. She'd hold out her hand for him to shake on the deal. But he was too big, no less than two hundred and fifty pounds, not older than forty, strong. The dose she could deliver through his hand would make him mightily sick, and that was all.

"And if I don't?"

"Then I start watching you, too, missy. And I don't figure it'll be too long 'til you fuck up and I slam your ass in jail." He chortled. "You might not even have to fuck up. You might get hurt one night. Know what I mean?"

Judith nodded.

"Alright then. Beat it."

Judith turned to walk out of the cemetery. The man held his ground. When she was ten yards off, he said, low and mean, "I'll be watching, little girl."

She stopped and turned to him. "I know."

The big cop shrugged at her, then focused his interest on his cigarette.

Judith pivoted and walked on. She peeled from her left hand the poison-tipped glove, the silk sheath and condoms, then the dry glove from her right. She snapped them away in her purse. Her hands had grown dewy inside the gloves; the chill nibbled now at her bare skin.

Only then did she ball her fists.

Aurora Heights
Arlington, Virginia

IN HER POWDER-BLUE maid's uniform, Judith pulled back the curtains from the big picture window and dusted the furniture clustered in front of it. She made a mix of ammonia and water in a bucket to clean the many panes of the window. When Mrs. P. set out a snack in the mid-afternoon, she and Judith sat on the sofa to eat and chat in the daylight.

Jacob and his wife returned from the funeral at two o'clock, an hour after Judith. Husband and wife went to their separate portions of the large house and did not speak to either of the maids. At three o'clock, Judith told Mrs. P. that all her work for the day was finished and she was leaving. The old cook shook her head at more secretiveness from Desiree and said nothing. Judith robed herself against the cold and walked to her Nash.

She didn't know the big cop's name. She didn't need to.

Washington, D.C.

THE TIN-PAN VOICE ON the radio startled Lammeck.

"Car one, car one, calling Eyeball. I've got confirmation on a burgundy Nash, license plate SCR-310."

The answering voice of Eyeball—Dag—spat from the speaker.

"Give me your 10-20, car one!"

The Secret Service agent in car one said he was on New Hampshire heading north into Washington Circle. Lammeck listened while the agent updated his position: The suspect car was coming out of the circle, headed east on K Street in the early rush hour traffic.

"Got her!" Dag growled, triumphant. He instructed car one to follow and take no action.

"Professor! You hear me?"

Lammeck fumbled for his microphone. He'd spoken on the two-way radio only once, to test it when the agents had installed it in his car. Now he held the mike to his lips, pressed the talk button, and bellowed, "Yes!"

Dag said nothing and the radio went silent. Lammeck didn't know what to do next; he waited dumbly for Dag to instruct him. Through the afternoon, he'd been scanning the recent batch of government hiring files sent by Mrs. Beach. His front seat was scattered with folders. He put the mike down on top of one.

"...finger off the button!" Dag snarled through the speaker. "Goddammit, take your finger off the goddam talk button!"

Lammeck scooped up the mike.

"Sorry, sorry, Dag. I'm here."

"Talk, Lammeck, then let loose on the damn mike and shut up while I talk. Jesus! Now listen, I've got an agent following a burgundy '39 Nash, plate number SCR-310. Got that? It's her."

Lammeck did nothing for a moment, to be sure.

"Lammeck!"

He pushed the button again. "Got it, yeah, yeah."

"She was probably casing Pa Watson's funeral over at Arlington Cemetery. Hot damn, I knew she'd try a stunt like this."

Lammeck asked, "Where are you now?"

"Pulling out north on Seventeenth, headed for K. I got agents moving in for backup. You make for Vermont. If she heads straight east on K, we'll pass you and you get behind me. Get going."

Lammeck set down the mike and reached for the ignition key. Then, he grabbed for the mike, pressed the button again, and said, "Roger."

Dag belted, "Go!"

Lammeck cranked the engine and merged into traffic away from his constant view of the White House. Every vehicle around him shared his urgency; at 4:00 P.M. in the District, everyone pulling out of parking spaces prepared themselves to do combat to beat the coming gridlock. At F Street, he ran a red light, then gunned it to beat a trolley onto G Street. Horns blared; the trolley driver clanged his bell.

Lammeck shot north across another intersection, dodging cars and nailing his own horn. His clenched hands were damp on the wheel. He was not so reaccustomed to American driving on the right that his manic maneuvering was instinctive; twice after making turns, he found himself in the wrong lane.

Dag continued to guide his agents on the two-way. Once he reached K Street and spotted the '39 Nash, he coolly intoned his location and distance from the target. He ordered car one to back off. Dag was in his element. Lammeck listened while agents checked in with their own locations. Dag instructed all to avoid contact; they were merely to take up support positions on all sides and shadow him and the Nash. No one was to move until Dag gave the word. Lammeck did not trust his own driving enough to speak up, except when Dag shouted, "Lammeck!" He answered with a hurried "Ten-four," and gunned through every break he could find in the traffic, north toward K.

Dag coached him over the radio: "Don't answer, Professor. Just drive. There's two of them in the car. I'm a half a block back and I can see there's a guy driving and a dark-haired woman in the passenger seat. Who the fuck is the guy? Don't answer! We'll find out in a few minutes. Alright, team, alert, they're coming up on Franklin Square. Wait . . . shit! They've turned north on Vermont. Repeat, north on Vermont! They're headed toward Thomas Circle."

Lammeck heard this and stepped on the gas, obeying Dag's order not to answer. He ignored every traffic signal, veering sharply in and out of traffic, regardless of the direction it traveled, closing in urgently on Dag's droning radio voice. An opening in the southbound lanes gave him the shot at speeding past the cars ahead of him. He leaned on his horn. Adrenaline prickled in his veins.

Lammeck reached K Street and shot across through squealing cars to Vermont Avenue. He didn't know how far behind Dag he was; he couldn't look up from the pinball game of horns and bumpers all around him long enough to find out.

Had Dag said there were two people in the Nash? This could be a remarkable turn of events. Did Judith have another confederate in the city, just as she had in Newburyport? Was she part of some wide-ranging conspiracy, or was this guy driving just some unlucky boyfriend or patsy she was working to help her reach Roosevelt?

Lammeck fixed his mind on his driving. He intended to find these answers out and a lot more in the next few minutes.

Dag crooned on the radio. Lammeck's engine wound tight, and

he wove recklessly through packed traffic on narrow Vermont. Then Dag shouted over the radio, "Out of Thomas Circle now! Headed west on Mass. Ave. toward Dupont Circle."

Thomas Circle was still two blocks ahead. Was that Dag's olive drab Packard a hundred yards in front of his bumper, heading west on Massachusetts? Lammeck looked beyond the Packard for a burgundy Nash and did not see it.

He reached for the microphone. "Dag, is that you up ahead? Coming out of Thomas Circle?"

"No."

A moment stretched by on the radio. Another opening spawned in the southbound lanes of Vermont. Lammeck sensed it and charged ahead, making up ground toward Dag with his engine thundering and other drivers damning him. He swerved to avoid a Buick as it dove for the curb. Lammeck spun around Thomas Circle and lit out on Massachusetts, west toward Dupont Circle, five blocks off. He ducked and wove in and out of line until he forced an opening, drivers pulled aside to let him dash past with horns squalling.

"Lammeck!"

But Lammeck was going too fast to grab for the mike and respond. Dupont Circle had rushed up on him sooner than he'd anticipated. He hit the brakes and spun hard right, entering the one-way flow around the ring. His fender barely avoided two cars on his left, but he overcorrected and nudged a Ford on his right. This driver, a woman in uniform, shook her fist. Lammeck stayed in the circle, past the connection to New Hampshire and Connecticut, then past the continuance of Mass. Ave. at the opposite end from where he'd entered. The Ford Lammeck had nipped tried to follow him as well, to get him to stop. Lammeck couldn't stop, but he didn't know where to leave the circle. He grabbed the mike.

"Dag!"

"Mass. Ave. They're heading back the way they came on Mass. Ave. Lammeck, fuck! You passed me!"

It must have happened in the blur of traffic inside the circle. Lammeck scorched tires now, orbiting Dupont Circle again. The Ford he'd bumped got trapped in a slower clump and could not stay in his wake when Lammeck careened back out onto Massachusetts. He left the furious driver behind, still on spin cycle, and surged into the clear.

Dag and Judith and the mystery man were close ahead. He ducked into the left lanes of Mass. Ave., mashing the gas pedal. His stomach turned over, queasy from the unremitting nerves of the chase.

"Alright, Professor, I see you back there. Cool down, you're driving like a Red Baller. Just stay in your lane, okay?"

Lammeck gazed ahead. There was Dag's Packard, only five cars behind a Nash driving along Embassy Row. One more burst of speed and he could pull in right behind Dag.

He nailed the gas, closed on the bumper of the truck in front of him, and swung out, putting his driver's-side tires into the west-bound lanes. Cars honked and dodged while Lammeck roared past, until he was right behind Dag. The car at Dag's rear slowed out of fear of Lammeck and let him merge.

The radio wailed, "Goddammit, I told you to cool it!"

Lammeck grabbed the mike. "Sorry. I can see them, up ahead. You're right, there's two of them."

Before Dag could make any reply, the '39 Nash pulled out of the pack. A puff of exhaust billowed from its tailpipe as the car heaved into higher gear and took off, angling wildly into the oncoming lanes.

"Son of a . . . it's supposed to be *surveillance*!" Dag shouted into the radio. "Alright. Alright. Eyeball to all agents, all agents! Suspects are eluding. Headed east on Mass. Ave., approaching Thomas Circle. Stop traffic on all thoroughfares out of Thomas Circle. Repeat: Stop traffic on all thoroughfares out of Thomas Circle!"

Voices flocked to Dag out of the airwaves, with names of

streets each pursuing agent would block. Vermont, Rhode Island. Thirteenth, Fourteenth, Fifteenth.

"Lammeck, stay on my tail," Dag barked, "and don't do one damn thing else."

Lammeck left the mike alone and drove as he was told.

The Nash tried hard to escape, accelerating dangerously toward the traffic circle, careening into every lane. Dag was trying to throttle all routes out of the circle. If that worked, Lammeck would be face-to-face with Judith and her driver within minutes. Cornered, would they both bite capsules, too? Dag would be overjoyed if these two collapsed at his feet. But twin suicides would rob Lammeck of a once-in-a-million opportunity.

The Nash came up on Thomas Circle and barely slowed to navigate the curve. Dag pulled up tight on the car's bumper. Breathing hard, Lammeck struggled to stay close on Dag's rear. Traffic swerved out of the way once they saw a chase was on, but not one second passed when Lammeck was not narrowly avoiding some collision with a tree, car, or terrified pedestrian. He hung on grimly, heart hammering, keeping Dag's rear in front.

The Nash did not shoot out of Thomas Circle the way Dag anticipated: Instead, it tore the whole way around the ring, to fire back down Massachusetts the way they'd come in.

"West on Mass. Ave.!" Dag shouted to his team. "Someone shut it down! Mass. Ave.!"

Agents scrambled in their number to see who was closest. No one could get to Dupont Circle quick enough. They'd been outfoxed.

"Lammeck, it's up to you. I'm gonna guess at Dupont Circle they'll try to go back the way they came and head south on New Hampshire. Take Rhode Island to M Street! Haul ass to New Hampshire! Shut it down!"

"Got it!"

He tossed the mike aside scarcely in time to peel away from Dag's bumper at Scott Circle. After squealing three quarters of the way around the loop, he burst out onto Rhode Island. With horn blast-ing, Lammeck tore for M Street. The radio stayed silent; Dag was relying on Lammeck now and not his agents. At the intersection of M and Connecticut, Lammeck ran another red light, then merged onto M. Brakes smoked and a milk truck skidded sideways, but Lammeck only saw these things in his rearview mirror. He raced the quarter mile of M Street, shouting at drivers in his way, before pow-ering through a stop sign at Twenty-first. There, he took a sharp right turn at twenty miles an hour, accelerated to travel another fifty yards, then slammed on his brakes.

He rocked to a stop in New Hampshire Avenue, blocking the two left lanes. Cars shrieked, drivers lowered their windows to shout. Lammeck grabbed the mike. "Done!"

Dag made no answer.

Lammeck got out of his car. He was a big man breathing heavily, pumped from the chase. Aggravated drivers were slow to approach him. They stayed behind their open car doors issuing colorful curses. Lammeck ignored them. He strode into the right lanes headed north toward Dupont Circle. These he could not block with his car. A few autos slid past, one driver flipped him the bird. He looked up the road, feeling sweat cool on his neck.

Two cars running south were coming his way, barreling in the open, wrong lanes. Lammeck saw one green Packard, chasing a burgundy Nash.

He glanced back to his car. There wasn't time to move it into their path.

He stepped in the middle of the northbound lanes to shut off the rest of the traffic. More horns blared at him. Then he turned to the fast-approaching Nash and held up his palm.

Both engines could be heard howling from two blocks away, even over the angry honks from the blockaded cars. The Nash was going too fast to take any turn off New Hampshire. It would come through where Lammeck stood. Or it would stop.

He flexed his knees. He would not die for Roosevelt.

The Nash showed no signs of slowing. Drivers on both sides of Lammeck altered their shouts from curses to warnings. "Hey, buddy! Get out of the way!" "Hey!"

The Nash tore into the block where Lammeck stood. Dag's car was hot on its tail. A man drove the Nash. Through its windshield, Lammeck could see eight white knuckles on the steering wheel. Beside him sat a dark-haired woman.

Lammeck held his ground.

The Nash hit its brakes, tires screaming. Smoke boiled from the wheel wells. But its momentum was too great. The car skidded past, as Lammeck leaped right, out of the roadway. Landing heavily on his side, he smelled burning rubber.

Dag's Packard skidded past. The green car screeched into the cloud of the Nash's straining brakes. Twenty feet past Lammeck, both cars jumped the curbside and crashed through a row of hedges. The sound of wrecked metal and crunching glass jolted Lammeck off the ground and got him running with others to the tangled, mashed cars.

By the time he reached where they'd come to rest in the middle of a lawn, Dag was already on his feet and handling his sidearm. Blood trickled from a gash in his forehead as he waved everyone away, cursing.

"Stay back, dammit! Lammeck, keep 'em back!"

All the bystanders and Samaritans came to a stop; Dag's demeanor, his handgun, and the blood on him made him commanding. Lammeck approached the Nash ten steps behind Dag. Steam hissed from both cars, shrouding the scene. Lammeck looked about for something that had been broken off, a tree limb or shard of metal, something he could use as a weapon. He found nothing, so he undid his belt. He knew a dozen ways to defend himself, or kill, with a strap. He'd taught Dag all of them.

Dag halted several feet from the smashed driver's window of the Nash. The man behind the wheel was slumped forward, his face twisted away. The passenger beside him whimpered; she was hurt.

Dag screamed, "Get your hands where I can see them. *Now!*" Only the crying woman obeyed. The driver didn't move.

Approaching the stove-in door, Dag kept his pistol trained. He yanked the door open to the screech of bent metal.

The driver fell out, limp as a fish. Dag followed him with the nose of the pistol. The man wore a Georgetown University sweater.

Dag muttered, "What the fuck?"

Lammeck edged closer. Lying on the cold grass, with a lump on his forehead that would take a while to go down, was a boy. Eighteen, maybe, nineteen at most.

Blood oozed between the fingers of the simpering woman, from her busted nose. Dag aimed his gun straight at her shining eyes. Lammeck leaned into the open car door, his hands ready with the belt.

She wore a sweater from a local high school, Western. She shook her head, pleading with Dag not to shoot.

Dag stiffened, then lowered his gun, disgusted. Lammeck stood there with his belt dangling in his hands, as if he might spank these two children.

Dag toed the cold-cocked kid on the grass.

"Wake up, asshole," he said, prodding the boy in the ribs until he heard a moan. Lammeck threaded his belt through the loops of his trousers. He walked around the passenger side of the car. With a finger he made a spinning motion to get the terrified girl to lower her window.

"Shut up," he said before she could whine through her dripping fingers. Blood dotted her Western sweater.

"One thing," Lammeck said curtly, leaning on the windowsill. "Where did you get this car?"

The girl looked away, to where the boy struggled to sit up. Dag kneeled to put an arm under his back. The boy set a hand to the growing bump on his forehead, then fell back into the grass. Lammeck was certain Dag was asking the same question, in an even more vexed tone of voice.

"Where?" Lammeck insisted.

The girl sniveled into her palm. She squeezed shut her bleeding nostrils.

"We . . . We found the keys in it."

On the other side of the car, Dag cursed so loud it echoed. Lammeck almost laughed.

Washington, D.C.

JUDITH HAD NO TROUBLE finding him. Because he was a bully, he did not like to be defied. And because he thought his target was weak, he followed through on his threat.

When she left the Tench home, she spotted him. A parked Ford only a block away issued a wisp of smoke from a window cracked an inch. From the back of the bus riding east into the District, he was easy to keep an eye on in traffic. Once she was in her apartment, she waited to let him get into position, to freeze a bit in the falling temperatures. She put her hair up under a black watch cap, donned a dark jacket and pants and black leather gloves, then slipped out a window on the unlit side of her apartment. She found him leaning on a porch rail one block away from her front door. The dot of a cigarette betrayed him in the inky alley.

She ducked into the shadowy space below an outdoor flight of wooden steps and for three hours watched him watch her dimly lit apartment. He ran through two packs of cigarettes and stomped his feet, blowing into his thick mitts. She heard him curse to himself. When a citizen of the alley, an older black man, walked up to inquire what he was doing there, he flashed a badge and said, "Buzz off. Police business."

Four hours after nightfall, he ground out a last cigarette and turned away. Judith moved out behind him. She stayed in the shadows, closing the gap to him while he walked down the center of the alley. He was a large blunt thing among the smaller people and humble homes here. He took no precautions, never looked around him. Judith knew this sort of man, arrogant because of his strength.

She trailed him out to New York Avenue. She would not take him in the alley; the landlord's boy had already fallen there, and she was careful never to shed blood in any single location more than once. The big man strolled west, his long coat billowing at his knees, into the block between Fifth and Sixth. He headed toward the parking lot of Precinct No. 2. Judith quickened her pace, but not so much that he might hear her footfalls. The tarmac was empty and the police parking lot, with its scattering of police and private vehicles, badly lit.

He moved into the lot. She wended behind him, careful of silence and confident he was not vigilant. She closed in, four hushed steps behind. He stopped at a sedan. When he dug his right hand into his pants pocket for his keys, she struck.

The first knife she drove into the flesh beneath his right shoulder blade. She left her feet to punch the six-inch Filipino Kriss blade deep, to freeze this arm away from the pistol harnessed under his left armpit. The cop grunted and staggered, the knife in his back like a dart. He spun, awkward with the right hand trapped in his pocket. Judith dodged a wild blow from his left arm, then in the same instant popped up in front of him, her chest against his, pressing the point of another six-inch dagger into his chin.

She hissed, "Make one sound and this goes into your brain."

He attempted to lower his chin to look straight into her eyes, but found the knife preventing it. Gazing down at her past his cheeks curled in pain, he clamped his mouth shut and inhaled shakily through his nostrils, shocked and afraid.

He stumbled backward to lean against the driver's side of his car. She laid close on him, sticking the curvy Kriss blade into the stubble below his jaw, just short of drawing blood. With her left hand she dug under his armpit for the pistol, an S&W revolver. She tucked the gun into her own waistband.

He grimaced. The knife in his shoulder blade was against the car roof. He opened his lips slowly, quaking, to speak.

"T . . . take my wallet. Take what you want."

Judith said nothing.

"Look, I'm a cop. You won't get away with this."

Judith answered, "Do you know who I am?"

The man's face constricted; his breathing spurted while he tried to identify his assailant. She relaxed the knife under his chin an inch so he could lower his eyes to see her. There was no sign of recognition in his eyes. She pulled off the watch cap and let her hair tumble down.

"What the fuck?" He blinked, incredulous. "You're the fucking maid."

This was all Judith needed to hear. She was just the maid.

She stepped back to straighten her arm, to speed the stroke. She did it forehand, palm up, with a follow-through so powerful she turned her back and had to look at him over her dipped right shoulder. His mouth worked but he did not make a sound. Blood gurgled out of the long incision across his throat, bubbling on air leaking from his severed windpipe to resemble a necklace of scarlet pearls. He could only clutch at his throat with the one hand, blood dripping between his fingers. Sinking to his knees, the cop did not take his terrified eyes off her. Judith ignored his wide final stare and moved behind him to pluck the blade from his shoulder blade. She took his wallet before he fell over.

She would throw the pistol into the Potomac later. She removed the cash from the billfold and left the emptied wallet in a garbage can where it could be found.

I ask you to judge me by the enemies I have made.

—FRANKLIN D. ROOSEVELT

MARCH

CHAPTER TWELVE

March 1
Aurora Heights
Arlington, Virginia

MRS. P. ENJOYED THE ride to the Tench home. The entire trip from the Chevrolet dealership in Falls Church, the old woman giggled and slapped her own big knees and Judith's.

"You paid de man *cash*," she declared, shaking her head as though she'd witnessed a marvel. "He 'bout soiled hisself when you did that. Mm-mm-mm. Five hundred dollar."

Judith pulled to the curb beneath the great bare oak in front of the house. She set the parking brake and reached for the ignition.

"No, no, honey, not yet. Let it run one mo' minute. I can't get enough of that sound. A colored girl paid de man *cash*."

Judith sat back and let the car idle. She tapped the gas pedal once to race the engine for Mrs. P., who whooped as though she'd been tickled.

"You 'member de way he kep' callin' everything 'baby'?" Mrs. P. did an impersonation of the salesman, thickening her already husky voice: " 'This baby over here, she do this, and this baby over here, she do that. This baby really go, that baby only got ten thousand miles on her.' Baby everything."

Judith nodded.

Mrs. P. smacked Judith's knee one more time. "I'd sho' like to see the pee-pee that can make a baby *dis* big!" The old woman gaped her mouth wide in shock at her own vulgarity, hacking up a cackle that sounded like she was gagging. Judith laughed along. It felt good to have ridden that public bus into Virginia for the last time.

She cut the engine. Mrs. P. sighed. They got out of the seven-year-old used car, deep blue with cloth seats, a big motor, a radio, and a heater. Feet on the ground, they were maids again. The old woman's demeanor cooled with the first step across the lawn.

"Desiree."

"Yes, ma'am?"

"That aunt of yours died up in Boston. You say she sent you de money jus' befo' she passed?"

"Yes, ma'am."

"How come you ain't gone to no funeral?"

Judith grinned privately. This old woman was canny and watchful as any detective.

"She died last summer, Mrs. P. The money got held up by lawyers. I just got it last Friday when I went to the post office."

"Mmm-hmm."

They reached the front steps. Mrs. P. dug in her purse for the key. Mr. Tench was traveling in the South this week, inspecting naval bases in Norfolk, Charleston, and Jacksonville. His wife had left yesterday to join him, to stop in on relatives in South Carolina, then the pair would go on to Florida for another week of sun.

The old woman unlocked the door and pushed inside. She did not glance at Judith while she hung her coat on the hall tree.

"Sent you cash, did them lawyers?"

Judith moved in front of Mrs. P. to face her. She paused while the old woman hoisted a skeptical eyebrow. Judith squared her shoulders and looked down at her inquisitive American friend.

"Money order."

Mrs. P. breathed deeply, as though smelling a pie to test if it was done.

"Mmm-hmm."

She walked away, patting Judith's shoulder as she departed. She mumbled, "Girl, girl, girl," and went to the kitchen. Judith suspected that the old woman believed the car was bought for her by Mr. Tench. She did nothing to dispel that notion.

Judith worked the rest of the morning dusting and sweeping. Mrs. P. scrubbed the kitchen floor and appliances. They labored in different parts of the house, but Mrs. P. made lunch and they ate together, as they always did. The old woman made no more mention of the car, chattering instead about a new movie she'd seen, *House of Dracula,* where all three of the great monsters—Dracula, Wolf Man, *and* Frankenstein—show up at the same time.

After lunch, Judith did the last of her chores distractedly. The mail was expected by one o'clock. Today, for an unknown reason, the postman came late, just as the several clocks in the house began their quiet grindings that foretold the chiming for two o'clock. As the bells tolled, the mail slot creaked open and closed. A handful of letters tumbled to the hall floor.

Judith put down her dust rag. She walked into the kitchen to find Mrs. P., to tell her good-bye, and found her at the sink. She kissed the old lady on the cheek. Mrs. P. pretended to snub the buss at first, but let it land.

"You know what you doin'," the woman huffed and went back to wringing a dishcloth. During their first days of working together in this household, Mrs. P. had never asked why Judith left promptly each day at two. At the beginning of February she had not inquired why Judith stopped that practice, and did not ask yesterday why it had resumed. Judith assumed Mrs. P. came up with her own reasons, the way the old lady did for everything about Desiree that did not fit. Today, Mrs. P. clucked her tongue, wagged her old head, and disapproved quietly of one more immoral and exciting thing Desiree must be doing.

Judith went to the hall. Snatching her coat and handbag off the tree, she bent for the day's mail. Rifling through it, she found what she was looking for. She stuffed one envelope in her pocket. The rest of the Tench mail she stacked neatly on the hall table. Then she left.

Washington, D.C.

MRS. BEACH PEERED OVER her glasses at Lammeck. "Good afternoon, Hardy. Where's Laurel?"

Lammeck eased the door shut. He pointed a finger like a little pistol. "Nice, Mrs. Beach. Very funny."

She blinked at him, expressionless. "I'm sorry you think so. It was intended as withering sarcasm."

"I've fallen out of favor that fast, have I?"

"We're result-based around here, Doctor. Yesterday's results dictate today's opinion. The chief is expecting you."

She looked away and Lammeck was dismissed inward. He opened the door to Reilly's office. The chief stood when Lammeck stepped inside.

"Professor."

"Chief. Look, about yesterday—"

Reilly waved a hand and smiled. "She give it to you bad?"

"Let's just say she was waiting for me."

"I apologize. Mrs. Beach is a luxury for me. I get to be the good cop. Anyway, what happened? Sit."

Lammeck took a leather chair and Reilly settled his thick frame behind his desk.

"She set us up. She knew we were watching for her. Those kids found the car at Thirty-fifth and R with the keys in the ignition and a window down. They took a joyride. The boy's a sophomore at Georgetown. The girl's a senior at Western High. That's it."

"Except for the part where you blew Dag's surveillance. Now I've got one wrecked car, one dented car, and a whole handful of citizen and D.C. cops' complaints. Anything I missed?"

Lammeck shrugged, wondering what had happened to Reilly's role as the good cop. But he wasn't in the mood to be stuffed into Reilly's doghouse. Lammeck was, after all, a private citizen. He glared straight back at Reilly.

The chief asked, "How did Judith know?"

Lammeck was ready. It was one of the two reasons he made this appointment with Reilly. First, to tell him:

"It was your fault."

Reilly eyed Lammeck hard, then leaned forward, elbows on his desk. Lammeck continued before the chief could rebut.

"You increased the security around the White House. If you'd asked me, and you didn't, I would have tried to stop you. Judith saw that. Hell, anyone walking past on the sidewalk could see it. The sudden extra guards tipped her off that something was different. She probably tried to make contact with her connection in Newburyport to check it out and came up empty. So she went through the same logic I did and figured out the car she was driving was hot. Then she dumped it and made a monkey out of me, fair enough. My guess is she bought another. And she's too smart to have bought it anywhere close by. Out in Virginia or Maryland, for cash, I'll bet. We'll never trace it. That's the bad news."

"So there's good news?"

"What happened tells me that after a lot of trouble on my part, she and I are finally thinking alike."

Reilly eased off his elbows. He leaned back in his chair, tapping fingers on his blotter.

"What was I supposed to do, Professor? Hang the President out to dry? Not after you convinced me that there's a very gifted and extremely dedicated level-six killer in town. Exactly what steps should I take? Now that I *am* asking you."

Lammeck inclined his head in a show of appreciation, then launched ahead.

"I've told Dag a hundred times, Chief, but it's not sinking in. Judith's not going to come from a direction where you can spot her. You won't catch this woman sneaking over the White House lawn or setting up a rifle in a window somewhere. She's going to come out of a shadow, from some corner you've overlooked. She's going to be a guest of one of Roosevelt's friends or some big shot at a dinner, at a birthday party or a wake, some kind of occasion where you think you've got every angle covered. She'll be a cook or a maid, or a socialite, or anything in between. But I guarantee you that another hundred agents around the White House won't save the President."

Reilly listened and never stopped his finger tapping.

The chief asked, "So what do we do? Just wait on her?"

"Keep your guard up. Make sure there's no new hires of domestic help in the White House; shut Judith completely down along those lines. Double background checks on every hotel or public location the President visits. Keep the number of guests he entertains to a minimum."

"And what else?"

"I assume you don't want me taking part in any more car chases."

"You assume correctly."

"I'm going to keep trying to anticipate her. For the first time in two months, I'm beginning to sense I'm right behind her. Every time we close off another avenue, it limits her choices, and I get that much closer."

Reilly finally stopped tapping.

"Professor, I'll keep my peace on just how peculiar it is that you can think like a female Persian assassin. Or that you spend all night and day dreaming up ways to murder my president. That being said, how can I help you?"

This was the second reason Lammeck had set up today's appointment.

"I need an open invitation to every embassy party, State Department reception, gala, whatever, that goes on in the District. I want a list of functions all the way down to cocktail parties, weddings, and christenings thrown by senators, congressmen, lobbyists, Cabinet members, and White House staff."

"You getting bored in Washington, Professor?"

Lammeck cleared his throat. "You and Mrs. Beach have the same sense of humor, did you know that, Chief? It's belittling and funny at the same time. It's enough that I put up with Dag's perpetual bad mood. But I'd appreciate it if when I visit this office you and your attack dog out there spare me your wit and do what I ask. I'm not here to make friends or be your pincushion. Understood?"

"Loud and clear, Professor. We work hard around here and maybe we get a bit punchy. I apologize for myself and I will so inform my Doberman. As for Dag, I can't help you with him. You're on your own there. What else?"

"I need you to vet every one of those functions I mentioned. No one attends without a written invitation off a prepared guest list. Anyone who brings a female guest who's not a family member has to personally vouch for that guest, and I want names and addresses for every one of them."

Reilly gave Lammeck an indulgent smile. He shook his head.

"That's a big job, Professor, and, frankly a little naïve of you. With the war winding down and the end of blackouts last year, Washington's throwing more parties than Versailles. Everyone from ambassadors to senators is hosting a shindig to jockey for influence after the peace. We've got Cave Dweller old-money socialite parties all the way to the Cuban embassy and the aluminum lobby. Remember, Washington's the only major capital in the world that's not occupied or close to the front lines. So every dethroned king and queen and exiled leader in the world is here. And I got to tell you, Professor, the local hostesses are falling on them like junkyard dogs on a soup bone. I can't police them all or keep track of who's attending what. I don't have the manpower to do it."

"I can go over to the FBI and ask Director Hoover."

"You're playing hardball."

"Like you said, he's your president."

"I still can't do it. Neither can Hoover."

"Listen, Chief. I'm not trying to catch her at these parties. I want her to catch us."

Reilly looked confounded.

Lammeck leaned forward, pressing his case: "Just give me enough agents to be a visible presence, to get people noticing at these functions that something's up. I need her to smell a rat. Now that you've let the cat out of the bag, I need her to know we're right on her ass. She won't know how many social events we're watching, but she will sniff that we're on the prowl for her in that arena and that'll spook her away. I want to herd her down to the fewest number of possibilities. Take me at my word, Chief. This woman has the ability and the cunning to find a way in. I need to slam as many doors in her face as I can. That's the only way I can catch her."

Reilly resumed his Irish smile.

"I'm sure you meant *we*, Professor."

Lammeck stood, finished. Reilly kept his seat.

"I'll have Secret Service credentials sent to your hotel," the chief said. "Flash that paperwork at any embassy or office in D.C. and you're in the door. You have any trouble, you call Mrs. Beach. She'll take care of it."

Lammeck knew this to be true.

"Thank you, Chief. Sorry about that bout of bad attitude there."

"No problem, Professor. I look at it like this: I'm sure you really are thinking like our gal assassin. And I'm hoping she doesn't like me very much, either." Reilly changed his mind about sitting and stood for Lammeck. "Now get out of my office and go find her, so she can tell me that herself."

March 3
Washington, D.C.

"STAND STILL."

"It's too tight."

Dag fidgeted like a boy in his First Communion suit. Lammeck struggled to button the starched white shirt at Dag's neck.

"If you'd gone to pick up your own tux, you could've had it fitted. I had to guess your size, so you take what you get."

Lammeck stood back, the button secured. He watched Dag manhandle the clip-on bow tie. Lammeck took a seat on the edge of his hotel room bed. The mattress was covered with the files and party schedules Mrs. Beach had sent over for this week's events.

"You've never worn a tux before, have you?"

"Why would I? Pansy clothes."

"Well, stick a shiv in your pocket and you'll feel more comfortable."

"I might." Dag finished and presented himself stiffly for inspection. Lammeck tucked and tugged a few items into line. Dag would pass, but, Lammeck wondered, for how long? He expected Dag's clothes to wilt and the cummerbund to pop at any moment.

"Let's get you to the party before you go back to being a pumpkin."

Dag said nothing in the Blackstone Hotel elevator, but busied himself digging fingers around the tux, prying it loose from his frame here and there. Climbing into Dag's replacement government car in the lot, Lammeck noted how it seemed Dag had already driven this vehicle hard. Pages of the *Post*, paper coffee cups, coins, and emptied Goody's Headache Powder packets spoiled the floorboards. Lammeck sighed and shot his cuffs.

On the drive, Dag finally asked, "Okay, walk me through this."

"What do you know?"

"All I got was a call from Reilly telling me to put on a monkey suit and go with you to the Luxembourg embassy instead of staying out on the street looking for her. Why I should do this, I can't fucking fathom. But I'm sure you have a reason, Professor. Good or bad, you've always got a reason."

Lammeck gazed at Dag and admired him for a moment. This bony, jangly man had killed three German guards in the forests of France to escape. Dag was a hard pill to swallow, but he was always bold, and though the agent lacked subtlety he was dutiful and stubbornly loyal. Dag was capable of killing, he was willing to die, and this made him heroic.

"There's only two types of people who get in to see FDR. The great and the small. The people who serve and those who get served. I think Judith is working both angles. Tonight, we're working one side of that."

"You think she's honey-trapping some ambassador or something?"

"I have no idea. But I want Judith to see Secret Service agents every time she turns around. I want to funnel her down to the path of least resistance. That's where we'll find her."

"And exactly where will that be?"

"I can't begin to guess."

Dag shoehorned an aggravated finger into his tight shirt collar.

"You have no goddam idea what you're doing, do you, Professor? You haven't from the start."

Lammeck grinned. Surprisingly, Dag grinned back.

At the embassy, the agent would not give the keys to the teenage valet for parking, but put the car right in front of the building and left it, flashing his credentials.

"Uh-uh," he said to Lammeck. "No teenage kid is getting my keys. Not after the other day."

The two ascended the steps to the Luxembourg embassy with a

formal, perfumed crowd on all sides. Though Luxembourg was still occupied by the Germans, the free Dutch maintained this embassy as well as their own with income from their colonies. Starting last August when Paris was liberated, the French embassy had returned to full swing. The Russian embassy celebrated a new victory against the Nazis every week. The British delegation mounted lavish events to compete in the last frontier of dominance left to them in Washington, the social network. The many Latin American embassies, roundly ignored before the war, now assumed the mantle of keeping Washington amused in the stead of so many European embassies who'd had their lights put out. Lammeck, on the steps of his first embassy reception, had no notion of the magnitude of Washington's drive to socialize with itself.

Lammeck and Dag were met at the door by a handsome young embassy functionary who took only a passing interest in invitations. The young man raised his eyebrows at Dag's Secret Service badge, then directed them to a sign-in book. Inside, diplomats and their belles danced, gaggled and gossiped, swapped emptied champagne flutes for full, ate and laughed with heart. Lammeck's spirits, already worried, sank. Reilly was right. There was absolutely no way to police this. And there were two other large embassy events plus a dozen cocktail parties scheduled within five blocks elsewhere on Mass. Ave. and Sixteenth Street, just on this one Saturday evening. Other agents were covering those functions, but the task was gargantuan. In this silken world, Judith could be anywhere.

"Jesus," Dag breathed, entering the great hall. Looking at the gowned and coiffed women, Dag stopped pulling at his tux and began to preen. He smoothed a palm over his hair.

"Dag, listen," Lammeck called over the din of a five-piece jazz band and international nattering. "There's maybe four hundred people here..."

Dag's eyes stayed on the dancing, gabbing crowd, an attractive bevy.

"Dag!"

The agent's head snapped to Lammeck. "Alright, alright."

"There's four hundred people in this place, and maybe a dozen of them have any shot at ever getting to Roosevelt. I'm going to look over the guest register and see who's here. Congressmen, presidential staff, celebrities, ambassadors, anyone who jumps out at me. You find the host and flash your badge. Get in some conversations, let the word out that the Secret Service is around. And please, I beg you, if you can't be pleasant, be polite."

Dag spit in both palms and rubbed them together, as if he were about to grab an ax handle.

"You betcha, Professor. I'm on it. Polite." Dag laughed, walking off. "Sure."

March 8
Washington, D.C.

JUDITH CLOSED THE LITTLE post office box door.

At the counter, she canceled the box. This morning she wore her government girl clothes, a cornflower blue wool skirt with matching jacket and white blouse. A March of Dimes pin was attached to her lapel above a blue silk carnation. On other days she'd come in dressed in her maid uniform. The old black mailman behind the counter smiled as he handled the paperwork. He asked if she was moving away. Judith said probably. He said he would miss seeing her. "I can't figure you out, girl."

"If you did, I'd have to marry you or kill you," Judith replied pleasantly.

The geezer cackled. "Maybe we could do both. Just kill me slow-like."

She winked.

The D.C. mornings had finally brightened and warmed. Awaking crocuses and daffodils lent some color to the long-sullen earth.

Judith did not like the chilly, enclosing dawns of the mid-Atlantic winter; the concrete and marble of this city cosseted the cold deep into the day. She missed the distant African sierras and the warmth of her own home.

Judith walked to her car in the post office lot. She drove five blocks west and quickly found a parking spot on Fifteenth, with a clear view of the White House's east and south gates. She left the car to walk for a newspaper and coffee.

Judith would not go to work at either of the Tench households today. The unhappy couple was still out of town and would not be back until the middle of the month. With a *Post* folded under her arm and a coffee heating her palm, she strode one circuit around the White House, peering at the Secret Service traipsing the greening grounds, sweeping it with dogs and automatic rifles. Clearly, Roosevelt was back in his fortress.

Something had changed in this operation. Someone was forcing her hand.

No mail had come from Newburyport in seventeen days.

She walked away from the White House, east down Pennsylvania Avenue. Her steps were slow, dodging through the morning cascade of workers headed to their desks in the Departments of Commerce, General Accounting, Internal Revenue, Justice, Trade, all aligned side by side on the avenue. Over the heads of the throngs on the sidewalk with her, the U.S. Capitol filled the horizon of the broad boulevard, like a giant at the other end of a seesaw. Judith was not bothered by the magnitude of America and its national city, its spires and columns, traffic, hordes of workers, monuments, or all the Secret Service men panning for her. She was not in a battle with them for Roosevelt's life. Someone hoping to go unnoticed, just like her, opposed her.

In this kind of one-on-one combat, the first rule was to find the weapon. Ignore all but the weapon.

She guessed who it had to be: the expert, the one the Secret Service had brought in. He was the large, handsome man who'd stood with the rumpled agent at the inauguration. In several coded letters, the old woman in Newburyport had written Judith as much as she could find out about him, before she'd fallen silent two and a half weeks ago. Before the security around the President had increased a hundred percent.

On the eastern side of the Capitol stood the Library of Congress. Inside the caverns of shelves and great labyrinth of desks and leather chairs, it was a simple matter to ask for and receive the doctoral dissertation of Mikhal Lammeck.

DUSK GATHERED ON JUDITH waiting in her Chevrolet. Again, the President did not venture from his compound for one of his afternoon drives. Since returning nine days ago from the Crimea, Roosevelt had only set foot off the White House grounds for the funeral of his old friend Pa Watson, an address to Congress on the following day, and a weekend train trip from which he'd returned last night. In the face of so little exposure, Judith maintained the patience of a hunter. She knew the man would emerge at some point, would lead her somewhere, and that would be the key. Or she would finally find a way in to him. Either way, this strategy— preparing, waiting, quickly exploiting—had always worked for her. It would again.

But tonight, on watch in her car, Judith noted an unfamiliar pang in her gut. The sensation was not fear, but may have been the kernel of it. She sat with it, tried to taste it. Concern, yes, and a bit of curiosity. Never before in her career had anyone seen her coming. Certainly, she had never been the hunted.

Through the morning and afternoon in that giant library, Judith had read many of Lammeck's papers. He was clearly an expert in the history of her craft. He was also, according to a June 1942 article in the *New York Times,* a professor at St. Andrews University. Now he was here, in Washington, dredged up by the Secret Service.

His very specialized body of work and his otherwise unexplained presence, first in Newburyport, now here in Washington, convinced Judith that he was the mastermind behind the government's campaign to track her down.

Good for the professor, she thought; some hands-on experience.

She admired his scholarship, an analysis of the effects of political murders across the recorded span of mankind. At the heart of all his commentary, Lammeck had staked out a wonderful position, made all the more so because Judith shared it.

According to Lammeck's doctoral dissertation from the University of Rhode Island, the world had seen two types of assassinations: those that stabilized, and those that destabilized, history. Lammeck deemed that a killing either served history's purposes by helping along the greater imperatives of the time and place, or it upset history's applecart. Only with the clarities of time and distance did each assassination's impact—or lack of it—became clear to the historian's eye.

Interestingly, this professor hypothesized that, across millennia, history herself, by accident or design, reacted in marvelous ways to the killings. History paved the way for those murders she approved of. To illustrate, Lammeck made much use of ancient Rome, Europe's royal houses, and Judith's own bloody Middle East. History, he claimed, often left a door unlocked, a guard asleep, a horse hobbled, a thick fog for a wrong turn. In most of these cases, the leaders and events that ensued after a political murder only hurried along some political inevitability that history had preordained. For the others—the ones Lammeck termed the "wild cards," those who thought they could alter history with a bullet, a blade, or a few deadly drops—their out-of-the-blue killings seemed to have even less effect. History may have been sent wobbling, but she always righted herself in time to disavow the murders, reducing them to violent orphans. The killers themselves were usually tripped up by the same sort of strange coincidences, again showing history's intervening hand. Those unwanted and uncalculated assassins were dealt with swiftly and just as quickly forgotten. That is, until Professor Lammeck rediscovered them, and preserved them.

Lammeck's conclusion: History was not easily bumped from her course.

Judith had benefited many times from happenstance: the door left ajar, the drunken secret, the snoozing dog. History favored Judith. That was why she knew she would kill Roosevelt.

She sensed that the formidable professor thought she could do it, too.

In her car, Judith waited. She spent the hours listening to her second-favorite radio station, the more talkative WMAL. She learned that last week Hitler had ordered the destruction of all Germany, every store, factory, road, and electric wire, claiming his nation was unworthy of surviving if it could not win this war. At Hitler's eastern threshold, the Russians were amassing three huge armies on the Oder River, the Führer's boundary with Poland. To Hitler's west, the American army gathered along the Rhine. A Lockheed Constellation had set a speed record for the route between New York and Paris. The favorite to win the Oscar next week for Best Motion Picture was *The Lost Weekend,* and the movie's star, Ray Milland, was a shoo-in for Best Actor. Joan Crawford was the front-runner as Best Actress for *Mildred Pierce.*

Sunset fell on Judith tapping her foot to "Swinging on a Star" by Bing Crosby.

She started the car and joined the exodus of workers, many of them in uniform, wheeling into the streets. Roosevelt would not appear today. And even if he did at this late hour, Judith's interest lay elsewhere.

She drove to the hotel she'd followed Mikhal Lammeck to, the Blackstone, seven weeks ago, after the inauguration. She bundled up in her brown coat and a wool blanket against the dropping temperature, eating grapes from a paper sack, wondering if he was still checked in at this address just three blocks north of the White

House. She didn't wait long for her answer: With the last sun giving over to street lamps, Lammeck emerged, alone.

The professor was decked out in a tuxedo and overcoat. Judith wondered what he would do if he knew she was watching. He was a big, bearish man in his beard, and the bow tie and ruffled shirt tamed him only a little. He moved well, sliding into his government Chevy.

Judith followed the Chevy out of the parking lot. Because of the tuxedo and the time of his departure, she guessed where Lammeck was headed, and he proved her right.

Massachusetts Avenue. Embassy Row.

She did not follow him more. There was no need for that tonight. But the professor was closing the gap.

MRS. P. CAME HOME to find Judith in her rocker, wrapped in the quilt the woman had given her. Judith rose to give the old maid her place. Mrs. P. waved her back into the seat.

"I be out in a minute. Set still."

Judith rocked, gazing over rooftops at the Capitol dome, the statue of Freedom capping it. City lights knocked out the stars and the sky stretched blank.

Mrs. P. came out on the porch in slippers and a housecoat. She'd draped a pink blanket over her shoulders. Judith watched her arrange herself on the steps. Mrs. P. produced her tobacco pipe and lit up. Judith breathed in secondhand smoke and craved some tobacco, or even some of her own hashish, but rejected the idea.

The old woman did not speak until she'd taken several noisy draws on her corncob. She contemplated the same sky as Judith in silence. Judith waited.

At last, Mrs. P. said, "You know, I had me a husband once."

"No, I didn't know. Did you have children?"

"Yep. Got two. They long growed up. The girl's in Kansas City. The boy, I don' know."

Judith rocked, and the small squeals from the chair's joints filled the silence. The mouth of the pipe glowed red in Mrs. P.'s grip.

"You got you a man, Desiree?"

Judith squelched her laughter.

"I don't know. Maybe."

The old maid sucked on her pipe and studied the sky. No one trod the alley. A record played somewhere in the building, a ballad by the colored American jazz singer Billie Holiday.

"You ain't gon' tell me 'bout that Mr. Tench. I don' wanna know 'bout him and you."

"No, ma'am. I'm finished with him. Someone else."

"That's good. You don' work for this man, too, do you?"

"No, ma'am."

"Y'all fuckin'?"

Judith suppressed another chuckle. "No, ma'am."

"Good. Get to know each other fust."

Judith rocked, thinking of something to say.

"We've started going to parties."

"That's nice. Showin' you off."

"I think he's trying real hard to get to know me."

Mrs. P. drew deep on the corncob and released a thoughtful cloud. "You gettin' to know him?"

"I'm just starting to. He's very impressive. Very smart. A little scary, maybe."

"Don' know if that's good, a woman scared o' her man. I was scared o' my Earl." Mrs. P. grinned. "Turned out I was right, too. Man got hisself throwed in jail. Almost killed a fella in a fight."

"Over what?"

"Over me."

Mrs. P. raised her pipe to the evening, some tribute. Or, Judith thought, an apology.

She turned in the darkness to face Judith. "He a he'p to you? Some men, they jus' want a woman to be good to them and don' do the return. You don' want no man like that. And that's most of 'em."

"Yes, ma'am. He's a help. He makes me be better. I have to be at my best around him."

Mrs. P. liked this. She tried to speak too soon after a puff and coughed out her first few words. "That sound good. You do that for him?"

"Oh, yes, ma'am. I'm sure I do."

"Now ain't that somethin' for you, Desiree. Maybe get you off dis here porch, get you goin' how you ought to be. You ain't meant to be cleanin' Miz Tench's house, girl, we both know that. So you go on with yo'self. Maybe you bring your man 'round sometime. Lemme meet him."

"I don't know, Mrs. P. I don't think that's going to happen."

The old woman stiffened. She bounced on her big rear end and grabbed at the ends of her pink blanket to keep it from falling off her.

"Oh, I don' like that at all. Mm-mm, no ma'am, a man you can't bring around to yo' friends. A man you can't show where you live. No, Desiree, that ain't right. You got to have a man you can be yo'self with. You special, honey, with all your plottin' and goin's-on. You got you a head on your shoulders, honey girl. You some kind of different, and a man got to be able to see that no matter *where* you livin' an' *what* you doin'." Mrs. P. waved the smoking pipe to make her point. "Naw, girl, you did *not* tell me your man can't meet me. Mm-mm."

Judith waited. Mrs. P. was not done.

"See, I knew the minute you started telling me about this fella. He makin' you be better, like you ain't good enough as you is. See, this the kind o' nonsense gon' hold you *back*. I had me a man like that. I walked out on Earl's bad ass, and he come after me and got hisself throwed in jail for it. That's right. Don' make no never-mind where I sit on no damn *bus*. Ain't no man gon' own me, tell me he can't come to my home and meet my friends. You got to get rid of a man like that. You got to toss him off like *chains,* girl."

Mrs. P. snapped her fingers. Like that, she was finished and resumed a quiet and intent sucking on her corncob.

Judith rocked again and considered. The two women sat while Billie Holiday sang another sorry tune behind the building's tar-paper walls. A cluster of kids came down the alley. Mrs. P. called, "Hello, chi'rrun." Judith did not speak.

After they'd passed, she said quietly, "I apologize, Mrs. P. I didn't mean to imply anything by what I said."

The old maid kept looking off. "That's alright. You go on and do what you gon' do."

Judith let a minute settle, then rose from the rocker. She stood behind the old woman and laid a hand to her shoulder.

"Take your chair. I'm going inside. Thank you."

Mrs. P. hesitated, then set her own calloused hand on top of Judith's. She rose and with a long sigh settled in her rocker.

"Can I drive you to work in the morning?" Judith asked, standing in the shadows of the porch. "So you don't have to ride the bus?"

Mrs. P. grinned. "That be nice, Desiree. Thank you."

Judith made a move as if to go inside. Then she said, "Oh, and I'd like the keys to the Tenches' house, and the one in Georgetown, too. I've got some time tomorrow, and I want to finish up the silver before they get back."

"Alright."

"And I'll pick up the mail again. It's probably all over the floor."

"You know it is."

"Mrs. P.?"

"Girl, go inside. You don' got to say no more. We straight."

"I just wanted to tell you one more thing."

"What?"

"You're right. He's holding me back."

The old woman started up the rocker, satisfied.

"Well, then," she said, "you know what you got to do."

CHAPTER THIRTEEN

March 9
Washington, D.C.

LAMMECK AWOKE EARLY, SMELLING of cigarette smoke. It was a pub reek, beer and ashes, but without the banging head. Before rising from his pillow, Lammeck sniffed his armpits. A shower was in order.

In the bath he turned on the water and brushed his teeth while steam warmed the tiles. With a measure of disapproval, he checked himself in the mirror. His cheeks were chubby; his bare belly filled both pinching hands. Today was the two-month anniversary of his arrival in Washington, D.C. Over that time, he'd not broken a sweat once. He'd spent all his time in cars and planes, on sidewalks, in chairs. He missed his studies, his students and weapons, his research and manuscript.

He stepped into the shower, considering his latest strategy. Over the past week, he'd been to twenty-six receptions and cocktail parties. At every one, he flashed his Secret Service letterhead, sent Dag into the fancy crowd like a hound into the brush, and mounted his most suspicious, scrutinizing face, as though he knew what he was looking for. Instead of making smart chat and finding his duty pleasant, he alienated everyone he talked with. It couldn't be helped: His purpose was to find out if they belonged at that shindig, and if they did, who was their guest? Lammeck intended to set tongues wagging, hoping a tendril would reach Judith's hidey-hole and she would back away or make some next, glaring move. Along Mass. Ave., he was beginning to be recognized as an unwanted omen at the door, like a crow at a wedding.

Soaping up, Lammeck grabbed his lapping waist again and lifted. He shook his head and spat into the tub.

"I can't keep this up."

And why should he, he wondered? For Roosevelt? A president, judging from the newspapers, half of America couldn't tolerate? Who for four years sat on his country's hands and let Germany terrorize Europe at will, at a cost that no one will ever reckon? Who now in his fourth term seemed too tired even to govern, now that he'd made himself king? Lammeck thought again of Gabčik and Kubiš, and grew disgruntled that since his arrival in America his two dead heroes had barely come to mind. He could not let himself forget them; that would be like forgetting your way in a forest. The U.S. was that forest, and Lammeck realized that he'd gotten lost.

And why should he continue to protect the prerogative of the Secret Service in this case? Why not bring in the FBI? Hoover had far more manpower; the FBI was a fearsome investigative agency. Why should Lammeck be dragged into Reilly's turf war? What had Reilly, Dag, and Mrs. Beach done for him except dragoon him into their witch hunt, away from his real work in Scotland? Even if he did manage somehow to stop Judith, there would never be an official word said about it. A massive cover-up would blanket the whole affair; Roosevelt himself might never know about it. America's thanks would come in the shape of a handshake from Reilly and a ticket back to Scotland. Maybe someone years later would discover a secret file and write about it.

"A little while longer," he grumbled into the shower spray. After that, he decided, he would skip the handshake and just take the ticket home. Then they could send Hoover after Judith. Or maybe Mrs. Beach.

Lammeck snorted at the image of the two women tangling, and in his imagination rooted for the assassin.

He stepped out of the shower to towel off.

And if we do find her? Will there be a chance to talk?

No. Dag will kill her.

Lammeck strode out of the bath. Naked, he began to conjure a conversation with Judith. Where would he start? What would the encounter be like? He saw himself beside her, unconcerned with what she looked like for the purpose of his daydream. It would be like talking to John Wilkes Booth, Cesare Borgia, or Brutus. He would ask . . .

He glanced at the clock—7:22 A.M. An envelope had been pushed under his door.

He tucked the towel around his waist and snagged the envelope. It was addressed in florid handwriting to Dr. Mikhal Lammeck, Room 540.

He tore across the envelope. Into his hand slipped an engraved invitation. At the top of the card, in embossed stamp, was a gold-foiled coat of arms. The paper was thick and ivory-colored, inviting the bearer to a reception at the Peruvian embassy tonight at 7 P.M.

Lammeck dressed impatiently. The elevator operator lowered him to the Blackstone lobby. Only a few people lingered there in leather chairs, occupied with cigarettes and the spread wings of morning papers. Lammeck approached the desk clerk.

The wan, tired man with a pocked face looked up. "Good morning, Dr. Lammeck."

"Jock. Did you just have this envelope sent up to my room?"

"Yes, sir. I'm sorry if we woke you."

"No, it's not that. Do you remember who gave this to you?"

"Yes, sir, of course. About ten after the hour this morning, it was dropped off here by a Negro woman."

"What did she look like, Jock? This is very important."

The morning clerk did not hesitate.

"Oh, I saw her real good. I guess she was about this tall . . ." The clerk held a flat hand out just below the level of his own shoulders, at perhaps a height of five two or three. "She was pretty dark. Looked to be, I don't know, maybe sixty something. Older, maybe. Tough to tell with those old colored ladies sometimes. And she was thick. Not fat like some, but heavyset. You know. She was wearing a kind of raggedy overcoat . . ."

"Did she say anything?"

"No, sir. Just tossed that envelope on the counter and walked off."

"Did you see where she went? Did she get into a car?"

"Don't know, Doc. I wasn't paying that much attention. I been on the midnight shift . . ."

Lammeck thanked the clerk and walked back to the elevator.

The woman Jock described couldn't have been Judith. Five foot two, squat, elderly? The beautiful, looping handwriting on the envelope probably did not belong to the woman who'd delivered it.

Who sent the invitation? Reilly? Mrs. Beach? Would either have used a little old black woman as a courier? Dag? Who else knew or cared where Lammeck was staying?

If it came from Judith, then she was very close. She knew his hotel, and she knew where he'd been searching for her. And if she knew these things, what else did she know?

Lammeck returned to his room and sat on the bed. He considered calling Dag to tell him what had happened. He set his mind loose down the road of what would happen next.

Dag would insist they both go to the Peruvian embassy tonight, and that they go in force, with armed agents manning every way in and out. If this was Judith, they'd trap her, nab her, and call it a day.

But what if she smelled too big a rat—Dag and his rigid, surreptitious, dangerous bunch—and didn't show?

If she meant to kill him, why invite him to a public place like an embassy ball? She knew the Blackstone, clearly she was following him. She could take him out a million other times and places that carried far less risk of exposure, when he wasn't expecting her, when there wasn't the potential of a Secret Service dragnet around him. The only smart reason—and she was extremely smart—for arranging a meeting like this was to talk. Did Judith want to turn herself in? Unlikely. Why did she need Lammeck? What did she want?

And suppose this envelope didn't come from Judith at all. What if it was just what it looked like, an invitation offered by some Peruvian diplomat, or even a random woman—or man—who'd taken enough interest in Lammeck to track down his hotel and chance a rendezvous? Lammeck concocted several innocent reasons for this invitation, a few of them creepy but none of them Judith. If one of those scenarios held true, he would lose more credibility with Dag and Reilly than he could ever recover. He might get his wish and be sent packing for home. That would be a retreat at a time and circumstance not of his choosing. Lammeck hadn't brought the hunt all the way from Massachusetts to be spanked by Mrs. Beach and shipped back to Scotland with his tail tucked between his legs. No.

He would go to the Peruvian embassy tonight. He'd be careful, quiet, and watch his own back. But there was no choice but to go alone.

AT THE DOOR, LAMMECK presented only the invitation. The card was taken from him by a woman in the foyer with Asian eyes and warm hands who dropped it into a decorative carved box. He said his name was Dr. Lammeck, and this satisfied her. Lammeck could tell she had no notion of security; she was just processing people into the event with her smile and lovely skin.

He signed the guest book and scanned the preceding page. Gene

Tierney, Oleg Cassini, Mrs. Nelson Rockefeller; senators and society names filled the spaces ahead of his. In a twinge of vanity he scribbled "Ph.D." behind his name.

Moving inside, Lammeck was slowed in a reception line. His nerves tingled, on edge in a fusion of worry and excitement, what he imagined it felt like to be on the verge of combat. But he was not a soldier like Dag; he was a teacher. Over the past five years, his war service had been spent in forests and darkness training young men to lay mines and spigot mortars, to shoot with silenced rifles, and to set explosives for sabotage. Nothing he'd learned or taught in that time would help him right now. He was accustomed to wearing tweeds or fatigues, not a tux; his talents had been honed only for classrooms and the woods. The packed embassy was nothing like his preferred terrain. This was a bash, public, perfumed, and raucous. Here the objectives moved, smoked, gossiped, and flirted. Every person and thing was exposed, lit and loud, which meant nothing stood out. Here, Lammeck had no skill or sense he could trust.

At the head of the reception line, he shook hands with the Peruvian ambassador. The man was a head shorter than Lammeck, nodding with vigor to every guest. Next was the ambassador's wife, who bowed Lammeck onward. He visualized Judith in line, returning this little Peruvian woman's bow. Judith would walk into the room tonight just as he did, unescorted. She would look around, for the best positions, for the exits, for adversaries. And for him.

Lammeck felt his heartbeat quicken. He wiped his palms on his jacket. He shot his cuffs to clear his sleeves, fingered his bow tie, and advanced into the throng.

There had to be at least five hundred crammed into this room. She was here. He was sure of it, and instantly was just as certain that he was nervous, mistaken and misled. She was not here. Lammeck's stomach churned with embarrassment that he was being hoodwinked again.

He walked to the food table, jumpy, scrutinizing every woman he passed or who sidled by and looked up at him. He measured them for the attributes he figured Judith must have: dark hair, height, muscle. In return he got smiles or upturned noses. Some of the men escorting the women bounced territorial looks off him. If Dag were at his back, the two of them could challenge the room. The thought of Dag made Lammeck once again question the wisdom of strolling in here without him.

The banquet table featured the usual selections of war-rationed foods, mostly chicken, though all were garnished and presented with a tropical theme in what Lammeck supposed was the Peruvian manner. The open bars did a sprightly business, and butlers slalomed through the crowd bearing trays of champagne flutes. Lammeck moved carefully, swinging his shoulders to avoid collisions with well-heeled guests bearing loaded plates or overfull highballs. He paid attention only to the women, pausing to listen above the music and examine them, appearing to them, he was certain, like a gigolo on the make. For the most part, he was ignored. This suited him, and wounded him, too. He felt even more intent and out of place. He hovered and eavesdropped: With the designer Oleg Cassini somewhere in attendance, much of the conversation concerned fashion. The women of Washington were tired of wearing separates, that conservative theme of the war years intended to give the impression of owning more outfits. They wanted longer hemlines. And fuller skirts. Now that Paris had been liberated for six months, the big dress houses were back in business. A few women at the reception were actually wearing designs by Balenciaga or Fath, and someone claimed she'd spotted a Schiaparelli. Lammeck plucked a champagne flute from a fleeting tray. The band struck up a noisy medley of Glenn Miller tunes.

Lammeck tipped the champagne and drained it. He stood still. Looking for Judith here was foolish. If the invitation did in fact come from her, she surely wouldn't allow herself to be spotted in this crowd; she was far too talented for that. No, clearly it had fallen to him to be the one located. That, by contrast, was going to be easy. Lammeck's height and girth, planted in the center of the ballroom floor, created a new traffic pattern of dancers and shifting cliques. He was larger than any man he could see in the room. If Judith was searching for him, here he was.

Lammeck drank another glass of champagne. He exchanged glances with two dozen women, all dressed well, a few of them wearing the lengthy French outfits the other women coveted. He believed he might have caught sight of the elusive Schiaparelli. One woman, a tall brunette wearing tortoiseshell glasses, circled past twice. On her third circuit, she stopped in front of Lammeck holding two champagne glasses.

"Freshen you up?" she asked.

Lammeck accepted the drink, placing his empty glass on another of the silver trays that bobbed through the crowd.

The woman wore a black silk dress that fell in deceptively simple folds to her ankles. The neck was cut high to showcase a diamond necklace; the shoulders were padded; the sleeves stopped below the elbows. A black sash cinched the waist. Not much of her showed outside of the gown, but inside it she was shapely. She wore no perfume he could detect.

She raised her glass to tip it against Lammeck's. He hesitated, wondering what to be suspicious of. He sniffed his champagne while she cocked a quizzical eyebrow. Satisfied, he clinked the lip of his flute to hers, but did not take a swallow. The woman drank on her own, gulping her glass. She lowered it and openly sized him up. Lammeck put his full glass on a passing waiter's tray; she set down her emptied flute. He returned her blue-eyed gaze. She cracked a smile. Lammeck did not.

"Shall I lie to you?" she asked.

Lammeck went very still. The expanse of the embassy vanished; the clatter of the band and dancers, all the sounds and images of the vast, ornate room, funneled away until he was focused only on this woman, like a crosshairs.

"What do you have in mind?"

"Oh, I could give you a fake name. Tell you some fairy tale. But you are far too clever for that, aren't you, Professor?"

Lammeck eyed her. Empty hands. Small handbag over her shoulder. Her voice bore a soft accent on the *R*'s, almost Irish. Skin the color of damp sand, stretched smoothly over an athlete's powerful physique. Hair a coppery brown color, twisted in elaborate curls.

"Clever? I don't know. You should have tried; I might have believed you. You don't look like I thought you would."

"Is that a compliment or an insult? Actually, I thought I look quite fetching tonight. Are you saying you didn't think I would be pretty?"

Lammeck made no reply.

"You like this gown? It's a Hattie Carnegie." Her fingertips brushed the diamonds at her throat. "These are real." She leaned in, coaxing and relaxed. "It's all borrowed."

He thought about seizing her by the arm. But he remembered the three bodies in the Newburyport morgue. Otto had tried to take her in a fight, and he'd been bigger than Lammeck.

He struck with his voice instead. "Are you turning yourself in to me? Judith?"

At her name, the woman's jaw slacked. Quickly, she regained herself.

"That disappoints me. Not in you, Professor, well done. But in her. She told you my name?"

"She's dead."

Judith drew back her head and stared through her spectacles, down her nose: "Did you kill her, Professor?"

"No. She bit a cyanide capsule."

"Well, good. I considered taking care of her myself. She was sloppy. But I try to keep the extra deaths to a minimum. It's unprofessional. Anyway, no, Professor, I am not turning myself in. You don't have me anywhere near that cornered. Especially since you came here alone. Tsk, tsk, whatever were you thinking?"

She put a hand to her hair, smoothing a chestnut curl onto her shoulder. She wore a wig, Lammeck realized.

"So," she asked, "shall we sit?"

Lammeck shook his head. "I can talk to you in your prison cell."

She smiled gaily. "Oh, you *are* the dogged pursuer. I was certain you would be. That's why I wanted us to meet. But actually, I meant that we ought to sit for your sake. You see, any second now, you're going to start feeling the effects of the poison."

Lammeck went ramrod stiff. His eyes started to go wild on her, he wanted to grab her and shake. He bit his lower lip and breathed until he could respond:

"I didn't drink the champagne you gave me."

She smiled and wagged a finger between them. "No, I didn't spike your drink. You're a big man and I couldn't get enough in there for an immediate reaction. Besides, a poisoned glass of champagne, that's such a cliché."

"What did you do?"

"Just a short, quick syringe in your back while you were elbowing your way through the crowd looking for me. You probably felt it as an itch in that handsome but rented tux."

"You're lying. I didn't feel anything."

"You wouldn't. I'm extremely good at my job, Professor, and you've been very distracted. So, shall we?"

Lammeck stood in astonishment. She moved away, gesturing him to follow through the crowd. He fell in her wake, restraining himself from running at her. Every step behind Judith revealed more reasons for him to be afraid. His mouth had gone terribly dry and the lights seemed to blaze in the ballroom. The words "immediate reaction" went off like fire bells in his brain. He snagged another champagne from a waiter. He drank it walking, spilling some on his shirt.

Reaching an empty table, she took a seat. Lammeck sat beside her, so close his shoulder touched hers.

She looked at him through the tortoiseshell eyeglasses. He struggled to keep his mind clear, to scour her for more clues. He noted that the lenses were regular glass.

"Aren't we cozy?" Judith remarked. She added, almost sympathetically, "You're thirsty. That's the first stage. Judging by your size, I suppose we've got twenty minutes before you start to get delirious. Then . . . Well."

Fighting terror and the urge to choke her, Lammeck demanded again, "What did you do?"

"What I had to do to get your attention. And to keep you from trying anything heroic. You're not a hero, I hope, Professor."

Lammeck's lips began to feel dry and hot. His throat thickened as if he'd swallowed cotton.

"What did you give me?"

"I'm not going to tell you that just yet. But trust me, what I injected you with will kill you."

"Do you have the antidote?"

She recoiled teasingly. "Of course. But first we talk."

"No. The antidote. Now."

Lammeck shifted to his left, nearer to Judith, to close the distance between them. In a single smooth motion, he pressed his left hand to his right forearm and bent the elbow. Then he lapped his left arm across the back of her chair, to keep her in it should she bolt.

He stuck the muzzle of the 9mm Welwand in her rib cage, tilting the silencer upward. If he fired, the bullet would pierce her heart.

"Now," he repeated.

She peered down into his cupped hand, at his thumb on the trigger.

"A sleeve gun! Professor, that's marvelous." She tried to lay a hand near it but Lammeck crammed the muzzle deeper into her ribs. She did not flinch. "Well, that *does* change the dynamic, doesn't it?"

"Give me the antidote. Or I swear I'll kill you right here."

They sat close like lovers, his arm around her back. She spoke, fearless.

"No, you won't. Be reasonable. Only I know what I injected you with, and only I have the antidote."

"I'll find it on your body."

"I'll save you the trouble. If you look in my handbag, you'll find four more syringes. All of them are numbered. One is the antidote, the other three are more ... poison. And I'm sorry to say there won't be time for you to get them to a lab."

Lammeck's throat began to burn as if he'd swallowed salt. "If I die, you die."

"Well, Mikhal ... I may call you Mikhal? ... let us make sure you don't die, then."

"What do you want?"

She set an elbow on the table to turn fully to him. He kept the Welwand pressed to her torso, gripping the gun out of sight below the tablecloth.

"I want you to get out of Washington. Leave me to do my job."

Lammeck shook his head. At the motion, his vision swam, the room throbbed with light.

"Mikhal, I can handle the Secret Service. I haven't the faintest worry about Reilly and his men. But you. I've read your writings. I know a clever man when I see one. Frankly, I'm concerned how well you've guessed at what I'm doing from such little evidence."

"Not so little. We found your knife."

Judith clapped her hands above the cocked 9mm in her gut. "You did! Good, I thought it was lost in the ocean. It's extremely valuable, but I suppose you know that. Please make sure it gets into a museum somewhere. I should like to visit it someday. Where was it?"

"Under Otto."

"Ah, yes. The big man on the beach. Well, I wondered." She nodded at the recollection. "I did not want to do that, Mikhal. Believe me or not."

"Sure. And what about Arnold?"

"The husband? Another necessary evil."

"How'd you do him?"

"You haven't figured that one out yet? You disappoint."

Lammeck licked his lips. Judith saw this and raised a hand for a passing waiter. She called, "Two big glasses of water, please." She returned her eyes to Lammeck. "The thirst will get quite bad. We'll make this as quick as we can for you. Now, Arnold, the husband. What do you think?"

He recalled the skinny corpse and the circumstances. Gunshot hole in the temple, massive exit wound. Cordite on the right hand. Spent round found low in the living room wall. No suicide note.

Lammeck blinked and lowered his eyes. The room flared again. He looked into Judith's midriff where the Welwand nestled, angled up into her silken sash.

The sash.

He looked up, wincing.

"Thuggee."

"Yes," she applauded. "You know the Thuggee! Show off for me."

"Followers of the death goddess Kali in India. They strangled victims using a wide silk scarf with a coin rolled in it. Arnold let you into his house that night because you had Maude King with you, a woman he knew. Then you choked him with a sash, but just to the point where he passed out. No bruises, no bugging eyes. When he was on the floor you put the pistol in his hand and fired."

"Bravo, Mikhal, bravo. You are quite the scholar."

"You murdered three innocent people."

Judith set a gentle hand on Lammeck's wrist above the Welwand. He did not shirk her off. One flick of his thumb and she would be bleeding out of her heart. Then he would have to guess which syringe would save him and which would have him lying beside her dead on the floor. She said nothing but looked into his eyes, silent while the waiter set two glasses of water on the table.

"Listen to my offer, Mikhal, and I won't have to kill you. Please drink. I know you're thirsty. Go ahead, don't worry. The waiter doesn't work for me."

Lammeck pulled his left arm from behind her and finished one glass, then the second. He knew a fair bit about poisons; too many of them had a raging thirst as the opening act. He couldn't begin to guess what she'd stuck him with.

"Talk," he said, wiping his lips, then returning his arm as a barrier behind her.

"First of all, I have no interest in killing you. Certainly with that gun in my midsection, I have even less. But as I said, I'm a professional, not some insane political murderer out of your history books. I kill only for pay or necessity. And trust me, the moment I see you marked by either one, I will kill you without hesitation. Anytime, anywhere. I believe I have demonstrated that tonight. I can drop you with a touch and you'd never see it coming. Bodyguards wouldn't stop me."

"All the more reason for me to pull the trigger tonight."

"Perhaps. But let's see if we can't come to an understanding first. And please, if you need more water, let me know and we'll get it for you. Also, swallowing and talking are going to become difficult sometime soon, and your eyes may become sensitive to light. You'll start to feel a little numb, too. If this gets too bad, tell me and we'll, as you Americans say, cut to the chase."

Lammeck eyed her purse on the tabletop. "Show me the syringes."

Judith complied and cracked open her handbag. Inside lay four needles, numbered with marked tape one through four. She clicked the purse shut, leaving it on the table between them.

"Listen to me, Mikhal. You're the world's most eminent scholar on the history of assassination. I assume you were brought into this case by the Secret Service as an advisor and not to have your own life put in jeopardy. And it is, my dear, in terrible jeopardy. Now, as the terms of your employment do not cover this risk, you have every reason to walk away, with no disgrace. You're an academic, not a soldier. I mean no disrespect by that. You're a brilliant man doing important work elsewhere."

Lammeck's pulse surged in his ears. Sweat popped on his brow but he would not free a hand to wipe it. Judith saw this. She touched his forehead with a cocktail napkin.

"There," she murmured.

Lammeck fingered the Welwand's trigger.

"No," he said.

Judith continued, undaunted, as if she'd expected that answer. She spoke with confidence:

"You're not pursuing me because you want to stop me. You're chasing me because you need to find me. To interview a real Assassin in the flesh for your research. If you kill me, and especially if you die too, this all goes unrecorded, undocumented, and history will never know of it. Trust me, you will not be made famous for it. Your Secret Service and the American press don't even mention that your President is a cripple. Do you believe they're going to trumpet an assassination plot against him? Do you think the Secret Service and the FBI will want it known that I got this close, and that you, a mere civilian, a scholar, was the one to stop me, not them? No, Mikhal. If we're lying beside each other dead like Romeo and Juliet, the story will be that I killed you with poison and you killed me with a pistol you snuck into the embassy. We'll be explained away as angry lovers or forlorn wretches or something equally mundane. We'll be buried and covered up, and the president I have been hired to dispose of and you are risking your own neck to protect will live instead. No, we both need to live and do our very important jobs."

Lammeck blinked. He was trembling now. He steadied himself.

"There ... there's no way I can trust you. I let you walk out of here, how do I know you'll give me the right antidote? What keeps you from trying this shit again tomorrow with another needle in my back?"

Judith nodded. She raised a soft hand below his chin, caressing his cheek.

"Absolutely correct. So I'm willing to make a good-faith offer, a sort of down payment. I will tell you some of my own history right now, just a bit of it, for your studies. And I promise that if we both survive each other and this war, I will tell you the remainder at another time and place. You can put it all in your book. You can ask me anything you want. The woman who killed Roosevelt. Imagine."

"You'd never do that."

"Why not? I'm being paid well enough for this to stay invisible the rest of my life. Try me. But decide quickly, Mikhal. From the look of you, I figure we have only another ten minutes."

"Give me the antidote."

"Give me a question."

He snarled, "Give me the fucking antidote." Judith had him pegged, he knew, he was no hero. He was angry, and he'd been stupid, and though those often resemble courage, they are not the same.

"Be patient, dear, aggression and a touch of mania are to be expected. And of course, fear. Concentrate and ask me a question."

Lammeck clamped his mouth. The lights in the room bedeviled his eyesight. Sweat gathered in his brows.

"Who are you working for?"

"That's for later. Ask another."

"The woman who dropped off the invitation?"

"She's nobody interesting to you, trust me. Ask me where I come from."

Lammeck cut his eyes to the purse. He could grab it, take his chances, one in four, of sticking himself with the right needle. But there was still eight or nine minutes. He could shoot her any time before then. The purse would be there. And she was right: He wanted to know.

"Where are you from?"

"That's much better. I'm from a pretty little village named

Shahrak, right on the Alamut Road, in what you would call the Valley of the Assassins. It's a place of extraordinary beauty, with vines and corn, broom and tamarisk, even oak and walnut trees. And you can see Alamut Rock in the distance on a clear day."

"So you are..." Lammeck's tongue was slurring; he cleared his throat. "You are Persian."

"Yes. My ancestors were *fida'i*s, Hasan-i-Sabah's disciples. We've lived in that valley for a thousand years. My father was a muleteer. I remember him in his red Pahlavi cap, eyebrows white from dust. I grew up in a mud brick hut next to a stream. As a girl I wore a pair of scarlet trousers with beads sewn at the ankles. I milked goats and sheep and made yogurt. I spun wool for carpets and patted dung cakes for fuel. We stacked the cakes on our roof to dry. I was a very happy child."

Lammeck ran his thumb over the trigger, to make sure he maintained control of the Welwand, digging the silencer again into her ribs. Judith did not react.

"What happened to you?" he asked.

"You must understand, Mikhal. Growing up female in Persia is the same as growing up in shackles. A Muslim girl is supposed to be pious and meek. I was neither. It's a country where weakness is death. If you're not strong, or you don't have a protector, you're nobody. Women are *zaifeh*, powerless. So we are sheep, unless we have a husband. An old Persian saying goes: 'Even the earth trembles beneath the feet of the unmarried.' Girls are married off before they reach puberty. When I was ten, my father gave me as a wife to a wealthy landlord who'd seen me in the village."

Lammeck's mouth had stopped making spittle. Each breath was becoming painful.

"You could have said no."

"That's such an American response. I expected better from you, a man of the world. In Persia, we're accustomed to being bullied. Conquered, ruled, kept illiterate by the Turks, by our own kings, it doesn't matter. Centuries have taught Persians to bend with the wind, to hide behind cleverness. Never let your actions be the mirror of your heart, my father taught me. Stealing is a national art, did you know that about us? We are wily, and thus we survive. At ten, I kept my mouth shut, and went where I was told. My father was given a tidy sum for me, and he genuinely believed I was headed for a better life than he could ever provide for me in Shahrak. My mother, of course, had no voice in the matter. My new husband took me to Tehran. As it turned out, he was a very kind man, an influential man, and a friend of Reza Shah. He treated all of his wives and children well. I was educated at the American school. I learned to read and write, dance, paint, sew; I became an excellent calligrapher, fluent in French, and a dab hand with an épée."

Lammeck kept his eyes hard on Judith, but the ebony of her dress had begun to bleed into the air around her. The music in the ballroom took on an almost howling quality. Again, he fixed on the handbag, measuring his chances.

"Finish up," he rasped.

"Of course. How inconsiderate of me, nattering away while you sit there dying. Do you want me to stop now and have you shoot me? Or should I at least round off my story?"

Lammeck tried to chuckle at his predicament; it seemed insane. But his mounting panic would not give him the luxury of a laugh.

He lifted his head, defiant. "Finish up."

"My husband was constantly annoyed with me. I was not the pliable material he believed he was purchasing in that little Assassins' village by the stream. I called him *Agha* instead of *Ghorban*, which is the equivalent of calling him 'Sir' instead of 'He for whom I sacrifice myself.' I refused to stay in the harem. I wandered about the grounds and even into the city, and he would cane me for it. I stood on the walls every morning and watched the camel caravans leave Tehran. I wanted desperately to go with them, tired of being *zaifeh*. So, I made my plan to leave my husband."

Lammeck growled, "Did you kill him?"

Judith stroked his gun arm. "I can see I do need to hurry up, dear

Mikhal; you're getting surly. No, I did not kill him. Among many of his collections was a set of antique knives. While he slept I buried one in the pillow next to his head. The other I kept, which now unfortunately is in the possession of the Newburyport police. I slipped away from *Agha* and went back to my father, who promptly threw me out. He said I had left his house in a white dress, and the only way I could return was in a black one. I was not going all the way back to Tehran just to kill my elderly husband and become a widow. And if I couldn't trust my family, I couldn't trust anyone. So I left Persia. I hold no love for Islam, it's too harsh to women. It reduces us to servants and beggars in *chadors*. That's why, when I started my career as an assassin for hire, I took the name of Judith, a Jewish heroine. Just to continue to be annoying."

A tremor shuffled across Lammeck's shoulders, the beginning of convulsions. He didn't have much time before he lost control over the weapon wedged in Judith's gut. Then she would leave him to die.

"I've trained very hard, Mikhal. I've studied under some of the best in the world, in Syria, Egypt, Istanbul, some in Europe. I've worked all over the globe. I've even done one job here, in Washington, for the Russians. Do you know who it was? Stay clear-headed for me. We're almost done, you and I. Think back to 1941," she prodded. "Bellevue Hotel."

Lammeck rummaged in his collapsing thoughts for the name. He recalled the murder: an ex–NKVD operator, a defector and Trotskyite on the run from the Soviets. Wrote a tell-all, *I Was Stalin's Agent*. Lammeck shut his eyes to concentrate, then snapped them open, aware that he'd taken them off Judith. She hadn't moved an inch.

"Krivitsky. Walter Krivitsky. Shot in the head."

She was pleased. "The police called it a suicide, but nobody believed that. Really some of my best work. My clan prefers the dagger, as you know, and certainly poison. But the Soviets specified I shoot him, to be certain. Poor old Trotsky, he got an ax in the head, so by that standard Krivitsky got off lucky. The Russians were extremely generous to me. In my line of work, it helps to be nonpolitical."

Lammeck's fingers had grown numb on the Welwand. His pulse raced. The room seemed aflame with flashes and flicking sparks.

"Enough," he croaked. "The antidote. Or you die first."

He didn't care if it was the poison making him say that. He knew he could do it.

Judith leaned in. "Mikhal, listen. You and I are the same, do you know that? I believe in God, that all things are in His hands. You believe, too, but you call your god History. We are both part of something much greater than ourselves. We are cogs, you and I, in the one clockwork. Now, pay attention. I'm going to give you the antidote. And you are not going to prevent me from doing my job."

Lammeck almost lowered the Welwand, but hardened his hand on it. With an open palm, she tried to push the weapon away. He thrust it back into her belly.

"I will stop you," he said.

She shook her head in a mournful, leave-taking gesture.

"No. You won't. I suspect after this evening you won't even get close. But if you do keep trying, and I become aware of you one more time, my dear, I will have to stop you instead. My mission is too important. Roosevelt has to die, Mikhal. If you knew why, you might even agree."

At this, Judith pushed back her chair. Her torso faded from the muzzle of the Welwand. She began to stand.

With his left hand Lammeck threw her back into the seat.

"Sit down!"

"Easy," she crooned. Judith waved her hands slowly, to mollify him. "Don't give in. We're almost done. Mikhal, listen to me."

"Shut up." Lammeck had gone hoarse; in his ears, his panting made him sound like a wounded animal. "Give me the syringe." He shoved the handbag toward her. "Done talking. Do it."

Judith complied. She snapped open the purse. Spreading the mouth of the bag, she showed him the four glass syringes.

"Which one?" he demanded.

She shook her head. "None of them."

Lammeck was stunned. She didn't have the antidote! He was going to die. He wanted to cry, but grief was swamped in confusion and rage. He braced to pull the trigger, to take her with him. He tried to separate his voice from the delirium of the poison, and knew that he no longer could do so. He heard other words in his head, not his.

Judith. She was talking to him.

". . . not here. Are you listening? Don't use these. All four of them are more poison. Mikhal?"

She put her fingers under his chin to raise his head and fix his eyes on hers.

"I gave you one-thirtieth of a gram of scopolamine. It was a powerful dose."

Lammeck repeated, "Scopolamine."

"Yes, good." Judith acted cheered by his fleeting attention. "Now, look here. Put out your hand."

Lammeck complied, glad to have any course other than death. Before he could catch himself he'd let loose of the Welwand. The elastic drew the weapon back up his sleeve. Judith set a brass token in his palm.

"This is a coat-check number. A syringe of physostigmine venenosum is in another purse I checked. It will reverse the scopolamine. You'll have a rough night, but you will not die if you get up and go now."

Judith snapped the handbag on the table shut. Lammeck heard the click in the torrent of sounds in his brain. She tucked it under her arm and rose. Lammeck did not stop her.

She leaned down.

Close to his ear, she whispered, "Remember, Mikhal: Anytime, anywhere, I can kill you. But not tonight. Now go. You'll make it."

Lammeck squeezed his right hand for the Welwand. It was gone. He shivered his head to clear it, and made a bark deep in his throat to speak. He laid his left hand to his elbow to reclaim the gun but she was already steps away, beyond the lethal range of the Welwand.

Judith crossed her hands over her breast. The diamonds at her throat sparkled. She bowed slightly.

"*Befarma-ri*, Mikhal. Go with God."

Lammeck lost her in the crowd and the thumping of his heart. He opened his right hand and stared at the token she'd left. What was the last thing she'd said? Go now, Mikhal. Go with God.

Go.

Lammeck ripped out of the chair, spilling it behind him. He staggered, catching himself on the shoulders of a dancing couple. The woman squealed when Lammeck drove her behind him with a sweep of his big arm. He walked clumsily, then broke into a zigzagging trot. The embassy's foyer seemed an impossible distance away, broken with undulating shapes. Lights hurt him and he squinted, blinding himself more to the crowd, making him collide with someone at almost every stride. He knocked women aside, a few men down, swimming through them all to the front door. At his back he heard shouts, but these fell in the sea of his burning blood and he pressed on.

At last, ready to buckle, gasping, he brushed aside a handful of gowns and tuxedos to slap the token on the counter of the coatcheck closet. The woman with Asian eyes started in disgust at him.

"Sir," she said, "please wait your turn."

"Now," he said, trying to make a fist to bang it, but he was out of strength. The woman did not move, defying his rudeness.

Lammeck focused on her with his last bit of clarity.

He hissed, "Fast..."

From behind, one of the guests Lammeck had shoved aside snipped, "Just give it to him, will you? We'll wait."

The girl took the token, then pivoted for the crowded racks. Lammeck gripped the counter like a plank at sea and clung there, waiting, counting moments with his wild heart. His torso shuddered, another convulsion.

"Here, sir. Now, if you please."

The girl set a black evening bag on the counter. Lammeck snared it and collapsed, his back against the half door of the closet. He tore trembling into the bag for the needle.

CHAPTER FOURTEEN

March 10
Washington, D.C.

LAMMECK LEFT THE DOOR locked and did not answer. That did not stop Dag. The agent quit knocking, disappeared, and must have flashed his badge downstairs because he came back with a woman from housekeeping who let him in.

Dag stood beside the bed. Lammeck rolled away, groaning. Dag pushed back the drawn curtains. Noon light blitzed the room. Dag tugged on Lammeck's shoulder to make him lie faceup.

Lammeck opened his eyes to a sour face. Dag dropped a thin folder on Lammeck's belly.

"What the hell's going on with you, Professor? You want to explain this?"

Lammeck tested his throat, to say his first words in fifteen hours.

"Break it off in your ass."

His voice remained strained, but he'd made his point and turned over on the ignored folder.

At his back, he heard Dag peel off his wrinkled raincoat and toss it on the sofa. The phone receiver was lifted from its cradle and a button stabbed.

"Gimme room service. A big pot of coffee to room 540. Pronto."

A chair skidded beside the bed.

"I don't care if you close your eyes or you're half dead. I want to know what happened."

Throughout the night, Lammeck would have settled for half dead. He'd been packed into a taxi at the embassy and carried back to the Blackstone after heaving his address to some Peruvian security guard. At the hotel, the black bellhop hauled him to the elevator, then Lammeck stumbled on the old man's arm to his room and bed. The clerk had to peel him out of the tux, whispering to Lammeck, "I know, big man, I know." For eight hours, until dawn crept around the fringe of the curtains, Lammeck struggled to breathe; he vomited a half dozen times after crawling to the toilet, then dry-heaved off the edge of the bed for an hour. His joints burned with every movement; his head spun in a dizzying whirl of pain and nausea. He recalled waking dreams or hallucinations, but nothing specific, just images of heat and ache out of order and all reason. It seemed that he'd fallen asleep only moments before Dag barged in.

Lammeck forced himself to flop over on his back. He stared at the ceiling out of eyes he did not want to see in any mirror.

"Judith." Her name was more croak than word.

"We'll get to her in a minute. First, I want to know why Reilly's office got six phone calls this morning about you being a junkie? And that means I got one big one from him. We've got pissed-off diplomats, including the Peruvian ambassador himself, bitching about you jabbing a needle into your thigh on the floor last night in the middle of their embassy. We got reports of you shoving people out of the way and falling on your ass to give yourself an injection. An injection, Professor! You want to tell me what this is about before I have the D.C. cops arrest you?"

Lammeck lay there wishing he could laugh; he mustered only the energy to prop himself up against the headboard.

With a raw throat, he told Dag of the invitation slipped under his door yesterday morning. The little old black woman who'd delivered it. Judith at the embassy, her physical description and what he thought were her disguises. Their face-off, with the poison gaining in him and the 9mm Welwand in her gut. He explained how she'd killed Arnold. Everything she'd said about her background. She'd done Krivitsky in '41. And Dag had been right all along: FDR was her target. The antidote at the coat-check closet, and his manic race for it. He finished with Judith's request that he back away from the investigation, or she would kill him for certain next time.

Dag listened without comment, an incredulous look plastered on his face. When he was done, Lammeck sank back into the bed.

"You mean to tell me," Dag said, "you went to that embassy by yourself, knowing damn well that invitation under your door came from Judith?"

"I . . ."

"Shut up. You took a firearm into an embassy, and ended up sticking it in Judith's ribs when she showed herself to you. And while you were passing out from poison that somehow you were stupid enough to let her poke you with, she admitted she was here to kill the President. Then you let each other get away, on the condition that you back off and allow her to kill him. And if you don't, she'll just kill you some other time. Did I leave anything out?"

Lammeck rolled to his side, facing away from Dag. "That sums it up."

Dag groused, "That's too goddammed far-fetched to be a lie." Lammeck heard the agent's derisive laugh to himself. "So what'd you tell her?"

"Since I was dying at the time, I told her I thought she made a very good point."

· · ·

DAG PACED WHILE HE got dressed.

The constriction in Lammeck's throat eased enough for him to comment on the indignities he'd endured in the past eighteen hours in the service of the United States government. Dag made no reply, shuffling around the room while listening to Lammeck carp. Dag was prepared to take a bullet for his president, and so he clearly lacked sympathy for Lammeck's current aches and pains.

Lammeck slouched into the bath for a shave and a shower. When he came out, he saw Dag had laid out his suit for him.

"Reilly's real eager to see you, Professor. Chop-chop."

Lammeck took his time climbing into the clothes, to gather himself and be defiant. Dag's authority over him had begun to chafe weeks ago, but last evening's near-death experience—almost dying and almost killing—added to his sense of liberation.

Traffic on the way to the White House was gnarled, even on a Saturday morning because of the six-day workweek. Even so, Dag reached the west gate before Lammeck was ready. Something had fallen out of balance about time. Last night seemed an eon ago, and only an instant ago. It seemed like the poison and Judith were all he'd ever known, as if he'd experienced birth and death in the fifteen minutes he'd been with her. He'd spent his adult life studying killers, plus the last several years training them—Dag, Gabčik, Kubiš, all were men who'd gone out and taken lives. Last night Lammeck, who'd always been squeamish around blood, came within a flick of his thumb from joining the rank of killers, then joining the dead. How could this not change a man, to stand on the lip of both abysses? Lammeck knew he'd been granted an insight, not just for his research on assassins and history. Last night, for the first time, he realized how much he did not want to die. He'd been witness to the terrible power held by someone who could take life without hesitation. He'd faced that person. And he believed, for moments, he'd been that person.

Dag led him to the West Wing and Reilly's office. Inside, Mrs.

Beach gave Lammeck a bemused smile, as though she were un-decided if she'd been proven right or wrong about him. Lammeck stopped in front of her desk and pressed his palms on her blotter.

"What?"

She blinked innocently behind her pince-nez. "I beg your pardon?"

"Say it."

"Say what?"

"No crack? No snide remark at my expense? Because I've had it, Mrs. Beach. Just so you know."

"I'll consider myself warned, Doctor. Dag, he's inside. Gentlemen."

Lammeck rolled his head on his neck like a gunfighter, waiting for another word, but she'd already returned her attention to her paperwork.

Reilly waited in his chair. Also in the office sat a young man with a sketch pad and a box of chalks. Dag took Lammeck's elbow, pulled him close, and whispered, "Just a physical description. Nothing else."

The artist stood to greet Lammeck. Lammeck shook the artist's hand and shot Reilly a nod.

Reilly said, "Rough night, I heard," making no pretense of his displeasure. "I look forward to the details when we're done here. This is Special Agent Decker."

The young artist asked a series of questions about Judith's ap-pearance. As best he could, Lammeck laid out for him her features: angular jawline, high cheeks, vibrant blue eyes, dark brows, reddish-brown hair that was probably a wig, glasses also a fake. Lean and tall, five foot ten. She emerged out of Decker's strokes as if out of a mist. In twenty minutes, with shoulder-length hair shaded black, Judith was in the room with them. But the likeness wasn't exact; Lammeck's recollections were marred by his memory of pain. Lammeck wasn't sure if anyone other than him could really recognize her from this depiction. Even so, he found the face on the page compelling, like a calamity.

Decker turned the pad to show Reilly.

"She's a looker." The chief nodded to Lammeck. "You sure about your memory?"

Lammeck shrugged, and kept himself from snapping: *She tried to kill me. I almost killed her. I was kinda busy.*

"Thank you, Decker." Reilly dismissed the artist.

When the young man was gone, Dag spoke first: "We're saying she's a stalker. A crazy hate-mailer. That's it."

Lammeck came out of his chair. "A what? She's not just some nut job. She's dangerous as shit, and she's here to kill the President. You can't cover that up!"

"We can," Reilly said, "and we are. Professor Lammeck, eight weeks ago when you first got here, Dag told you only a handful of people in the world knew there was something in the wind that might—just might—turn out to be a plot against our president. Now that we know there's a full-blown assassination attempt brewing here, we haven't changed the strategy of keeping a tight lid on it. Every agent we have in the field right now who sees that sketch will think he's looking for some weirdo wandering the White House grounds or circling the streets somewhere. We've put out the word that she may be armed, and that's all. Frankly, we get five nut cases a day who say they want to kill Roosevelt, so one more'll come as no surprise. You said you wanted a presence and that's what I've given you. But understand me clearly. I'm not taking any risk of this leaking. The Boss knows we've beefed up his security. That's the extent of what he or anyone outside this office knows. My people are trained not to ask. We're still in a world war and I will not have the country or the President distracted from that. We can handle this without spreading the news all over Washington. Believe me, sufficient precautions are being taken to keep the President safe. Sounding the alarms won't help. Now sit down."

Lammeck returned to his chair. Foreboding weighed him down.

"Who's we, Chief?"

"Professor, I can't undo what you know. Right now you are in on one of the biggest secrets in the whole United States. I heard you mention to Mrs. Beach on your way in that you have 'had it.' It's my unpleasant duty to inform you that, whether or not you're considering quitting this case, you are not going home. You are not leaving my protection or control. You haven't 'had it,' Professor, unless and until I say you have. That means until this woman is stopped. Or the war is over, at which point I assume whoever hired her will call her off. Then you can go, and we'll keep an eye out for her ourselves."

Lammeck glanced at Dag for no reason—he knew he would find no support there—other than to look away from Reilly in astonishment.

"I'm being held prisoner?"

"That's one scenario. The other is you continue to cooperate with us. Your choice. House arrest in your hotel or you stay on the team and help us catch this bitch. And Professor: If you have any ideas about calling the press or a lawyer, if you even think about fucking with me, you will very quickly see what authority the Secret Service has put at my disposal. I assure you, you'll be impressed."

Lammeck came to this office ready to lambaste Reilly and Dag, to thump his chest and leave in an indignant huff for being unappreciated, and put in harm's way. Abruptly, he realized just how badly he'd miscalculated.

"You didn't tell the ambassador."

Reilly laughed at this, ridiculing. "Come on, man, use your bean. You think I'm going to tell anyone how a Persian assassin drugged you?"

"*Drugged* me? She *poisoned* me!"

"Alright, she poisoned you. Trust me, it was a hell of a lot easier to tell the ambassador of Peru that you're a diabetic who doesn't manage his insulin shots very well than to let the cat out of this particular bag. Oh, and for good measure I threw in that you're known to be pretty rude when you've had a few too many and your blood sugar gets out of control."

"But..." Lammeck choked, stunned, "...but I'm a scholar. I have a reputation. That was an antidote. I could have *died*!"

Smiling, Reilly waved this objection away. "The U.S. government will make it right, Professor. Once this is over with, and President Roosevelt can be told, believe me, your contribution will be acknowledged through the proper channels." Lammeck didn't understand, and Reilly made himself clearer. "That means Harvard, Yale, Stanford, whatever you want. Okay?"

"You trying to buy me off?"

"I'm trying to shut you up. And I'm trying to keep you on the team." Reilly's demeanor eased. "Christ, Professor, you *found* her."

"She found me."

"Just like you said she would. But not exactly the result we were looking for."

"What are we talking about, Chief?" House arrest was not an option, and going back to Scotland was off the table. Reilly was asking him to keep his life on the line: Judith had made it perfectly clear that she would not think twice about removing him if she felt too much heat again.

Reilly glanced at Dag, who took over.

"Number one, you're off the front line. No more parties, no more tuxes. She knows you now and she's too dangerous for you to be left dangling as bait. If you get hurt as a civilian, that looks bad on my résumé. Two, new hotel. Three, you report where you are and what you're doing every day to me or Mrs. Beach. And believe me, all three of us are being punished with that one."

Lammeck readied a reply. Before he could snap, Dag grinned.

"Look, Professor, lighten up. This is what we've got to do. The chief and me signed up for this kind of thing, but you got dragged into it. Honestly, we have a better shot at her if you're with us. Please don't make us have to babysit you in your hotel until this is over. You're already a major pain in the rear. Can you imagine what you'll be like if we have to do that? Cut us a break, okay?"

The devil and the deep blue sea, Lammeck thought. Reilly versus Judith. One led to house arrest and the U.S. government as an adversary, the other to potential death—or a potential wealth of knowledge for his career. What was the right thing to do? The brave thing? Unbidden, perhaps because Judith was Persian, Lammeck thought of Nadir Shah, the goatherd who, in the mid–eighteenth century, rose to head of his family, chief of a bandit clan, then became the military leader who drove the Afghans and Turks out of Persia. Once he became Shah, Nadir turned into a despot who waged many wars and built pyramids of skulls from those who opposed him. As dangerous as the man was, he was finally assassinated in 1747 by four of his bodyguards; Nadir killed two of them before being cut down himself. Just bodyguards, Lammeck thought. Anonymous men who did the courageous thing. Lammeck wanted to know their names, to give them their due.

He said to Reilly, "Why not."

"Thank you," the chief replied. "You should know, Mrs. Beach really does like you. That's just how she shows it."

Judith appeared to like him, too. She'd tried to kill him. Those two women had in common an odd stamp of affection.

"You went alone," Reilly said. His temper eased now that Lammeck was back in the fold. "That was gutsy and stupid. Why'd she let you go, Professor? She had you dead to rights."

"I stuck a 9mm Welwand in her rib cage. We struck a deal. We both walked away."

"Joseph, Mary, and Jesus." Reilly shot Dag a disbelieving look.

"Okay," Dag said, rubbing his brow. "Number four. No more firearms, Professor."

. . .

March 12
Aurora Heights
Arlington, Virginia

JUDITH SLIPPED THE KEY into the Tenches' front door. She stepped around a scattered heap of mail to hang her coat on the hall tree. She sifted through the envelopes and this time left the invitations alone. She arranged the mail neatly on the sideboard.

Upstairs, she took Mrs. Tench's gown out of a dry cleaner's cardboard box and returned it to the woman's dressing closet. She fingered several of the gowns, then held an azure patterned silk to herself. It had sweeping long lines to the floor and would bring out the color of her eyes. She returned the dress to the hanger. Closing the closet door, Judith sighed. She would not get the chance to wear that dress.

The Tenches were scheduled to return home tomorrow. The die was cast for Judith to leave this household. She would wring the mister another couple of times for what he was worth, but held little faith anymore that he was the path. Instead, she'd made some other promising connections in her embassy evenings. Several powerful men had asked for her phone number. She'd refused, taking their cards and saying she'd call them, a scandalous and intriguing thing for an attractive woman to do. One bullfrog-necked power monger claimed to be the chief of staff for a senior New York congressman. He was unmarried, full of himself, and ripe.

Downstairs, she sat in the bright kitchen. This was her favorite room in the house, because Mrs. P. kept it a sanctuary. Judith considered making Jacob a gift out of this kitchen; it would be a simple thing to make his wife very sick. A sprinkle of corn cockle on a Parker House roll. A dash of meadow saffron in a glass of milk. Baneberries in a slice of pie. His skinny, unstable wife would have to see a doctor, probably go to the hospital. Jacob would have to pay some attention, make certain she was cared for. Maybe he'd look closely for the first time in years and see who he married, then make some decision, one way or another. Maybe the wife would be the one to act. But the camel needed to be pulled fully into the tent before those two fortunate and wretched Americans would speak to each other about it.

Judith stood to go, leaving that decision for another day. Probably Mrs. P. would take the blame for making the woman ill, her cooking would be faulted. She'd be fired. That would be a complication Judith didn't want.

She donned her coat, locked the house, and drove away. The day was a token of spring, under a blue sky with early blossoms in the rich yards of the neighborhood. Tomorrow Judith would tell Mrs. Tench she would be quitting soon and would need a referral letter. The woman's reaction would dictate how well she ate in Judith's final days in her employ.

She drove east across the Potomac. As always, Memorial Bridge was packed with cars, buses, and military vehicles. Frequently, the bridge was shut down while hearses and mourners filed slowly to Arlington Cemetery for some soldier or sailor's burial, backing traffic up for a mile into downtown D.C., injecting a frozen gridlock into the heart of the city that took hours to filter away.

Finally reaching Seventeenth, she turned south to motor past the Blackstone Hotel, for no reason other than it was a touchstone, where Lammeck had been. The professor had surely been relocated by now. She didn't need to know where he'd gone. If she saw him again before her mission was finished, it would be because he'd sought her out. She hoped against that.

In any event, he was alive for now. She'd set up the rendezvous at the embassy to scare him off, with no intention to kill him unless he proved to be some unrealistic academic or repressed champion who wouldn't back down. As it turned out, he was exactly those things, but also something less, and that saved his life. Though he'd actually checkmated her, though he certainly had gumption, and their encounter had been exhilarating, she was never in real fear that he could pull that trigger. Judith knew the eyes of a killer, and

Lammeck—even in pain and fright—did not have them. In him, she'd seen a clever man worth keeping a vigil on, but not one to fear. This confirmed the suspicions she'd had before meeting him; extremely rare are the people who can kill face-to-face. If cold-bloodedness were a common trait, Judith would have had no career.

Mikhal Lammeck posed no threat. For now, letting him live served her purposes, for every dead body she created was a compli-cation, and another crumb dropped on a trail that might lead to her. There had already been corpses aplenty on this job.

Besides, in the unlikely event the professor proved her wrong, she'd keep her word to him. She'd kill him.

For twenty-five minutes she drove up and down the eastern rim of the White House grounds, until a parking spot opened. Judith was pleased; she'd expected a longer wait. The sooner she was against the curb, the sooner she was out of the line of sight of agents prowling the streets and sidewalks. The time was one-thirty. The President never came out of his big white residence and its grounds before three o'clock. Judith walked away from the car, slipping eas-ily into the stream of workers on the sidewalks. She was accus-tomed to being packed in with people on all sides; Cairo was just as crowded, but less frenetic. The men and women on the move here in Washington had a world to win with their fast steps, and this made every stride important, dedicated. She waited in line to buy a soft pretzel and a bag of warm chestnuts from a vendor, then strolled away in the multitude.

Today was the first pleasantly warm day since her arrival. She'd heard of the beauty of Washington's springtime, the fabled cherry blossoms beside the reservoir. She walked west toward the classic façade of the Lincoln Memorial, alongside the narrow Reflecting Pool. This path, designed to be a promenade beside monuments and tourist attractions, was just as choked with human traffic as any sidewalk or street in the center of the city, for this was the location of more than half a mile of temporary, four-story wooden office buildings thrown up for the Navy Department on the long banks of the artificial pond. A covered walking bridge, connecting the two sides, cut across the middle of the pool, breaking the view. Judith marveled that Rome, Athens, Constantinople, Peiping, the centers of history's empires, had managed to avoid architecture this homely in order to fight their wars.

She took a bench in the sun and ate beside the shallow pond. She imagined this white city, blushing in pink blossoms, with its leader dead. She passed her mind's hand over the landscape, draping pillars and domes with black, painting the sky a rainy gray for a grand procession, an imperial mourning. She would transform both this city and the world it affected with its guns and money. She would do this vast thing.

Judith ate slowly, enjoying the day and her anonymity in it, regardless of how hard Lammeck and his wrinkled agent companion sought her out. She had something on her side they could not counter. Time. Her acts of history carried no schedule. Six months, a year on the outside; her employers never specified, trusting to her abilities. Sooner was always better—it showed proficiency—but patience was sharper than any blade, more lethal than the keenest poison. She had all the funds she needed, and the papers to assume another half-dozen identities. Judith had many strengths as an assassin, but her greatest was her discipline. She knew how to circle and watch for the beckon, listen for the cue, for history to call her onto the stage where only she and her target would stand before no audience.

She tore off a bit of pretzel for a tolerant pigeon.

It could be any day, she thought. Why not today?

Judith rose from the bench, to amble in the spring warmth back to her parked car.

At ten minutes to six, Roosevelt emerged for the first time since his return from Yalta. He did so in his accustomed fashion, in his armored limo flanked by Secret Service cars crammed with agents. With headlights on, the little caravan crept away from the south gate. Judith let some traffic fill in between them, then pulled out.

Roosevelt was always easy to follow on his motors away from the White House. His driver never made attempts at evasion. His motorcade used no sirens or lights, and obeyed every traffic signal. Clearly the Secret Service had not curtailed the man's movements because of her. Did he even know an assassin was on his trail? From a hundred feet behind the limo, Judith projected herself into the seat next to the crippled man, an invisible eye on him. No, he didn't know about her. Roosevelt's minions were protecting him from Judith in every way they could, even from knowledge of her. Why? Because the old man was burdened enough. How sad, to need these occasional drives just to feel mobile in the world. To have such power and still crave a simple ride in a car. Judith envisioned the old man's face fixed to his window, a slow and ill gaze watching his sunny country slide by. He was ruler here, but he must also be alone inside his walls, trapped and betrayed by his body, in need of fresh air and a change of scenery. For the first time, Judith sensed the tragedy of this president. Even in an America ascending, he was intended for sacrifice, as the great almost always are. That time was very near, just as she was. History had removed its grace and protection from Franklin Roosevelt, and put Judith there instead.

She sensed they would meet soon. She felt this in her hands and heart, and in her purpose, all stronger than his.

The motorcade turned west toward Georgetown. The President's window was cracked open; smoke leaked from a cigarette. Judith followed the three cars, maintaining a two-block distance from the trailing vehicle. She guessed the motorcade was headed again out to Rock Creek Parkway so the President could get some wind in his hair. She was wrong. Instead, the cars turned into the residential streets, among the fine brick homes and wrought-iron railings. Judith sped to shorten the gap to the motorcade; she did not want to lose them in these tight avenues.

The three cars drove not far into the neighborhood behind several embassies, then stopped on Q Street in front of a high brownstone. Judith held back. An agent stepped out of the lead vehicle and went to stand beside Roosevelt's passenger door. The President did not get out of the limo; instead, a tall woman came down the steps from the house without anyone going to fetch her. She'd been waiting for them.

The agent opened the limo door for her—more smoke escaped—and closed it; the motorcade continued with the woman seated in the back beside the President.

Judith moved in their wake. She drove past the brownstone, glancing up to take the street number, 2238. In a tall window, watching the cars disappear, stood a very robust white woman. She wore a maid's uniform.

Judith didn't trail the President and his female guest. She drove back to the White House. She parked in sight of the south gate. At twenty minutes to seven, the three vehicles returned.

At midnight, one car left the south gate, returning to Q Street.

March 13
Georgetown

JUDITH REACHED FOR THE bottle of maple syrup a split second behind the big woman. She smiled, retracting her hand. "I'm so sorry. You saw it first. You go ahead."

The woman returned the smile and took the item; Judith grabbed the bottle behind. The old maid pushed her cart farther along the aisle. Judith lagged, feigning interest in other groceries until the woman laid hold to a tin of cling peaches. Judith appeared at her wide shoulder, waited, then again took the second can.

"Funny," she said, "it's like we're shopping for the same person."

"Yes." The woman nodded and peeked into the wire basket over Judith's arm to see they also had Wheateena Biscuits in common.

Judith made a show of running her gaze down the woman's girth, not to take in her size but the solid black maid's outfit with its lace collar beneath her unbuttoned coat. Judith wore a very similar uniform, purchased that morning.

"I've never seen you around," Judith said. "Are you new in the neighborhood?"

The woman laid a plump hand to her breast and quaked with a giggle. "Me? *Non,* there is nothing new about me at all." This woman was like Mrs. P., old and possibly much older than she looked. She was moonfaced and pleasant eyed, and she was not American.

"Where are you from? You have a beautiful voice. Oh, I'm sorry, I don't mean to be forward." Judith took the wire basket from her right arm and with shy eagerness extended her hand. "My name is Desiree."

"And I am Annette. Desiree. *Un beau nom.* Do you know what that means?"

"A beautiful name."

"You know French?"

"I grew up in New Orleans speaking Creole French. My daddy is colored but my mama's Cajun."

"Well, well." Annette jiggled again with laughter. "We are a pair, *oui*? Perhaps we are long-lost sisters."

The woman turned to continue her shopping with Judith at her side. The two chatted in their common tongues and plucked a few of the same things from shelves, though Judith did it once for comedy and put the item back. To Judith's questions, Annette played out a quick version of her story: her hometown of Toulouse, coming to America as a young widow looking for work after the tribulations of the last war, then a long employment as the private *servante* for a rich *madame* who was recently widowed, who was up from South Carolina for a visit with her sister here in Georgetown. Despite Annette's energy, she grew flush and breathless talking and rolling the cart. Judith could see her health was not good.

Judith got her groceries first, filling only one bag. Annette had three bags. Judith offered to help her carry her load back to the house of the madame's sister.

"*Merci, chère.* But I will carry them alone. I do not want to be seen so old and fat that I require the assistance of a skinny girl."

Judith took one of Annette's bags. The older woman did not resist.

"But you do need the help, *ma soeur.* It's no trouble. Come on."

Judith walked beside the huffing woman. She made most of the conversation to spare Annette the exertion of talking. She explained that she was new in Washington and worked for a crazy lady whose husband had a big job in the government. She didn't like the capital all that much; it was so much bigger and more crowded than what she was used to back in New Orleans. She was considering going home, or maybe getting a different job, somewhere in the countryside.

This took them to the steps of the brownstone. Judith walked the grocery bag to the top of the steps. There she said good-bye to Annette.

"I'll see you around," she promised. The big woman watched her down the steps and held up a hand in farewell. At the sidewalk, Judith pivoted to walk on. Just before she could stop and call out, the older woman spoke.

"Desiree, are you free this evening? My madame, she is going out for dinner. I will ask if I may go to a dinner myself. With a friend."

Judith cradled her own bag of groceries with both arms, swinging them just the right amount with girlish humility.

"*Avec plaisir,* Annette."

AFTER SIX O'CLOCK, JUDITH tailed one dark car from the White House to Q Street. When the tall woman again came down the steps and was chauffeured away, Judith parked on P Street, then walked to the brownstone to collect Annette.

Approaching the home, Judith felt a pulse of affection for Desiree, her alter ego. Tonight, Desiree was dressed like a white woman, to counter any possible problem in the restaurant. Though America's capital was not officially segregated, Washington still found ways to be less than evenhanded toward its blacks. This took the shape of poor service, sideways glances, arms-length engagement. Judith wore heels, a slimming charcoal jacket and matching skirt, and her hair in a tight French twist. This evening needed to go smoothly.

Annette came to the door dressed more humbly, in a plain olive frock and flats. She seemed self-conscious until Judith swept the old maid down the steps with assurances of her beauty. Judith chided herself that she'd overshot the mark in her dress, drawing needless attention and comparison.

"I've got us a table at a nice restaurant, just three blocks from here," she said, switching the conversation.

"*Merci.*"

Judith strolled at the big woman's pace. Annette laid out the duties she served for her madame: She was dresser, cook, housekeeper, and confidante. She'd been with her lady for twenty-five years, since the first days of her marriage. The *monsieur* had died one year ago next week. He was many years older than the madame. "And you, Desiree?"

"Me, I'm just a housekeeper right now. And I serve at table sometimes. But I can do anything. I can cook French, Italian, Middle Eastern, anything. I can sew and write invitations. I can garden, too."

Annette smiled her approval. "You say your madame is crazy. She must be, to use you so little. Eh?"

The two giggled. Judith did not want to hurt this cheerful woman.

At the restaurant, the waiter took their coats and seated them. Annette ogled the fancy interior and clientele.

"I'm buying," Judith said. "It was my birthday last week and my mama sent me some money to have a nice meal out. And that's what I'm having. With you."

She asked Annette to select a wine. When they were settled and the entrées ordered, Judith asked, "Who is your madame?"

Annette sipped from her glass. "Mrs. Lucy Mercer Rutherfurd." With no reason between them to defend her employer, she added, "She is a very fine woman."

"I'm sure. What does she do?"

Annette shrugged, confused by the question. "She is a widow. I suppose she travels. She tends to her properties. Do?" The woman chuckled. "What does your madame do?"

"Cries half the day, hoots like a barn owl the rest of the time. Like my old daddy used to say, I can't tell if she's going south or bowling."

Again, Annette seemed confounded, but her good nature made her enjoy the odd idiom. Judith poured more wine.

"Annette, who was that picked up your lady?"

The Frenchwoman shook her head. "That I cannot say, *chère*. How do you know this?"

"I was so excited about having dinner with you tonight I got there a little early. I saw a big black car pull up and she got in. The fellow that opened the door for her looked like some kind of body-guard."

Annette squinted over her wineglass. "And so he is. But I cannot say for whom. It is a most powerful man."

"Oh, I wouldn't tell anybody. We're friends. And you ought to be happy for her, seeing somebody new so soon after her husband died. Must be a load off poor Mrs. Rutherfurd's heart."

"It is, it is. They are old friends, she and this man. But I cannot say. It is a big American secret."

Judith held her wineglass below her lips, pretending to think hard. She set the glass down, swilling wine over the lip onto the white tablecloth.

"Oh, my stars. Is your lady dating somebody in the government?"

Annette shrugged. Judith saw how the old Frenchwoman wanted to hold back the secret, but also how she would enjoy the credit that revealing it would bestow on her with young, admiring Desiree.

"A senator?"

"Desiree, you must stop. I cannot say."

"Not the President?"

"Shhh."

Judith borrowed a phrase from Mrs. P. "No she is *not*!"

Annette worked her hands at Judith as if shooing bees away, still shushing her.

"The *President*? I knew it. That was the Secret Service picked her up."

"Desiree, lower your voice." The old woman flattened both palms on the cloth and looked to see who might be listening. "She is not dating the President."

"She is *too*."

"The President is a married man. Mrs. Rutherfurd is a proper widow." Annette wagged a finger. "The two have known each other for thirty years. That is all."

Judith sat back in her seat. "Oh, my stars." Then she leaned forward, to lap her hand over Annette's meaty arm. "Girrrl," she clucked, then sat back again, grinning. She topped off Annette's wineglass in a show of admiration.

Judith waited moments to let Annette's mood bubble up. The old maid had let the secret slip and had to recover. Judith aided her with a hand over her heart.

"Swear to God, Annette, I will never breathe this to a soul. I swear. But, it is so exciting."

This helped the Frenchwoman smile again, and to play the classic role of veteran and complaining servant.

"It is more trouble than you might think." She sighed dramatically. "Believe me."

"Do you ever get to meet him?"

"Yes, several times. But of course only most briefly."

"Have you cooked for him?"

"*Oui.*"

Judith leaned across the table to confide, "Oh, I would kill to cook for him."

Their own meals arrived then. Judith ate mussels; Annette had ordered a chop. Judith called for another bottle of wine. She pressed Annette for details of her mistress's relationship with the President of the United States. The old maid sighed, hemmed and hawed. Judith drew out the tale with patience and well-timed gasps.

In 1914, while Franklin Roosevelt was assistant secretary of the Navy, his wife Eleanor had hired a social secretary to help keep up with the many obligations required of a rising young political star. At the suggestion of her uncle Theodore Roosevelt, Eleanor hired Lucy Mercer, a girl from a formerly good Washington family whose father had fallen out of grace through alcoholism.

"Mrs. Rutherfurd has always been a lady to her fingertips," Annette added, "even when she was twenty-three."

Young Franklin Roosevelt saw this, as well, and was sufficiently moved by it to begin a romance with Lucy, despite his marriage and five children. Eleanor was kept in the dark. Franklin and Lucy attended parties together and dined in public during Eleanor's absences from the city.

"Eleanor Roosevelt is a marvelous woman," Annette was careful to add. "She is a leading light for women everywhere."

Three years later, in 1917, with the war on and Washington's social life curtailed, Lucy's work for Eleanor lessened and she was dismissed by Eleanor. That summer, Lucy enlisted in the Navy as a female yeoman and was assigned to secretarial duties in the Navy Department that kept her near Franklin. The affair between the two blossomed. Gossips in Washington wagged tongues, but Eleanor refused to listen, believing it was below her station to do so.

In the summer of 1918, Roosevelt traveled abroad to inspect

naval facilities. In September, he returned to New York, sailing on the ship *Leviathan*. Eleanor met the boat at the quay, in time to see her husband carried ashore, incapacitated on a stretcher. The diagnosis was double pneumonia; several sailors on the *Leviathan* had already died at sea from the disease.

At their Manhattan home, Eleanor unpacked her sick husband's luggage for him. In it, she discovered a ribbon-wrapped packet of letters from Lucy Mercer.

The affair was in the open at last. It was then closed down as quickly as it had come to light.

"Mrs. Rutherfurd believes," Annette said, downing more wine, "it was the President's mother who stepped in and sorted this out. Eleanor wanted a divorce, but the *grande dame* who controlled her son's money said *non*."

Sara Roosevelt would not give Franklin another cent, and he would not inherit the family home in Hyde Park, if he divorced Eleanor. The old woman feared for her son's political career, at a time when divorce was social suicide. Besides, Lucy was Catholic. Marrying a divorced man presented a huge obstacle for her faith, as well as for mother Sara's staunch Protestantism. The whole episode was written off as a disgrace, but a private and contained one. Both Franklin and Lucy promised never to see each other again.

With his love affair over, his marriage altered, and the Great War done, Roosevelt was ready for a change. He ran on the Democratic ticket as vice president alongside James Cox in the 1920 election, the first ballot in America to allow women voters. The Democrats lost, and Franklin returned to the private sector.

Lucy, too, altered her life. In 1920, the twenty-eight-year-old accepted the hand of a wealthy fifty-eight-year-old widower, Winthrop Rutherfurd, who'd hired her as governess to his five children, none of them out of their teens, after the passing of his wife three years before. Over the next twenty-four years, she cared for Winty and family on his estates in New Jersey and South Carolina. She bore him one more child, a daughter, Barbara.

In 1921, while on vacation in Canada, Roosevelt, at thirty-nine years of age, was stricken with polio. For the next seven years, he concentrated on rehabilitation, seeking water treatments at Cape Cod and in a little town in Georgia, Warm Springs. By 1928, he'd strengthened his arms and back enough to swing in and out of a wheelchair and walk with the aid of leg braces and a cane. That year he was elected governor of the state of New York. Four years later, he was President.

"Mrs. Rutherfurd saw every one of his inaugurations," Annette declared with pride, "from a car with the Secret Service. But she was there, always."

The two who had vowed never to see each other again kept their promise for three decades, although they had not pledged to stop writing or speaking on the phone. Sometimes they would chat in French to keep White House operators from listening in. With the passing of grande dame Sara in the autumn of 1941, "and the pressures the President had been under for so long," explained Annette, the old friends renewed their acquaintance in person. Soon after Franklin's mother's funeral, Lucy traveled to bring her ill husband Winty to Washington, D.C., to Walter Reed Hospital for treatment of a stroke. While in Washington, she and Franklin laid eyes on each other for the first time in almost a quarter century. Thereafter, whenever Lucy was in Washington, she came to the White House for dinners, or the President called for her at sister Violetta's house. After Winty died in March of 1944, at age eighty-two, Lucy not only increased her visits to the White House, but also saw Roosevelt at Hyde Park and at the Little White House in Georgia. The President began to divert his train to pay Lucy house calls at her estates in New Jersey and at her home in Aiken, South Carolina.

"That is why Mrs. Rutherfurd has come to Washington. To visit with the President." Annette wagged a finger. "And shame on anyone who says different. She is a lady," the loyal old maid repeated, "down to her fingertips."

Judith set down her fork, done with her mussels. Annette had hardly touched her pork chop. She'd talked nonstop for a half hour; once the secret parted the woman's lips, there seemed no room for anything to flow in the other direction except wine.

Annette saw the cooled chop and lifted her silverware.

"Fini," she said, waving the knife across her face the way Mrs. P. might have done. *"C'est tout ce que je sais."* That is all I know.

Judith watched Annette tuck in. She poured the last of the wine.

"Annette."

The woman answered around a mouthful. *"Oui?"*

"Thank you. That's a terribly romantic story. And like I promised, I won't tell a soul."

"I believe you, my dear. The reporters, they already know. But they do not say. With a war on, why make something of it? He is a sad man. Very lonely. And not well. Are we to say he does not deserve an old friend?"

"No. Of course he should see your madame."

"Bon. The President is a great man."

Judith let the old maid finish every morsel of the chop, then asked if they would have dessert. Only coffee, Annette answered, patting her belly.

When the waiter had filled the cups, Judith asked, "When do you leave?"

"The madame is visiting at the White House this week. Next week, we will take the train south to Aiken."

Judith lowered her eyes into her coffee and sipped with contemplation. She went silent, and waited for Annette to notice.

"Desiree, *qu'est-ce que c'est?"*

"Annette, I know we just met and all. But I have a favor to ask."

The big woman smiled and cocked her head. Judith leaned past the coffees to put her hands on the maid's wrists.

"I want to come work for Mrs. Rutherfurd."

Annette did not pull her arms from under Judith's hands, but breathed deeply with reluctance.

"*Chère,* I do not know if this is possible. Madame is a very private person."

Judith squeezed. Eagerly, she said, "I'll work for half wages. Just 'til I can prove myself to you both."

Judith felt the flesh of Annette, the depth of the other woman's softness. She quickly calculated how much belladonna it would take to make the woman too sick to work, but not to kill her.

"Annette, I can be a help. I don't mean offense, but I see how difficult it is for you to get around. Those groceries we carried tuckered you out pretty good. I can do anything you need me to do." She took her hands from Annette's arms, satisfied with her assessment.

"I don't want to go back to New Orleans. And I can't stay in this city; I hate it here. Please, Annette. Will you talk to your lady for me?"

Annette sat back, shaking her head. "I do not know how I can do this. . . ."

Judith smiled appreciatively. The tablecloth lay bare but for the coffee cups. Judith would wait a moment, then make the scene pleasant and whole with a laugh and an admission that maybe it was too much to ask. She would invite Annette to a good-bye luncheon tomorrow while her lady was at the White House. Or order more coffee tonight and slip the poison from her purse into the maid's cup. Or help her into her coat with a touch to the neck. Or something.

Annette gazed at Judith. Those eyes would dilate and blur. The heartbeat in her great breast would be audible from several feet away. Her pulse and breathing would triple in rate. She would collapse into fever and convulsions. She would, if Judith were careful, survive. Judging from her weight and age, tissue and color, she would have a lengthy convalescence. She could not travel back to Aiken the day after tomorrow. She would be visited often by her new friend Desiree.

Under Judith's stare, Annette stirred in her seat.

"You say you will work for half?"

"Absolutely. Just feed me and give me a bed indoors, and I won't charge her a full wage until she says different. That's how sure I am she'll like me."

Annette sighed, resigned but pleased. "Ah, *chère,* you are right. I could use the help. I am not so young and lovely as I once was. I will ask the madame. I make no promises. Will you have a letter of referral from your current employer?"

Judith clapped. At that moment the waiter brought the bill in a leather binder. Judith eagerly snapped it off the tablecloth. Annette inclined her head in gratitude.

"She came home just today. I'll see her first thing in the morning and ask her to write me one up."

On the walk back to Q Street, Annette told her to come tomorrow at four o'clock.

"If the madame agrees, you must be ready to leave with us next week. Can you do that?"

"I'm ready right now."

At the front door of the brownstone, Annette set a hand to Judith's shoulder. "You know, we are going to South Carolina. It is segregated. Here, this city is not. You have left that behind once in New Orleans. Are you sure you want to go back to it? I must suppose it is hard to live that way."

Judith kissed the old maid on the cheek. "You know why I'm good at what I do, Miss Annette?"

The woman's eyes crinkled at the proud question. "Tell me, *chère.*"

"Because no matter what happens, I know my place."

She spun on her heels and skipped into the darkness.

CHAPTER FIFTEEN

March 14
Fort Myer
Arlington, Virginia

LAMMECK PLANTED HIS FEET square and hard, flexing at the knees. Both eyes stayed open, the way he trained his Jeds, keeping the periphery available to spot secondary threats. He sighted, right-eyed, down the short barrel at the end of his extended arms, the left hand cupped under the butt. In quick succession, he squeezed off six rounds, pressing the trigger with the first fold of his index finger. The paper man forty feet away shivered and tore.

Lammeck set the smoking gun on the counter. He tugged off his earmuffs and hauled on the clothesline to spool the target to him. The paper sprinted forward on its wire rail.

A Colt .38 Super Automatic was not Lammeck's first choice. He'd bothered Dag for a Smith & Wesson .44. Dag refused him that sidearm, claiming "God forbid" Lammeck would ever use that hand cannon in a crowd; the rounds would go right through whoever he hit—especially a woman—and knock down somebody else. Dag didn't want Lammeck carrying a gun at all, rule number four. But Lammeck insisted he be provided a pistol, and not a lightweight

.22 but something with punch. If he was going to be looking over his shoulder for Judith, he wanted more than a sleeve gun between them next time.

Dag relented and handed over a favored weapon from his rival agency, the FBI. This morning he gave Lammeck the Colt. Lammeck chose a 130-grain round, which flung the bullet at 1300 fps. That would be as accurate and powerful as any cartridge this .38 could fire. Lammeck wanted to be able to stop her the moment he saw her, from whatever distance. He had no desire to get close to Judith again.

The paper torso halted abruptly in front of Lammeck's station. The target flipped at him and he snagged the lower edge, yanking it out of the clips. Concentric circles branded the chest of the silhouette. Lammeck had put four rounds inside the rings, one on the outer edge. The sixth round he'd purposely pulled out of the circle and aimed at the big-eared head. He'd missed, leaving a bullet hole that would have taken off an ear but not stopped the body. Lammeck folded the target and set it behind him. After reloading a fresh magazine, he stuck a new paper man into the clips, pulled on the rope, and sent it back into the line of fire.

After an hour's practice at the range, Lammeck grew satisfied with the sidearm. He snugged it into the holster under his left armpit and left the military base, located outside the western rim of Arlington Cemetery. He drove into the late morning for the White House.

Stopping at a convenience store in Rosslyn before the Potomac, Lammeck paid a nickel for a *Washington Post*. He parked in a government space on Executive Avenue, across from the Ellipse. His appointment with Reilly wasn't for another hour, at one o'clock. He spread the newspaper across the steering wheel.

Tedium was settling on Lammeck fast. Prevented by Reilly and Dag from actively searching for Judith, he'd been relegated to stakeout duty and cogitating. Others would take the bit and run when he next got an idea about where she might turn up. In the meantime,

Lammeck was reduced to spying on the White House grounds, scratching his head in his new hotel, and reading the papers to keep track of the war.

Judith had vanished again. After encountering her up close, and almost paying for it with his life, Lammeck firmly believed she could get to Roosevelt. The woman was ruthless, focused, invisible. Worse, she would wait as long as it took and use whatever means presented themselves. Judith seemed at peace with her role in history as a murderer; she was even somewhat moral about it, regretting the collateral deaths. On top of that, she had associates, unwitting or otherwise, like the old colored woman who'd delivered the invitation to the Blackstone. By contrast, Lammeck was isolated and lonely.

Every passing day, Judith blended deeper into the fabric of Washington, and beyond that, America. No question; she would not relent. But he would, Dag and Reilly and Mrs. Beach would, because Judith would lull them into it. Just five days after surviving the Persian, Lammeck was already tired of sifting the long hours for a clue or an insight. He saw the hubris that Reilly carried as chief of the President's protection detail. Dag had been infected with it. We can handle it, they said. No clamor, no all-out search, raise no hue and cry. Every night that FDR laid his head down to sleep, they figured they'd done their job, maybe even scared her off. Lammeck was certain that they hadn't.

Reilly and Dag thought of Judith as a killer. She was not. She was an assassin. For four years in Scotland, he'd trained assassins. Dag, one of them, had forgotten what he'd been willing to do.

Reilly had told Lammeck he could go home only when the war was over. This presumed that Judith was working for an enemy. Lammeck had no basis to speculate who she worked for, though Reilly's reasoning was sound. Still, if the two keys to Lammeck's liberty were catching Judith or the war ending, he was betting on peace happening first. He scanned the *Post* for articles on the state of the war.

Last week, the Allies took an intact bridge across the Rhine in the little town of Remagen. General Bradley had flooded a hundred thousand troops into the German heartland before the bridge fell into the river. The Marines had just about captured all of Iwo Jima. Manila was liberated. Wreckage in Berlin from Allied air raids was estimated at 87 percent. American dead, wounded, and missing since Pearl Harbor was estimated at 859,587. In Parliament, Churchill announced that "Victory lies before us—certain and perhaps near." Lammeck wandered farther into the paper, glancing at his watch for his upcoming appointment still thirty minutes off. *A Tree Grows in Brooklyn* began its third week at the Roxy Theater in New York. Judy Garland would be opening soon in *Meet Me in St. Louis*. Nationwide there was an acute shortage of fats; citizens could help by turning them in to their butcher. Several early advertisements for Mother's Day touted sales of hats, candies, and flowers. Chuck steak was 30 cents a pound, lamb 35 cents, spinach 9 cents, tomatoes 25 cents. These were better prices than what Lammeck had paid in Scotland.

He set the paper aside. Afternoon foot traffic around the White House picked up as staffers plied their way back to their desks from lunch. Lammeck caught himself vetting each stroller, every vehicle, for some suggestion of Judith. He shook his head at how he'd tumbled into the paper for fifty minutes, ignoring the street and his task, forgetting everything but the little clock on his wrist and the world in small print and pictures. To goad himself, he created Judith in the noon sunshine, walking with poison in her purse, with a dagger sheathed and hidden against her thigh. Did she, for one minute, forget Roosevelt? Did Gabčík and Kubiš forget Heydrich?

"No," he said aloud.

Lammeck got out of his government car to walk in the crowds. He gazed hard into every tall woman's face, knowing she was not among them, but forcing himself to look anyway. Quickly, this game became artificial, plainly too small an effort in too great a pool of faces. Lammeck stopped at the corner of Pennsylvania

Avenue and let his burst of fervor drain away. Of course, Judith counted on this erosion, and he couldn't stop it. He looked around one more time in case she was watching, to see herself winning. Lammeck threw up his arms, to tell her it was so. He turned back for his appointment with Reilly.

Walking to the west gate, he saw a dark Packard pull in from Pennsylvania. The guard at the main gate recognized the vehicle and driver and waved them through. Lammeck watched the car head around the half-moon drive for the north portico, the front door to the White House.

He entered through the west gate, showing his Secret Service credentials. After checking his .38, he headed down the long West Wing hall. Inside the office door, Mrs. Beach pointed to a chair.

"The chief's not here."

Lammeck looked at his watch. He was right on time.

"When's he coming back?"

"You can ask me whatever you were going to ask Chief Reilly."

"Reilly's not coming?"

"The chief said you could ask me, Dr. Lammeck. Do so or good day."

Lammeck dug fingers into his beard and observed Mrs. Beach, who didn't even bother to hold his eyes. She typed while he considered her. This was how far he'd fallen; Reilly didn't keep Lammeck's appointments anymore. Had Judith set this in motion on purpose? Did she know he would make an ass of himself spiking his thigh right on the floor of the Peruvian embassy? That there could be no honest explanation coming out of Reilly's office? She'd taken Lammeck right out of the game without killing him. Fucking brilliant.

"Mrs. Beach?"

"Yes, Doctor?" She continued typing.

"Alright. I suppose Reilly would have passed this request on to you anyway."

"I'm sure."

"I'd like to see the President's daybook."

"His what?"

"FDR's schedule. Where he goes, who he sees, hour by hour. Who keeps those records?"

"They're kept by the White House usher, and we sometimes cross-reference with the steno pool. The President's schedule is off limits. You must know that, Doctor. There's a war on. The President's movements are strictly confidential to his staff and this office."

"I am part of this office, Mrs. Beach."

The woman took a second to adjust her pince-nez on her nose. Perhaps she paused so Lammeck would reconsider that statement, so she wouldn't have to do it for him. He did not, and she continued with cold precision.

"Doctor, you may have enjoyed flaunting your Secret Service credentials to get into diplomatic parties and restaurants. But you are not a member of the Secret Service, and your credentials exist at the pleasure of Chief Reilly. Neither you nor God Almighty is going to compromise the security of the President of the United States—"

"That's what—"

She cut him off, "—and access to the information you have requested would do exactly that. I cannot approve your request, Doctor."

"Are you saying I'm a security risk?"

"No, Doctor. I'm saying this Judith woman has demonstrated that she can find you whenever it suits her purposes. And the next time she comes knocking, we cannot have her getting her hands on a full repository of the President's whereabouts and plans. You understand."

Lammeck got to his feet.

"I do."

He stomped toward the door, making up his mind to confront Reilly before the day was out.

"I *can*, however," Mrs. Beach stopped him before he turned the doorknob, "give you access to the records you're asking about, but only after a three-week lag time."

Lammeck faced her. She peered up at him over her glasses, implacable and placid.

"So I get it cold."

"Cold enough, Doctor, so that it can do no harm. Take it or leave it."

"I'll take it. Date it back to January one, this year."

"I'll have everything sent to your new hotel. It will be delivered to you personally, for your signature."

"Of course. The desk clerk's a spy for the Germans."

She ignored this. "I should have it ready by noon tomorrow. Needless to say, you are responsible for the privacy of those documents."

"I'm not sure they're hot enough off the presses to make much difference."

"You disappoint me, Doctor. I expect you to see that they do make a difference. Or why give them to you? Anything else?"

Lammeck recalled the dark Packard pulling into the grounds.

"Who was in the car that just arrived at the west gate?"

"That was Chief Reilly. He went to pick up an old friend of the President's for lunch at the White House."

"Does this old friend have a name?"

Mrs. Beach managed a face balanced between an annoyed glare and a bemused grin of tolerance. She made no reply.

"I can follow that car when it leaves, Mrs. Beach. Save me the trouble."

"Her name is Mrs. Paul Johnson. She came for lunch. Mrs. Johnson and the President go back a very long time. She is above reproach, I assure you."

Lammeck inclined his head to the secretary. "I'm sure Mrs. Johnson appreciates your faith in her."

Lammeck stalked out of the office. He collected his pistol and strode back to his car. A softball game had started on one of the fields in the Ellipse. Lammeck bought a hot dog from a kiosk and took a seat on the grass in the unlikely spring warmth.

Aurora Heights
Arlington, Virginia

"YOU'RE LEAVING?"

Mrs. Tench took a seat on a divan. She produced a kerchief and fanned herself as if she had the vapors. "Do you have another job?"

"I might, ma'am."

"But . . . but I need you here. I can pay you better. Is that it? Do you need a raise?"

"No, ma'am. The pay's fine."

"Then . . . ?" Mrs. Tench shook her head at the carpet and curtains, the tabletops and silver that were about to be abandoned. "Then what is it? Is it me? Have I been too difficult?"

"No, ma'am. You're fine. I just don't like the city. I'm trying to get a job in the countryside. It's more to my liking."

Judith knew to ask for the letter of reference quickly, before this mercurial woman's mood turned sour.

"Desiree, I . . ." Mrs. Tench stood, jamming the lace kerchief into her pocket. Judith cringed; she'd waited too long. "I am *very* disappointed in you. Do you have any idea what kind of lurch this leaves me in? Do you know how difficult it is to find adequate help in Washington? I've been good to you, have I not?"

Better than you know, Judith thought.

"Yes, ma'am. But I got to move on and I figured I should tell you straight off."

"Is there nothing that will change your mind?"

"I'm afraid not."

"Well, I hope you know Mrs. P. will also be extremely hurt by this." The woman checked Judith's face for some twinge of regret, then said icily, "Fine. I can see you've made your decision. Can you at least stay 'til the end of the month? Mr. Tench and I will be hosting several parties to mark our return home."

"I can't say, ma'am. Probably not."

Mrs. Tench brought her rail-thin hands up to her temples, edging closer to one of her fits. Judith wedged her words in before the woman could disappear into the house for a crying jag.

"I'll do my best to stay as long as I can, ma'am. Alright? I'll ask."

This mollified Mrs. Tench enough to lower her arms. "Fine," she sniffled.

"Also, I'll need a letter of reference. If you don't mind."

"And what shall I say, Desiree? That you deserted your last employer?"

"I'd rather you not." Judith smiled. "But at least that would show how much you missed me."

Mrs. Tench shook a finger. "Don't try to charm me, missy. Alright. I'll be in the library writing your reference. Please bring me a vodka tonic on ice."

Judith watched the woman whirl away in a flurry of thin wrists and skirt. She went to the liquor cabinet in the salon to mix the drink, then to the kitchen medicine cabinet.

In the library, Mrs. Tench took the cold highball glass and swapped Judith an envelope, then looked away peevishly. Judith left the library to read the handwritten note:

TO WHOM IT MAY CONCERN:
    Desiree Charbonnet is a fine girl. You may hire her.

                                        Mrs. Jacob Tench
                                        Arlington, Virginia

Judith dusted until the woman called for her customary second highball. This Judith also made with rubbing alcohol, even stronger than the first. She delivered it to the library and told Mrs. Tench it was almost two o'clock, she would be leaving for the day, and thank you for the reference letter.

Judith put on her coat and stood in the front hall, not wanting to cheat herself. She waited, making no sound. In five minutes, Mrs. Tench shouted from the library for Desiree. Judith waited to hear the woman retch, then turned the doorknob silently and slipped away.

Washington, D.C.

AT THREE O'CLOCK, THE same black Packard pulled out of the north drive of the White House. The car turned left on Pennsylvania. It continued west through Washington Circle, past the Rock Creek Parkway, toward Georgetown.

Lammeck followed at a safe distance into the tony residential lanes. On Q Street, at the steps of a brownstone, the car halted. Mike Reilly got out and opened the door for Mrs. Paul Johnson. The woman held her skirts nicely when she climbed out of the backseat, very ladylike. Tall and graceful, she was measured in her movements. Reilly even bowed a little at the waist when she took her leave of him. From a block away Lammeck could tell she had a creamy complexion and long legs.

He waited until she was halfway up the steps before driving forward. Once Mrs. Johnson reached the landing, Reilly drove away down Q Street. Lammeck slipped in behind. He got only a glimpse of her before she disappeared through the front door: early to mid fifties, short gray hair still seasoned with auburn, soft figure; she probably was lanky years ago. In profile, Mrs. Paul Johnson was beautiful.

Lammeck drove off when she entered the home. Before bringing his eyes back to the street, he caught sight in a window of a large-framed figure, a white woman in a black maid's uniform. She was at least as old as Mrs. Johnson, and one and a half times the size.

Lammeck drove off. As far as he could tell, Mrs. Paul Johnson appeared legitimate, and her maid was definitely not Judith.

Georgetown

"COME IN, *CHÈRE*, COME in. Give me the coat. There, *bon*. Ah, what have you done to your hair?"

Judith patted her temples with shy fingertips. Her hair stopped now above her shoulders.

"I cut it back."

"I see this. Did you do it yourself?"

"Yes. Why, does it look bad?"

"No, no, it is *belle*. But you had such lovely hair."

And now, Judith thought, I do not. Mrs. Rutherfurd would not be asked to compare her own beauty to Judith's.

Annette spun her to see the new cropped style from all sides. She said, "You did not mention that you are also a fine hairdresser. Perhaps you will cut mine. Make me look like an elf."

"Do you really like it? Some of the Hollywood stars are wearing their hair this short now. Like Bette Davis. Oh, and Ingrid Bergman."

"Yes." Annette nodded. "*Casablanca*."

Judith lowered her voice, to imitate Bogart speaking to the French inspector played by Claude Rains in the movie: " 'Louis, I think this is the beginning of a beautiful friendship.' " The two women giggled.

Annette nudged her round bosom close to whisper, "The madame is in a fine mood today. I have spoken with her about you, made very big boasts. I have told her that I am needing some help, I am not so young as before. She is waiting in the parlor with her sister." Annette clasped her hands. "I have hope, Desiree."

Judith arranged her black skirt and blouse. She'd chosen to again wear the maid's uniform similar to Annette's, to show she was ready to join the team. The old maid led her to a set of pocket doors, then patted her arm and slid back one tall panel.

Inside the parlor sat two very similar women, clearly sisters. One, the taller and younger, stood and approached with an open hand.

"My name is Mrs. Lucy Rutherfurd. This is my sister, Mrs. Violetta Marbury. This is her home. Welcome. It's Desiree, yes?"

Judith curtsied. "Yes, ma'am."

Mrs. Rutherfurd laughed at the formality. "No need for that, child. Please, sit down."

The woman's voice flowed from her warm and dark like pouring tea. A fluid ease marked her movements, especially for a tall woman in her fifties. Her sister inclined her head in a gentle greeting. Mrs. Rutherfurd sat beside her sister on a wide sofa as Judith took a straight-backed Windsor chair. The two mature women arranged themselves in composed poses on their cushions as if sitting for a portrait, hands clasped in their laps, shoulders square. This, thought Judith, is an American breed, the upper class.

Mrs. Rutherfurd let a moment settle in the parlor, unhurried. She made the few seconds elegant by letting them be quiet. Judith found more calm during her first minute in Mrs. Rutherfurd's presence than she'd experienced in months with Mrs. Tench. Judith spilled a long breath and fidgeted.

Mrs. Marbury piped up, "Don't be nervous, Desiree." The woman's voice was as clement as her younger sister's. "Annette has told us all about you. If half of what she says is true, you're a dream." The sisters smiled at each other. They were mild women, tender-hearted, as unsuspecting as they were trustworthy. They were, Judith thought, ideal for their roles as accomplices.

"Yes, ma'am." Judith tried to sit up and arrange herself the way

Lucy and Violetta did in their chairs, so primly. Judith caught the sisters exchange an approving glance.

Mrs. Rutherfurd asked, "Tell me about yourself."

Judith gave the sisters the New Orleans story. She invented a mother and father working in factories, a Catholic girls' school where she learned her letters before she quit and went to serve as a housemaid in a big French Quarter home. An old white patroness who sent her on to high school, a Cajun restaurant where she got the hang of cooking. Her desire to see some of the world, the bus ride to Washington. Her few months struggling with the big city. The accidental meeting with Annette. Then she produced the terse reference letter from Mrs. Tench. Judith rose and walked it across the carpet to Lucy.

"It's not a long letter," she explained demurely. "The lady didn't want to see me go, I reckon. But she said it was alright and gave me that."

The sisters took a moment with the note. Violetta remarked that she knew of the Tenches, but not personally. She asked what chores Judith had done in the Tench household.

"Everything but cook. And I'm a good cook." Quickly, she added, "Maybe not as good as Annette, though."

Lucy and Violetta looked at one another and communicated something silent. Judith imagined pretty Lucy Rutherfurd doing this for Roosevelt. She saw Lucy sitting with the crippled man at meals or in his study, listening intently, holding herself back and drawing him out. Judith had seen many photos of the President's wife, Eleanor, who was also his second cousin. Eleanor had unfortunate teeth and an ample figure. She was almost as renowned a personality as her elected husband, traveling and speaking across the nation, exercising her own authority and fame, maneuvering always to advance her causes. This woman perched beside her sister daintily in the elegant parlor had little in common with Roosevelt's wife. Eleanor Roosevelt was an admirable and historic woman. Lucy

Mercer Rutherfurd was vain with her pearl skin, select with her words. Lucy was, in Judith's understanding of Western men, a perfect companion.

"Annette tells me you've offered to work for half wages, until you prove yourself to me. Is that so?"

"Yes, ma'am."

"Please go into the hall and ask Annette to join us."

Judith stood, impressed with how effortlessly Mrs. Rutherfurd issued an order. Apparently she was not all lace and smile.

Judith fetched the big French maid, catching her standing close on the other side of the pocket doors, probably after listening through them. The two entered the salon. They sat side by side, matching the sisters.

Mrs. Rutherfurd spoke: "Desirée, why would you offer to work for so little pay? Not only does it put a prospective employer on alert, it is bad for you personally. Hear me, girl, you are to never sell yourself short. I have tried to avoid that in my own life, not always successfully, but I have always found it to be a good policy. Now, Annette?"

"Yes, madame."

In French, the lady addressed her old maid. "I am disappointed that you would encourage this girl to do such a thing."

Before Annette could speak, Judith replied, also in French: "Begging your pardon, madame, but it was not Annette's idea. It was mine alone. I want so badly to work for you."

The sisters cocked their heads simultaneously, like birds. Again, they exchanged looks, this one transparent. They were impressed.

"*Oui?*" asked Lucy.

Judith lowered her eyes. "Yes, ma'am."

Lucy waited, blinking at Judith, employing her habit of letting time settle before continuing. She said, "Desiree, I have one more question for you. I believe I already know the answer, but it is a prudent person who asks and makes certain. Are you discreet?"

"You mean can I keep a secret?"

"Yes. Exactly that."

Judith paused before speaking, adopting Lucy's way. She amused herself with the ridiculous nature of the question to an assassin, but kept that off her face.

"Yes, ma'am. I can keep secrets. You have my word on that."

Lucy nodded. She said, "Excuse us for a few minutes, please, Desiree. Annette, please stay seated."

Judith was not left in the hall long. Annette came out in a tizzy, hustling Judith away from the pocket doors.

"She will pay you ten dollars a week, and of course your room and board. After three months, if you are both happy she will raise your money. You have the job, Desiree! This is *magnifique,* yes? We will be like them, sisters!"

Annette explained that one week from tomorrow, on the 22nd, at eight in the morning, the three of them would all leave Violetta's house for the train station. By that night, they would be at home, Ridgeley Hall, in Aiken, South Carolina.

"You can do this, honestly?" Annette asked. "You can leave your place behind and come with us?"

"I've got nothing but some luggage."

Annette dug into a pocket of her apron for a five-dollar bill. "Here. Mrs. Rutherfurd gives this to you for a taxi when you return with your bags. Be here by seven, yes?"

Judith took the money; it would be odd to refuse. She adopted Annette's animation and clapped, bouncing on her toes at the front door while she put on her coat.

Annette ushered her happily onto the landing. She blew Judith a kiss through the closing door. "*Au revoir, chère.* I will see you next week. I know we are going to get along."

Judith laughed and allowed herself a pun that only Lammeck, wherever he was, whatever dead end he was following, could catch.

"*Avec la merveille.*"

Famously.

. . .

March 21
Washington, D.C.

THE WEATHER HAD WARMED during the daylight hours, but at dusk the temperature dipped with the sun. Judith needed Mrs. P.'s quilt to sit and rock in the old woman's chair.

Sweat chilled her neck where her hair had been. An hour of training left her panting and soaked. She wrapped herself in the quilt and came out on the porch for the final time. Judith breathed in the cooling alley, exchanging greetings with black men strolling home from work, and with women herding their children inside from the falling dark.

Mrs. P. waddled up the alley well after the sun was down. She carried mesh grocery nets in each hand; her bowlegged gait made her teeter between them. Judith swept aside the quilt to help the old woman carry her bags the last yards to her door. Mrs. P. did not hand them over, shrugging out a heavy sigh.

"My burden, child. I'll carry it. You get back under that blanket, you got nothin' on but yo' pajamas. What you need all them muscles for anyhow?"

On the porch, Judith pulled the blanket out of the chair. She swaddled herself in it again and took a seat on the steps to leave the rocker for Mrs. P. Minutes later the old woman came out of her apartment. She'd changed from her maid's outfit into a wool housecoat and stocking cap. She flapped her lips like a horse, "brrrr," and collapsed into the rocker.

The two said nothing for a time. Judith looked over her shoulder to find Mrs. P.'s eyes closed, but her swollen ankles pushing the rocker in rhythm. Finally, the old woman cleared her throat.

"So, you gone, huh?"

"Yes, ma'am. Tomorrow morning."

"Mrs. Tench 'bout to be tied up. You should see de girl she hired to take yo' place. Dumb as a dog in a shirt."

"Is Mrs. Tench feeling better?"

"Yeah, just had a tetch o' flu or something."

The rails of the moving rocker creaked on the porch deck. Mrs. P. let them be the only sound for a while. In her way, the old black maid had the same gentility as Mrs. Rutherfurd.

"How come you ain't told me where you goin'?"

Judith shook her head to herself in a small motion, so Mrs. P. could not see it. No one had tried to mother Judith in twenty years. Her own mother had let her be sold as a child to a husband, then would not overrule her own husband to take her daughter back in. Judith said nothing to Mrs. P.'s question.

"Uh-huh." Mrs. P. rocked harder, pointing. "I see how you do me. Just gon' slip off and to hell with ol' Mrs. P."

"Yes, ma'am. All but that last part. Not to hell with you at all. You've been a good friend to me. You've done more than I can tell you."

"Shit," Mrs. P. chortled, "that can't be much. You don't tell me nothin' anyway. I got to figger everything out 'bout you by my lonesome. I still don't know what you up to. Anyway, you just go on."

Judith turned back to the alley. Dinner odors crept from the crevices of the poor buildings around them. Cabbage and stews, fried breaded meats, pork sizzling in pans, a sweet apple Betty— Judith pressed into her memory these mementoes of America's forgotten folk living in the heart of its grand capital city. Later, from Cairo, she'd look back on them.

She sensed the end coming soon; she'd found the way in. After taking a four-day break—probably because his wife was in town— Roosevelt had visited with Mrs. Rutherfurd three days in a row, including dinner tonight on the eve of her return to Aiken.

"What you gon' do if I call the po-lice?"

Judith did not move.

"You've got no reason to do that, Mrs. P."

"I bet they find a reason if they look at you good enough. I tell 'em you some kind of international crook or somethin.' Maybe

I call ol' Hoover up the FBI. What you think he gon' say? 'Yes, Mrs. P., I be right over. Maybe your Desiree some kind of spy.' That's what he'd say. Then I bet you do some talkin', yes ma'am."

Judith waited. The rocker's rails squeaked.

"You got a big secret, girl. At least admit that much."

Judith turned her face to the alley. She thinned her lips.

"Yes, ma'am."

"Well alright. I got *that* outta you. That's *somethin'*."

Judith's papers, cash, and kits were packed. She'd thrown out her expensive shoes and business dresses, keeping only one plain dress and a pair of flats. The apartment glistened clean. She'd paid up the next six months for the garage where her car was kept and doubled the lock. She could disappear in thirty seconds. Tomorrow morning she'd be on a train to South Carolina. No one would think to look for her there. Perhaps she didn't have to do what loomed in front of her. But Mrs. P. kept talking.

"Desiree, if that's your name?"

"Yes, ma'am."

"Tell me one thing. Just one."

"If I can."

"Whatever it is you doin', you ain't taking nothin' from no black folk, are you?"

Judith stood and strode in front of the rocker. Mrs. P. quit the chair's motion and gazed up, unafraid and curious.

"No, ma'am. I am not."

Mrs. P. studied Judith for a long moment, then nodded.

"You ever comin' back?"

"No."

"You gon' stay outta trouble?"

Judith smiled. "That's a lot to ask, Mrs. P."

"I'm gon' worry."

"I know. I'm sorry. I can't tell you how much I wish you wouldn't."

She moved behind Mrs. P.'s chair. She pressed a hand to the

woman's back for her to lean forward. Judith lowered the mantle of the quilt around her shoulders, tucking the blanket around Mrs. P., closing it across her breast. Then Judith walked in front and leaned to touch her lips to the dark forehead.

She backed away, keeping her eyes on this clever, loyal woman she could not leave behind. Mrs. P. tugged the quilt more tightly around her; she seemed saddened by Judith's parting kiss. Judith headed to the door of her building.

The old cook called across the porch, "Who gon' keep an eye on you after me?"

Judith paused, then opened the door. Without looking back, she softly answered, "No one, I hope," and thought there had been too many already.

The old woman sat on the porch a long time, past midnight. She appeared to be waiting. Judith came back onto the porch. The alley was vacant and dark.

Mrs. P. asked, "What you gon' do if I scream?"

With a speed that surprised Mrs. P. so that the old woman pushed back instinctively in her rocker, creaking the old rails, Judith clamped a hand over the old maid's mouth.

"This."

Mrs. P. made no struggle in the chair. Beneath her pressing palm, Judith felt the lips shut. Mrs. P.'s eyes widened but her arms stayed at her side. Close into Judith's face, the woman nodded. Judith eased her fingers, but kept them close.

"Who are you?"

"I'm standing here because you ask that question, Mrs. P. I wish you hadn't."

The old maid nodded. "It's too late, ain't it?"

"Yes, ma'am."

"I ain't gon' make this easy for you."

"Don't fight me."

The woman snorted. "What I'm gon' do? I can't fight you. But I ain't gon' say some bullshit like I'm ready to cross over Jordan. Girl,

I ain't. I'm a old woman but I like living. So you go ahead on. Then you go to hell."

With her free hand, Judith undid the black silk scarf from around her waist. A silver coin had been sewn into the center of the sash in the ancient Thuggee technique. Judith whirled behind the old woman, whipping the silk tight around her throat, the coin centered over her windpipe.

"Yes, ma'am," she whispered.

Judith gripped the scarf with both hands and leaned back, pulling hard enough to cut off oxygen. Mrs. P. struggled, she couldn't help herself, clawing at the black wrap around her neck. She lasted only moments, then passed out, limp, eyelids down, mouth open. Her arms relaxed in her lap. When Judith let go, the rocker whined, righting itself.

Judith moved in front of the old woman, tucking the sash away. With the index fingers of both hands, she felt along the sides of Mrs. P.'s throat, for the pulse in the carotid arteries. She found it, left and right, the blood dimmed but still coursing. The woman did not stir. Judith checked the alley one more time. It remained empty and still.

She applied more pressure now, using not just her fingertips but the length of her fingers to prevent bruising, even against the dark skin. Within two minutes, Mrs. P.'s breathing ebbed and quit. The throb under Judith's fingers stopped. The blood to the old woman's brain had been choked off. The cause of death would be explainable, but untraceable. She'd simply been put to sleep.

Judith opened the door to Mrs. P.'s building. The hall was quiet. The coloreds in these apartments were working people; their days started early. Judith opened the door to Mrs. P.'s room. She returned to the porch and lifted the dead old woman across her shoulders. Careful to make no sound, she hefted Mrs. P. onto her bed. Judith returned to the porch for the blanket, and spread it across the woman.

Back in her own room, Judith lay awake, watching the drawn blinds for dawn.

A man in high public office is neither husband nor father nor friend in the commonly accepted sense of the words.

—ELEANOR ROOSEVELT

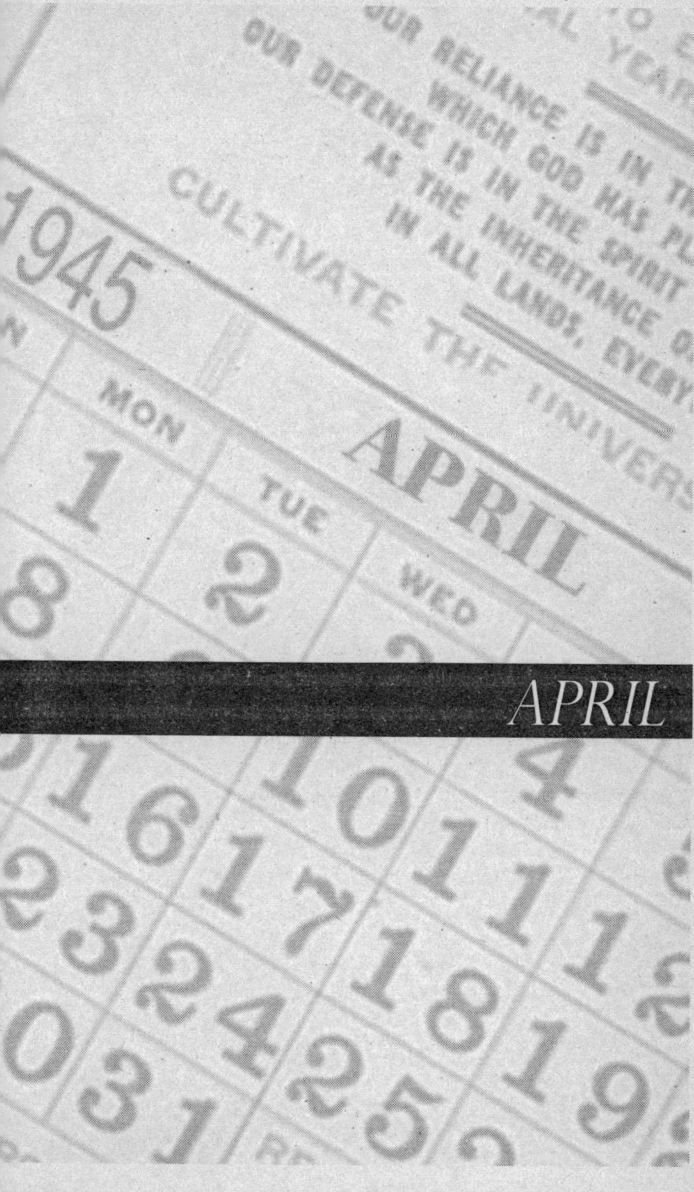

APRIL

CHAPTER SIXTEEN

April 1
Washington, D.C.

"GIMME THE SPORTS."

Lammeck lowered the front page to rummage in the untidy pile of Sunday news next to his eggs and coffee. He handed the Sports to Dag, who tossed back the Local section badly folded, its proper creases ignored. Lammeck refolded the sloppy sheets and arranged them on the stack. He forked some egg, then spoke from behind the raised paper.

"You're getting on my nerves."

On the other side of the black-and-white curtain, Dag snorted. "Sorry, honey."

Lammeck stopped reading and listened to Dag mumble over his sports. Dag cursed racehorses in Florida, spring baseball, and all the scrubs and women playing the games because of the war. He slurped his coffee and banged the cup down on the saucer. Lammeck worked his tongue in his cheek, then went back to his world news.

Patton and Montgomery had crossed the Rhine. The Pentagon was worried Hitler might head south and set up shop for a resistance movement in the mountains. Stalin and the Russians had three million men in Poland on the German border, waiting to steamroll to Berlin. Marines were poised to land on Okinawa, island-hopping and spilling blood all the way to Tojo's backyard.

The pages spread in Lammeck's grip rattled. Dag was tapping on them. Lammeck furled the paper. "What?"

"Let's talk."

"What's the matter? Need more pin money?"

Dag stared. "You still got that gat under your arm?"

"I shower with it."

"Good. Keep it close. That'll help keep me from choking you."

The two exchanged blank looks, gunfighter glares. Lammeck cracked up first; Dag laughed and looked away, shaking his head.

Lammeck gathered the newspaper and set it out of the way. He signaled the waitress for more coffee.

Dag asked, "You coming up with anything?"

Lammeck waited for the girl to pour the coffee before answering.

"Nothing. Mrs. Beach sends me a packet every few days from the President's schedule, always three weeks old, sometimes more. I go over it and over it. The guy barely sees anyone during the course of a day. A few senators, some staff, maybe a Cabinet member. His wife when she's around, which is rare. One of his sons when they're in town. His daughter Anna seems to be playing hostess at the White House, and her husband John is around a lot. For some reason the crown prince and princess of Norway are living at the White House, so Roosevelt eats dinner with them once in a while. He visits the doctor's office a bunch. He doesn't seem to be able to work a whole lot, spends most of his time avoiding it or resting from it. A car ride twice a week. Takes the train to Hyde Park every other weekend and doesn't lift a finger while he's there. Most of the time he takes one or both of his old-maid cousins with him. The Canadian prime minister is a favorite pal. Three secretaries who come and go. Every one of them has got security clearance a mile deep. Whenever I do see a name with Roosevelt I don't recognize, I

check it out. False alarm every time. And that's it. Outside of his immediate circle, almost nobody gets to see him. He's like the damn
Wizard of Oz. And Dag, you know this: The man's sick."

Dag listened over the warmed coffee. "You can't find her?"

Lammeck let the question linger, feeling the sting of it. It wasn't
really a question.

"I can't find her." Lammeck spread all ten fingers in the air.
"Poof."

Dag finished his coffee. He gestured for the check. "I've been
talking to Reilly about what to do with you. You're starting to get
on his nerves, too."

"I have that effect when I'm held against my will."

"Fair point. Anyway, with the war looking like it could wind
down pretty soon, and no trace of our Persian gal anywhere, he was
thinking of maybe letting you off the hook sooner rather than
later."

Lammeck tapped his thumbs on the linoleum tabletop. "Is this an
April Fool's joke?"

"Nope. And regardless of what you think of Mrs. Beach, the
chief, or me, we appreciate what you've done. The fact is, we've got
the situation under control. As much as it can be. And frankly, it
looks like you're out of tricks, Professor."

Lammeck smiled, not bothered by the assessment. "I'm an old
dog. When?"

"Give it another two weeks. Let Patton and MacArthur kick
some more ass. That'll definitely put the war on the downslope.
That ought to spring your cage. What are you gonna do, head back
to Scotland?"

"That's where my work is. For now. I'll have to see what happens
after my book is finished."

"Your assassins book. Yeah. Too bad our little gal isn't going to
get her own chapter."

"I wouldn't worry. Over the course of four thousand years of civ-
ilization, there's no shortage of material."

Dag looked into his empty coffee cup. "That's fucking sad."

When the check arrived, Lammeck said he'd take care of it. Dag stood from the booth. Lammeck stayed seated to finish the newspaper. Walking past, Dag patted Lammeck's shoulder. His palm landed on the harness of the holster.

"Hey, Professor."

"Yeah?"

"Be careful."

Lammeck gestured to the hidden .38. "What, with this?"

"No." Dag paused. He seemed to be saying more than good-bye for this morning. Oddly, his face softened. "I mean . . . you know, just be careful, okay?"

The agent strode off. Lammeck called at his back, "I'm just an historian, Dag. We academics never get into trouble if we can avoid it. That's your job."

April 3
Aiken, South Carolina

TO WORK IS TO worship. This Muslim adage played in Judith's head.

Suds nibbled at her elbows, her hands probing into the kitchen basin for the next dish to wash. Warm water lapped at her forearms. The open window ushered in an afternoon breeze and a robin's warble.

On the marble counter beside her, Annette finished tucking the last crisscross of crust over a rhubarb pie. The old maid set the pie in the icebox, next to the evening's pot roast. Potatoes waited in a colander to be peeled. Once the dishes were finished, Judith would take the spuds outside to the rear portico where the breeze was flavored by the lawn and nearby horse barns.

Annette slipped a crockery bowl and wooden spoon into the suds between Judith's arms, then went to the dining room to fetch the last teacups and napkins. Deeper in the house, in the ballroom, a visiting neighbor played piano. Mrs. Rutherfurd stood in the backyard under a parasol, listening to the singing bird.

Annette returned with hands full. She was so stout she could not get close to the sink to place the china cups into the water without brushing against Judith's hip. For a moment, Judith leaned into the Frenchwoman.

"You go ahead and take a nap," she told her. "I'll finish up and take care of the 'taters."

Annette stepped to the middle of the kitchen floor to consider. The marble slab needed to be cleaned of flour and dough; the dining room table had to be set for four; in an hour the roast should be put in the oven; the dishes needed to be rinsed, dried, and put away; the tile floor needed mopping.

"*Chère,* the kitchen is my responsibility."

Judith pulled her hands from the sink. Bubbles clung to her knuckles.

"Annette, I'm sorry. I don't mean to be doing your job. I was just . . ."

"I mean you are too kind to do your work and mine also. How you can do so much is a mystery. Thank you. Yes, I will go lie down for a while. When I wake, I will find some chore of yours to do. Or I will make you a special cake all for yourself."

Annette approached to hug Judith before leaving for her third-floor bedroom.

Judith swung back to the sink. Before she sank her hands again in the dishwater, the robin flapped to a new branch close to the window. In the yard, twirling her umbrella, Mrs. Rutherfurd followed the bird's flight. She caught Judith's eye. The two women lifted their chins at each other, sharing the robin's voice. Judith listened, then dropped her hands into the water and found the bowl, swishing it with a dishrag, thumping the basin holding the other plates and glasses. Watchful Mrs. Rutherfurd smiled from the yard to hear the song of Judith's work.

When she'd finished in the kitchen and the dining table was set, Judith strolled through the big first floor with a duster. Little presented itself for attention. All three floors of Ridgeley Hall were spotless, and had been since her arrival two weeks ago. She carried the bowl of potatoes outside to the portico. The robin took fright and winged off its branch.

With the bird gone, Mrs. Rutherfurd turned for a leisurely walk to the fence line to stroke one of her neighbor's ponies. Judith watched her turn away. There was nothing dowdy about the woman, even in the privacy of her backyard. She wore an ankle-length skirt and long-sleeved blouse to protect her skin; she carried the parasol across her shoulder like a woman in an Impressionist painting. She was well aware of her place in the order of her home and in southern society. While at all times Mrs. Rutherfurd remained pleasant, Judith's administration as a servant was left to Annette. Mrs. Rutherfurd made little conversation with her, even on the train south from Washington and during Judith's first days here. Mrs. Rutherfurd had given her a tour of the home, including the dents in the floor beside Mr. Rutherfurd's bed that the old man had made in his last days by banging his cane for attention. Most of her talk was reserved for the description of household duties. Annette was in charge of Mrs. Rutherfurd's toilette, hair, closets and dressing room, as well as the kitchen and daily menu. Judith's tasks were to clean, make beds, do laundry, and serve at table. Time off from chores was not discussed; the assumption was that when time was needed, it could be requested.

An age-old line was drawn in this house between servants and mistress. Judith accepted it, and judged that she was less pleasant to her own house staff in the Cairo compound. She considered that, when she returned, she, too, might hire a French maid.

Ridgeley Hall encompassed more than enough space for privacy; the three women lived well here. On the third floor, Judith and Annette occupied two of the nine bedrooms. The rest served as closets for Mrs. Rutherfurd's outfits and the children's memorabilia.

The second floor held five bedrooms. Winthrop's room remained as it was in his last invalid days, a morbid place to dust. Mrs. Rutherfurd had her own bedroom, and the others awaited visitors. The first floor was a maze of sitting rooms, library, ballroom, breakfast and dining rooms, porches, pantries, and halls. Across from the house, on the other side of the dirt tract called Berrie Road, lay the Palmetto Golf Club. Winty had been chairman of the grounds committee there. The few homes on their street occupied the heart of thousands of forest acres riven with riding trails for Aiken's horse set.

The mansion's tales were stored in Annette's expansive breast. On several evenings, when Mrs. Rutherfurd had gone to bed after a toddy or a round of cards with friends, Annette sat with Judith at the hewn oak kitchen table. The two poured Mrs. Rutherfurd's sherry into coffee mugs in case they were caught nipping. Annette told Judith about Mr. Winthrop. The monsieur had been twenty-nine years older than Lucy Mercer when they married. He'd been powerful and manly, a lifelong Republican, a hunter and gamesman. His first wife was chronically ill, and when she passed away he turned his attentions immediately to his pretty young governess. His love for his young second wife was possessive, often smothering. Lucy raised his five children and the one child they shared. Lucy became adored, as well as restored, in this house, and on the lush estate in northern New Jersey. She'd been a loyal wife and mother. Many times, Annette made a point of Lucy's loyalty. Not once did she mention, and nowhere in the grand house was there evidence of, Franklin Roosevelt.

April 8

MRS. RUTHERFURD TOOK HER Sunday brunch in the breakfast room. Judith served her sweet tea and bacon-wrapped melon wedges. The room was sunny for the lady's morning paper, facing south over rhododendrons toward the golf course. When she was finished, she asked Judith to go to the kitchen to fetch Annette, then invited both servants to take seats at the table.

"Tomorrow morning," she began, "an old friend of mine, a portrait artist named Madame Elizabeth Shoumatoff, will arrive. She is driving down from New York City with a Mr. Nicholas Robbins, a photographer. Now, Desiree?"

"Yes, ma'am."

"Do you recall in our first meeting when I asked if you could keep a secret?"

"I recall that very well, ma'am."

"Excellent. I am about to tell you a secret I need you to lock away in your heart."

Judith nodded eagerly, portraying the desire to be fully inducted into the society of this household.

"On occasion, the President of the United States allows me to pay him a visit. He and I are old friends from many years ago, long before he was president. I assume that Annette has said nothing about this to you?"

Judith assured Mrs. Rutherfurd this was the first she'd heard of it, and proclaimed it wonderful news.

"He's a great man, Mrs. Rutherfurd. You're lucky to have him as a friend."

"Yes," she said, preening, "I am blessed to know him. Anyway, now that you've been included in our circle of trust, you must safeguard this knowledge. Needless to say, the movements of the President during wartime are extremely hush-hush. America's enemies would dearly love to know where he is every moment of the day. And frankly, the President's political opponents here at home would love to make something of our friendship that it is not. If you understand me."

She spoke to Judith as if to a clever child, in firm tones, unambiguous terms. No trace of the impoverished daughter of an alcoholic, the social secretary, the mistress, or the governess, remained in this woman. She'd become a dowager, a wealthy widow, the confidante of the President. Lucy Rutherfurd was uncomplicated because she'd made herself into one simple thing, a highborn woman.

Judith gave a nod. "Yes, ma'am." Behind her solemn face she thought it odd that the one person in all her missions whom she had not completely fooled was Mrs. P., the most unrefined of them all. Lucy Rutherfurd would sit Mahalia Pettigrew down at this table and speak to her loud and clear like a pet. And Mrs. P. would walk away, do her chores, and later mumble more insight and wisdom behind her corncob pipe than a hundred of the President's friends could ever tell him. Judith snuffed a bit of regret, knowing her mission was intact and she was safer without Mrs. P. back in Washington talking about Desiree, gossiping on the bus, worrying and wondering where the girl had gone off to. Judith suppressed the pang she felt for the crusty old cook's killing, as gentle as she could make it. She set the distraction aside, then leaned forward to Mrs. Rutherfurd, to portray a hunger for more of this refined woman's secrets.

"Tomorrow, Madame Shoumatoff, Mr. Robbins, and I will drive to Warm Springs, in Georgia. The President has been resting there for two weeks at his Little White House."

Roosevelt had telephoned Aiken every day for those two weeks, to chat with Mrs. Rutherfurd in French. Judith had eavesdropped. She knew where Roosevelt was.

"Madame Shoumatoff has already painted one portrait of the President for me. I have engaged her to do another, this one for my daughter. Mr. Robbins will attend to take photos because the President can't pose for very long. He is a very busy man, and sometimes he tires quickly. Desiree?"

"Yes, ma'am?"

This was the moment Judith had swum ashore for on New Year's morning. Over four months she had killed and plotted killing, for the next words Lucy Rutherfurd uttered.

"I will leave you in charge of the house. I think you're certainly ready for that. Annette and I will be gone for a week. Annette, please prepare my luggage. Pack for spring; I expect the weather will be warming."

Annette beamed at her madame. "And I will prepare us a luncheon."

"Splendid. Thank you, ladies."

Judith was on her feet before Annette could push back and stand.

"Ma'am?"

"Yes, Desiree?"

"Since Annette has got so much work to do to get the two of you ready to go, I thought maybe I could cook dinner tonight. If it's okay with Annette . . ."

Mrs. Rutherfurd looked at her French maid for agreement.

"That would be perfect," the lady of the house said. "Make something special."

"Oh, I will, ma'am."

April 9

IN HER BARE FEET, Judith ran through the hall. She plunged down the servants' stairwell, taking the steps three at a time to the second-floor landing. She made as much noise as she could, letting herself become breathless, to seem panicked.

She ran the length of the second floor, slapping her hand against the wall once to announce her off-balance dash. Stopping at the far bedroom door, she panted loudly. Her knock was perfectly tuned between urgency and respect for the early morning hour.

"Mrs. Rutherfurd! Ma'am!"

Behind the door, the woman grunted, drowsy and tentative.

"It's almost one in the morning, Desiree."

"You got to come quick, ma'am. Upstairs. It's Annette."

Shuffles on the other side of the door revealed the woman was out of bed, quickening into her satin robe. In moments, the door flew open. Judith stepped back to let Mrs. Rutherfurd lead the way through her home, flicking on lights as she went.

Hurrying, Mrs. Rutherfurd asked over her shoulder, "What's the matter with her?"

"I don't know, ma'am. A minute ago I woke and heard her throwing up. I went down to her room to see. She's lying in bed, white as a ghost. I think it might be her heart. I can't tell."

"Alright girl, stay calm. I'll see to Annette."

At the steps, Mrs. Rutherfurd gathered her robe and climbed fast. Judith kept on her heels. The odor of vomit crept down the long hall from Annette's room. Mrs. Rutherfurd did not hesitate.

"Get a mop and bucket, Desiree," she ordered, entering the maid's room. Judith watched the lady sidestep the mess and sit on the edge of the narrow bed, clicking on a table lamp. Mrs. Rutherfurd cast Judith a stern glance. "Go, child!"

Judith lit out for a closet in the hall. Behind her, Mrs. Rutherfurd crooned, "Annette, dear, dear, let me look at you."

Judith returned to mop away the contents of Annette's stomach, the bits of a dinner served almost five hours ago. She fetched damp rags for Mrs. Rutherfurd to wipe Annette's mouth and lay across her brow. The lady took the old maid's pulse, then laid her graying head across Annette's bosom, listening. Judith watched Annette wince with the pounding in her chest.

Mrs. Rutherfurd stood from the bed. "Desiree, you stay with her. I'm going to call the doctor."

Judith swapped places with her employer, who swept downstairs to the phone. Annette's eyes stayed closed. Judith laid her hand over Annette's heart, seeking the beat beneath the ribs and layers of fat. Irregular thumps reached her palm with no rhythm, just random thuds like someone throwing objects against a wall.

She'd expected Annette's reaction to the foxglove to arise sooner, around bedtime at ten. A pinch of the herb had been sprinkled on the maid's baked squab, and blended in her mashed potatoes as garnish. It must be her size, Judith figured. She worried she may have miscalculated the dosage for good Annette, too much or too little.

"I'll be back in a minute, *chère*." Judith went to her room to make an emetic, a mixture of strong mustard in water. With a hand behind Annette's neck, she coaxed the maid to drink, then held Annette's head while the woman vomited again into the mop bucket. "We need to clean your tummy out," Judith whispered. The woman's pulse echoed in Judith's arms. The digitalis made her old heart slow and contract hard, squeezing like a bellows. Her face was gray. "*Bon*, Annette," she said, "you'll be fine."

Mrs. Rutherfurd returned to check on Annette's condition, and to say she would wait for the doctor downstairs. The extra vomiting had paled the maid even more. Her breathing became more labored.

By the time the doctor stomped up the servants' steps thirty minutes later with Mrs. Rutherfurd in tow, Annette's pulse had gathered some steam. Her heart had begun to remember its tempo and her pallor pinked. She was exhausted and woozy.

The doctor took Annette's vitals with stethoscope and thermometer. The big maid talked a little, lapsing in and out of French complaints that the doctor did not understand. Mrs. Rutherfurd smiled indulgently.

The doctor asked questions about what Annette had eaten recently. Mrs. Rutherfurd answered with the evening's menu, proclaiming that all three of them had eaten the squab and mashed potatoes. The doctor asked Annette how she felt and got a wheezy response that her chest did not hurt so badly, and that, oddly, for several minutes, her vision had turned everything blue. The doctor handed Mrs. Rutherfurd a packet of activated charcoal to further clean out Annette's system in case the illness was food-borne. Her heart had been put through a bad strain, he advised. She must stay in bed for a few days' rest.

At half past two in the morning, Mrs. Rutherfurd saw the doctor to the door. Judith stayed upstairs beside Annette. The old maid shook her head at Judith.

"You," she said, raising a weak and plump finger. "You made a wonderful squab. Did I mention that?"

Judith took the woman's hand into her lap.

Mrs. Rutherfurd returned. She walked around the bed to sit on the far side of Annette. She took the maid's other hand and cut off the table lamp. The three women sat in the light spilling from the hall.

"Annette, I don't know what to do. We're expected at Warm Springs tomorrow afternoon. But the doctor was quite clear that you should not travel. I could put off the trip, I suppose."

"*Non, madame.* You must go. He is the President. You do not cancel a visit with the President."

Mrs. Rutherfurd stroked Annette's brow and looked across her to Judith.

"I'll be fine," the old maid insisted. "The worst is over. You can take Desiree with you."

"No," Mrs. Rutherfurd answered. "Desiree will stay here. She must look after you."

"Madame, this girl will be wasted here with me. Take her with you. She will be a great help to you, better than me—she is younger and quicker, yes? And she is a master with hair." Annette reached a fond hand to Judith's temple. "She cuts her own, did I tell you? See?"

Mrs. Rutherfurd hedged. "I don't know."

"The doctor will look in on me. You will ask a neighbor to check. I will sleep tonight like a child and see you go in the morning with your friends to visit the President. Desiree should meet him, madame. This is a wonderful chance for her." Annette beamed at Judith. "She would not say so for herself."

Mrs. Rutherfurd released Annette's hand. She stood beside the bed and spoke down to both women.

"I will call the doctor in the morning. If he agrees to drop by twice a day, and I can get Mrs. Lawrence to bring you dinner, Desiree may come. Desiree, does that meet with your approval?"

"Yes, ma'am!"

"Then I bid you both good night. Annette, please do not frighten me like this again. My own heart can barely take it. Desiree, make certain you pack before you go back to bed."

The lady left her maids. Judith did not follow until Annette fell asleep. In her room, she packed quickly, everything.

MADAME SHOUMATOFF AND HER photographer Mr. Robbins arrived just after breakfast. The painter pulled into the drive, crunching gravel beneath a great Cadillac convertible with the top down. Mrs. Rutherfurd clapped to see it and sent Judith upstairs to the closets to find her a hat with a scarf tie for the ride to Georgia.

Annette stayed in bed, doctor's orders, eating from a breakfast tray brought by Judith. The old maid's face had regained much of its color, but her arms and neck remained rubbery and gray. Judith was now sure she'd overdosed her; the big woman's condition was weaker than Judith had estimated. Annette would recover, though there was no way to know what permanent damage her heart had suffered. Once Judith had found a straw hat with a white silk tie, she stopped in to say good-bye to Annette.

"We're going now. Will you be okay?"

"Yes. I'm glad it worked out this way. At our first dinner you said you wanted to meet the President. And when the madame asked if I had told you anything about him, you kept my secret. You did that for me. *Bon.* I am here and I will be fine. And you are in for a treat."

Judith sat beside the big maid. "We all are. Except for you, I'm afraid."

"Don't worry. But wait until you see the President. He will look worse than me, right until the moment he sees the madame. Then, it is like a magic how she cheers him. You'll see. And you will come back and tell me everything."

The old maid pulled Judith's face close to kiss her.

Before Judith could leave the room, Annette added, "Beware, *chère*. He loves women. He will flirt."

Judith grinned. "I might have to smack him."

Annette hooted at this. Judith left her laughing.

Downstairs, Mr. Robbins busied himself cramming Mrs. Rutherfurd's luggage into the trunk. Judith carried out her own small valise. The photographer found space beside his cameras, Shoumatoff's easel and paints, and their several bags.

Judith set out snacks for the travelers. Mrs. Rutherfurd introduced Judith to her painter friend and the photographer. She explained why Annette would miss this trip, and that she would be replaced by Desiree, whom Mrs. Rutherfurd described as "extraordinary." Madame Shoumatoff, a Russian émigré, inclined her head royally. Mr. Robbins, also some foreign sort but with an Americanized name, stood and politely shook her hand. Judith cleaned behind them as they munched, and when they were ready to leave, the kitchen was spotless.

She got in the backseat beside Robbins. Shoumatoff would drive. The painter set the Cadillac on low mixture to increase the car's mileage and pulled away from Ridgeley Hall, onto the clay road. Across the way, white-clad golfers and caddies trod the course. Judith laid back her head and watched the canopy of old maples and pines accelerate above her.

The mood in the open car was merry. The ride to Warm Springs was expected to take until four o'clock. The President himself would meet them in Macon. Madame Shoumatoff proved to be an able captain of her large landcraft, peeling down the country roads at an exhilarating rate. Mrs. Rutherfurd pressed down her hat. The tips of the scarf tied under her chin flapped behind her like doves.

Robbins had never met the President before. Madame Shoumatoff thought it a good notion for Mrs. Rutherfurd to brief the photographer and the maid on the man, his Little White House, and what they could expect ahead.

Mrs. Rutherfurd turned in her seat to address Robbins and Judith. Silk wings beat about her face until she tamed them with a free hand.

"President Roosevelt is the most brilliant man. He is engaging and quite the charmer. As you know, he was a victim of infantile paralysis when he was young. Out of the public eye, he uses a wheelchair to get around. The press never shows him in his chair—and, Mr. Robbins, that will include you. No photographs whatsoever of the President without his permission. You will both see him in his wheelchair, and you are to make no mention of it whatsoever. Now, Desiree. You should be aware, the President fancies himself a ladies' man."

Desiree lowered her eyes. "Annette told me."

"Did she? Well, then I shall move beyond that point and trust to your common sense. He also considers himself an architect. Honestly, he's not very good. You will find the Little White House quite small and austere, and not the most comfortable of places. This too shall go without comment."

Madame Shoumatoff took a hand from the wheel to swat at Mrs. Rutherfurd. "Don't tell them things like that, Lucy."

Mrs. Rutherfurd shouted through the wind. "They know who he is, Shoumie. For heaven's sake, he's been President for twelve years! I want to tell them who they *don't* know he is."

She pivoted back to Robbins and Judith.

"Franklin Roosevelt is the dearest person in the world to me. But it's important we all understand what sort of man he is and what his situation is so we do not tax him. First, he is not physically well. To be truthful, his heart is a concern. He has worked extremely hard these last few months, what with his long journey to Russia and the war. He may appear quite thin to you from what you have seen of him in the news. This trip is a vacation for him. He's already been down in Warm Springs for ten days, and we will only be staying for three or four ourselves, long enough for Madame Shoumatoff to do her work. The President needs his rest, and we must do nothing to interrupt that. Desiree, you are along on this trip to assist me, Madame Shoumatoff, and Mr. Robbins. I do not intend to further burden the President nor his staff with our presence. They all have enough on their plates for the moment. As for the President, he always bounces back, and he will this time, too."

Madame Shoumatoff glanced in the rearview to catch Judith's eye, to see how she reacted to being assigned to care for all three of them. Judith left her face expressionless, as if this instruction were natural. Shoumatoff switched her reflected gaze to Robbins. She called over her shoulder in her Russian accent: "He is a lonely man. I saw this when I painted him before. Even though he is the most powerful person in the world. I try to capture this. The power. And the isolation."

By now the Cadillac had crossed the state line, rushing west into Georgia, approaching Augusta. Mrs. Rutherfurd smiled at her artist friend, appreciating the talent required to depict on canvas the man she carried in her heart. She took up the theme Shoumatoff had initiated.

"Over the past few years, the President has had several personal losses that have affected him deeply. He'll play them close to the vest; he's not the sort of man to grieve openly. He's very much the Yankee stalwart like that. But in the last year alone he's suffered the deaths of his old friend Pa Watson and his secretary Missy LeHand. His former headmaster from Groton, Dr. Peabody, passed away before this last inauguration. Dr. Peabody had given the invocation at every one of Franklin's ceremonies and was like a father to him. Louis Howe, his old political mentor, died a few years back, and now Harry Hopkins, his closest advisor, is so ill the two hardly see each other anymore. When Franklin's mother passed away four years ago, the poor soul wore a black armband for a year."

Shoumatoff lifted her voice to add, "After the old lady died at Hyde Park, the biggest tree on the property came crashing down."

"That's something," Robbins said, smiling over at Judith. Shoumatoff continued, regaling them through the wind with her impressions of the President from her brief visits with him, how he ate alone many nights, how his famous uplifted chin and cigarette holder masked a spirit that often flagged in his tortured frame. She repeated how these were the mysteries and opposites she strove to paint of Roosevelt. Robbins nodded in fascination, mentioning that he too hoped to capture these qualities on film. Mrs. Rutherfurd's face soured but she did not stop Shoumatoff from chattering on. Judith noted how the two artists seemed impressed with the myths of Roosevelt—the crashing tree, the lonely meals. Lucy alone was pragmatic, figuring how to help him and, plainly, to love him.

Morning drifted into early afternoon. Neither Mrs. Rutherfurd nor Madame Shoumatoff turned anymore to speak to the backseat. They kept their conversations to themselves. Robbins, whom Judith determined must be eastern European in origin, closed his eyes and let the sun and air brush his face. Judith watched great swaths of the American South fly by. The road rose and fell over easy hills green with young crops, weeds, and fresh, bright leaves. The land was carved into broad fields by antique fences long left unpainted, or by creeks. Cattle, sheep, and chickens moved in the emerald shade or amber patches of sunlight. Elder white folks and Negroes hung laundry on lines, rode clattering tractors, padded beside the road leading swaybacked horses or mules by tethers, and children who ought to have been in school ran on dusty feet or in moccasins. Every town the Cadillac motored through was small and whitewashed; the road they were on was always the only one through town. Everyone they passed stopped to stare at them. Judith smelled the poor rural warmth and thought how different America was in its regions, how far she'd come from the cold swells off Newburyport, the ghetto alleys and marble heights of Washington, and how close she was to the finish of it all.

By four o'clock, Madame Shoumatoff was lost. The Cadillac zoomed past a sign claiming that Warm Springs lay behind them. She pulled over, exasperated. Mr. Robbins took control of the maps. Mrs. Rutherfurd twittered nervously, but left the navigation to the two immigrant artists. Judith kept her eyes on the sky, on falcons and crows against the very deep blue, until Mr. Robbins convinced the ladies in the front seat what direction they should travel. He led them to two more wrong turns. Mrs. Shoumatoff's foot grew heavier on the gas pedal until Mrs. Rutherfurd calmed her, saying the President had enough tragedies on his hands. Mercifully, a sign clearly pointing the direction and distance to Macon emerged out of the lush landscape.

The Cadillac arrived thirty minutes late to the designated spot in Macon. Nothing indicated the President was anywhere near: no Secret Service presence, no crowd. Madame Shoumatoff muttered in Russian. Mr. Robbins traced the map with a finger and declared they should head directly for Warm Springs. Mrs. Rutherfurd searched the street in vain.

The car roared out of town with certainty, headed in the direction Mr. Robbins dictated. Fifteen minutes later, Madame Shoumatoff announced she was convinced they were lost again. Mr. Robbins blustered over the map. Finally Mrs. Rutherfurd exerted her authority. "Keep going this way." She pointed ahead through the windshield. Shoumatoff drove on. Robbins shrugged at Judith, privately unsure.

Ten minutes passed on the swervy country route. Tall maple trees leaned over the road, shading it and presaging the cool approach of dusk. Mrs. Rutherfurd hugged herself, eager to be there, not wanting to stop to raise the top and make herself even later. The Cadillac hurtled into green obscurity for another half hour, racing in the direction of Mrs. Rutherfurd's intuition, until ninety minutes after they should have met the President in Macon they arrived in the tiny town of Manchester. Barely slowing to cruise down the main street, Madame Shoumatoff gave a whoop. Mrs. Rutherfurd clasped her hands at her breast. A crowd had gathered around another open car, a Ford parked at a pharmacy. Several men in dark suits, out of place in this small burg, monitored the women milling in their cotton dresses and the men in overalls around the vehicle. Madame Shoumatoff parked close. Mrs. Rutherfurd opened her car door almost before the Cadillac had halted. A pair of Secret Service agents came to shepherd her through the crowd. When the people parted, Judith spotted the President of the United States, twenty feet away, sliding aside in the rear seat, a Coca-Cola in his hand, greeting Mrs. Rutherfurd, who climbed in beside him.

Washington, D.C.

LAMMECK CROSSED HIS TIRED legs on the stone bench and gazed at a giant African orchid. High overhead, the great glass dome of the Botanic Garden presided over air artificially moist and close. Late sunlight flowed through the glass into a tropic mist, highlighting bizarrely great leaves and jungly twists. Lammeck took a deep breath of falsity and longed for the real chill and mists of Scotland. Not just the weather, but the freedom.

Yesterday he completed his walking tour of the National Gallery and the Freer Museum of Art. Last week he finished the Smithsonian, the Air Museum, and the Arts and Industries pavilion, along with various monuments, statuary, and points of interest. This morning, before the Botanic Garden, he'd visited the National Archives. Now Lammeck rested, done with Washington as a tourist and with no more professional reason to be in this city.

That made his next stop a foregone conclusion.

Lammeck exited the beautiful gardens into a crisper, natural air. He strolled west along the one mile that was the Mall toward the White House. Entering the southwest gate, he again showed the Marine on duty his creased Secret Service letterhead that granted him entry. The afternoon ran late, past five o'clock, and he wasn't sure he'd catch the cantankerous secretary before she left for the day.

Lammeck checked his .38 at the gate and entered the West Wing. At the end of the long white hall, opening the office door, he thought himself in dubious luck; Mrs. Beach was still at her station.

She looked up from her typewriter. "Doctor. I haven't seen much of you this past week. Dag mentioned you're not checking in as often as you used to. Keeping busy?"

"Yes. I can barely keep up with my duties. And my social calendar is just chockablock."

"Splendid. If you're here to see the chief, he's out of town until the middle of next week. I'll tell him you dropped by."

"Where is he?"

"He's with the President, Dr. Lammeck. That's his job."

Lammeck took a seat in front of Mrs. Beach, to inform her he was not in the mood to be turned away. "And where is that?"

She pressed her pince-nez up on her nose, a gesture he'd learned to interpret to mean she was ready to be cantankerous.

"And the reason for your interest is . . . ?"

"Because, damn it, I want to get the hell out of here and back to my work in St. Andrews. Tell Reilly you can keep Harvard and Yale and the rest. I don't need a payoff. Just let me out of here. And I want to go now. Get him on the phone."

Mrs. Beach smiled with the stolidity of a career bureaucrat.

"I understand your sense of urgency, Doctor, but unfortunately it is not one this office shares. I am not going to disturb Chief Reilly from his duties protecting the President simply to pass along an administrative matter. It, and you, can wait for his return. And just to show you I'm not hard-hearted or untrusting of you, Chief Reilly is in Georgia, with the President."

She tilted her head to imply that was all she had for Lammeck. He was undaunted.

"Call him."

"No."

"Where's Dag?"

"Agent Nabbit is also on assignment out of the capital. He's doing advance work for a trip the President will be making soon. We have not forgotten your Persian, Doctor, no matter what you may think of us. We're quietly doing our job. We are, after all, the *Secret* Service."

Lammeck had run into the stone wall he'd expected. But he hadn't figured on having to wait until next week for Reilly to get back to settle this. The notion set his foot tapping with impatience. He stood from his chair.

"Mrs. Beach. I'm bored, I'm useless, and, worse, I'm getting fat. I want you to do everything possible to send me home the minute Reilly gets back."

The secretary knit fingers and rested them across her keyboard. "Doctor, I assure you that you're just as important and handsome as you were the day you first walked in that door. As for your being bored—here."

She reached for a folder on the credenza behind her and handed it over. Lammeck flipped it open and knew immediately this was another set of yellow typed pages copied from Roosevelt's daily schedule. The dates covered the week of March 11th through 18th. Four weeks old.

"This saves me a courier. Good day, Dr. Lammeck. And rest assured, though you'll be missed, I'll do everything I can to expedite your leaving us. Somehow, we'll fend for ourselves."

Lammeck grimaced his good-bye to the secretary. He took the folder into the hall. Walking absentmindedly for the gate and his gun, he scanned the first few pages. For the date of 3/11/45, he read:

1140—to office

1145—Chinese ambassador

1200—Budget Director Harold D. Smith

> 1245—Sec. of State Edward R. Stettinius, Jr.,
>   Adolf A. Berle, Acting Brazilian Min. of
>   Foreign Affairs Pedro Leso Velloso
>
> 1330—returned from office
>
> 1330–1455—(lunch—Sun Parlor) Mrs. John
>   Boettiger, Sec. of State Edward R.
>   Stettinius, Jr.
>
> 1635—to office
>
> 1830—returned from office via doctor's office
>
> 1945—(dinner) ER
>
> 2125–2245—Dorothy Brady, secretary
>
> 2345—retired
>
> ER–2330—left for Raleigh, NC

Nothing out of the ordinary. A typical short day for the tired and ailing President. A few hurried appointments, lunch with his daughter and secretary of state, then after dinner, Eleanor headed for Raleigh, leaving him alone again. This report was as stale and dormant as Lammeck himself felt. He was only a few steps down the hall when he turned to the next page, March 12. What he saw stopped him in his tracks.

> 1120—to office
>
> 1125—Sec. of State Edward R. Stettinius, Jr.,
>   Comdr. Harold E. Stassen, Rep. Charles A.
>   Eaton, Dean Gildersleeve, Sen. Tom
>   Connally, Rep. Sol Bloom, Sen. Arthur
>   Vandenberg (Delegates to San Francisco,
>   Cal., UN Conference)
>
> 1145—War Sec. Henry L. Stimson, Adm. William D.
>   Leahy

1200—Sen. Lister Hill (Alabama)

1230—Herman Baruch

1340—returned from office

1340–1440—(lunch—Sun Parlor) Mrs. John
            Boettiger

1750—motoring

1840—Returned, accompanied by Mrs. Rutherfurd

1930–2230—(dinner—Study) Col. and Mrs. John
            Boettiger, Mrs. Rutherfurd

Who the hell, Lammeck wondered, was Mrs. Rutherfurd? It was a name he'd never seen nor heard anywhere near Roosevelt, much less someone whom the President picked up in his limousine, and who then had a private dinner with Roosevelt plus his daughter and son-in-law.

Quickly, Lammeck checked the schedule for the next day, March 13th. There she was again, Mrs. Rutherfurd for dinner at 1915. She enjoyed two hours with the President, plus Anna and John Boettiger, and the Canadian prime minister, Mackenzie King. Again on the 14th, Roosevelt lunched with Anna and Mrs. Rutherfurd, then that evening ate dinner with Mrs. Rutherfurd alone.

On the 15th, she was gone. That day, Eleanor Roosevelt had returned from North Carolina.

Lammeck reversed direction. He'd gone no more than a dozen strides down the hall, and used only half that number to return to Mrs. Beach's door. The doorknob was still in his grip when he started speaking.

"Four weeks ago, a Packard brought an old friend of the President's to lunch. You told me that woman's name was Mrs. Paul Johnson." Lammeck rattled the yellow sheets, Mrs. Beach looked up at them. She stayed tight-faced and glaring. Lammeck continued, giving her no chance to interrupt. "It says here someone named Mrs. Rutherfurd came for lunch that day, not Mrs. Paul Johnson."

The secretary inhaled, an impatient retort on her lips.

"Quiet," Lammeck snapped, leaving the woman with her mouth open. "There *is* no Mrs. Paul Johnson. I want to know right now who this Mrs. Rutherfurd is, and why you were covering her up with a false name."

Mrs. Beach remained stony, working her jaw below a hard stare.

"Mrs. Rutherfurd is off-limits to you, Doctor."

"Too late for that. Georgetown, 2238 Q Street. I followed Reilly's car when she left the White House. Either have me arrested right now or I get in my own government car, drive over there, and ask her why she only comes to visit when the President's wife is out of town."

Mrs. Beach sighed, pointing to a chair. Lammeck folded into it.

"Doctor, this is a potential hornet's nest. It requires delicacy. With apologies, that is not a trait anyone here associates with you."

"At the moment, that sounds more like your problem than mine. Who is she?"

Mrs. Beach pulled down her pince-nez to rub her eyes with her fingertips. Lammeck had never seen her without the sharp-edged frames perched across her nose. He read this gesture as a victory, like watching an enemy fort take down its flag.

She composed herself before answering, leaving the glasses on the desk. Succinctly, Mrs. Beach summed up the President's relationship with Lucy Mercer Rutherfurd. The woman was exactly as she'd been described to Lammeck previously, a dear friend of Roosevelt's, and above reproach. But there was a new twist to the tale: She was not just an old acquaintance, but an old flame. Thirty years ago Lucy had almost broken up the Roosevelts' marriage. Caught and chastised, FDR vowed never to see Lucy again. Nonetheless, over the years, the President and she had kept in touch by letter and telephone. The President took an interest in all of

Lucy's stepchildren, getting military commissions for two of the Rutherfurd sons. Lucy's calls were passed through to the President by Louise Hackmeister, the chief White House operator, under the code name Mrs. Paul Johnson. In recent years, Lucy had begun to visit the White House in person under that same name, a thin protective guise in case Eleanor ever got a gander at the usher's or operator's logs. Ever since Lucy's husband died last year, her visits had become more frequent. Just last month, Roosevelt grew tired of the "Mrs. Johnson" deceit, instructing the staff to admit Mrs. Rutherfurd by her real name. Four weeks ago, when Lammeck asked about the visitor, Mrs. Beach had called Lucy by her code name, partially out of long habit, mostly to keep Lammeck off her scent. "Needless to say," the secretary conceded, "that didn't work."

Eleanor would not be at all pleased to find her husband had renewed visits with his former sweetheart. Even the President's daughter and sons were in on Lucy's visitations. The children liked her and viewed her as a tonic for their sick father. They accepted the deception of their mother as the price they paid for the man's rare comfort and pleasure in these difficult days. The President had also visited Mrs. Rutherfurd at her estates in Allamuchy and Aiken. The pool reporters, along on these train trips and left to wait on the sidings, seemed content to let the Boss have his diversion.

"Mrs. Rutherfurd is quite different from Mrs. Roosevelt. She is more...congenial. The President enjoys her company; he is the Boss; and on this topic, Doctor, I will say no more. Except to repeat that, for obvious reasons, Mrs. Rutherfurd remains off-limits to you. To a great extent, she's out-of-bounds even to us."

Lammeck sat back, satisfied that he'd wrung from Mrs. Beach all he was going to get. If he pressed much further, she might take him up on his bluff and have him arrested. He'd spoken to her pretty roughly to get this far. Though delicacy might not be his strong suit, he wasn't stupid.

"Thank you, Mrs. Beach. One last question. You say Mrs. Rutherfurd lives in South Carolina. Who's at Q Street?"

The secretary replaced her glasses on the bridge of her sharp nose. Lammeck guessed this heralded the end of her patience.

"Why do you need to know, Doctor? Is it important?"

"I have no idea. I can only guess that if you don't tell me, it is."

"Point taken. That is the home of Mrs. Rutherfurd's sister, Violetta. At present, so far as I know, Mrs. Rutherfurd is not there, but at her property in Aiken. So you do not need to drive to Georgetown."

"Agreed."

Lammeck recalled the big maid he'd seen peering through the Q Street window when Lucy returned from her White House lunch.

"You said Mrs. Rutherfurd has two estates. I assume she has staff. What do you know about the people who work for her?"

Mrs. Beach cocked her head. Lammeck readied himself to escape.

"As I've said more than once, Mrs. Rutherfurd enjoys a special status with the President. We do not pry too deeply where she's concerned. We trust her because the President trusts her. To do otherwise would be to second-guess and displease the man we all work for. Understood? Good. Now, is that all? I should like to go to my own home before the night is over. You are not the only one tired of being in my office."

Lammeck rose, thanked the woman again, and left. Only seconds behind him, she locked up, sounding stern even with her keys. At the gate he reclaimed his pistol. Mrs. Beach strolled off in her direction, and he went his through the dusk back to the Carlton Hotel.

In the hotel parking lot, Lammeck opened his car. He checked the glove compartment. For three months he'd driven little more than slow circles around the White House. Mostly, he'd walked.

He'd accumulated more than enough gas ration coupons to drive to South Carolina.

. . .

Warm Springs, Georgia

MADAME SHOUMATOFF LEFT THE Cadillac to join Mrs. Rutherfurd in the President's car. When Mr. Robbins took the wheel of the big convertible, Judith asked him to raise the top against the cold. She stayed in the backseat, lowering her face against curious eyes and the day's failing light.

On the drive away from Manchester, one Secret Service car led the way, while the other filed in behind the Cadillac, bracketing it into the motorcade. Judith kept watch on the roads and turns leading to Warm Springs. On the way, Mr. Robbins attempted conversation. Judith maintained her shyness to quash it.

Darkness overtook them by the time the convoy reached Pine Mountain. The four cars slowed but did not stop for a raised barrier at the head of a gravel road. Two Marines saluted the vehicles. Judith watched Roosevelt, surrounded by women, lift a thin white hand to the soldiers.

The road wound downhill through pine forest and uncut scrub. Judith marked the direction and landscape. No man-made light broke through the branches and night; Roosevelt's retreat had no neighbors. The gravel road to the cottage threaded more than a mile from the main highway through the wooded dark. Judith could not spot security patrols or sentries.

Minutes later, electric glows cut through the leaves. The cars rounded a last bend. Down a mild slope, in a break in the trees, stood a white cottage, lit up and hospitable. Both Secret Service vehicles braked outside one final raised barrier. The President's car and the Cadillac proceeded past the Marines, crunching along a circular drive to the front door of the Little White House.

Beside the drive, an entourage waited in the grass. Three men wore suits; two others stood in naval officer blues. They were joined by seven women. Everyone together descended on the President's

car, greeting Mrs. Rutherfurd and Madame Shoumatoff. Mr.
Robbins got out of the Cadillac, neglecting Judith in the rear. She let
herself out and stood motionless, hands behind her back, to draw
no attention. Mr. Robbins strode to the welcoming party and received introductions to the President, his staff, and the other guests.
Judith watched the Secret Service agent who'd driven Roosevelt's
Ford reach into the open backseat to lift the President, then deposit
him into a wheelchair. Roosevelt appeared limp in the bulky agent's
arms. No one in the crowd seemed surprised or distressed, least of
all Roosevelt, who never took his happy eyes off Mrs. Rutherfurd
while he was boosted into the air. All the women smiled grandly. The
men watched, measuring every aspect of the President. Judith stood
beside the Cadillac, ignored until Mrs. Rutherfurd addressed one of
the ladies, a stout black woman, before joining the group moving
indoors. With a pleasant demeanor, this woman approached Judith.

"You're Desiree?"

"Yes, ma'am."

The woman, wide as a teapot, reached to shake hands. Hand-
shaking was not something Judith had seen an American woman do.

"I'm Lizzie McDuffie. I do the housekeeping when the President's
in town."

"Pleased," Judith said with a short curtsy.

"Mrs. Rutherfurd asked me to show you where to unpack her
suitcase. Then I can show you where you'll be staying with me and
Daisy Bonner, the cook. Daisy's right over there."

Lizzie pointed out another woman, white and cut from the same
dumpy, friendly cloth. Daisy Bonner waved. Judith smiled in return.
She reached into the trunk for Mrs. Rutherfurd's suitcase.

"That looks heavy," Lizzie said. "You need help?"

Judith hefted it in one hand. "No."

"Great." Lizzie grinned. "Your Mrs. Rutherfurd says Annette is
feeling poorly. When you get home, please tell her I asked after her."

Two square outbuildings framed the main cottage. Both stood uphill fifty paces from the front door. Lizzie led Judith to the structure on the right. "Up them steps there. Your lady and her painter friend will be bunking above the President's two cousins. The photographer fella will stay in town at the Warm Springs Hotel with all the reporters. You and me and Daisy are over there, above the garage. I got a cot all set out for you."

Judith stepped up into the small frame building. The interior was simply four paneled walls and a heart-pine floor covered with a hook rug, two narrow beds, two cane chairs in the corners. Doilies and lamps rested on two tables, and yellowed framed prints did little to decorate the space. Clearly the President included others in the humble theme of his refuge in the piney woods. Judith admired the lack of opulence; it was not what she expected from a king.

She carted the weighty luggage up the stairs. Lizzie tagged along, chatting, oblivious to Judith's lack of response. This room was no different from the one below, equally spartan with twin beds and plain décor. Judith imagined Mrs. Lucy Rutherfurd, wealthy matron, widow, and close friend of the President, curled on one of these cots, sharing the tiny room with an immigrant painter who looked like a snorer. Judith smiled at love and the odd places it could lead. She laid the contents of Mrs. Rutherfurd's bag in the drawers of an old dresser.

In quick order, Lizzie led Judith back to the Cadillac to fetch her own luggage. Carrying her cheap valise, Judith followed the housekeeper to the second outbuilding, then up a staircase leading above the garage. Lizzie gestured at an iron cot in the small bare-beam foyer. Lizzie and Daisy had their own little rooms and beds. Beside Judith's cot waited a chamber pot. She did not unpack her bag under Lizzie's eyes, but slid it beneath the bed frame.

The two stepped outside to the cool mountain eve, peering downhill into the cottage windows at the excitement for Lucy's arrival. In the dark woods around them, Judith heard nothing but the flap of a hunting bat and a warm Georgia breeze.

"What now?" she asked Lizzie.

The housekeeper moved forward, eager to get back to minding her guests.

"Let's go help Daisy in the kitchen," she said.

FRIENDS AND ASSOCIATES SWIRLED around Roosevelt. Judith stood in the entryway looking into the parlor; there'd been no room for her in the kitchen alongside the two hefty servants. Daisy Bonner had ushered her out politely by the elbow. "I'll have use for you shortly, dear," the cook had said, adding, "but I will say, you do take up less space than Annette."

Everyone seemed glad to see Mrs. Rutherfurd. Even a chubby Scottish terrier panted for her attention. Inside, the cottage was hardly better appointed than the outbuildings. Naval prints adorned the walls, books filled a few shelves, a big stone fireplace awaited colder evenings. The tables and chairs were pedestrian, the carpet just another hook rug. The only ornate possessions were several model wooden ships on the mantel.

None of the Secret Service agents had come inside the crowded cottage; their job kept them on its perimeter. Roosevelt's wheelchair faced away from Judith. She caught only glimpses of his profile; he appeared ashen and gaunt with ruby cheeks. But his words sailed above the packed den, a kite of a voice that rose because it was thin. He laughed at something a woman—probably one of the cousins—said. He turned to Mrs. Rutherfurd, seated at his shoulder, and cried, "Don't you just love it?" Judith caught a glimpse as Mrs. Rutherfurd touched his shoulder at whatever jest had been made. Roosevelt covered her hand with his for a moment. The two shared a gaze as if they were alone. Judith put her hand in her pocket and fingered a small vial of white powder.

"She's good for him."

Judith turned to look into the handsome face of a dapper black man.

"Yes, sir."

He smiled a palisade of white teeth. The veins in his hands and the width of his shoulders showed strength.

"You don't have to 'sir' me, girl. I'm Arthur Prettyman, the President's valet. If you come with Mrs. Rutherfurd, then I'm glad to see you."

Judith pulled her touch from the bottle in her pocket to take the valet's offered hand. "I'm Desiree."

"I heard. You know who any of those people are? Beside the ones you came with?"

"No."

"Alright. The one young fella in the naval uniform is the President's doc; the other is his pharmacist and masseur. Over by the fireplace that fella is a secretary, just like the two ladies he's talking to. Now you keep an eye on those other two gals standing either side of your Mrs. Rutherfurd. They're the President's cousins. Treat them nice and stay out their way. And you already met Lizzie and Daisy."

"Yes. Thank you."

"I hear your Mrs. Shoumatoff is going to do another portrait of the Boss. And that other fella's a photographer, is he?"

Judith nodded.

"Seem like nice folks," Arthur mused.

"How's the President feeling?"

Arthur seemed surprised at the question from a colored maid. He mulled his answer, staring into the room at his charge.

"He's alright. He's good. Listen to him." Judith saw plainly on the valet's brown face how hopeful he was.

Roosevelt's voice still crowned the room. All the women gave themselves over to his charm. They gazed down at him adoringly, except for Mrs. Rutherfurd, who sat at his level and shared whispers. In return, Roosevelt tossed them brisk words and flicks of his thin wrists, burning the candle as bright as he could with the pale wax of his flesh. Arthur saw this and loved the President for it, fooling himself. All the people in this house fool themselves, Judith thought. Even Roosevelt.

Lizzie came around the corner, curling a finger to summon Judith to the kitchen. She left Arthur and slipped through the main room, catching snatches of the voices of Shoumatoff and Robbins telling tales about getting lost this afternoon. The President egged the story on with a jovial "No! That's the wrong turn! Ha!"

Judith entered the kitchen only a step before Daisy thrust at her a platter of snacks, crackers with tiny meats and pimento cheese. "Serve those," Lizzie called from the stove where she stirred a great pot that smelled of stew.

Judith turned to face the room, the tray in front of her. She strode into the gathering. Many hands plucked treats from the tray. She made her way to the President. She stopped, one step from his wheelchair. The two locked eyes.

"Hullo," he said.

Judith bent to lower the platter for him. The President glanced without interest at the snacks, then straight into Judith's eyes. He froze then, as if he saw something familiar. Judith suspected he did, for she did in him. His face bore the coldness she recalled in the eyes of Agha, the old husband who'd bought her as a child; the icy distance she'd seen, too, in her father's face when he denied his own daughter her return; then in the many eyes of her assassin teachers; and in the looks of the dozen targets she'd been paid high wages to kill, all powerful men and women. The chill had taken root in her eyes, as well. It could be recognized only by another of the same kind. It was the frigid gaze of one who knows that other people are to be used for a purpose, then discarded. Roosevelt, riveted on her, began to speak.

Immediately Judith straightened and softened her own expression. The President blinked and paused, surprised at the maid's abrupt withdrawal. For a second his mouth hung open. Then he began to cough.

Judith leaned in again. The President covered his mouth with a knotty fist. Mrs. Rutherfurd patted his back, and the gathering paused. The color in Roosevelt's cheeks fled. The collar of his shirt was at least one size too big for his neck, where tendons bulged from the strain of his hacking. Close, Judith took a deep smell of the living man. She shifted the platter to one hand and reached for the President's arm, squeezing as if to comfort him. She knew then his weight, his condition, his dose.

The naval doctor pressed through the crowd. He pushed in front of Judith and knelt to look into the President's face. As he did this, Roosevelt regained control; the coughing subsided. The doctor hovered, making certain the spell was gone before he stood aside.

With a linen handkerchief, the President wiped his mouth. Beside him, Mrs. Rutherfurd surveyed him with deep concern, lapping a hand on his forearm where Judith's had been seconds before. The room regained its lost kilter, growing voluble again. The circle of women around Roosevelt lit their glances on him in fresh competition for his return gaze. Judith held out the tray to Mrs. Rutherfurd. She selected a small hot dog with a toothpick through it. Judith moved the platter again to the President's reach.

As he did before, he paid scant attention to the food. Instead, he looked again at Judith, now with a sudden tired melancholy.

"No," he said, "thank you. I haven't much appetite." His voice was not that of a dying man, not weak, but firm and misleading.

Judith smiled, pulling back the tray.

She would not act tonight. She didn't know the land, the security layout, or the size of the Marine detail, and couldn't trust the direction to the main road through the dark forest.

"Maybe tomorrow, Mr. President."

CHAPTER SEVENTEEN

April 11
on Route 1
Sanford, North Carolina

LAMMECK ORDERED COFFEE AND a steak. A waitress, red-headed and gum-chewing, brought the coffee. She scratched her head with the eraser of her pencil. Outside, a lumber truck hit its brakes to slow for the turn into the diner.

"Your steak'll be up in a few."

"Thank you."

"Where you from, honey?"

Lammeck dug fingertips into his sockets. His eyes felt dry and were likely red.

"Washington, D.C."

"That's a ways off. You drive all that today?"

"Since dawn." He'd driven it at thirty-five miles an hour, the national wartime speed limit, behind tobacco, livestock, and lumber trucks. He'd followed old ladies, farm tractors, and military convoys. Another two hundred and fifty miles remained to Aiken. Lammeck expected them to be just like the first two-fifty.

"Shoo-wee," she sang and popped her gum. "I been to Washington.

Saw the monuments and all. I was a young girl, but I remember it. Jefferson and Lincoln and the Capitol building. It was nice."

Lammeck was the only customer in the diner. At four in the afternoon, the day was too early for dinner, too late for lunch. He said, "Actually, I'm glad to be getting out of D.C. for a little while. I've been cooped up there too long."

"Yeah," the waitress agreed, "travel's nice." She looked out the windows. "That your car with the government plates?" His was the only car in the lot with the lumber truck. "You from the government?"

Lammeck didn't feel like explaining himself. His circumstances were complex. He was road-weary and hungry. It was easier to say, "Yes."

"What do you do?"

Again, Lammeck gave her a shorthand explanation. "I'm with the Secret Service."

The waitress slapped one palm over her rouged lips and studied him. She filled his coffee mug with a fresh pour.

"You know President Roosevelt?" she asked.

Lammeck blinked, trying to decide whether to stop this pretense or string it out. For a moment he envied Dag, who could answer her truthfully, give the woman a thrill, maybe even get a small one back. That would feel wonderful, he thought, after being ostracized and under what amounted to house arrest for a month at the Hotel Carlton. He'd had to put up with a near-fatal poisoning, then the constant threat of Judith's shadow returning. And the way Reilly had hung him out to dry with the Peruvian embassy. There was Dag's constant backbiting, Mrs. Beach's disdain and unvarnished bitchiness. Taking orders, being given nothing in return but stale information. He'd driven from Washington partly to do his job, as little a thing as that had become, but mostly to perform an act of rebellion, because Mrs. Beach would be furious. Mrs. Rutherfurd was off-limits, she'd told him. Lammeck thought: *off-limits, my ass.*

"Sure. I know FDR."

The waitress bent to peer between Lammeck's elbows on the tabletop.

"You got a gun in there?"

Lammeck opened his jacket. He wore the shoulder holster and the pistol everywhere; it had become one of the few sources of esteem left to him. He whispered. "It's a .38 automatic."

He closed the coat over the gun. She gawped. "Can I go tell my husband?"

"What's your name?"

"Mabel, sir."

"Mabel, I'd rather you keep this between you and me. After all," Lammeck grinned, stealing from Mrs. Beach, "we are the *Secret* Service."

She bounced on her toes like she had to pee. "Please, mister. Just Bo. I swear. Please."

Lammeck nodded. Mabel checked his coffee mug before hustling to the kitchen through a swinging door. She returned beside a tall man with a homemade cigarette stuck on his lower lip, a greasy apron, and a head topped by a beat-up mockery of a chef's cap.

"Bo," Lammeck nodded. "How's that steak coming?"

The man pincered the cigarette off his lip. "Right up, sir. You bet."

The trucker had entered the diner and arranged himself at the counter. He rotated on his stool and said, "Hey. Some java?"

Bo didn't turn but waved a hand behind him, batting the trucker's request back at him.

"You know the President, do you?"

"Yes."

"Can you give him a message for me and Mabel? Just a short one?"

"Sure."

Bo took off his hat. He held it over his heart.

"Tell him," Bo paused to look down at his wife for her agreement. "Tell Mr. Roosevelt we'd vote for him another twenty times.

He's the greatest man America ever produced, bar none." Bo glanced again to Mabel, to see how he'd done. "Ain't that right?"

She bobbed her head at him, then at Lammeck.

The trucker heard this. He piped up, "That goes for me, too. The old man's alright."

Bo grinned at the trucker and jerked a thumb over his shoulder for Mabel to give the man his coffee. Mabel leaned close, touching Lammeck's sleeve. Quietly, she said, "That steak's on the house, sugar."

Bo remained, beaming. "Mister, you mind?" The cook had lowered his voice, too, remounting his battered toque on his head. "Lemme see that gat you got in there."

Lammeck pulled back the flap of his jacket to reveal the snugged pistol. Bo snapped his head forward, then backed away pointing both index fingers.

"Whoa! I'll get on that steak for you," he said.

When the meal arrived, Lammeck ate slowly, with too many miles left to be in a hurry. Mabel brought no check. Lammeck left a good tip. She pointed at him like Bo did, with two fingers. "You promised," she reminded him. The trucker tipped his hat when Lammeck walked by.

He rode south again. Route 1 ran all the way into Aiken so he had no worry about missing turns. He cozied up behind more laden trucks lumbering south. With a full stomach, and his gladness to be out of Washington, he drove slowly, admiring pink and white dogwoods sliding past. Shrubs of quince flowered sunset red against the green of the Carolinas. Soon, dusk flattened the light and Lammeck drove on behind his headlights, thinking no more about Mrs. Beach or Reilly, but of the free steak and coffee he'd received in the name of Roosevelt. Lammeck still didn't like the President, liked him even less with the knowledge of Lucy Rutherfurd, and how Roosevelt was going behind his wife's back, even involving his children to do it. Nothing would change Lammeck's mind about Czechoslovakia, or Gabčik and Kubiš, or a dozen other grudges over lost lives and liberties that America might have better defended. But, for the first time, he felt the urge not just to catch the President's assassin and get famous for it, but to actually protect the man, admitting it was for no better reason than for people like Bo and Mabel and that unnamed trucker.

He decided to drive until ten o'clock. That would bring him close to Batesburg, where he'd take a room for the night. In the morning there'd be just twenty-five more miles to Aiken.

He'd deliver Mrs. Rutherfurd the message from the diner. Let her deliver it to the President. Then he'd go back to Washington, tell Dag or Mrs. Beach where he'd been, and get himself tossed in jail or thrown out of the country.

The Little White House
Warm Springs, Georgia

MRS. RUTHERFURD SAT ON one of the cane chairs. Judith stood behind her, admiring the set of the woman's shoulders, square and poised. The small bedroom was empty; Shoumatoff had gone for a walk. Judith dug her fingers into the graying hair on Mrs. Rutherfurd's head to spread the pomade evenly.

Mrs. Rutherfurd sighed, relaxing. "You have quite strong hands, Desiree."

"Yes, ma'am."

"Was your mother a strong woman, also?"

"No, ma'am, she wasn't."

"Your father?"

"He threw me out, begging your pardon, ma'am."

Mrs. Rutherfurd considered this under Judith's kneading fingers. "That's hard."

"It's alright."

"Then you must have made yourself strong."

"Yes, ma'am."

Mrs. Rutherfurd exhaled. "That's always best," she mused softly. "I'm sorry for not knowing that about you, my dear. I guess I might have asked before."

The lady dropped her chin to her chest. Judith guessed from this that she had more to say.

"I have never been a strong woman, myself. I've been reliant my whole life."

Judith paused at this odd volley of candor from Mrs. Rutherfurd. The woman noted Judith's hesitation.

"I apologize. I'm feeling a bit wistful just now. Annette and I often talk when she's working on my hair."

"It's fine, ma'am. You go ahead."

"No, I suppose I'll be quiet and let you do your magic."

Judith worked the perfumed cream along the woman's temples and over her crown. She pulled a comb through the damp strands, parting the hair on the right, then sculpting waves above the ears and at the brow. She used clips to hold the hair in place until the gel could stiffen.

On Shoumatoff's cot, Judith had laid out for Mrs. Rutherfurd a dark blue dress with white piping, a double strand of pearls, and eyeglasses linked to a gold chain. Earlier that afternoon, the President had asked Mr. Robbins to take a photograph of Lucy before dinner to match the ones taken of him. The woman had selected an outfit that would work on the opposite side of a cameo. Both the President and his sweetheart would be in dark garb and pale complexion.

"Desiree, would you mind rubbing my neck a little? It feels stiff."

Judith peeled down the collar on Mrs. Rutherfurd's housecoat. She worked with vigor, bringing up a sanguine flush. Mrs. Rutherfurd did not complain but lolled her head as Judith's hands closed around her throat.

"Do you know," the woman said, "that the President has shared with me the instructions for his funeral? He has left in his will very clear orders not to be embalmed, or seen in public in an open casket. Eleanor's to be buried beside him after she passes. Both graves will reside in his mother's rose garden in Hyde Park."

Mrs. Rutherfurd let Judith massage for several more seconds, then asked, "Why do you think he would tell me something like that?"

"Sounds to me like he doesn't want to have any secrets from you."

The lady considered this. She shook her head, disagreeing. Judith stopped her massage.

"He's thinking he will die soon," Lucy Rutherfurd said.

Judith admired the healthy glow she'd worked in the woman's neck.

"Yes, ma'am."

Mrs. Rutherfurd adjusted her terry-cloth collar. She rose from her chair. Without turning to Judith, she stared at the dark outfit arrayed for dinner.

"Treasury Secretary Morgenthau is expected to join us tonight."

"Cook told me."

"The Morgenthaus are very close friends of the President's wife. They are neighbors of the Roosevelts up in Dutchess County in New York."

Mrs. Rutherfurd moved to the small dressing table to sit before the mirror. Judith watched the handsome face gazing into her own aging eyes.

"Do you think Franklin did that on purpose?"

Judith moved behind her to remove the clips. Mrs. Rutherfurd's hair took the curls perfectly.

"The President knows what he's doing, ma'am. You've said so."

"Bring me the pearls."

Judith lifted the twin strands from the cot. Sharing the mirror now, she lowered the necklace around Mrs. Rutherfurd's throat.

"You didn't know him before," the older woman said. "He was the most vibrant man. Even after the polio hit him, though we didn't see each other for thirty years, even while I raised another man's family and a child of my own, Franklin has always been the center for me. You only see him now, Desiree. Not the real man. He's changing. In front of my eyes. He's letting go. And the world is letting go of him, you can tell from the newspapers, and all the friends who've gone on before. The world and he are weary of each other. But I'm not. I can't let go."

Mrs. Rutherfurd cupped the pearls in her hand. Her eyes fell from the mirror, away from the reflected pearls to the real orbs in her fingers.

"I'll be down presently."

Judith went outside into the Georgia dusk. She looked down the gentle slope at the curtained window behind which Roosevelt napped before his evening meal. She wondered at Mrs. Rutherfurd's conjecture upstairs, about the dinner invitation to Morgenthau. Was Roosevelt really preparing to reveal the return of his old love? The old man was clearly ill. He would not face the American voters a fifth time. Who could tell him he couldn't see Mrs. Rutherfurd? His wife? She and mother Sara had already done that years ago and it didn't take. His staff? His children? They all approved of her. Who was there to tell the most powerful man in the world "No"?

Judith was there. She had the power in her pocket. With a sprinkle, she could deny him absolutely. Would killing Roosevelt make her more powerful than he? She had no one to ask this question, except Roosevelt himself. She projected her thoughts past the darkened window of the cottage to sit beside the old man's bed. Am I, she asked his waking eyes, more powerful than you? No, he said. Murder is a small thing. The taking of a life is not the equal of the life itself. You're wrong, she said. He waved a spectral hand: Do you think I couldn't have you killed if I knew what you were going to do? Of course I could. Power isn't killing, my dear. Power is not needing to kill and still getting what you want. Now leave me alone; I'm tired and I've earned my sleep. In her mind, Judith passed her hand across the President's eyes to close them and return him to slumber. She stood beneath the sighing pines, looking away into the woods, eager to be away in that wind, hidden under it and running home, finished with questions.

Over the past two days she had studied the placement of the Secret Service sentry boxes surrounding the Little White House. She'd plotted the routes of the Marine detachment patrolling the perimeter. She knew the ways deeper into the mountain and the directions of each road leading off it. At every meal, Judith had slipped into the kitchen to help in little ways, until cook Daisy Bonner was accustomed to her presence. She'd watched the President chatting with his ladies, the two cousins and Mrs. Rutherfurd. They helped with his stamps, or knit or smoked on the veranda while he read his mail in the sun. Shoumatoff set up her easel and worked her brush slowly, squinting at Roosevelt, who could only pose for short periods. Mr. Robbins took pictures of the old man after arranging him in a blue Navy cape, having him grip a scrolled paper. The President could not hold a smile for long, until he caught sight of Mrs. Rutherfurd moving to the easel to peek. Then he beamed. Over the last forty-eight hours he appeared to gain a little weight and color, the "bounce" that Mrs. Rutherfurd predicted. He had tanned his gray cheeks on a picnic this afternoon with his two cousins at the highest spot on Pine Mountain. Judith could kill him tonight. She could poison him and flee into the woods, a shy and terrified girl screaming "The President's dead!" In the flurry of activity that was certain to follow Roosevelt's collapse, no one would think to run after a panicked maid.

Judith looked up the slope in the direction of the main road. A car at the gate waited for the Marines to lift the bar. The vehicle passed through and rounded the crushed stone driveway to the house. The rugged-looking driver, an agent named Reilly, got out to open the rear door. The man who emerged then to enter the house must have been Secretary Morgenthau, arriving early for dinner.

Judith held her ground. The agent drove past her toward the gate, then stopped. Reilly got out and left the engine running.

"It's Desiree, right?"

Judith lowered her face to answer, "Yes, sir."

The agent stopped several strides away. "Desiree what?"

"Charbonnet."

Reilly mulled this with a cocked head. "You're not French, too, are you? Like Annette?"

"No, sir. New Orleans Creole."

"Uh-huh. Your people still there?"

"Yes, sir."

"Lift your head, girl."

Judith raised her eyes and put her tongue behind her lips to appear timid, and to misshape her face slightly. Reilly ran his eyes over her head to toe.

Out of the cottage behind her, the two cousins came into the dying light. They walked past, greeting Reilly. One woman asked Desiree to go tell Mrs. Rutherfurd they were gathering for dinner.

Reilly watched them head down the hill. "Desiree, I think you and me ought to sit and talk some. We haven't had the chance to get to know you. I just have some basic questions I need answered. You understand?"

"Yes, sir. But I got to go right now. I got to fetch the missus, and help in the kitchen. I'm serving."

"Tomorrow, then."

Judith watched his broad back return to the car. When he pulled away, she pivoted for the cottage to deliver the cousins' message to Mrs. Rutherfurd.

No, Agent Reilly, she thought. She listened to the sundown breeze on the mountain rustling the new leaves. Not tomorrow.

Before Judith reached the cottage door, Mrs. Rutherfurd stepped out. White skin offset the deep blue of her dress, making the pale pearls a striking contrast. The woman's cheeks stood out, rouged and hearty. With a lively tread, she strode up to Judith.

"I've changed my mind. I have decided that I'm looking forward to our dinner with Mr. Morgenthau. What do you think, Desiree?"

Judith had no immediate answer. She paused to calculate. Mrs.

Rutherfurd waited only a moment, then moved away, trailing a hand at Judith's back to nudge her to come along. Judith fell in behind, the place of a servant.

. At the front door, Mrs. Rutherfurd tugged open the screen. The little black terrier bounded to her ankles. Judith stepped behind and eased the door shut. In the parlor, Mr. Morgenthau stood at Mrs. Rutherfurd's arrival, while the cousins kept their seats. Arthur wheeled the President from his bedroom into the den. Roosevelt wore a blue suit, and a starched shirt that again betrayed how he was shrinking.

The man's sagging face brightened on seeing Mrs. Rutherfurd. She paused in the doorway, clutching the pearls to her breast. Over her shoulder, she whispered to Judith, "A strong girl can change her mind. Can't she?"

Before turning for the kitchen, Judith touched Mrs. Rutherfurd's arm. She leaned forward and whispered, "Sometimes."

April 12
Aiken, South Carolina

LAMMECK DROVE SLOWLY DOWN Laurens Street, Aiken's main thoroughfare. The town was awake: Strollers, a few cars, and a dozen horses and riders ambled along the avenue and grassy median.

He parked at a restaurant where two horses stood tied to a hitching post. An elderly couple at a sidewalk table sipped morning coffees to the sounds of hooves on pavement and spring songbirds. Inside the restaurant he ordered coffee and eggs, and went out to sit in the morning.

Lammeck struck up a conversation. The older couple knew immediately where Lucy Mercer Rutherfurd lived, at Ridgeley Hall across from the Palmetto Golf Course on Berrie Road, just south of downtown. Lucy was quite well known, they told him. President

Roosevelt used to visit when old Winthrop was still alive. The Army Signal Corps would lay lines all the way through town out to the Rutherfurd home. The Secret Service closed off the clay road leading in and out of Ridgeley Hall and the country club, causing considerable inconvenience. Lucy was well liked, and the six Rutherfurd children were all respectable, though they were not known as horse people.

Lammeck drove south with directions to Berrie Road. He entered an expensive neighborhood, amazed at the residents out so early riding over trails and fields. With little trouble, he found the stately brick home opposite the golf course. Golfers and caddies drifted around the lush greens. After three months in wintry, hectic Washington, and four years in Scotland training Jedburghs, Lammeck wondered: Where in Aiken was the war?

Before knocking, he rested his right hand just inside his coat lapel, near the grip of the holstered .38. Lammeck did not want to find Judith here, but would not let himself be surprised to find her anywhere.

His rap was quickly answered. A stout woman filled the doorway. Lammeck recognized her: This was the maid he'd seen in the window at the Q Street house in Georgetown. This morning she wore not her domestic uniform but khakis and a cotton blouse.

"Good morning. I'm Mikhal Lammeck. I hope I'm not calling too early, but is Mrs. Rutherfurd at home?"

The woman smiled and shook her head. "I'm sorry, but Mrs. Rutherfurd is out of town until the middle of next week."

Her accent was unmistakably French. She made no motion to close the door and cut Lammeck off.

"Is she with President Roosevelt?"

The big maid started. She blinked at Lammeck while he produced his letterhead from Mrs. Beach.

Looking over the rumpled sheet, she asked, "Don't you already know where she is?"

"No, ma'am. Mrs. Rutherfurd's movements are quite the well-kept secret, even inside the Secret Service. Is she in Warm Springs with the President?"

"Come inside, please."

Lammeck followed her into the spacious foyer, to a seat in the living room that could double as a ballroom. She plopped opposite him on a plush sofa.

"My name is Annette. I have been Mrs. Rutherfurd's housemaid for many years. I do not reveal her whereabouts to strangers just for the asking. Regardless of a piece of paper. You understand."

"How many years have you worked for her?"

"Twenty-five."

Lammeck nodded. "Of course. But you understand I have a job to do, protecting the President. There are circumstances, Annette, I can't share with you."

She shifted on her cushion. "Circumstances?"

"Dangers," Lammeck said dramatically.

Annette gasped and covered her mouth. "Is the madame in danger?"

"I can't say. I can't protect her if I don't know where she is. But, yes, if she is with the President, she could be exposed to ... circumstances."

Annette shook her head, considering what to do. Lammeck waited.

"Madame Rutherford left two days ago. She is in Georgia, with the President. I stayed behind. I became ill and could not go."

"Ill? Are you better now?"

Annette nodded vigorously, now quite willing to talk to Lammeck.

"Yes. The night before they left, I fell very sick. Then by the next afternoon, I was tired but fine. The doctor had no explanation."

A fuse sparked in Lammeck's gut. "The night before?"

"Yes."

"Was it sudden?"

"Yes. I went to bed, and just like that," she snapped her fingers, "I could not breathe and my heart hurt. I vomited many times."

"You said 'they' left for Georgia. Who are 'they'?"

"Why, Madame Shoumatoff, the painter. Mr. Robbins, her photographer. Mrs. Rutherfurd, of course. And Desiree, the other maid." Annette spoke as if she disapproved that Lammeck did not know all these things in advance.

Lammeck scooted forward on his seat. "Tell me about Desiree," he urged. "How long has she worked for Mrs. Rutherfurd?"

Lammeck feared the answer he got.

"Three weeks."

In an instant Lammeck recalled the poison in his veins. He cursed under his breath.

"What is it? What?"

"Where did Mrs. Rutherfurd meet Desiree? Please don't tell me it was in Washington."

Annette recoiled, falling back into the sofa. She covered her lips again. Lammeck took this as her answer.

"Is she tall? Athletic? Is she blue-eyed with a brown complexion? Annette, is she?"

"*Mon Dieu . . .*"

"Where's a phone?" He shot to his feet. Annette pointed through one of the doorways. Lammeck bolted out of the great room through a narrow hall, entering a library. On a large polished desk sat a phone. He dove for the receiver and plunged a finger into the dial.

Before he could spin the 0 for the local operator, he stopped, his finger still in the slot. He froze, staring at the walls of books.

"She won't believe me."

Lammeck ran through the conversation he would have with Mrs. Beach: Doctor, I told you *not* to leave Washington. I told you *specifically* not to bother Mrs. Rutherfurd. The President is not dead, Dr. Lammeck, despite the fact that this Desiree has been with him for two and a half days already. No, I will *not* call Chief Reilly, the chief is on the scene and in control, as always. Stay where you are, Doctor. I will be sending a state police escort to take you into custody.

Not a conversation at all, Lammeck determined, but a scolding. Then he'd get arrested. There'd be no advantage to calling Mrs. Beach, except that he wouldn't have to drive himself back to D.C.

Lammeck returned the receiver to the cradle. What if the Mrs. Beach in his head was right? Roosevelt wasn't dead; if that was the case, the whole world would know. What if she did call Chief Reilly in Georgia, and Desiree turned out to be just some coffee-colored, athletic, blue-eyed maid from Washington? The Secret Service would look like clowns in front of the President and his dear friend, the untouchable Mrs. Winthrop Rutherfurd. Reilly and Mrs. Beach's vengeance on Lammeck would know no bounds.

There was one answer, and Lammeck hated it. He would have to drive to Warm Springs right now. If Desiree the maid turned out to be Judith, and he wasn't too late, he'd confront her and maybe, just maybe stop her before she killed him and the President. If she wasn't Judith, Lammeck would be in just medium-depth shit.

He called a thank-you to Annette before sprinting out the door. He spun tires in the gravel leaving the estate, with Annette hailing from the doorway for him to come back and explain. Leaving Aiken, Lammeck ignored the thirty-five-mile-per-hour speed limit.

April 12
The Little White House
Warm Springs, Georgia

JUDITH HAD GUESSED RIGHT: Madame Shoumatoff was a snorer. She heard the woman sawing as she tiptoed up the guest-house steps to wake the ladies for breakfast.

Shoumatoff woke quickly, while Mrs. Rutherfurd languished, half asleep. Judith laid out the Russian's morning garb and poured fresh water into the porcelain basin. Mrs. Rutherfurd roused only after Shoumatoff was out the door. She seemed reluctant to begin the day.

A tension that had cropped up yesterday hung over Mrs. Rutherfurd's morning toilette. She complained of the rivalry for the President's attention that had risen between her and one of the cousins, Daisy Suckley. That was why she hadn't gone on the picnic in the afternoon. And last night at dinner, Bonner had served pancakes and soup, an odd combination. The cook, in the manner of all good cooks, believed a man could be made well by serving him his favorite dishes. Mrs. Rutherfurd praised the meal when she saw the President's pleasure; Cousin Daisy sniped at pancakes for dinner and drew a mild rebuke from Roosevelt, which only sharpened her attitude toward Mrs. Rutherfurd. Secretary Morgenthau had proved to be a dour presence, only wanting to talk about politics and dismantling Germany after the war. Roosevelt cut him off, preferring to spend the evening recalling their boyhoods in the Hudson Valley, the frozen river and snowy hills. Roosevelt turned melancholy when he spoke about Pa Watson, Missy LeHand, his mother, and many of his departed friends. Morgenthau lost interest and left early. The mood of the night was ruined. Mrs. Rutherfurd did not sleep well beside the snores of Shoumatoff.

Listening with closed mouth and busy hands to the woman's mundane plaints, Judith prepared her for breakfast. By necessity, many times in Judith's career she'd gotten close to those who'd stood near her intended targets. In each instance, the rich, the powerful, beautiful, or famous, griped and obsessed over the same ridiculous things every person was vexed by. They were as subject as paupers or simpletons to pettiness and jealousies, little squabbles for private power, personal schemes, and slights that kept them awake at night. No hand was so great in the world that it could rewrite its human heart. Combing the woman's hair, Judith let

Mrs. Rutherfurd prattle on. She thought, not for the first time, how her work had ruined her ability to admire anyone ever again.

Once Mrs. Rutherfurd was out the door, Judith took a walk in the woods, east toward State Route 194 leading to the town of Warm Springs. She carried a handbag and made a point of straying past the Secret Service sentry boxes, waving at the agents sunning themselves on stools, and at the Marines patrolling the fence line. She let them all see her in her maid's uniform. In addition to dodging Reilly, she also avoided standing in the wings inside the President's tiny cottage, watching the pair of cousins wriggle like rude piglets for Roosevelt's glance, or bearing Mrs. Rutherfurd's pliant manner, Shoumatoff's artistic airs, and the President's frail philandering. Judith strolled alone, enjoying the blooming Georgia woodland. She had in one pocket her passports and the rest of her American money. Inside the handbag were a linen skirt and blouse, and flat leather shoes. Everything else, her poisons kit included, she would leave behind. This would make no difference; by the time they looked, they would already know what she had done. In her other pocket rode the vial of cyanide powder.

Judith stayed away until late morning, covering the eastern grounds, showing herself to every guardian of the President's retreat and staff member in her path. She left the handbag under a great oak that would be easy to locate again. When the sun had risen high and she walked on her own shadow, she turned around.

Route 22
outside Sparta, Georgia

IN HIS MIRROR, LAMMECK watched the state trooper's bantam saunter. The skinny cop wore a wide-brimmed straw hat, and the belt of his sidearm slanted across his hips like a gunslinger's. He stopped at the rear of the car to hook his thumbs in his belt and consider the Washington, D.C., license plate. When he was done, he moseyed to Lammeck's open window, staring through dark lenses. Another car went past, swirling dust and pollen behind it.

"Mister."

"Officer."

The trooper peeled off his sunglasses. He narrowed his eyes.

"Can I see your driver's license, please?"

Lammeck had out his wallet, and the letter from the Secret Service.

"Officer, I know I was speeding."

The man reached for the license. "That makes two of us."

"I'm with the Secret Service. I have a really important message for President Roosevelt. He's at Warm Springs. Here, take a look."

The trooper ignored the offered letter. He looked up from Lammeck's driver's license.

"Mikhal Lammeck?"

"Yes, sir."

"This is a Rhode Island license. Says here it expired two years ago."

"I've been out of the country."

"Doing what, sir? You ain't in uniform."

"Training."

The officer tilted his head, awaiting a further explanation. Lammeck paused, pretending reluctance. Then he grimaced, as if letting a secret slip under duress. "Training spies."

The trooper didn't bite. "Mmm-hmm."

Lammeck held out Mrs. Beach's letter. The trooper took it this time. Lammeck watched the man's eyes work down the page.

"I don't think the federal government has given you permission to speed in my county, Mr. Lammeck. Nor to drive with an expired license."

Lammeck accepted the return of the letter. The trooper hung his thumbs on his belt again. He pursed his lips.

"Spies, huh? Like behind enemy lines and such? You some kind of expert?"

"Yes, sir. You could say that."

"You wasn't making your way across Hancock County like no spy. You was doing fifty. Where you comin' from?"

"Aiken."

"And you're headin' all the way down to Warm Springs. That's about a hundred eighty miles. You plan on speeding the whole way?"

"It's crucial I get to President Roosevelt quickly."

"Mmm-hmm. And I suppose I'm holdin' you up?"

"That's a trick question, Officer."

The trooper grinned. "You know, if it was Tom Dewey you was in such a fit to go see instead of ol' FDR, I wouldn't say what I'm about to."

"And that is?"

"That is, Mr. Lammeck, that my mother and father got bread on the table, that my big brother's fighting in Germany in a war we're about to win, that I got this here job, and that the Baldwin County line's another ten miles up the road. How 'bout I give you an escort?"

"Thank you, Officer. And thank you from President Roosevelt."

The trooper returned his shades over his eyes.

"You hang on," he said before pivoting for his vehicle. "We're gonna do seventy. After that, you're someone else's problem."

The Little White House
Warm Springs, Georgia

THE PRESIDENT SAT IN the glow of the open French doors. Light brightened his cheek and forehead, and highlighted the maps of veins in the backs of his hands. He wore a red necktie instead of his preferred bow tie, and a dark gray suit and vest beneath a navy cloak. A breeze ghosted from the porch to lift his wispy hair.

Madame Shoumatoff rose from her easel, talking incessantly in accented English. The President is to hold his head a little more to the right, he must please lift his chin a bit. She took from her pocket a tailor's tape and measured Roosevelt's nose. Cousin Polly Delano entered the room with a spray of wildflowers and set about arranging them at the dining table. On the sofa, Cousin Daisy Suckley knit. Mrs. Rutherfurd sat beside her, hands in her lap, with the quiet face of a child told to sit patiently.

Judith stayed out of the bright room, hanging back from the doorsill unnoticed. Little Fala snuck into the foyer to sniff at her ankles, then trotted off to curl at Cousin Daisy's feet. Shoumatoff returned to the easel and took up her brush. Roosevelt squirmed in his chair, tiring but trying to please the painter because this portrait was for Mrs. Rutherfurd's daughter. Shoumatoff added a few watercolor strokes to the canvas, and made more conversation to keep the President focused in his pose. She asked if he had liked Stalin when they'd met at Yalta. Yes, the President said, but he believed that Stalin had poisoned his wife. Only Shoumatoff did not laugh.

Roosevelt asked his cousins how the day's plans were shaping up. That afternoon he was scheduled to attend a barbecue in town; in the evening, a minstrel show. Daisy replied she'd heard everything was on schedule. The weather would stay fine. Roosevelt assured his ladies they would enjoy both events. Shoumatoff continued to dab her easel, silent now that the President had taken hold of the conversation. Out of the blue, he mentioned he might resign the presidency to take the job of heading the new United Nations, which was to hold its first meeting in San Francisco before the month was out. No one reacted, expecting him to laugh the statement off. He did not. Judith looked to Mrs. Rutherfurd. She seemed far off, mesmerized in the noon light by her admiration of the man. He's not going to retire, Judith thought. He says things to please people. He said that to please Mrs. Rutherfurd. If Judith had believed him, she might have walked away. Her job was to kill

Franklin Roosevelt, President of the United States, not head of the United Nations.

Hassett, Roosevelt's secretary, entered with the day's mail pouch. He encountered Judith in the foyer. He smiled, likely assuming that Judith waited in the wings until she was required.

"How's the painting going?" he asked.

"I don't know."

He moved toward the room, saying, "I'm sure no one will mind if you take a peek."

Hassett's arrival called a halt to the posing session. When eyes turned to him, Judith was noticed. She moved toward Mrs. Rutherfurd.

"Ma'am."

"Desiree, where have you been?"

"Out walking, ma'am. It's such a fine day. I'm sorry, was I needed?"

"No, but please let me know when you are going to be out of earshot."

"Yes, ma'am."

"We'll be serving lunch soon. You should ask Cook if you can be of help."

"May I look at the painting, first?"

Mrs. Rutherfurd caught Shoumatoff's eye, then gestured to ask for permission. The artist nodded and waggled fingers for Judith to come. Judith moved along the wall, watching Hassett lift a table in front of the President's chair. Roosevelt screwed a cigarette into a holder, allowed Hassett to light it, and set about the mail. Judith slipped behind Shoumatoff. The painter took no notice. She continued to work the canvas, filling in the President's red tie.

On the canvas, Roosevelt's face appeared complete. His upper torso was gathered beneath the shoulders of the dark cape, of which only the collar had been colored in. Shoumatoff had captured the President faithfully, but not generously. Oyster folds hung like crepe below his eyes. The eyes themselves bore a farseeing weariness. The whole of the painting, even unfinished, spoke of his illness and his struggle against the gravity of the grave.

The President sat engrossed in the papers laid before him by his secretary. He wielded a fountain pen above one page and said to the room, "Here's where I make a law." Judith watched him scratch his name. Hassett set the paper aside for the signature to dry. Roosevelt signed several pages, then Hassett lapped each over a chair arm or seat back like white laundry. The secretary hung one sheet near enough for Judith to see the signature; the scrawl was weak and barely decipherable as "Franklin D. Roosevelt."

Shoumatoff went to the President to straighten the cape across his shoulders. She tried to engage him again in chat, to lure him back into pose. Hassett, who made no secret of his dislike for the painter or the quality of her work, harvested the disarray of signed papers. He reminded the President that Agent Reilly would be leaving soon for San Francisco to arrange the upcoming UN trip. Roosevelt asked him to tell Reilly to come up after lunch for final instructions. Hassett left the room. With the secretary gone, Roosevelt kept his attention on the remaining work stacked on the tables. He lifted his head a few times, not at the painter but only to smile at Mrs. Rutherfurd.

Judith watched the room, silent as a shadow. Shoumatoff added touches to the portrait. The two cousins read and knit, nothing they could not set down in an instant for a laugh with Roosevelt or to tend to him somehow. Mrs. Rutherfurd, as quiet as Judith, asked for nothing but to be close by. The Filipino houseboy Joe came out of the kitchen to set the table for lunch. The President peered up to see Joe laying out the dishes.

Roosevelt spoke Judith's mind: "We have about fifteen more minutes."

She slipped from behind Shoumatoff, again keeping close to the wall and the fireplace. She entered the kitchen. Daisy Bonner had the oven door down, checking on fresh rolls that perfumed the small kitchen. Judith asked, "Miz Bonner, can I help?"

"Can you cook, girl?"

"Yes, ma'am. Right well."

"Alright. The President can't eat much at any one sitting, so I been feeding him bits before and after. You whip him up a nice warm bowl of corn gruel, and that'll settle his stomach for lunch. The bag of meal's in the cabinet. Milk's on the back porch in the icebox."

Bonner chopped vegetables for a salad. Judith paused to admire how the woman handled a knife, then fetched the milk and corn-meal. Setting a pot to heat on a burner, she mixed the gruel, stirring to keep the milk from skimming.

Bonner did not watch Judith. In a minute, when the gruel had thickened, the cook lifted her nose.

"That smells nice," she said. "What'd you add?"

Judith ladled dollops of the mush into a bowl for the President.

"Almond extract."

The cook came close to sniff. She pointed a finger to dip it into the bowl and sample.

Judith smacked the woman's hand. "No, Miz Bonner. That's for the President."

The cook straightened, surprised. Judith ignored her. She arranged the bowl on a simple wooden tray with a napkin and spoon. Entering the room, the President looked up from his papers. He made space on the table.

Roosevelt flicked his eyes to Mrs. Rutherfurd. He cast her a smile that said *I'm sorry, I have to eat this bland, pulpy mess.* Mrs. Rutherfurd beamed in return, forgiving. Judith paused to let the two complete their final dialogue. She wanted to slip out of her body presenting the gruel to Franklin Roosevelt, just for a moment, to step invisibly beside Madame Shoumatoff. She would whisper, "Pay attention, woman. Paint *this* moment."

Roosevelt blinked, away from Mrs. Rutherfurd. His face fell, resigned, as he watched the steaming bowl land on the table in front of him. He lifted his glance to Judith.

"Goody," he said.

LAMMECK'S LEGS AND BACK throbbed after five hours on the road. His eyes and nerves felt frazzled from breaking the speed limit through two states, watching for cops behind every rural billboard and clump of brush. Finally pulling into Warm Springs, he had to urinate and the car needed gas. Stopping at a filling station, he told the attendant to top off the tank. In the Whites Only bathroom, the soles of his feet and the meat of his rump tingled from the memory of the long ride.

Washing his hands, Lammeck took his first look of the day in a mirror. He was untucked and wrinkled, radiating urgency. He looked like Dag: tense. If Judith was with the President, the man was only alive at her discretion. Lammeck had no idea why she was restraining herself, but every second he delayed increased the danger. If he looked this rough when he arrived, he'd never get past the first tier of guards. He washed his face and hands, straightened his suit, shirt, and tie, and made himself walk back to the car instead of sprint. The attendant gave him instructions to the Little White House, just five minutes away.

Lammeck did not speed out of town. He recalibrated himself, calming down. The .38 was fully loaded but he checked the magazine anyway. The feel of the pistol in his hands helped smooth his nerves. He slipped it in place near his armpit and patted it, the one thing he was confident of.

Within minutes, Lammeck found the turn to Roosevelt's wooded retreat. He checked his watch. A few minutes before one. The sky shone dazzling blue, birds twittered in the soft-leaved maples lining the entrance.

Three dress Marines guarded a gate across the shady lane. Lammeck braked at the command of a white-gloved hand.

"Afternoon, sir."

"Corporal. I've got an appointment with Secret Service Chief Reilly." Lammeck produced the dog-eared letter from Mrs. Beach.

The Marine perused the page. "This don't mention any appointment, Dr. Lammeck, sir. And this letter's over a month old."

Another Marine checked a clipboard. He shook his head at the corporal; Lammeck was not on their list of visitors.

Lammeck opened his hand and gestured at the car. "Corporal, take a look at the dust on this thing. I drove all the way down here from D.C. yesterday and this morning. Chief Reilly is expecting me to be on time. And if you know the chief, you know I need to keep moving."

The soldiers exchanged glances.

"I'm a special consultant to the Secret Service, fellas. And..." Lammeck peeled back his lapel to show them the Colt .38 in its harness, "...I'm carrying this. That's all I can say." He let go of the coat to conceal the gun quickly, importantly. "Now raise the gate, or Chief Reilly will put your heads on the stake next to mine."

The corporal considered Lammeck with an unsure wince. While he glared, another soldier lifted the gate. Lammeck saluted and drove through.

The road wound a mile through dogwood, pine, and oak on sloping fields. Insects buzzed over sunny acres. Lammeck kept his foot light on the gas pedal. Another gate, this one guarded by Secret Service agents, crossed the road ahead. On the other side of that gate waited a classic damned-if-you-do, damned-if-you-don't situation. He was going to surprise and piss off either Reilly or Judith. Pick one, he thought.

Lammeck talked his way through this gate also. Again he displayed his paperwork and the pistol, letting the agents assume that only a prominent man would show up with both, and dusty D.C. plates to boot. Lammeck drove on, catching his breath, but he could do nothing about his hurried heartbeat when he saw, around a downhill bend, the Little White House.

. . .

THE PRESIDENT PUT ONLY two spoonfuls in his mouth. Judith concealed her excitement behind Desiree's servile mask. When Roosevelt swallowed the second time, Judith knew it was enough. She sensed the bonds of this man's life break, and with them the life of Desiree. The two would die together.

Judith took the tray to the kitchen. She meant to rinse out the bowl in the sink but Daisy Bonner, still pouting from the slap on her hand, ushered Judith out of her domain. "I'll get that," she said, pointing at the cooling gruel. Judith did not argue, figuring if the cook tasted it now, that was her fate. Judith left the tray on a sideboard where the cook ignored it. She slipped into the den to stand against the wall. The table was set for lunch. Madame Shoumatoff painted silently, unable to reengage the President. The knitting cousin Suckley focused on her needles and crimson yarn. At the table, the other cousin arranged a vase of cut dogwood blooms. Roosevelt glanced back and forth between piles of papers on two card tables within his reach. Only Mrs. Rutherfurd watched him. And Judith.

Roosevelt's cheeks seemed flushed around his tilted cigarette holder. He took the holder from his lips and set it in an ashtray. His head bobbed between the stacks of work, then fell forward. His hands fumbled at nothing in the air. Suckley set aside her knitting, rising from the sofa. She stepped close to Roosevelt and bent to look in his face.

She asked, "Did you drop something?"

Roosevelt raised his left hand to his temple. He pressed there with shaky gray fingers. The hand went down, then the right came up to cover the whole of his forehead. He did not look at his cousin, but gazed down and muttered. From her place against the wall, Judith barely made out what he said: "I have a terrific pain in the back of my head."

Judith cut her eyes to Mrs. Rutherfurd. The woman's composed smile was gone. She leaned forward on the sofa, ready to act somehow. Cousin Suckley urged Roosevelt to lean back. The President settled against the cushion in his regal cape. Judith caught him glancing at Mrs. Rutherfurd straight ahead. Then his eyelids half closed, and Mrs. Rutherfurd rushed forward as he slumped.

At her easel, Shoumatoff shouted, "Lucy, something's wrong!" Beside the President, Suckley asked, "Franklin, are you alright?" Roosevelt's mouth sank open. Mrs. Rutherfurd landed on her knees next to him. All she could offer was an open hand to his cheek. The Russian painter stood behind her unfinished painting and screamed.

At the sound, Arthur the valet plunged out of the bedroom. Cook Bonner and houseboy Joe erupted from the kitchen. Quickly the six formed a huddle around Roosevelt. In a burst, Suckley explained what had happened. Lucy waved a kerchief dipped in camphor under the President's nose to revive him, but to no effect. Arthur and Joe took action, linking hands under the President to lift him out of the chair. The wool cape wrapped him like a shroud. The Delano cousin took hold of his feet. He was slack in their arms. His breathing grated. When they carried the President past her, Judith saw only whites under his drooping lids.

Mrs. Rutherfurd, Suckley, and the cook stood aside, fists in their mouths. Shoumatoff had seen enough. The Russian ran from the house, shouting at the agent outside, "Call a doctor!" Inside, Suckley took hold of herself. She darted to the phone, telling the Warm Springs operator, "Get a doctor up here, quick!" Mrs. Rutherfurd stared at the entrance to the President's bedroom, balling her hands, white-faced.

Shoumatoff hurried back into the cottage, bustling for her easel and paints. She gathered fast and carelessly, tucking the unfinished painting under her arm. She saw Mrs. Rutherfurd standing still.

"Lucy! Lucy, we have to go. Now!"

Mrs. Rutherfurd seemed not to hear. "What?"

"We have to go! I will call Nicholas at the hotel. Pack everything!"

Mrs. Rutherfurd did not take her eyes from the wall behind

which Roosevelt lay. Arthur, Joe, and cousin Delano were in there with him. They loved him, too. She moved toward the bedroom.

With a gentle touch to her shoulder, Judith intercepted the woman. Mrs. Rutherfurd did not take her eyes from the doorway. She tried to walk past. Judith stiffened her hand.

"Mrs. Rutherfurd, no."

At Judith's voice, the woman's fixation on the doorway broke.

"Excuse me?"

"You need to listen to your friend. You need to disappear." Judith used none of her Negro accent, none of her deference. She squeezed once on the woman's arm, then released it.

"Disappear," Judith repeated.

Mrs. Rutherfurd gazed at her for a moment with the same sad acceptance with which the President had looked at the poisoned gruel.

Shoumatoff, laden with her paints and canvas, called from the foyer. "Desiree! Come and pack!"

Judith walked away. Before exiting the front door, she glanced back. Mrs. Rutherfurd had not moved, steps from the President.

Judith paused in the foyer, to let Shoumatoff climb the slope and reach the guesthouse. Then she left the Little White House.

In the driveway, a Secret Service agent sat in his car, speaking into a radiophone. Judith darted past him. She thrust her hands through her hair, making certain to run awkwardly. She dashed past the guesthouse, up the hill, away from the gate and into the woods, screaming, "The President's dead!"

LAMMECK PARKED IN THE drive, behind a dark federal car. Before he'd taken two strides toward the white cottage, he knew something was wrong.

Out of one of the smaller guesthouses, a woman joggled down the hill. Judging from the flail of her arms, she was frantic. Behind her, a Cadillac waited, its trunk open. She hastened to another woman treading up the slope. Lammeck recognized this one: Lucy

Rutherfurd. She walked unhurried, stunned. The frenzied woman gripped Lucy with both hands, gave her a shake, then headed for the front door of the Little White House. Lammeck reached under his coat for the pistol. He touched it, then took away his hand. This was not the place for an unknown man to be running with a firearm in his mitt. Lammeck broke into a run and beat the woman to the cottage door.

He flung open the screen door. Leaping through the foyer, he landed in a larger room with a fireplace, a table set for lunch, other tables with documents spilling onto the floor, and two standing women chewing on their knuckles.

He huffed at them, "Where's the President?"

One, the shorter and more frumpy of the two, pulled her hand from her mouth to mutely point. Lammeck dove for the doorway.

He stopped at the threshold. The three people around the bed turned to see who had arrived. They didn't know him, and Lammeck did not recognize them: a black man, a brown man, and a well-dressed older woman. The man on the bed, he knew.

Franklin Roosevelt was being undressed by the black man. His shined shoes had been set carefully beneath the narrow bed, below his stocking feet. The downed President lay swathed in a great cape. His tie and shirt were undone. All three turned back to attending him, ignoring Lammeck. Lammeck looked at the ashen face, heard the labored breathing, and knew the President was good as dead.

"Who the hell are you?"

Lammeck whirled to face a big man, the agent who'd been in the car out front.

"Lammeck. No time to explain, but I'm working with Reilly. Tell him I'm here. Come over here."

He stepped the agent away from the President's bedroom. In the den, the woman who'd followed Lammeck into the house snatched down an easel, scooped up tubes of paint.

"What's your name, Agent?"

"Beary."

"Alright, Beary, when did this happen?"

"Just now. Maybe a minute ago."

"There was a maid who came with Mrs. Rutherfurd. Young girl, tall, brown skin."

Before Beary could answer, one of the women standing at the sofa, again the dowdy one, said, "Desiree."

"Desiree. Yeah, that's her. Where is she?"

Beary pointed outside, up the hill. "She ran off right before you pulled up. That way, into the trees."

"Beary, get on your horn right now! Tell everybody you can, Reilly, the Marines, state police, all of them to lock this place down. No one gets in or out."

Lammeck flew out the door, offering no explanation. He was sure Agent Beary would not take orders from a man he didn't know. He'd hesitate, check with his boss Reilly first. That would be all the room Judith needed.

In the shady yard, Lucy Rutherfurd was still struggling up to the path to the guesthouse. Lammeck had no time to spend on her. Judith had run northeast. Lammeck tore after her.

He put the .38 in his hand and ran. Lammeck was not built for pursuit, and the months in Washington had robbed him of his conditioning. He sucked air and pumped his arms as hard as he could, kicking up leaves, crashing through brush. Judith could breeze over this, he knew, and he had no chance to catch her. He ran on, fighting himself. The Colt swinging in his fist grew heavier.

Lammeck plowed ahead. Dead foliage made the footing unreliable. He could not run in a straight line for all the tree trunks; dodging them sapped him even faster. His gait eroded until he came to a standstill, hands on his knees, bent and gasping. Then he saw something on the ground.

In the bushes ten feet from where he stood, at the foot of a thick oak, lay some clothes. Lammeck stood erect, marshaling his breathing. He lifted the .38, scanning the barrel in every direction up the hill. He sidestepped through the leaves, eyes and pistol on watch for motion in the forest. Standing over the clothes, he looked quickly down. At his feet lay a black maid's dress, set off with white piping and lace.

His hands tightened on the Colt. He stood rock still, searching the woods for the sound of crunching leaves, the flash of a figure between the trunks.

"Hello, Mikhal."

Lammeck swung the gun to her voice, straight ahead uphill. He did not find her.

"Judith."

"How incredible to see you. I wondered who was making all that noise behind me. At first I thought someone was riding a horse."

"I don't see you. Come out."

"Is that a Colt .38?"

"Yes, and it's goddam heavy."

"I can tell. You look winded."

"I am."

Judith laughed.

"When Allah wants to give us strength, He sends labors to make us strong."

Lammeck took a deep breath to compose himself. He stood straight now, feeling his pulse racing in his temple and hands.

"Come out, Judith."

Sixty feet up the slope, her head leaned from behind a wide oak. Her hair was shorter than the wig she'd worn at the embassy.

Lammeck said, "He's dead."

"Or he soon will be."

"How'd you do it?"

"You'll figure it out soon enough. Did you visit Annette?"

"Yes."

"How is she feeling?"

"She's fine."

Slow and two-handed, Lammeck brought the pistol dead center on her face.

"It's over," he said.

"No, it's not, Mikhal. Not at all. I still have a long trip home. So if you'll excuse me, I need to be going."

Lammeck tightened the first fold of his index finger against the trigger.

"Put your hands where I can see them, and step in the open."

Even at a distance, Lammeck could see the white of her smile and blue glint in her eyes.

"That's a big gun, and not very accurate. Plus it's an uphill shot, I'm a rather small target, and you're exhausted."

Lammeck fired. The bullet blasted a chunk off the center of the tree inches from her ear. At the splatter of bark, Judith ducked behind the trunk. The blast's report echoed across the woods. Birds fluttered off to quieter branches. Slowly, she slanted out again.

"One-hundred-thirty-grain round," he called out, training the barrel on her forehead. "And for the record, I'm a fucking expert shot."

"My, you are."

"I'm taking you back."

At this, Judith stepped full from behind the tree. She wore a dark blouse above a green skirt. A black purse hung over her shoulder. She looked like a woman ready to go shopping, in colors perfect for running through a forest.

Lammeck made his way up the slope, holding her steady in the gun's sight. She did not raise her hands but joined them at her waist, tapping the thumbs impatiently.

"Believe me, Mikhal. The last thing anyone wants you to do is bring me back."

Lammeck winced at this. The statement made no sense. He continued to climb the hill, eyes cocked behind the gun.

"Listen to me," she said. "Your job was to stop me. It's too late for that. My job was to kill him. Both of us are done. Let's go home."

Lammeck continued to approach, halfway to her now. Judith

lifted a foot to move backward up the hill. Lammeck shifted his aim and sent a round past her. She snapped her head around at the bullet's whisper close to her cheek. She froze.

In silence except for his steps on the forest floor, Lammeck closed the distance to five yards. Then he stopped, keeping the Colt aimed between her eyes.

"Drop the purse."

Judith let the black bag go. Lammeck closed the gap two more strides. She sighed as if his caution were needless.

"Mikhal, I'm not armed. Honestly, I wasn't expecting anyone to come after me. I did a very good job back there of setting myself up for this panicked little run. Only you, my amazing dear. Only you. Who could have guessed?"

Lammeck pointed at the earth. "Sit down."

Judith made no move to comply.

Never lowering the Colt, Lammeck surged forward. With a tiger-fast blow, he shoved her shoulder and swung his big leg behind her, sweeping her feet. She went down hard, flat on her back.

Lammeck retreated a step. Judith grimaced. She rolled to her side to rub her rump.

"Ow. But nice. I didn't think you were that type."

"We're not even yet."

Lammeck lowered the pistol. A slug in her thigh would clip her wings while they waited for the agents or Marines to follow the sounds of his gunfire and arrive. Then he'd turn over the President's assassin.

"Wait."

Lammeck glanced up.

Judith held one hand in what looked at first glance to be the OK sign. Between her finger and thumb was a gray capsule.

"I will not be captured, Mikhal. You know that's not an option."

Lammeck raised the gun from her leg to her chest. She propped herself on an elbow, brandishing the capsule close to her lips.

"Go ahead," she said. "Or I will."

"No, you won't."

"Mikhal, you disappoint me." She sucked her teeth, making a *tsk, tsk*. "Who should understand an assassin better than you? Think about it. No one ever kills the high and mighty of this world without first accepting that death and a little infamy might be the only payoffs. Some even go looking for them. It's always been that way. From Egypt to Alamut Castle, right up to this pretty afternoon in your America." Judith shrugged, nonchalant, the pill pinched at her lips. "If that little old lady in Newburyport could do it, you know I can."

Lammeck blinked, amazed. She lay at his feet, beneath his weapon. He held what he thought was complete sway over her, but she acted as if he had no power at all. At that moment he realized fully in whose presence he stood. Gabčik again, and Kubiš. Agrippina, Charlotte Corday, Booth, Gavril Princip. This woman with poison inches from her tongue wasn't answerable to him; moments ago, she had changed the course of a century. Mikhal Lammeck was nothing more than an interpreter, a manservant, of the history she created.

"Killing me serves no purpose," she said.

"It'll stop you from ever doing this again."

"No, it won't. Stopping *me* doesn't stop me." She sat upright. "Pull the trigger if you think that's true. But the next king to die will still die. You go ahead and watch. You write it down. Then remember I told you."

Unbelievably, Judith rose from the ground. She brushed sticks and leaves off her skirt. She arranged herself one-handed, never taking the capsule from her lips. She slid her eyes off Lammeck only to reach down for her handbag.

"But you're not going to shoot me, Mikhal. I know well what a killer looks like, and so do you. Back in the embassy, when you had that cute little Welwand in my ribs, the moment I looked into your eyes I wasn't worried."

Again, Lammeck centered the .38 on the space between her eyes. Five feet from the end of the barrel, Judith's expression didn't change. She fixed her eyes on Lammeck's face.

"You realize what that .38 will make the back of my head look like. Even worse than Arnold's."

Involuntarily, Lammeck flinched, remembering the husband in Newburyport murdered by Judith.

"I know," she said, softening, "it must have been gruesome. And I know it affected you. You'd like to be a killer, Mikhal, you'd like to know what it's like. But I'm afraid your destiny is to report rather than participate."

"Maybe I'll prove you wrong."

Judith smiled, disarming. "Oh, don't be like that, Mikhal. It's not an insult to your manhood to have a woman say that you're good and gentle and can't murder someone. But I haven't got the time right now to make you feel better about it. I must go. You understand."

Lammeck shook his head. "You're not leaving here."

She nodded, contradicting him. "History, Mikhal. She's speaking very clearly at the moment. She needed the President of the United States dead; that's why she sent me to do the job. Now that it's done, history needs me alive."

He asked down the barrel of the Colt, "How do you know?"

She laughed again and pointed between his eyes, matching his weapon with an assassin's finger.

"For the second time you disappoint me. The answer's astonishingly simple." She spoke across her turned shoulder, past the pill still hovering at her mouth.

"History sent you to stop me. *Befarma-ri,* Mikhal."

Lammeck drew a bead square in her back, into the heart.

"Don't."

Judith smiled. In an instant, she took off up the hillside with amazing fast strides, accelerating like a wolf. Lammeck held her just above the gun sight, following her up the hill. For seconds she stayed within the range of the Colt's heavy cartridge. He drew a breath to yell at her again.

He let the breath go, and with it, Judith.

In the last yards of the Colt's reach, for no reason he could understand—he figured he'd sort everything out later; after all, that was *his* role—Lammeck fired.

She didn't break stride up the hill. As the shot echoed, Judith lifted both hands above her head. Lammeck could not tell if this was a gesture of victory or farewell.

She vanished.

OUR RELIANCE IS IN T
WHICH GOD HAS PL
OUR DEFENSE IS IN THE SPIRIT
AS THE INHERITANCE O
IN ALL LANDS, EVER

1945

CULTIVATE THE UNIVERS

MON

TUE

WED

MAY

MAY

1

8

2

16

10

4

23

17

11

30

24

18

19

31

25

CHAPTER EIGHTEEN

May 9
Washington, D.C.

DAG LIFTED LAMMECK'S DUFFEL into the trunk and slammed
the lid. The two climbed into the government Packard. Pulling
away, Lammeck didn't look back at the hotel, at the passing White
House, or the sunny city. Washington hadn't been much of a home
to him; he was glad to leave. His kept his eyes fixed on the road,
even when he spoke to Dag.

"You didn't need to do this."

"Yeah, I did. I got you into it. Least I can do is drive you out of it
to the airfield."

Dag headed south on Fourteenth Street. He slowed to let a crew
of street sweepers with big-wheeled trash cans get out of the way.
Newsprint, whole or cut into confetti, trash, liquor bottles, hats, and
clothes littered the streets from yesterday's immense celebration.
The Germans had officially called it quits. Every person in America
who was able to had kissed someone, drunk a toast, and tossed
something in the air. Lammeck had tottered back to his hotel last
night covered in lipstick and smelling like a tramp. The celebration

had been his send-off. This morning, he awoke late with his head aching and his bag packed for Scotland.

Easing beyond the sweepers, Dag chatted. "Now if we can just get this crap over with Japan. I hear the Marines are closing in on Okinawa. And the Aussies are making their move on New Guinea."

Lammeck let the words hang unanswered. Dag let out a long breath.

"Sorry I haven't been around much, Professor."

"Really? I hadn't noticed."

"Aw, cripe. Give me a break. Truman's a lot tougher to guard than Roosevelt."

"The guy's got legs that work."

"That's mean, but accurate."

Dag swung left on Independence, then veered onto Virginia, headed east for the Anacostia Bridge. For blocks, the two men let silence flow between them. The day was pleasant and Lammeck was finally set free, but the mood in the car curdled until Dag stopped at a street light. The Capitol dome rose blocks away on their left. With no motion or wind, the quiet in the car grew even more uncomfortable. Dag broke it.

"I read your report."

Lammeck nodded, not turning his head from the red light.

Dag snorted. "I can tell you this much for absolute sure. That report is going to set a record for how deep it gets buried. Top Secret doesn't even *begin* to describe it."

"Great. I finally achieved my life's work. I wrote an historical document that'll become the standard for no one reading it."

The rumpled agent, even in this weather wearing his raincoat, sped the car beneath the changed light. Dag chuckled.

"Christ, Professor, give it up already. What did you expect? That the United States government was going to announce in the last days of a world war that the President had been murdered? And we don't even know by who? What do you think that would have done to the nation's morale? To peace negotiations? There would've been a witch hunt bigger than the fucking Inquisition. The whole globe might have gone right back up in flames. And that's probably exactly what whoever's behind this wanted. No goddam way, uh-uh. Your report got buried and it stays buried. Roosevelt had a brain hemorrhage. The old man died of natural causes, hardening of the arteries. End of story. Forever."

Lammeck glared at the rolling road, the flag-decked buildings, the banners and bunting draped over every railing and windowsill. Confetti lay trampled and filthy everywhere. The city wouldn't be clean, or fully sober, for days.

"Shame your Persian gal got away. I would've liked a little talk with her before I put a bullet in her brain."

Lammeck said nothing.

"You had your chance though, huh? Three shots."

"Yeah."

"You get a good look?"

"Not good enough, apparently."

Dag tapped fingers on the steering wheel.

"You know, you might not have had the chance to read Agent Beary's report. He said, judging from what he heard, he thought there might've been two minutes between your second and third rounds."

"She was hiding from me."

"She's a good hider."

Now Lammeck glanced at Dag. The agent kept his eyes on the road.

"She say anything?" Dag asked.

"No."

"She didn't mention what a surprise it was to find you one minute behind her all the fucking way down in Warm Springs, Georgia? Nada?"

"We didn't talk."

"Okay, sure. So let me get this straight. You chased her uphill into the woods, starting about a minute behind her and a hundred pounds heavier, and you caught up, probably while she was changing out of the maid's uniform. You got close enough to fire twice with a handgun and missed both times. All of sudden she hid, though you'd just had her in your sights good enough to squeeze off two rounds. You looked for about two more minutes and couldn't spot her. She said nothing and did not take a step on a forest floor covered with dead leaves. Then you saw her again one last time and you took your last shot. Missed again. Then poof. She's gone. That about how it happened, Professor?"

Lammeck watched Dag's profile, until the agent turned his head to face him.

"Exactly how it happened, Agent Nabbit."

Dag grinned. "Just asking." He returned his attention to the road. "You know, 'cause I spent a few days down there walking around where you were shooting at her. I dug two of your slugs out of two different tree trunks. Both dead center. And to tell you the truth, the woods seemed kind of thin to me. There just weren't that many places where a woman at a dead run could duck completely out of sight from a man close behind shooting a .38 Colt at her with a 130-grain round. A man who's an expert shot. So you're right, Professor. Judith was incredible. For that matter, so are you."

Lammeck pulled his gaze from Dag's grin. The car crossed the Anacostia River to the naval air station on the south bank. With no more talk, Dag drove through the security gate, credentials in hand. He parked in front of a hangar. Turning to Lammeck, he rested an elbow on the seat back.

"Professor, it's been a real pleasure and an honor. Mrs. Beach and Reilly send their fond regards and farewells, of course. Reilly says you can keep the hand cannon." Dag poked a finger across the seat at Lammeck's underarm, touching the leather sheath around the pistol. These days Lammeck strapped on the gun with his morning coffee, taking it from under his pillow.

"What else did Reilly have to say?"

Dag shrugged. "Not much. Just that if any mention of what you know ever appears in print, or anyone ever hears about it, emphasis on the word 'ever,' then Scotland ain't far enough, and that Colt under your arm ain't big enough. The full weight of the United States government will be applied to destroying you and your career. Again, *ever*. So don't think in terms of leaving some legacy behind. The chief ordered me to hear you say that you understand."

"Loud and clear."

"Good. "

"What about everybody else?"

"Everybody who could be lied to, was. Lucy Rutherfurd, the cousins, that painter and the photo guy, the President's domestic staff, even the Marines. They've all been told you were chasing off what you figured was an intruder on the Little White House grounds, firing in the air. You were some local cop, that's all, with a letter from Mrs. Beach to help out on occasion. No explanation beyond that. As for the maid Desiree, the line on her is she got spooked when Roosevelt keeled over, and ran off. She had a police record and didn't want to be around when the cops showed up. She's gone; it's that simple. The doctors who were at the Little White House and examined the President got roughly the same speech you've been given. Oh, and the flatfoot Massachusetts cop Hewitt sends his regards. Says with the war over he's going to go to college and join the Secret Service. How 'bout that?"

"You've always been persuasive, Dag. What about the poison? Cyanide?"

"Bingo. Just like you figured. In the mush Roosevelt ate before lunch."

Dag offered his hand. After a moment, Lammeck shook it. The two got out of the Packard. Dag retrieved Lammeck's duffel from the trunk. A hundred yards away on the tarmac, a silver Lockheed glinted, waiting. Lammeck looked at a windsock blowing his direction, east across the Atlantic.

Lammeck grabbed the bag. Dag walked beside him a few steps, then stopped. He raised his voice above the spinning propellers.

"I'd like to say I'll see you again. But it's not something you'd want to hear. Because, Mikhal, if I do see you again—"

Lammeck interrupted him. "I know, Dag. I won't see you."

Dag winked and turned away first. Lammeck watched him go only a few strides, then headed for the plane.

May 20
St. Andrews, Scotland

A STIFF BREEZE OFF St. Andrews Bay clipped at Lammeck's back. Across the campus, university pennants and Union Jacks billowed from their cleats against every school building wall, against the castle ruins on its spit beside the water, and from the cathedral tower at the east edge of town. The wind rippled the crimson capes of students returning from Sunday services, exam studies in the library, or the many medieval crannies of the town. Lammeck walked with the wind, aimless, with nothing to do but amble the cobbled streets amid green lawns.

The University had preserved his office and his position. He was welcome to stay and teach in the upcoming academic year. With the war in Europe over, and the one in the Pacific drawing to a close, the school braced to swell with returning servicemen and women. For the present, Lammeck had no official duties. The training of the Jeds in the western hills had shut down while he was in America. *The Assassins Gallery* lay on his desk in his flat on Muttoes Lane. He'd spent his first week back rereading the finished chapters. He found them dull and too conclusive. His writing on the political history of assassination was steeped in study, but lacked fascination; since his return, he'd determined the subject was not so dry as he'd once imagined. Lammeck considered that he might rewrite the whole book, spice it up with some adventure and humanity, turn it into something for a wider audience than just his fellow scholars.

But this morning he could not focus on his pages. Lammeck chose instead to take a long stroll and stir up a thirst.

. . .

SHE DID NOT SIT at his table but slid into a booth across the tavern. Lammeck made no outward reaction, though every klaxon in his mind and body went off. He forced himself to be motionless under her bemused gaze. She looked stunning under a broad-brimmed straw hat, in a white polka-dot dress, a shimmering emerald pashmina about her shoulders. She grinned at Lammeck past shifting patrons, through the smoky pub air. She let the shawl collapse down her shoulders to show her arms were tanned and bare. Her hair was longer now.

A boy, the proprietor's lad, wiped her table with a rag. Before he could leave, she snared him by the arm. Lammeck watched her take from her purse a sheet of paper and a pen. She scrawled something, creased the page, then gave it to the boy with a coin. The lad hustled through The Cross Keys' drinking traffic to Lammeck's table.

"For you, sir."

Lammeck slid a shilling across the table. The boy looked at it, frowning. "The lady gi' me a hae' crown."

Lammeck reached slowly to take his shilling back. The boy snatched the coin from under his fingers, left the note, and took off.

Lammeck pulled his eyes off her long enough to unfold the page. She'd written, *May I?*

He flipped the sheet on its back, recognizing on it the FBI sketch of Judith.

Across the room, she waited, framed in the green curtain of the shawl, in the soft light beneath the straw hat. She raised her hands in a mock surrender. Keeping them up as though Lammeck held a gun on her, the cashmere dangling off her elbows, she rose and came to ease into his booth.

"Put your hands down."

She dropped them. "Aren't you going to pull out a pistol or something? I'm not sure what to say to you without a gun between us."

"Or somebody poisoned."

"Fair point. I'll behave if you promise to."

"Who are you this time?"

"Colleen Duckworth. A very rich Canadian widow."

"My condolences. You've got a tan."

"It's warm where I live."

"I think it's warmer where you'll end up."

"Touché, Mikhal. You're still taking shots at me. At least that one hit. But what do you say to a truce?"

They looked up at the approaching waiter.

"What are you having?" she asked Lammeck. "I'm buying."

"Stout."

Judith said to the waiter, "Apparently he likes his beer the way he likes his women. Dark and bitter. Two, please."

Lammeck took in the details of her. Polished nails, stylish dress. He'd not forgotten her face but was reminded by her shoulders above the drooped shawl how muscular she was.

"What are you doing here?"

"The Scottish spring is the most beautiful in the world. I've been thinking about taking up golf. And I made you a promise, Mikhal. Or don't you remember?"

Judith put her elbows on the table to set her chin in her cupped hands. "Don't look so surprised. Surely you haven't forgotten me."

This is how she works, Lammeck thought, how she gets inside. She plays charming, plays stupid or smart, beautiful or dull, innocent or naïve. He kept his mouth shut, glaring at her, probing for her intent, or threat.

"It's a purely social visit." She leaned off her hands and sat straight. "Can't a lady drop in?"

"You murdered Roosevelt."

"No, I didn't. He died from a cerebral hemorrhage. It was in all the papers."

"You killed three people in Massachusetts."

"Yes, I did."

"You caused the death of your accomplice, Maude King."

"Indirectly."

"Before Mrs. Rutherfurd, you worked as a maid for Under-secretary of the Navy Tench. You've been tracked back to an apartment in one of the colored alleys. There's no proof, but—"

She interrupted him. "Yes, Mikhal, I killed poor Mrs. Pettigrew. And my landlord's inquisitive son Josh. And the policeman hired by Mrs. Tench's family to follow her straying husband. I never knew the cop's name. But he followed Jacob to me."

"And no further," said Lammeck.

"Well put."

"Six civilian murders and one assassination of a president." Lammeck's voice carried disdain. "You were a regular killing machine."

"The civilians were regrettable, but beyond my control. You understand."

"I understand you should get the electric chair for every one of them."

She blinked and waited without expression, letting the notion hang between them. Then she said, "You know I never will. And if for one moment I believed you intended to bring me before your precious justice, I'd . . . I didn't come to renew old antagonisms with you, Mikhal."

Lammeck studied her grin and stunning blue eyes, all focused on him like a Cheshire cat, ready to disappear.

Lammeck said, "I'm one of a handful of people in the world who's aware of what you've done. You and I both know it's going to stay that way. So why'd you come to Scotland? To gloat?"

Judith took off the broad-brimmed straw hat and laid it carefully on the seat beside her. She ran a hand through her hair. She smiled beguilingly. The FBI poster could never do her justice.

"For two reasons. First, just as you say, I got away with it. No-one's looking for me. There's no bounty on my head. I'm retired, and I'm in the clear. Oh, I'd still consider doing another job if the money was ridiculously large and the target was intriguing enough. But for now, rest assured I have no reason to fear you or to hurt you. That could change, but that is entirely in your hands. Second, you had a gun on me twice, and both times you let me go. A girl gets to appreciate that sort of thing."

Lammeck had not forgotten the sting of her parting words in the Georgia forest. *History sent you to stop me, because history knew you wouldn't.* He'd stewed over this for weeks. Now, with Judith unarmed in front of him, he wanted to assault her, stand her up from her chair and slam her to the bar floor as he'd done in the woods. Then ask her to comment again what she thought he was made of.

The waiter brought the beers and left. Lammeck waited with the glasses on the table.

"Would you like to swap beers with me?" Judith asked, her eyes merry. "Shall I take a big swallow out of yours first?"

"Yes."

She lifted her own beer. "Don't be absurd. Drink."

Lammeck watched her gulp and wipe foam off her lip. Only then did he lift his beer and drink.

"There, that's better. This is what history wants. You and me sharing a pint. How's your book going, *The Assassins Gallery*? Is there a chapter about me?"

"No."

"Pity. But I didn't think there would be. I suppose it would get you in some pretty hot water."

"There's no chapter because there's no evidence. It's all vanished. And I'm not worried about hot water."

"What if they sent me?"

Lammeck fingered the sweaty beer glass. "You're retired."

"I know." She leaned across the table. "But humor me. What if *I* were your hot water?"

"Then we'd both better worry."

Judith sat up fast, clapping. "That's better!"

"I need to know something. Then I'll decide about the chapter."

"These are my conditions. No questions about my past work. No questions about where I live or who I am. I will never compromise my own security. Understood?"

Lammeck cared about none of this.

"Who'd you work for?"

"Ah, that's the big one, isn't it? For an historian, anyway. Who wanted to change history so much they killed a president?"

"Tell me."

"Guess."

"Just fucking tell me."

"Just fucking guess."

Lammeck took another swallow. He licked his lips, and said: "It was an international action. Some nation. I don't believe any of Roosevelt's domestic enemies were behind it. You showed up in a sub. Industrialists and politicians have a lot of money. They don't have subs."

"Correct. But which country?"

"Reilly thinks it was the Germans."

"But you don't agree?"

"No. By the beginning of this year, the outcome in Europe was a foregone conclusion. Germany was going to lose. There were even efforts by the Nazis at high levels to negotiate some kind of peace shy of total surrender. Killing Roosevelt wouldn't have changed the military reality on the ground, not even a little. Stalin was agitating to pastoralize Germany, take all their factories, pour concrete in their mines, to keep them from militarizing again for a long time. Churchill was against it. He wanted a rebuilt Germany, along with a strengthened France, as a buffer against a powerful postwar Soviet Union to his east. Roosevelt was on the fence. Killing Roosevelt would have just passed that decision on to Truman, and no one knows Truman any better than you and I know our waiter. And what if you'd gotten caught? Roosevelt would've seen to it along with Stalin that Germany didn't have two sticks to rub together for another hundred years. That's a big risk. With the exception of Hitler, I doubt there was any support in the German high command for taking the President down."

"Alright. Next."

"The Japanese." Lammeck shook his head again. "By December last year, the Japs were on the run in Burma and the Philippines. Their navy just had its butt whipped at Leyte Gulf. Five months later, we're island-hopping straight to Tokyo. It's the same deal as Germany— killing Roosevelt won't alter the inevitable. The war's lost for the Japs. History isn't going to change for them, no matter who's president. So why risk it? There's no upside in targeting Roosevelt."

"You forget. The Japanese and Germans are vengeful people. It might have been no more than that."

"They're also incredibly pragmatic. I can't see them dedicating the resources this late in the war just for revenge. And again, if they'd been caught . . . if *you'd* been caught . . . a vengeful Germany or Japan is nothing next to a pissed-off America. Trust me. Besides."

"Besides what?"

"I don't see you working for them."

"Someone like me isn't motivated by politics. I work for the challenge and the money. But, no, you're correct. I wouldn't work for Hitler or Tojo. Theirs is not the world I want to help usher in. I'm not completely amoral."

Judith sipped her beer, eyeing Lammeck. "Then who has the upside, Mikhal?"

"The Russians. You did Krivitsky for them. So they brought you back for Roosevelt."

"Tell me why."

"No one else in the world right now is as strong as America except the Soviet Union. Things are shaping up to be a staring match across the globe, between communism and democracy. Stalin's not leaving the countries his armies liberated. Neither is America. The Reds feel they won the war in Europe almost by themselves, and as far as war dead goes, they pretty much did. The estimates I'm hearing approach eight million. I think it'll be more. With the fighting there barely over, why not upset the applecart? Rub out Roosevelt, put in the untested Truman. Take the new President to the wood-shed while the taking's good, before Truman gets his feet under him. Stalin's never shown the slightest scruple about removing rivals, and Roosevelt was his greatest rival. All the ingredients are there. Power grab. Available resources for the job. Precedent. And most impor-tant, history changed for the better—for them."

"True. All true."

Judith sipped her beer, keeping her smile behind the glass.

"So why am I wrong?" Lammeck demanded.

"For the exact reasons you're right, Mikhal. Stalin's Red Army has grown into the largest in the world. They've been bloodied and they've won, and they are now spread all over Eastern Europe. Despite agreements, Stalin hasn't pulled one soldier from the Balkans, Poland, or the eastern half of Germany. He's setting up puppet governments in every nation he's 'liberated.' And in Finland, Greece, Italy, Portugal, and Spain, he's got political support. Even in America there's an active Communist party. All of this was done on the watch of one Franklin Roosevelt."

"What are you saying?"

"That Stalin never had a better friend than Roosevelt. America was so bent on stopping the Nazis that it used Russia as proxy to fight them until she could get in on the fight, just as she did with England early on. But after the Reds won at Stalingrad, and showed the world the Germans could be halted on the steppe, Roosevelt shifted loyalties. The amount of matériel the Soviets were handed dwarfs anything the English got. And the Reds made good use of it, killing nine out of ten German soldiers in the war. Now they're putting together their own bloc of satellite nations from the ones they chased the Germans out of. At the same time, the United Nations is going to do everything it can to dismantle the old European colonial powers, while doing little to slow Russian ex-pansion. That leaves just two superpowers. The Soviet Union is soon going to be the equal of America for world influence and prestige. And they have America to thank for that. So why would Stalin murder his American benefactor?"

"He wouldn't."

"So who would?"

The answer came to Lammeck like an artillery shell, with a disheartening whoosh out of the air. Judith must have seen the shock on his face. She laid an open hand to his cheek. Lammeck was too stunned to avoid her touch.

"Poor Mikhal," she murmured. "Have you never been jilted?"

He stared past her, outside the hazy pub into the world where this impossibility came from.

"Churchill."

Judith left her palm against his skin. Gently she said, "I can't say if it was Churchill. But, yes, it was England."

"It wasn't about gaining power," Lammeck said as the reason exploded on him. "It was to stop the loss of power."

"Dead on." She withdrew her hand.

"Before the war, Britain was one of the strongest nations in the world. Now, after the war, their whole empire's going to be broken up. Churchill wants to keep the status quo, the old European balance of power. But Roosevelt intended to use the UN to end colonialism. The only thing Churchill had left to protect British interests was his alliance with America. Then, under Roosevelt, after Malta, that alliance shifted to the Soviets. So Roosevelt had to go."

"He was too tired, Mikhal, too sick. He was a frail, dying old man. I saw him with my own eyes. He wasn't going to be strong enough to be an effective force to help check Stalin. The British saw this at Tehran, again at Yalta. The time is now, the forces are moving. They figured Truman could only turn out better. Roosevelt was a great man, and a great president for America. I'm sure you historians will forgive him for the weaknesses of these past few years. But he wasn't an Englishman, and the once-great English can never forgive."

"Your accomplice, Maude King. An anticommunist."

"Vehemently so, I was told. She was recruited years ago, just in case."

"Why didn't they send you to kill Stalin instead?"

Judith shook her head. "A change of power in Communist Russia would affect nothing, Mikhal. The problem there is systemic; they all think alike. In America, a new President might just make a difference. And..." She paused, scratching her chin with a painted nail, "let's be honest: Stalin wouldn't have been so easy to kill."

Lammeck took up his beer. Judith had already finished her stout. He helped his throat to a long draught, then wiped his mouth on his sleeve.

"How does something like this happen? Did Churchill actually tell someone to murder Roosevelt? I can't believe that."

Judith shrugged. "One day Henry II was sitting with some of his knights, complaining about his maverick archbishop of Canterbury, Thomas Becket. He said, 'What cowards have I around me that no one will rid me of this lowborn priest?' Who knows if he meant it or he was just letting off steam. In any case, his boys took him at his word..."

"...and Becket was murdered in the cathedral."

"And became a saint. So it goes. Perhaps Churchill did nothing more than growl around one of his cigars one evening about how he wished such and such might befall Roosevelt. The wrong words in the right ears, and here we are." Judith whirled her hands. "Abracadabra. History."

The historian and the assassin sat with emptied glasses. Lammeck struggled with the immensity of what she'd just told him. He believed her; it added up.

"So, Professor. Have you made up your mind?"

"About what?"

"What drives history, events or individuals? Don't look so

surprised; remember I've read your work. What do you think? Am I a free agent of change or just a cog of history? When I killed Roosevelt, did I move the mountain of the future even an inch left or right? Or is the mountain still in the same spot? I'd love to know what you think. Please."

Lammeck eyed her. He enjoyed a quiet moment of irony, the theoretical assassin asking him his theory of assassinations.

"For the last five thousand years," he said, "until recently, surprisingly few people have actually affected world events. Moses, Jesus, Muhammad, Buddha, the great religions' prophets. A few dozen scientists. The wheel, gunpowder, electricity, steam and coal power, the cross, the Bible, the Koran—each of them transformed societies to their very core. But it's hard to come up with more than a handful of political leaders who have significantly affected the course of global history by living or dying. Movements rise and fade, conquerors win and lose. Few leaders prove irreplaceable. That's because power always comes from the people, even religious power, and it has vast momentum. Power is not a nimble thing. The ruling class understand that. But changes within the ruling class rarely alter their style of ruling, because they all end up thinking essentially alike. It's exactly the way you described how futile it would be to assassinate Stalin and make any difference in the Soviet Union. Or the Roman Empire's Caesars. Then there's always the counterweight to the ruling class, the radicals. Whenever the ruling class loses touch with the people, they protect their power by coercion and repression. These invariably give common cause to malcontents, who are themselves members of a class. As such, they're also interchangeable. One oppressed radical or another, just like one ruler, has turned out to be as good or bad as the next, with only varying degrees of vision and charisma."

Judith narrowed her eyes. "You mentioned 'recently.' What about it? And this better be good. I don't want to hear I've been wasting my time."

"Democracy changed everything. Over the last two centuries the real experiment with politics has been America. Europe comes close, but the Europeans' support of royal families and their status as colonial powers has perverted it. In the United States, the first nation on earth with no kings or queens, in what's become an open marketplace of competing ideas, the radicals themselves often get to be the rulers. But not like Lenin and his Communists. They may have harnessed widespread unrest, but they took control through bloodshed, and have to maintain it at the end of a cannon. That can't last. But America will. Because for the first time and place in history, one man or woman can make a difference based not on birthright or the size of an army, but solely by the power of an idea itself. And because of America's size and power, especially now after a victorious world war and the reduction of other traditional powers, the ideas of the American leadership will have global impact. A change in the presidency will affect hundreds of millions, for generations to come. Not since Rome has there been that kind of concentrated power. The difference is that in Rome, men ruled. In America, ideas rule. When you remove one man, you replace him with another. When you remove an idea, history changes. You may have committed the first assassination in all of recorded history that will actually have a profound political effect on the entire planet."

She fanned herself. "Me? Did you all learn this from me? Truly?"

"It's all I've been thinking about since I got back to my work."

"Well, you certainly take a girl's breath away. That was a beautiful lecture, Professor. I'm sorry I can't take your class. Now ask me what *I've* learned."

Lammeck tipped his head, to give her the implied question.

"I've killed thirteen men and women on assignment in my career. Four times that many, when you count the incidental deaths. Not in a single instance did I question myself about whether it was the right thing to do. Not once did I hesitate. Except for this last job. I let one frail old man live a few extra days. I took pity on him, frankly. You showed up a minute after I poisoned him. One little minute, Mikhal. I barely managed to get away. You know what that told me? That Allah still loves me. But it's clear that His love is down to one minute. I no longer can resist my doubts. So I can no longer be a part of history. History is not made by doubters. Only those without misgivings may stay. So," she asked, "what of your misgivings? What are you going to do?"

Lammeck cast himself forward into a future where he wrote what he knew. Where he hung in his gallery of assassination this folded FBI poster of Judith, below an image of Franklin Roosevelt. Where he charged England with the murder of an American president. He'd face derision, expulsion from academia, and, probably, some cold night, he'd face Dag or his British equivalent, maybe another of his own SOE trainees. In time, maybe a long time past his life, he'd be proven right. He'd be famous, with a name, known forever as the man who'd brought to light one of the great assassinations of the modern era.

"Before I answer that, I've got one more question for you. Why tell me? I know you made me a promise, but why keep it? If what you've done were made public, if people believed it, the impact would be..." Lammeck searched for a word to encompass the circumstances, "...incalculable."

Judith reached to the seat beside her, lifting her broad straw hat. "As I said, I don't know what the right thing is anymore. Killing clouds that in you. So I brought the truth to you. I believe you'll do the right thing. You're that kind of man."

Silently, Lammeck asked the same question Judith had answered in the woods: What did history need? Would it be served by exposing England? Would history be changed by the knowledge of this crime—and if so, for the better? And, not as important but more immediate, did history need Mikhal Lammeck, and—despite her confidence to the contrary—possibly Judith, alive or dead?

"You want to know what I'm going to do?" Lammeck gestured for her to set down her hat. "What I should have done five months ago when Dag came to drag me into this."

Lifting his hand higher, he caught the old bartender's attention across the tavern and called for two more beers.

AFTERWORD

President Franklin D. Roosevelt collapsed at the Little White House in Warm Springs, Georgia, at 1:15 P.M., on April 12, 1945. He was attended medically by Lieutenant Commander George Fox, pharmacist and masseur, and Lieutenant Commander Howard Bruenn, cardiologist, USNR. Due to the emergency, an internist, Dr. James Paullin, was called to come from Atlanta.

Over the next two hours, Roosevelt's condition worsened. Systolic blood pressure skyrocketed to 300, the limit the cuff could read; pulse quickened to 104. His left eye began to dilate. Roosevelt's bladder emptied. His breathing struggled, in a deep, rhythmic snore. Bruenn injected aminophylline and nitroglycerine into Roosevelt's arm to expand the arteries and lower blood pressure. His diagnosis was a massive cerebral hemorrhage in the occipital area, a stroke caused by a clot or a hardened artery that had broken and spilled blood into the skull, pressing on the President's brain.

By 2:45, FDR's blood pressure had dropped to 240/120; his pulse to 90 bpm. His breathing became irregular, with frequent pauses. His body snapped in and out of rigidity.

Dr. Paullin arrived at the Little White House at 3:30. The internist strode directly to the President's bedroom, where, within minutes, Roosevelt stopped breathing. Paullin injected a syringe of adrenaline straight into Roosevelt's heart. Through a stethoscope, Paullin heard only a few more heartbeats, then nothing. Dr. Bruenn listened for another minute and found no response. Paullin tried a blood pressure cuff and got no reading.

At 3:35 CWT, Dr. Bruenn pronounced, "This man is dead."

In Roosevelt's little bedroom, on the bedside table, lay a book, *The Punch and Judy Murders,* by Carter Dickson, opened to page 78, the beginning of a chapter headed "Six Feet of Earth."

ON THE FUNERAL TRAIN north from Warm Springs, cousins Delano and Suckley sat with Eleanor to keep her company. During their talk, Delano informed Eleanor that Lucy Mercer Rutherfurd had been visiting the Little White House when the President succumbed, and also that Lucy had been a frequent visitor to the White House with the knowledge and assistance of daughter Anna. Delano's rationale was that "Eleanor would have found out anyway." In fact, Eleanor was the only close family member, and just one of a few White House intimates, who did not know of Lucy's return into her husband's life.

Eleanor and daughter Anna Boettiger became estranged for years afterward, but later reconciled.

Eleanor died in 1962, revered as one of the great citizens of the world. Among the possessions found in her New York apartment, on her bedside table, was a clipping of a poem, "Psyche," by Virginia Moore:

> *The soul that has believed*
> *And is deceived*

Thinks nothing for a while,
All thoughts are vile.

And then because the sun
Is mute persuasion;
And hope in Spring and Fall
Most natural,
The soul grows calm and mild,
A little child,
Finding the pull of breath
Better than death ...
The soul that had believed
And was decieved
Ends by believing more
Than ever before.

Across the top of the clipping, in Eleanor's hand, had been scrawled the notation *1918,* the year she discovered the affair between her husband and Lucy Mercer.

ROOSEVELT WAS LAID TO rest in his mother's rose garden at the family home in Hyde Park, New York. British Prime Minister Winston Churchill did not attend the funeral. He did not visit Roosevelt's grave at Hyde Park until March 12, 1946.

Churchill lived another two decades. He was voted out of office just eight weeks after the end of the war in Europe, losing to the Labour candidate Clement Atlee. He became the Western world's leading bellwether against the spread of communism. In October 1951, Churchill was again elected prime minister, serving until 1955.

Upon his return from Yalta, Churchill remarked to his foreign secretary Anthony Eden, who insisted that pressure be put on

Roosevelt to insist that Stalin keep his Yalta agreements, "I am no longer fully heard by him [Roosevelt]."

Later, in his memoirs, Churchill considered the effect of FDR's declining health on the lowering of what he called "The Iron Curtain" across the middle of Europe:

> *We can now see the deadly hiatus which existed be-*
> *tween the fading of President Roosevelt's strength*
> *and the growth of President Truman's grip of the*
> *vast world problem. In this melancholy void, one*
> *President could not act and the other could not*
> *know.*

Before his own death on January 24, 1965, Churchill won the Nobel Prize for Literature, accepted the Order of the Garter, and became an honorary citizen of the United States.

SHORTLY AFTER FDR'S DEATH, Eleanor Roosevelt sent through cousin Daisy Suckley a small Shoumatoff portrait of her husband to Lucy Rutherfurd. From Aiken, May 2, 1945, Lucy wrote to Eleanor the following note:

DEAR ELEANOR,

Margaret Suckley has written me that you gave her the little water color of Franklin by Mme. Shoumatoff to send me. Thank you so very much—you must know that it will be treasured always—

I have wanted to write you for a long time to tell you that I had seen Franklin and of his great kindness about my husband when he was desperately ill in Washington, & of how helpful he was too, to his boys—and that I hoped so very much that I might see you again.

I can't tell you how I feel for you and how constantly I think of your sorrow—you—whom I have always felt to be the most blessed and privileged of women—must now feel immeasurable grief and pain and they must be almost unbearable—

The whole universe finds it difficult to adjust itself to a world without Franklin—and to you and to his family—the emptiness must be appalling—

I send you—as I find it impossible not to—my love and my deep sympathy.

> As always—
> Affectionately,
> Lucy Rutherfurd[1]

Roosevelt's daughter Anna arranged for Lucy to visit Roosevelt's grave in Hyde Park on June 9, 1945. On that day, Lucy was stopped by a guard, who advised her that her admission card was not valid, though it was signed by Anna Boettiger, Roosevelt's daughter. The guard telephoned Eleanor to obtain permission for Lucy to visit FDR's grave. Eleanor granted the request.

In 1945, Lucy told Madame Shoumatoff that she had burned all of FDR's letters.

Lucy Mercer Rutherfurd died of leukemia in New York City, on July 31, 1948, at the age of fifty-seven.

SHOUMATOFF'S PAINTING, WHICH HAS become known as *The Unfinished Portrait,* is on display at the museum of the Little White House in Warm Springs, Georgia.

Immediately upon learning of the President's death from U.S

---

[1] Lucy Rutherfurd to Eleanor Roosevelt, May 2, 1945; file: Russey-Ruz General Correspondence, 1945–52; Eleanor Roosevelt Papers, Part II: April 12 1945–64, Franklin D. Roosevelt Library.

ambassador Averell Harriman, Josef Stalin held the ambassador's hand for thirty seconds before asking him to sit. Stalin queried Harriman about the circumstances of Roosevelt's death, then sent a message to the U.S. State Department requesting that an autopsy be performed to ascertain if Roosevelt had been poisoned.[1]

IN THE LAST PARAGRAPH of Mike Reilly's book, *Reilly of the White House,*[2] he states:

> *I walked into the kitchen to collect the remnants of FDR's breakfast and took them to a [Georgia Warm Springs] Foundation chemist to be analyzed.*[3] *He found nothing, but a Secret Service man must check all credentials. Even Death's.*

SOVIET FOREIGN MINISTER V. M. Molotov, heading the Soviet delegation to the inaugural meeting of the United Nations held in San Francisco in April 1945, stopped in Washington, D.C., to acquaint himself with the new American President, Harry S. Truman.

During a meeting in the Oval Office, Truman upbraided the Russian minister, specifically over the Soviets' failure in Eastern Europe to abide by the terms of the Atlantic Charter guaranteeing liberated nations freedom from fear and representative government of their own choosing.

Put on the defensive, Molotov complained, "I have never been talked to like that in my life."

Truman replied, "Carry out your agreements, and you won't get talked to like that."

[1] Author's note: It does not strain credulity that Marshal Stalin recognized the handiwork of an assassin, having employed several himself.

[2] Simon & Schuster, New York, 1947.

[3] Author's note: No copy of this chemist's report has ever been found.

. . .

WALTER KRIVITSKY, BORN IN Russia in 1899, became a Soviet Intelligence officer. In 1923 he was sent to Germany in an attempt to start a Communist revolution. In 1933, he was transferred to Holland as Chief of Soviet Military Intelligence for Western Europe.

In 1936, Stalin began purging his government of officials whose loyalty he suspected or whose power he feared. Concerned for his life, Krivitsky defected to Canada in 1937, where he lived under the name of Walter Thomas. In 1939, Krivitsky gave the FBI details of sixty-one Soviet agents working in Britain, among them the Soviet moles Kim Philby and Donald Maclean. The British intelligence service, MI5, was not convinced by Krivitsky's testimony, and his leads were not followed up.

Krivitsky settled in the United States and wrote his memoir, entitled *I Was Stalin's Agent*. A repentant and fervid anticommunist, he testified before the House Un-American Activities Committee.

On the 10th of February, 1941, Walter Krivitsky was found shot to death in the Bellevue Hotel, in Washington, D.C. Initially, it was reported that he'd committed suicide. However, it has long been speculated that his hiding place was uncovered by a Soviet mole working for MI5, and he was murdered by Soviet agents. Krivitsky's death remains a mystery.

THE NAZI BOAST THAT the Czech town of Lidice had been erased from the map has been proven false. Several towns around the world have renamed themselves "Lidice" to commemorate the massacre staged by the Nazis in retaliation for the assassination of Reichsprotektor Reinhard Heydrich.

THE CZECH PARACHUTIST KAREL Čurda, who betrayed to the Gestapo his fellow SOE operatives including Josef Gabčik and Jan Kubiš, was hanged in Prague on April 29, 1947.

AUTHOR'S AFTERWORD

This novel is a work of speculative fiction. Even so, as in all my historical works, I have stuck closely to the true facts of recorded events. The times, dates, places, and many of the people in this story are actual and accurate to my abilities to research and make them so. Equally, the occurrences and characters that sprang from my imagination are as authentic as I could create them.

As is the case in every book I have written, several people and institutions contributed to this novel sufficiently to deserve appreciation and credit. *The Assassins Gallery* would not have been the story it is without the invaluable input and friendship of Mark Lazenby, who one day will quit his job as corporate shill and write the best lowbrow adventure-thriller novel ever. Again, my old comrade Dr. Jim Redington provided me with all the things medical and creepy I asked for. The FDR Library at Hyde Park was extremely helpful with records of Roosevelt's last months. My agent Tracy Fisher at William Morris was her usual extraordinary self, even while having her first baby. Bantam editor Kate Miciak continues to strive to make me a better writer with every manuscript I hand in, which she sends back laced with pencil marks of brilliant excision. Dr. Angus Goldberg let me use his family's flat in St. Andrews, Scotland. He and Capt. Mike Beach are two of my most valued sounding boards and admired intellects, as well as treasured sailing mates. And my wife Lindy stayed patient with my seven-day-a-week writing schedule, giving excellent advice with just the right blend of enthusiasm and skepticism, one of her many brands of genius.

David L. Robbins
Richmond, VA